BACK OF BEYOND

C.J. Box is the winner of an Anthony Award,
the Prix Calibre .38, the Macavity Award,
the Gumshoe Award, the Barry Award and
the 2009 Edgar Award for Best Novel. His
novels are US bestsellers and have been
translated into 21 languages. Box lives with
his family outside of Cheyenne, Wyoming.
Visit his website www.cjbox.net

BACK OF BEYOND

C.J. BOX

CORVUS

First published in the United States of America in 2011
by St. Martin's Press.

This edition first published in Great Britain in 2011
by Corvus, an imprint of Atlantic Books Ltd.

1 3 5 7 9 10 8 6 4 2

A CIP catalogue record for this book is available from
the British Library.

Hardback ISBN: 978-1-84887-298-1
Trade paperback ISBN: 978-1-84887-299-8
eBook ISBN: 978-0-85789-424-3

Printed in Great Britain by the MPG Books Group

For The Gauntlet (Jeff, Brian, Ken)
...and Laurie, always

Acknowledgments

The author would like to sincerely thank the many friends, relatives, and colleagues who assisted in the research, reading, editing, and publication of this novel, starting with Investigator Cory Olson of the Lewis and Clark Sheriff's Department in Helena, Montana, and including Investigator Larry Platts, Sheriff Leo Dutton, my friend Pam Gosink, and forensics guru D. P. Lyle, MD.

Thanks always to my first readers: Becky Box Reif, Molly Box, and Laurie Box.

Thanks also to John R. Erickson for the use of the lines from *The Original Adventures of Hank the Cowdog*, Puffin Books, 1983.

It's an absolute honor and privilege to work with the excellent and enthusiastic team at St. Martins Minotaur, including Sally Richardson, Andy Martin, Matthew Shear, Matthew Baldacci, Hector DeJean, and the absolutely peerless Jennifer Enderlin.

For Ann Rittenberg: You. Are. The. Greatest.

Who trusted God was love indeed
And love Creation's final law
Tho' Nature, red in tooth and claw
With ravine, shriek'd against his creed

—Canto 56, Alfred Lord Tennyson's
In Memoriam A. H. H., 1850

Part One

Montana

1

The night before Cody Hoyt shot the county coroner, he was driving without a purpose in his county Ford Expedition as he often did these days. He was agitated and restless, chain-smoking cigarettes until his throat was raw and sore. He drove right by the rural bars he used to frequent, not going in. Then the call came from dispatch on his cell phone: hikers claimed they found a burned-out cabin in the Big Belt Mountains to the northeast with maybe a dead body inside.

Even though it was the end of June the weather was unseasonably cold and it had rained in the valley for three straight days. That evening, before the clouds finally lifted and the sun died, he'd seen a dusting of snow on the tops of the Big Belts to the north and the Elkhorn Mountains to the south. *Snow.*

"Patrol has been sent up there," Edna the dispatcher said. He liked Edna even though she'd decided she was his surrogate mother and gave him pies and casseroles and tried to fix him up with Helena divorcees. She said, "My list says you're the one on call tonight."

"Yeah," he said. Cody was a Lewis and Clark County Sheriff's Department investigator. Detectives were automatically called to investigate any "unattended death," meaning accidents, suicides, or in the rare instance, homicides.

"Because you have nothing else to do," she said, mock joking.

"Not a damned thing," he said, deadly serious.

"Are you at home?"

"Yeah," he lied. "Watching the game on TV. Just a second, let me grab something to write on." He knew if Edna wanted to she could fire up the tracking screen in the dispatch center and find the location of his vehicle out in the county because of the GPS unit mounted under the front bumper. Or she could have at one time, before he dismantled it the month before because he didn't want anyone knowing where he'd been going or that he spent his other nights driving, driving, driving.

He pulled to the side of the road into the rough parking area in front of the Gem State Bar, the tires popping on the wet gravel. A single mercury vapor light on a pole threw dark shadows across the parking area. Pools of standing water from the recent rain reflected the light and the few stars that had appeared between night thunderheads. There were five other parked vehicles in front of the bar, all pickups. His pen was somewhere in the ashtray, which was spilling over with butts. As he pulled it out he noted the plastic barrel of the pen was rough with burn marks.

"Okay," he said.

"The cabin is located past Vigilante Campground on Highway 280, eight miles up Trout Creek on County Road 124. The map shows it's in the Helena National Forest, but maybe there's a private place up there."

He lowered the phone and sat back and closed his eyes without writing anything down. Outside his driver's side window, two men wearing dirty jeans and hoodies and ball caps pushed their way out the door of the bar. He recognized them as sapphire miners. Sapphire mining was a small industry in the county, and there were scores of one- and two-man claims that had been worked for years and still produced. The miner in the gray hoodie was practically as wide as he was tall. The one in the yellow hoodie was gaunt and skeletal with eyes sunk deep in their sockets. They were laughing and shoving each other. Yellow Hoodie had a twelve-pack of Coors Light under his arm for the road and he'd no doubt leave a trail of empties all the way up into the Big Belts to his little one-man mine. They looked up and saw him parked but didn't straighten up or try to act sober. He was just a guy in a muddy SUV to them because the vehicle was unmarked. Even the plates didn't give him away because they were skip plates. If anyone ran a check on them, they'd come back to a fictitious address and company name.

"Cody?" Edna asked.

"I'm here."

"Did you get that?"

"Yeah."

"The complainants called from the York Bar. They agreed to stay there until they met the officer so they could guide him to where the cabin is. Officer Dougherty was dispatched to the scene and he is there with them now taking their statement. Should I ask them to stay until you get there?"

"Not necessary," he said, "I know the cabin. Tell Dougherty to proceed—I'll meet him there. What did they say about a body?"

"Not much really. They said they thought it was an old place by the look of it and they poked around inside a little. They said that they think there's a body there because of the smell and what looked like a human hand, but they didn't actually see the body. They said it was raining hard and getting dark and they just wanted to get out of there."

"Male or female body?"

"They don't know. They said the hand might have been a glove or the arm from a dummy because it didn't look real."

He nodded to himself. Fire turned human bodies into sexless grotesques. He'd been on the scene where the fire was so hot the dead muscles of the arms and legs cooked and roasted and contracted the body into a fighter's stance: arms curled against the chest and knees bent, like a boxer in the ring. And the smell, like charred pork . . .

Outside in the parking lot, the two miners put the twelve-pack on the hood of a pickup and pulled out two cans and opened them. The spray from a can hit Fat Gray Hoodie in the face and he bellowed a laugh as he took the beer.

"Okay," Cody said to Edna.

He said, "Edna, call Larry. Tell him I need him."

Larry Olson, the only other detective in the five-man Criminal Investigations Division whom Cody thought was worth a damn. Olson was short, solid, and shaved bald; a flesh-colored fire hydrant who entered a room like a quiet exclamation point. Larry Olson was a Montana legend. He'd solved crimes by careful observation and exhaustive investigation. He wore suspects down. He wore his fellow detectives down. When an unsolved crime went on too long anywhere in the state, the call went out to "borrow" Larry Olson. The word was the only reason he stayed in Helena instead of going state or federal was that he wanted to be there for his three boys who lived with their mother in town.

Edna said, "Larry's not on call tonight."

She waited for him to acknowledge, but he didn't.

Finally, she said, "Cody?"

He held the phone out away from him at arm's length and made a gargling sound in his throat that resembled static. He said, "I'm losing the signal right now. Call Larry. I'll call back when I get a better signal," and closed the phone and dropped it to the seat. Overwhelmed with a wave of nausea and needing air, he pushed open the door and stepped outside, his boots splashing in a deep puddle.

"Good one," Skinny Yellow Hoodie said, laughing. "Right in the hole."

Cody ignored them as he bent forward, grasping his knees with his hands. He breathed in the moist mountain air, filling his lungs with it. Mixing it with the smoke. His eyes watered and he stood and wiped at them. Cold water poured in over the top of his low boots, filling his socks. He wished he'd worn his cowboy boots instead.

"You okay?" Yellow Hoodie asked.

"Fine."

"Want another beer? You could probably use one now."

"No," he said. They assumed he'd been drinking. Or, he thought, they recognized him from when he haunted the bars.

"This fucking rain, eh? Day after day. My dad said never curse the rain in Montana, and I never have. But this is motherfucking *crazy*. El Niño or some such thing. I heard the weatherman call it 'The summer without a summer.'"

Cody grunted.

"Want a hit?" Fat Gray Hoodie asked in a voice indicating he was holding his breath in, and Cody realized the man was holding a joint between his fingers. Cody's face must have cracked the miner up because he coughed and expelled the marijuana smoke in a cloud.

"Jesus Christ," the skinny miner said to Cody. "Don't mind him."

"Just being friendly," the second miner said, bringing the joint back up to his mouth.

Cody Hoyt was thirty-eight years old but often mistaken for being in his late forties. He had unkempt sandy hair, a square jaw, high cheekbones, a broken nose, brown eyes flecked with either gold or red depending on the circumstances and often described as either "mean" or "dead," and a mouth that twisted naturally into a cop smirk even when he didn't want it to. He wore jeans, boots, and a loose long-sleeved fishing shirt. Detectives didn't wear uniforms and dressed to blend into the community. He reached down and pulled the hem of the shirt up so they could see the seven-point gold sheriff's department badge on his belt.

"I got a card for this," the smoking miner said quickly, nodding to the joint.

Practically every sapphire miner in the county had a card signed by a doctor for medical marijuana use, Cody had found. And many of them grew plants in quantities and potency well beyond simple home use. It wasn't a coincidence that the miners used most of the same instruments—scales, small tools, hundreds of small Ziploc bags—dope merchants used.

Cody raised his .40 Sig Sauer in a shooter's grip.

"Really," Fat Gray Hoodie said, stepping back and dropping the joint, which extinguished with a hiss between his feet in the mud, "really, I got a card. I'll show you. Shit, I know I'm not supposed to smoke in a public place, but damn, my back started hurting . . ."

"Give me the rest of the beer," Cody said.

Both miners froze, then shot glances at each other.

"You want the beer? You can have it," Yellow Hoodie said. "Why the hell you want my beer? What kind of cop wants my fucking *beer*?"

"I don't," Cody said with a twisted smile. He holstered his weapon and climbed back into his Ford. He roared away, thinking he wanted that beer so goddamned bad right now he would have killed them both for it.

He'd heard a couple of maxims from Larry after they'd danced around each other for three months. Larry had stopped by his desk one afternoon when no one else was in the office, paused, leaned over until his mouth was an inch from Cody's ear, and said:

"I know you were a hotshot detective in Colorado and I also know your rep as a drunk and a screwup. I've heard about some of the things you used to do when you grew up here, and your crazy homicidal white-trash family. I've personally arrested two of your uncles and I sent one to Deer Lodge prison. I was shocked as hell when you moved back here, and even more shocked when the sheriff hired you on. I can only speculate that you've got something on him so big and nasty he didn't have a choice."

Cody said nothing, but locked in Larry with his best cop deadeye and refused to blink.

Said Larry, "If so, good for you. More power to you, brother. But since we have to work together, I called a couple of your old partners in Denver. They said you were crazy, violent, and unpredictable. They said you were a loose cannon and you were all over the place like a fart on a hot skillet. But they also said you were a fucking fantastic cop and you went at every case like a bulldog on steroids who wouldn't let go. That you nailed a child-porn king and a sitting Federal District judge in one fell swoop. But they said they didn't really want to ever work with you again because they wanted to keep their jobs and not spend half their fucking time defending themselves and you to Internal Affairs and the mayor's office.

"Me," Larry said, "I'll give you the benefit of the doubt. But don't ever screw me, and don't ever put me in a position I don't want to be in. Just do the job and show me what you've got, and you'll find out you can trust me. But you need to *earn* my trust because you brought a lot of baggage back with you to Montana."

Cody said nothing.

Larry continued, "There are four things you need to know about this place. One, we only get a homicide about once a year. But that's not good, it's bad. It's bad because most of these jamokes around here," he nodded toward the door to indicate the rest of the sheriff's department as well as the municipal police department across the hall, "never get enough experience to work a murder investigation smoothly. If the homicide is hinky and not a straightforward domestic or bar brawl, it's always the first time for most of 'em. They've grown up watching *CSI* and cop shows and they turn into actors they've seen on the screen instead of remembering their training.

"Second, the most important topic of every day is where to go to lunch. You'll find yourself discussing that particular dilemma more than anything else.

"Third, bad things always happen on a Friday, almost always after you're off duty. So if you're off duty but on call, you better not hit the bottle like I've heard you do.

"Fourth, and most important, take every possible fucking opportunity you can to eat and take a shit, because this county is thirty-five hundred square miles, a third of it roadless."

With that, Larry Olson stormed out of the room.

Cody thought of the third and fourth maxims as he drove up into the mountains. The rain had started again, and heavy-bellied drops smacked against the windshield as if they were committing suicide. The two-lane highway was dark and slick. Canyon Ferry Lake—so named because they'd built a dam to hold back the Missouri and submerge the historic river crossing—simmered like a stew on slow boil because of the rain. The dark wooded canyon wall rose to his left. He realized he was hungry because he hadn't had dinner. His vague plan had been to go to York and have a burger, but a burger without a beer seemed an impossible mission.

And he could use a toilet as well. There were outhouses at Two Camps Vista and another at Devil's Elbow. He hated outhouses because he could never not look down into the pit—sometimes using his flashlight—to see what was floating around down there. It reminded him of too many things.

The possible body in the cabin beyond Vigilante Campground made Cody's heart pound and his hands go cold on the steering wheel. His mind raced and scenarios formed. He immediately assumed the worst.

He dug out his cell phone and called Edna at dispatch.

"Is Larry coming?" he asked.

"He's not happy about it."

"I don't blame him."

"Quit pretending you're losing your cell phone signal when you aren't."

He sighed. "Okay."

After a beat, she said, "Should I call the Scooter?"

The county coroner, Skeeter Caldwell, enjoyed his job a little too much and was considered a pain in the ass to work with ever since he found out he was the only elected official with the authority to arrest the sheriff. Plus, elections were five months away and he wanted to keep a high profile in the local press. Nothing could be done with a body until the coroner arrived. He owned all bodies in Lewis and Clark County and they couldn't be touched or removed without his authority.

"Naw, I'll call him if we have to," Cody said. "I'll confirm it's a body first. The hikers could have seen anything. Lots of things look like hands."

"And I should ignore the call I just got from a drunken miner saying a sheriff's department employee tried to steal his beer outside a bar?"

"Yeah, you should ignore that," Cody said.

He drove just under control, taking the switchbacks hard, crossing the faded double center line with each turn. There wasn't a light bar on the Ford so he'd toggled on the switch that turned his headlights into strobes that flashed psychedelically on the wet canyon walls and pine trees. And froze two cow elk in their progress across the highway.

Cody cursed and swerved to the left, his tires dropping off the pavement into the muddy ditch, but he wasn't fast enough. One of the elk inexplicably bounded in front of him and turned her head toward him and their eyes locked a split second before he hit her solidly in the shoulder with the right front fender of the truck. The impact made the Ford fishtail. If it weren't for the front right tire still gripping the pavement, he would have hurtled left into the bank of trees. He jerked the wheel and the Ford bounced up out of the ditch.

He stopped in the middle of the highway, breathing hard, knowing if his brakes hadn't bitten he would have gone straight off the edge of the mountain into Canyon Ferry Lake. Rain drummed on the roof. A single headlight pointed out into the dark, lighting only the rain that slashed through the beam. He checked his side mirrors. In the red glow of his taillights he could see the other elk bound up the canyon wall but the one he'd hit was down, its legs churning, head writhing.

"Shit!"

His boot eased off the brake and he began to roll forward again, making sure he could still go forward. The Ford went a few feet before it stopped again. He needed to assess the damage. And he couldn't leave her suffering like that.

Chanting "*Shit-shit-shit-shit-shit . . .*" he got out and walked back along the wet asphalt in the rain and drew his Sig Sauer and shot her in the head. Her thrashing went manic until it stopped altogether. He couldn't shed the afterimage of her eyes boring into him before he hit her, even when she closed them now. It took five minutes to pull her off the roadway. She was heavy, wet, and smelled of musk and hot blood.

He took a quick look at his bumper. His right headlight was out and thatches of elk hair were caught in the grille. There was a six-inch gap between the frame and the hood. He could smell the sharp odor of burning hair and meat on the hot surfaces of the motor. He had a couple of thousand dollars in damage and years of jokes from the county maintenance shop guys and fellow cops ahead of him. But the Ford still ran.

"*Shit-shit-shit-shit-shit . . .*"

For his next trick, he climbed into the cab of the Ford to locate a dead body in a burned-out cabin.

"*Shit-shit-shit-shit-shit . . .*"

A body that, in all probability, belonged to someone he knew and trusted and admired and who had kept him tethered to normalcy the past few months by a single fraying thread. And he could feel the thread unraveling.

2

The rain had turned to slush by the time Cody Hoyt drove through Vigilante Campground and continued up the sloppy road along Trout Creek. The patrol officer ahead of him was easy to follow because of the deep fresh troughs in the chocolate one-track. His single headlight seemed to light up and suspend the cold viscous rain in midair.

He could never enter the campground—which the U.S. Forest Service contracted with the L&C Sheriff's Department to patrol—without remembering the keggers he used to attend there when he was growing up in junior and senior high. That's when it started, he knew. When he learned that when he drank he could feel like a superman. His muscles and attitude swelled and his reticence and common sense stepped aside. He recalled a fight with baseball bats, remembered the hollow sickening sound his twenty-eight-inch maple bat made when it connected with Trevor McCamber's forehead. Remembered the creamy white belly and thighs of Jenny Thompson under the blue-green glow of his dashboard lights . . . before that belly swelled with his son and he married Jenny in a drunken and hasty ceremony at a ranch outside of town. His best men had been Jack McGuane and Brian Winters, fellow seniors and best friends at Helena High. Brian thought the wedding was hilarious. Jack tried to pretend it wasn't.

Jack's parents spent the ceremony shaking their heads and looking toward the road to see if Cody's father and uncle Jeter would show. They didn't.

After graduation from high school, Cody and Jenny moved from place to place until finally he was back in Montana without her or his boy.

Cody Hoyt drove under the towering knotty pine archway and over an ancient wooden bridge barely nosing above the foam and fury of Trout Creek filled with runoff. Around a wooded corner was the cabin, and suddenly there were lights in the pure darkness: the headlights of a patrol cruiser trained on the charred remains of the structure, and a single round Cyclopean eye of a departmental Maglite swinging his way and blinding him.

This was the crime scene, all right.

Cody pulled up next to the patrol SUV. Inside the next vehicle, illuminated by the interior lighting, were two citizens. A man in his forties and a woman who looked to be in her early twenties huddled in the backseat. They looked cold and tired, he thought. The man needed a shave. The woman needed a hot shower. He nodded at them through two sets of windows and they nodded back.

The patrol officer, Ryan Dougherty, appeared at his driver's window, and tapped on the glass with the flashlight. In the process of doing it, he blinded Cody again.

Cody powered down the window, and said, "Would you *quit* shining that fucking thing into my eyes?"

"Oh, sorry." The patrol officer, newer to the department than Cody, was blond and baby-faced with a trimmed bristly mustache that said, *Here comes a cop!* and eyes that had not seen enough. In fact, Cody thought, Dougherty looked flushed, despite the weather.

"What happened to your front end?" Dougherty asked.

"Hit an elk," Cody said.

"On the way up?"

"Yeah."

"Bull or cow?"

Cody hesitated. "Cow."

Cody knew what Dougherty would say next. "Got a cow permit?" he said, grinning.

"Ha ha," Cody said, deadpan.

"I bet you'll be hearing that one a lot."

"I bet I will," Cody said, nodding toward the patrol vehicle. "Those two the hikers who found the cabin?"

"Yeah. I met them at the York Bar and they showed me the way up here. Here, I got their names . . ." Dougherty dug inside his raincoat for the notebook in his breast pocket. He was in uniform: brown shirt, tan pockets, and epaulets. The reason the dopers called them "L&C County Fascists."

"I don't need their names," Cody said. "Unless you think they did it."

"Oh, no. Not at all."

"Did they tromp all over the crime scene?"

"Just a little," Dougherty said. "It's hard to tell what they touched."

Cody said, "Why don't you ask them?"

"I can do that."

"Good. Put one of them in this vehicle and interview them separately. Walk them through their movements when they first saw the cabin. Find out which direction they came down, and what they did inside. Find out what they touched and if they took anything. It's amazing how many times citizens take souvenirs from a crime scene. If something sounds wrong or their stories don't match, come get me."

"Yes, sir," Dougherty said. The flush was gone from his cheeks. Cody could tell he was beating himself up for taking their story at face value.

"I'm gonna go take a look," Cody said.

"It's wetter than hell," Dougherty said. "The ash from the fire makes it all . . . soupy."

Cody glared at him. "Have *you* been in the crime scene?"

Dougherty looked away for a second, and when he turned his head back he said, "A little."

Cody's voice was ice. "How fucking little?"

"Enough to confirm there's a body. A big fat one."

Cody took a deep breath of wet air.

"You aren't gonna write me up, are you?" Dougherty asked. "I was thinking, Jesus, what if the person is still alive?"

"Don't lie." He repeated a sheriff's department bromide: "You lie, you die, Dougherty. You wanted to see a burned-up dead body. Everybody wants to see a dead body until they see one. Have you had your fill?"

"Christ, yes," Dougherty said, shaking his head. "I'll be seeing that *thing* in my dreams."

"Step aside so I can get my rain gear," Cody said.

His foul weather gear was in a heavy plastic box in the back of his SUV and there was no way to reach it from the inside, so he grabbed his Colorado Rockies baseball cap, jammed it on, and opened the door. The cold rain stung when it hit his bare face and hands. He could remember only one other time when he got his rain gear out, the previous spring when he was called to a ranch because the foreman thought he saw Middle Eastern terrorists photographing a missile silo. Turned out the photographers were farmers from India on an agricultural mission sponsored by the State of Montana and their interest was wheat, not missile silos. But it rained so rarely in Montana, Cody thought, that packing rain gear was almost silly. He didn't know a single person who owned an umbrella, for instance.

He leaned into the back of the Expedition while he wrestled with the box. It was jammed against the backseat and he had to pull it over the top of the rest of his gear—his long-gun case, large evidence box, canvas duffel packed with two armored vests, a survival crate the sheriff insisted they carry with them filled with a sleeping bag, candles, food, and water. While he threw the boxes around and got the one with his crime-scene clothing, he could feel the rain soaking through the back of his shirt and jeans. His boots were already wet from the puddle in the parking lot.

Even though it was getting more pointless by the second, he pulled on rain pants and slipped Tyvek booties over his wet boots. Instead of a raincoat he pulled on a full-length Australian oilcloth duster. Rain immediately beaded on the fabric.

His cell phone burred and he dug it out and saw the call was from his son Justin. Justin was an anomaly to Cody—miraculously, the only genuinely good person he knew. Justin was kind, selfless, and admirable. Plus he was tall and nice-looking and had a sweet temperament. Cody had no idea how he could have spawned such a child, given his own foibles and his long lineage of white-trash relatives. Every time Cody saw his son he looked for signs of his own obsessions and bad traits and had yet to see them. Justin was a fucking miracle at seventeen years old, Cody thought.

"Hey," Cody said. "This is bad timing."

"Hi, Dad. Sorry, but I wanted to ask you something."

"I'm on a crime scene," Cody said. "Can I call you back later?"

"Yeah, but do it quick. I'm gonna be gone for a while."

"Gone where?"

"Didn't Mom tell you?"

"I haven't talked to her."

"Oh."

"Look, Justin, this is a really bad time."

"You said that," his son said, not masking his disappointment well. "I wanted to ask you if I could borrow—"

"You can borrow anything you want of mine," Cody said. "Don't worry about it. I've got to go. Later."

He snapped the phone shut and crammed it in his pocket, feeling guilty and angry at himself for cutting off Justin.

———

Cody grabbed his digital camera and light setup and his favorite flashlight, a Maglite with an extension that held six batteries and could be swung like a heavy lead pipe—with the same results. It was better than that twenty-eight-inch maple bat. The long flashlights had been banned from most police departments, which Cody saw as a further sign of official wimpification. He turned toward the burned-up cabin.

As Dougherty escorted the female hiker into Cody's SUV, he said, "Look at you. You look like a gunfighter in that coat. I need to get me one of those. *Cool.*"

Cody sighed.

As he approached the cabin he tried to clear his mind of everything in it, including Justin's call, to make it a fresh whiteboard. He wanted to view the scene with absolute open-minded clarity. He knew this was his only chance to investigate the scene without anyone around. If there was a body, the place would be swarming with people within the hour. Skeeter would be there with his deputy coroner and perhaps a reporter from the Helena *Independent Record.* Skeeter would feign innocence as to why the reporter was there, but everybody would know he called her before he rolled. There might even be a team from one of two local television stations, although he knew they operated lean going into the weekends. And Sheriff Tub Tubman, also up for reelection, would no doubt arrive in his Suburban with Undersheriff Cliff Bodean just a few steps behind him. Mike Sanders, the other detective on call, might surprise him with his presence because the sheriff was there, no doubt bitching about the fact no one had called him. The forensics unit shared by the Helena PD would be present, as would the county evidence tech. So until the scene became chaotic, this was his opportunity to see it fresh. He couldn't do anything about the fact that the hikers had reported seeing a hand, but he tried to ignore that, also. He wanted to see the hand for himself as if he'd stumbled upon it. If there was a hand.

If there was a body.

Because if there was a body and it belonged to whom he thought and if the evidence pointed to a homicide, he'd personally go after who did it like a rabid dog until he took that person down. And he wasn't thinking Deer Lodge, Montana, where the state penitentiary was located. He was thinking Dirt Nap, Montana. Which was just about anywhere he wanted it to be.

Cody opened the beam on his Maglite as he approached on a flagstone footpath. He moved slowly, taking in not only the cabin itself but anything of note on the path, which was the only walkway to the place from a gravel parking area. Looking for anything out of place; a wrapper, a cigarette butt, a spent cartridge. He saw nothing unusual.

The cabin was originally built in the 1920s on the edge of a meadow that sloped down to Trout Creek. The twenty acres of wooded land that went with it was surrounded on three sides by the Helena National Forest. An agreement had been granted years before to the Forest Service for a public easement for access to the trails in the Big Belts. That's how the hikers stumbled on the scene.

The cabin was built of logs and had a deck overlooking the meadow in back and a covered porch in front. Tall spruce trees bordered it on three sides. Although it had fallen into disrepair in the 1970s, the structure had been expensively renovated and restored. At least before half of it burned down, that is.

The cabin was, quite simply, half the size it should have been. The left side was burned to the ground except for a black woodstove and chimney that leaned dangerously toward the creek. The right side was perfectly intact. He looked at the right side first, where the bedrooms and kitchen were. Rainwater coursed down bronze-colored logs, and there were lace curtains in the windows. A plaque near the front door read LEAVE YOUR TROUBLES OUTSIDE BEFORE ENTERING. He smiled bitterly at that.

He slowly circled the outside of the cabin, flashlight down, walking a perimeter he would later flag with yellow plastic CRIME SCENE tape to keep the press and public out. The ground was soaked and muddy. There was standing water in every depression. The grass was long and hadn't been mowed for a while. Long blades of it bent down as if depressed, heavy droplets on every point. He looked for footprints wherever the grass gave way to dirt. He saw none except for two sets of fresh hiking boot impressions. He shot photos of the footprints and checked to see if they were good shots on the display screen on the back of his camera. He knew where they came from, and glanced back toward the parking area. Dougherty had moved from interviewing the male in his Ford to the department vehicle where the female hiker had been asked to stay.

Then he carefully approached the burned-out part of the cabin, and twisted the lens of his Maglite to narrow and brighten his field of view.

The floor of the burned rooms consisted of black wet tarlike sludge; ash mixed with rainwater. It looked like wet black cement. Fallen timbers and collapsed framing stuck out from the soup. As did the woodstove, a charred black metal desk with a squared-off black box on top of it, and the metal frames of an easy chair, fold-out couch, and gun safe.

It all smelled of charcoal, smoke, rain, and damp. And something else: barbecued pork.

A tangle of wooden beams and wall joints had fallen on the metal skeleton of the couch. But protruding from the tangle was a swelled and waxy-looking arm. On the end of the arm was an outstretched human hand, the fingers splayed out as if to say *Stop!*, the hand so bloated he could barely see the glint of a gold wedding band on the third finger. The skin of the forearm looked crispy and black, like the burn on the side of a roasted marshmallow. Cody further narrowed the beam on the flashlight to a five-inch spot to peer further inside the load of burned wood. A naked thigh, the skin burned and split to reveal neon orange fat like a pig or a goose.

Cody closed his eyes and reached up and took his cap off and let the rain hit him in the face.

Larry Olson arrived a half hour later. By then, Cody had thoroughly photographed the scene. He'd placed plastic numbered tents near the body, the stove, the desk, and the couch. He'd set up his remote flashes on mounts that lit it up like daylight. The photos he saw on his display were sharp, focused, and thorough. He tried not to think about what he was shooting or who the body had belonged to. He shut off his mind from speculation, and made sure every possible angle and object was preserved digitally. He never once walked into the burned-out rooms, but did all of his shooting from outside. As he did, he found other objects of interest: a metal briefcase swimming in the black soup, the frame of a Winchester rifle with the stock and forestock burned off, a blackened bottle shape he recognized with such intimacy and disappointment that it was as if someone had punched him in the throat.

He looked up as Larry's flashlight bobbed along the flagstone path and eventually raised to take him in.

Larry said, "Nice raincoat. You headed to the OK Corral later tonight? You and the Earp brothers and Doc Holliday?"

"Yeah. I've got issues with Ike Clanton, that bastard."

Larry actually laughed. "Suicide? Tell me it's a suicide."

"I'm not going to tell you anything," Cody said. "I'm going to go back to my truck and burn one. I'll stay out of your way. Then I'm going to come back and listen to your initial theory. I've looked over the scene and I've got more than enough shots of it. And I've got a theory of my own, but I don't want to steer you one way or the other."

Because it was dark, Cody couldn't tell what Larry was thinking.

"Have you been in the unburned section?" Larry asked.

"Not yet."

"Good. Let's do that together."

"All right."

"Bad fucking night for this," Larry said. "You must really hate me to call me out on a night like this."

"I don't hate you, Larry. I want your opinion."

"Have you called the coroner?"

"Not yet."

"Jesus, Cody. You should have called him already."

Cody shrugged.

"I'll look things over and give you my opinion as long as you call Skeeter and the sheriff and we do this thing properly. Remember what I said. You remember, don't you?"

"Yeah, I do."

"A deal's a deal."

Cody nodded. He said, "Take as much time as you need. The scene is yours. I've got great photos, so you don't need to worry about that. Just look it over, tell me what you think. And I'll make the calls I need to."

Larry reached up and squeegeed the beads of rain off his shaved head with his hand. "I should have brought a hat."

"You can have mine," Cody said, handing him his cap as he passed. It was sodden and heavy with rain.

"Keep it," Larry said. Then: "Hey, what did you do to your unit? You've only got one headlight."

"Hit an elk on the way up."

"Yeah, I saw it on the side of the road. You must have been in a hell of a hurry."

Cody left Larry and walked toward his Ford. He looked up at the dark sky, hoping for an opening in the rain clouds. Nope.

"Hey, Cody," Larry called.

"What?"

"You got a cow permit?"

Cell service was spotty, so Cody shooed Dougherty and the hiker out of his Ford. As Dougherty climbed out, Cody said, "Any discrepancies in their stories?"

"No, sir."

"Good work. Keep them here for a while in case we have more questions, then take them back to the York Bar or wherever they're headed. Just make sure we've got contact details on them if we need to get in touch later."

The patrol officer patted his notebook. "I've got all that."

"Okay then," Cody said.

Dougherty paused. "So you aren't going to write me up?"

"Go. Just go. But remember, never shut off an area of inquiry in any situation. Never assume anything. Always assume everybody is guilty as hell but act like they're innocent to their face. Remember that. Everybody is guilty of something, every single one of 'em. It may not be this," he said, chinning toward the cabin. "But it's something. No one is clean and pure and perfect."

Dougherty didn't say *Yes, sir.* He just stood there.

"What?" Cody said.

"I hope I never get like you," Dougherty said, and went back to his truck.

Cody said to no one in particular, "I hope you don't, either."

It was warm and dry in his Ford. The windows steamed on the inside of the cab due to his wet clothing. He called Edna on the radio. While he talked to her he watched Larry Olson retrace his own steps around the cabin, shooting his flashlight about, moving slow.

"Edna, please alert Skeeter and Tubby—"

"You mean Sheriff Tubman."

"Of course," Cody said, glad she pointed that out since there were plenty of locals who monitored the police band. "Sheriff Tubman."

"What should I tell them?" Edna asked.

"We've got a body," he said, signing off.

He gave Larry plenty of time. Dougherty and the hikers sat in Dougherty's vehicle waiting for the word to be given for clearance to leave. As Cody waited for Larry to finish up, he glanced into the backseat. The male hiker had left his daypack, the idiot. Cody thought he may need to call Dougherty, tell him to bring the guy over to get his property.

Before he reached for the radio, he slung the pack up to the front seat and unzipped it. He kept the interior light off and the pack below the window so the deputy or hikers couldn't see what he was doing. The contents smelled of woodsmoke. He felt sorry for the hikers, having to camp night after night in the rain. How fun could that be? Plus, the female wasn't exactly a looker with her matted hair, hairy legs and underarms (he'd noticed), and no makeup. A typical Missoula or Bozeman bark beetle type.

The pack was heavy and he rooted through the balled-up damp clothing. He found a Ziploc bag with residue of marijuana. *See,* he thought to himself, *everybody is guilty.* He wondered if they'd purchased it from a sapphire miner. He put it back, and dug further, thinking maybe he'd find matches and an accelerant and close the case like a supercop. Instead, he closed his fingers around the loving and familiar and understanding neck of a full bottle of Jim Beam.

He whispered, "Oh, no."

Then: *I've got to make another call.*

Then: *To whom? Especially now.*

Then: *This is not happenstance. This is fate. And Fate says, "You need to drink this. It's why I left it for you to find. You'll need it to get through this."*

Before he made the decision he knew he'd make, he looked up and saw Larry walking toward his Ford. And he shoved the bottle back into the daypack and pushed it aside.

"Well?" Cody asked, opening the door and sliding outside. His boots hit the mud with two *squish-plops.*

Larry's shaved head beaded with rain and a rivulet ran down between his eyebrow and pooled on his upper lip. "I'm thinking accidental death with an outside chance of suicide, so I'm happy."

Cody grunted. They'd discussed it before, how at every death scene they hoped like hell it was a natural or an accidental or a suicide, that they'd be done with it in a matter of hours after they turned it over to the coroner.

"Show me," Cody said, "show me what led to your thinking suicide."

"Which means you're not so sure," Larry said.

"Which means nothing at all."

"Is suicide on your mind?"

"Constantly."

"You know what I mean. So, did you call Skeeter?"

Cody sighed, "Yeah. But given the distance and the rain, I figure we've got an hour before he gets here."

"Sheriff coming?"

"Don't know."

The two of them slogged down the flagstone path toward the scene, when Larry suddenly stopped. "Hey," he said, "An hour for *what*?"

"To come to a consensus," Cody said, widening the beam on his light to encompass the burned half of the cabin. "Okay, walk me through it."

Larry pinched down the beam of his Mag to use as a pointer within the wide pool of light. He started with the blackened woodstove.

"First thing I noticed," Larry said, "is the door to the stove is open. I don't see that happening after the fire started, do you? The handle locks down from the top, so a falling beam wouldn't hit it and knock it open. So I conclude it was open before the fire started. So what likely happened was our victim had a fire going—it's sure as hell cold enough this summer—and left the door open for some reason. The logs inside shifted or sparks flew out or something. Thus starting the blaze."

Cody said, "Go on."

"It's speculation until the arson team comes and looks things over, of course," Larry said while he slowly moved the beam of his light from the open door of the stove to the black muck that was the former hardwood floor, "but it looks like the fire started here a few feet from the open door and spread outward. The floorboards are completely gone right here, burned completely through to ash."

He danced his light around the edges of the structure, where the floor butted up against the concrete foundation. "See, there's still some floor left up against the foundation. So I'm thinking the fire started in the middle of the room and took off from there in all directions. Probably caught some curtains or the walls and climbed up to the ceiling, and then spread across the inside top of the ceiling. With fire burning the floor and all four walls and the ceiling, it was like an incinerator in the room. A fire like that sucks all the oxygen out, so our vic could have died from smoke inhalation before he barbecued—but that's for the autopsy guys in Missoula to tell us. My guess from working a few of these fire cases is he was dead before he burned, and way dead before the roof came down on him."

"Okay," Cody said, "why'd the victim leave the stove door open and crash on the couch?"

"The question at hand," Larry said, playing it like a game, "the question we must answer in order to declare it a suicide and go home and climb into our dry beds with our hot mamas."

Cody snorted. He had no hot mama at home, and neither did Larry.

Larry stepped carefully over the exposed foundation and sunk ankle deep into the black muck, cursing. He shuffled toward the couch frame and the body, the beam of his flashlight bouncing all over until it settled on a black stalk jutting up from the surface a few feet from the couch.

"You got pictures of this, right?" Larry asked, hesitating before he reached out.

"Yeah."

"Okay then," he said, leaning forward and grasping the black stalk and pulling it free. He held the bottle by the neck. "Here's our answer. Judging by the shape of it, I'd guess Wild Turkey. One hundred proof."

Cody concurred. He knew the bottle, even though the fire had puckered in the sides of it.

Said Larry, "No way to tell if it was empty, half full, or full. If there was any left when the fire burned this hot it would have boiled any-thing inside into vapor, which is a sad loss of pretty good bourbon. But it appears there wasn't a cap on it. Does Wild Turkey have a metal screw cap?"

"Nope," Cody said. "It has a cork plug kind of thing."

"Hmmm, then we'll have to get it analyzed to see if there's any cork or plastic residue inside the neck of the bottle. But I'd guess our victim opened this baby up and didn't cap it. Which means serious drinking to me. I mean, when a guy doesn't bother to put the cap back on between drinks, he's on a good toot. Right, Cody?"

Cody grunted with recognition.

"So the way I see it," Larry said, moving the flashlight to the black-ened arm and hand sticking out from the couch and debris, "is our victim was feeding the fire and getting pounded at the same time. Ex-cept maybe toward the end of the toot he didn't latch the handle on the stove completely. He staggered back to the couch with his bottle of Wild Turkey and had another drink and likely fell asleep. When the logs in the stove shifted they pushed open the door.

"Of course," Larry said, raising his flashlight to illuminate his face so Cody could see Larry's index finger posing pensively alongside his cheek, "first impressions can be wrong, especially in these conditions, and I'm never one to jump to conclusions no matter how much I want to will them to be what I want them to be. For starters, this isn't an optimal crime scene. In fact, it's a fucking horrible crime scene, which is why I don't want it to be anything other than a suicide. The rain changes everything, as we know. There's both bad and good aspects of this scene because of this goddamned weather."

Cody could tell Larry was at his best and wanted to be prompted.

"Like what?" Cody said.

"Well, the bad aspects are legion. It's been two or three days since the fire occurred, for one, so the scene isn't fresh. Rainwater has contaminated it if we try and look for trace evidence of any kind. Animals have been in here."

"They have?" Cody said, genuinely surprised he'd missed it.

Larry squatted and trained his beam so it shone from a lower angle into the tangle of debris around the body, illuminating a swatch of dark red striped with white. Bone white: ribs.

"Yeah," Larry said. "A badger or something got in here and fed through the meat to the bone. So that's just gross."

He stood, and said, "Continuing, the slop of ash and water within this foundation is wet enough not to retain any prints or tracks. So we can't tell if anyone besides us and the hikers were in here. Not that it makes that much difference, since dead is dead. But if there was someone else here with the victim we have no evidence of that. No empty glasses, or cigarette butts, or anything like that. If there were tire tracks out in the parking area or footprints in the dirt they're gone. We've only got what we've got. And if anything was left in this part of the cabin before the place burned down it's literally in the soup now.

"If an accelerant was used as part of a suicide I doubt there would be any trace of it left. Of course, hundred-proof whiskey might have had the same effect."

Cody nodded.

"But there's some good things," Larry said.

"Which are?"

Larry shined his light on the unburned half of the cabin. "The rain put the fire out before it took the whole place down. We might find something in there. That's where the kitchen and dining room are, and a bedroom. There's a lot of smoke damage, but who knows? We might find something.

"And the rain and cold might work a little in our favor," he said. "If the rain hadn't come no doubt the body would have been subject to the wick effect, because our victim was big and had plenty of fuel."

The wick effect was when fat smoldered—sometimes for days—and rendered the carcass a mass of black gelatinous goo.

"So because we have a great deal of the body left, the autopsy boys might be able to determine cause of death."

Cody centered his light on the frame of a metal desk and the black melted hulk on top of it. "We might even be able to recover something from the hard drive of the computer, I just don't know. I don't know if data on a hard drive can survive that kind of heat and this damned rain. But we might be able to recover something, if it's even worth trying."

Larry said, "And there you have it, folks," bowing and sweeping his hand toward the body like a performer done with his act, "an accidental death in a remote mountain cabin."

Cody said nothing. The rain drummed.

"What?" Larry asked, finally. "Are you thinking something else?"

"Let's take a look inside the rest of the cabin," Cody said. "Let me grab my gear."

"You're thinking something else," Larry said, his disappointment palpable.

All the walls were black with smoke, but the kitchen was neat and uncluttered. The table was cleared except for salt and pepper shakers designed to look like rising trout. It felt good to get out of the rain.

There were no dishes in the sink. There were unopened packages of meat and vegetables still in the plastic bags from the store in the refrigerator.

"Looks like he'd just been shopping," Larry said. "There's no old stuff in here at all, like maybe he'd been gone and just came back with groceries. And there's plenty here—two big steaks, some potatoes, salad in a bag. Like he was expecting someone or maybe just eating for two. I bet these steaks are still okay, considering how cold it's been."

Cody opened the dishwasher, hoping there would be dirty glasses or dishes inside.

"Shit," Cody said. "He ran the dishwasher before the place burned down, so we won't pull any prints from the glasses or plates."

"He was a clean drunk," Larry said, rooting through cupboards. "I'll leave all these doors open so you can shoot 'em if you want. It might be better in the daylight, though."

Cody checked under the sink. Cleaning supplies, garbage bags, the usual. He shined his flashlight into the garbage can, which was lined with white plastic. Garbage cans often held good stuff, he knew.

There were a few items inside, and he took the can out and emptied it on the table. Crumpled paper Dixie drinking cups, wadded-up Kleenex, shreds of cellophane, and the missing cork cap to the Wild Turkey bottle. Cody photographed the contents.

Larry saw the cap in the flash of the camera and whistled. "So we can assume he was on a bender after all."

Cody pushed the cellophane strips around with the tip of his pen.

"What are they?" Larry asked.

"Cigar wrappers, I think."

"So maybe he was smoking a cigar as well," Larry said. "But I still think it was the open stove."

Cody bagged the cellophane and the Dixie cups and the bottle cap and marked them with evidence numbers.

"What's with that?" Larry asked, observing.

"You never know," Cody said. "Maybe a print can be pulled."

Larry nodded his head but eyed Cody with suspicion.

"Got something here," Larry called from the bedroom.

Cody entered. Because the door had been closed, there was little smoke seepage or damage. The room was pristine compared to the kitchen; i.e., white walls, made bed, a half-full closet. Larry had his flashlight trained on an open suitcase on a cedar chest. Clothes were folded neatly inside. "He just got back from somewhere and hadn't even unpacked yet."

"That's what it looks like."

"Either that, or he was one of those anal types who packs the night before. But that doesn't account for the fresh food in the refrigerator. Plus, the place just doesn't seem lived in. It seems like it was closed up for a while and he just got here and immediately decided to get hammered. That's kind of weird."

"Yeah," Cody said. Cody's beam slid off the suitcase and rested on a battered leather briefcase next to the cedar chest.

"And something else, I just realized," Larry said. "There weren't any other liquor bottles in the kitchen. None. So unless he kept his bar out in the den where he burned up and every trace of it melted into the mud, the only bottle here was the one he was drinking."

"Um-hmmm."

"Which kind of makes me think he picked it up on the way here."

"Um-hmmm," he said, taking several photos of the suitcase, the closet, the bed.

"Hold it," Larry said, moving farther into the room. He illuminated a dresser with several items on top; a comb, a Delta Air Lines envelope, a paperback, a pile of coins, and a wallet. "ID," he said.

"Wait a minute," Cody said. "Before you pick it up let me take some shots of the layout and the stuff on the dresser. Then I want to superglue the room. Then you can check it all out."

Larry stared at him and Cody could feel his eyes on him in the semidark.

"Cody," Larry said, "what the hell are you doing?"

"Investigating," Cody said. "We're investigators, remember?"

"Fuck you. I'm saying accident and you're not. You're treating this as a homicide."

"I'm crossing every *t* and dotting every *i*," Cody said. "You know, like they teach us."

"Bullshit," Larry said, his voice rising. "You're trying to show me up."

"Not at all," Cody said, opening his case and finding the extra-large can of superglue Fume-It. In a closed room, the aerosol glue would fog up the space and collect on any latent fingerprints on the surfaces of the walls, counters, or mirrors. Fingerprints would show on the flat surfaces like floral flocking on wallpaper.

"I'll wait for you in the kitchen, you . . ." Larry said, not coming up with the foul name he wanted that fit the bill.

"Just be a minute," Cody said. "Close the door."

Larry slammed it shut so hard the rest of the house shuddered.

Before releasing the spray, Cody threw the briefcase on the bed and opened it.

Ten minutes later, Cody opened the door to the dining area. "Got some shots," he said. "The man was cleaner than hell. He must have scrubbed his walls. But I got some prints. Make sure we get the evidence tech to lift them."

Larry stood in the dark in the kitchen and said nothing. Then he shouldered past Cody into the bedroom. The dissipating fog of Fume-It made him cough. When he emerged, he pinched the flashlight between his jaw and shoulder so he could use both hands to hold the ticket jacket up and open it.

"Used tickets and a baggage claim check," Larry said. "Our man flew here on Delta from Salt Lake City three nights ago." He dropped the jacket on the table and opened up the wallet.

"His name was . . ."

"Hank Winters," Cody said.

"You knew him."

"Yeah. He was my sponsor."

3

"Sponsor?" Larry said. "Sponsor?"

As the realization dawned on Larry his face fell. "You mean, like Alcoholics Anonymous?"

"Yeah," Cody said. "He was my guy. I've been up here a couple of times. That's how I knew where it was and who he was."

Cody shined his flashlight to where the east wall of the room would have been. "That entire wall was covered with books. Hank was a collector and he had some really valuable first editions. He bought them all over the country when he traveled. Some of those books were really old and dried out. When the fire got to them I bet they went up like cordwood and probably made the fire even more destructive because of the heat of burning paper."

"But you didn't say anything. You were holding out on me."

"You mean knowing him? Or that I was in the program? Or that I think this wasn't an accident?"

"All of 'em, you son of a bitch. We work together. We talk to each other. No secrets. This is how you got in trouble down in Denver. This is why you're back in Montana. Damn you, remember when I told you never to put me into a position I didn't want to be in?"

Cody didn't shine his flashlight at Larry to see his face. He didn't need to. Larry was angry, and hurt.

"I wasn't holding out," Cody said. "I wanted your honest take on the scene. I wanted you to talk me out of what I was thinking. I hoped you would. You didn't."

Larry threw the wallet down on the tabletop. He started to say something but caught himself. Then, mocking, he said, "My name is Cody Hoyt. I'm an alcoholic *asshole.*"

Cody couldn't help himself. He laughed.

Larry looked up, surprised. "That's funny?"

"Yeah, it is. Tonight when I got the call, I nearly double-tapped a doper outside a bar for his twelve-pack of beer."

Larry looked at him. "How long have you been in AA?"

"Two months. Just two months. Fifty-nine days, five hours to be exact. Hardest time of my life."

Larry chinned the direction of the body. "And he was your sponsor? I don't know exactly how this works, but this guy Henry—"

"Hank," Cody corrected.

"*Hank* was your sponsor. That means whenever you felt like taking a snort you called him and he talked you down? Like that?"

Cody said, "Like that. But there's a lot more to it. Nobody can talk a drunk out of a drink except a fellow drunk. He was good, too. He appealed to my best nature."

"I didn't think you had one."

"I don't," Cody said. "But I've got a kid. I don't see him much, but he looks up to me because he doesn't know any better."

Larry's face softened some. Not much.

Said Cody, "My dad was a drunk. My mom was a drunk. My uncle was a drunk. My kid could go down the same road. I don't want him to. So I want to clean myself up. Not give him a role model, you know?"

Larry looked away. "I hate this kind of sharing. Men *talk* to each other, they don't *share.* Sharing's for assholes."

"Yeah," Cody said, "believe me, I hate this Oprah bullshit. But it is what it is. I'm learning to find out what it's like to be clean and sober. I've been pretty much drunk for twenty years. And you know what?"

"What?"

"It *sucks*. I don't know how you people do it—too much reality. But Hank was good because he understood and didn't try to act superior. He knew where I am now. He went through it himself, and he was a tough bastard. Marine. Desert Storm, in fact. And he did it all on his own. His wife left him years ago and he had no brothers or sisters. His parents were dead. He did the Twelve Steps on his own."

Moments went by. The rain thrummed on the roof.

"Well, good for you," Larry said. "I didn't mean to give you a hard time. But it seemed you were holding out, like testing me or something."

"I told you it wasn't like that."

Larry took a deep breath and threw his shoulders back. "So can we get on with this now? Can we figure this stupid thing out?"

"Yeah," Cody said, grateful.

"So what did Hank Winters do? Was he coming back here from a trip?"

"Probably. He was on the road most of the time. A pharmaceutical rep. His territory was the whole mountain west, from what he told me. He didn't tell me the specifics, but he was gone three out of four weeks a month. He stayed sober even though he was surrounded by temptation—all those airports and hotel bars. Think about it. He once told me, 'Even if you're not at home you can always find a meeting.' And he did."

Larry nodded. "So how could he be your sponsor if he was gone all the time?"

"I thought we put that away," Cody said. "But since you asked, I called him on his cell. He'd answer me any time of the day or night, wherever he was. I pulled him out of some big meeting once with a hospital and he took the call and talked me down for forty-five minutes.

A couple of weeks later he said he got beat out of a commission for five thousand bucks. But he took my call. That's the kind of guy he was."

"A good guy," Larry said.

"Yes," Cody said, looking down at his sodden boots and feeling his chest contract. "A saint. My saint. And not the type of guy who would buy a liter of Wild Turkey and drink the whole bottle alone. He just wouldn't do that. No way. That's why I think this wasn't an accident."

"Who would kill him? Somebody local? Any ideas?" Larry asked. But it was obvious he wasn't convinced.

"No idea in the world," Cody said. "But AA is its own world. We share—I mean talk about—the most intimate things in the world with each other. But other than his job, I don't really know much about him. That's the way it works."

Larry took a couple of steps toward Cody. His voice was low. He said, "Cody, I know you want to believe that. And you may be right. But shit, man, isn't it 'once an alcoholic, always an alcoholic?' I mean, maybe something happened. Maybe he just fell off the wagon. You can't say it doesn't happen."

"Not Hank," Cody said. But a kernel of doubt had been planted.

"Maybe just this once he fucked up," Larry said. "It happens. You *know* it happens."

"*NOT HANK,*" Cody said.

"Okay," Larry said, putting his free hand up, palm out. "I'm just sayin'."

"There's something else," Cody said, suddenly feeling as if the floor was buckling under his feet. "I checked out his briefcase."

Larry said, "And . . . ?"

"His coins were gone. He always kept his coins in a plastic sleeve in his briefcase. He'd bring them out whenever we met face to face and show them to me. He was so proud of them."

Suddenly, the kitchen flooded with light. Cars had entered the parking area. Cody could see Larry without lifting up his flashlight. In the glare of the lights through the rain-streaked windows, the surface of Larry's face and head was patterned with shadowed rivulets that looked like channels in an ant farm.

"Skeeter," Larry said, chinning toward the window. "Maybe the sheriff, too. At least three units. A whole shitload of 'em."

Cody didn't look over.

"The coins," Larry said. "Were they gold coins or something? Valuable? So you're saying maybe it was a robbery and a murder?"

Cody shook his head. "The coins weren't worth shit."

"So what are you driving at?"

"They're AA coins," Cody said softly. "Twelve-step program coins. One for every year from the local chapter. They're probably worth twenty bucks each, if that. There's a goddamned elk on the Helena Chapter ones. Hank had nine of them. I'm ten months away from getting my first one and I've never wanted something so bad. And they're missing."

Larry shrugged. "So your point is what?"

"They're gone," Cody said.

Outside, he could hear the sound of doors slamming and loud voices.

Larry said, "We better go out and fill them in."

Back out in the rain, Larry said over his shoulder, "My cynical cop mind tells me Henry, I mean Hank, tossed the coins away when he decided to go on a bender. You know, like symbolic."

"Not Hank," Cody said.

4

Sheriff Edward "Tub" Tubman and Undersheriff Cliff Bodean arrived on the scene in identical beige GMC Yukons with LEWIS AND CLARK COUNTY SHERIFF'S DEPARTMENT decals on the front doors. They parked side by side next to Larry's rig. Dougherty jumped out of his car to greet them. Both hikers remained inside his vehicle. As Larry and Cody approached, Tubman was unfolding his rain suit. His new gray Stetson rancher—an affectation that appeared the day after he declared he was running for reelection—was on the wet hood of his Yukon, the top of it already darkened from the rain. Cody was annoyed the sheriff didn't know enough to rest a good hat like that crown-down on a surface like real ranchers did.

Bodean was still in his vehicle and talking to dispatch over the radio.

The sheriff shot his arms through the sleeves of the suit but it got bunched around his head and he struggled. Cody was reminded of a turtle.

"Let me help you with that," Dougherty said, giving the back hem of the coat a yank. When he did, Tubman's head popped through the material and he came up sputtering.

"Damn thing anyway," he said, reaching for his hat. "So what have we got, boys?"

Tubman was short and doughy with a gunfighter's mustache and a tuft of hair that circled his round head like a smudge.

Larry and Cody exchanged looks, waiting for the other to start.

"A body, right?" Tubman said, annoyed. "You've got a body?"

"We've got that," Larry said. "Likely three days old. Male. Burned up in the fire."

Larry briefed the sheriff on the crime scene and what they'd found. He offered no opinions or speculation, just a solid accounting of the facts as they'd found them. He did it with such authority, Cody thought, that on the facts alone there was only one conclusion. He appreciated that Larry didn't even hint at their earlier discussion.

"Accidental death then," Tubman said with some relief. "Or what we like to call 'death by misadventure,' if you add in the empty bottle. Is Skeeter on the way?"

"As far as I know," Larry said. "Cody had him called."

"Let's hope he shows up alone without his fan club," Tubman said, shaking his head.

The sheriff nodded toward the hikers in Dougherty's truck. "Those folks the people who called it in?"

"Yes, sir," Dougherty said. "I questioned them separately."

"Did they check out?"

"Yes, sir."

"Are they county residents?"

Cody heard, *Are they voters?*

"No, sir," Dougherty said. "The man's a college professor from MSU. The woman's his student, apparently. They really don't want their names out, if you catch my drift."

Tubman smiled. "Too bad. Their names will be in the report. So tell the professor he better start doing some damage control with his wife."

Dougherty laughed.

"And get them out of here," Tubman said. "Take them back to their car so they can go home."

"Yes, sir."

Cody watched Dougherty get into his vehicle and start it up. He waited for the professor to remember his backpack in Cody's Ford, but the professor looked distraught. The woman stared out the window, as if contemplating what the rest of the semester would be like now. As they left the two of them appeared to be engaged in an angry exchange, based on the waving of hands.

Cody thought: *They left the backpack.*

Then he thought: *Fate.*

The bad blood between the sheriff and the coroner had recently come to a boil when Tubman was quoted in the *Independent Record* declaring that the cause of death of a twenty-five-year-old drifter found in Lincoln was due to an overdose of meth. He used the opportunity to make a case for increased drug-enforcement funding for the sheriff's department. The next day, Skeeter held a press conference for the newspaper and the two television stations and made a point of saying they were awaiting autopsy results and, "Maybe our local sheriff should just stop by my office to learn how we actually do our job, since he seems to somehow know things that haven't yet been determined scientifically."

Although the victim *was* later declared to have died due to an overdose, the war had begun over which one of the two would be the official spokesman for law enforcement in the county when it came to dead bodies. Because both men were running again and wanted as much authoritative face time in the press as possible, it was often an ugly race to the cameras for both of them.

Bodean opened his door and leaned out. "We've nailed down the owner of this place," he said. "Local man name of Henry Winters, age fifty-nine. No record."

"We found his ID," Larry confirmed.

"It didn't burn up?" the sheriff asked Larry.

"The wallet was in his bedroom in the side of the cabin that's still standing."

"I don't know him," Tubman said dismissively. Meaning Winters wasn't influential with the city council or a campaign contributor.

I did, Cody thought. He was angry with the sheriff's gut reaction.

Tubman took his wet hat off and looked at it in his headlights. "I gotta get me one of those plastic hat condom things so the felt doesn't get stained."

Another set of headlights strobed through the lodgepole pine trees.

"Who smashed up the unit?" Tubman asked, turning his attention to Cody's dented Ford.

"I hit an elk on the way up."

"I hope you've got good insurance," Tubman said, not kindly.

"I hope you've got a cow permit," Bodean laughed.

Cody cleared his throat. "I think it's a homicide."

Even in the diffused light from the headlights, Cody could see the sheriff's face darken.

"Larry thinks it could be accidental, but I don't. I think somebody killed Hank and tried to cover the crime by burning the place down. If it wasn't for the rain, he would have completely gotten away with it."

Tubman spat between his feet. "It *sounds* accidental, Cody."

"I'll give you that. But I knew the man. It wasn't an accident."

The sheriff turned on Larry: "Why didn't you say so in the first place?"

Larry shrugged. "We're still working it out," he said.

"Before Skeeter gets here," Tubman said to Cody, "tell me why you don't think this is what it appears to be."

Cody told him, leaving out the part about him being in AA. Leaving out the part about the missing coins. Saying he knew Hank Winters never drank alcohol.

"*That's* your reasoning?"

"Yes." Cody could feel Larry glaring at him but didn't look over. Hearing in his head, *Don't ever screw me, and don't ever put me in a position I don't want to be in.*

Tubman crossed his arms and shook his head. "So what do I tell the press? What do I tell that fucking Skeeter?"

"Whatever you want," Cody said. "I'm investigating it as a homicide."

The sheriff set his jaw. "I know you sometimes forget this, Hoyt, but you work for *me*. And from what I've heard, it's an accidental death. Do you dispute anything Olson told me?"

"No."

"Then keep your theories to yourself until you've got something a hell of a lot better than what you've got. The last thing I need right now is an unsolved murder leading up to the primary. Do you understand? It's an accidental death until you can prove to me it isn't. Like if the autopsy boys in Missoula find a bullet hole in his skull or a knife in his gut. Then we've got something that changes the situation. Got that?"

Cody felt a familiar rage building up in him. But he managed not to lash out.

"Got that?" Tubman said again.

"I hear you," Cody mumbled.

Deep in the trees from the direction of the main road he could hear the sound of a vehicle approaching.

"Oh no," Bodean said, zipping up his long yellow raincoat and turning toward the road. "Skeeter's coming."

"Shit," Tubman said, turning away from Cody, dismissing him. "Skeeter's been showing up places wearing a sidearm lately. He's trying to hammer home the fact that he's law enforcement. Let's see if the joker is packing."

Skeeter was called Skeeter, Cody'd been told, because he didn't like his first name, which was Leslie. SKEETER was stenciled on his vehicle doors. He pulled his four-wheel-drive behind Cody's Ford, blocking him, and jumped out quickly, already dressed for the weather. Before he zipped his rain jacket, Cody saw Skeeter was wearing a holster.

Skeeter Caldwell was tall, slim, and gaunt with deep-set eyes and a long bladelike nose and he'd recently had his teeth capped so he wouldn't look quite so much like a ghoul. But, Cody thought, he *still* looked like a ghoul.

"Sheriff," Skeeter said in greeting, nodding toward Tubman.

"Skeeter," the sheriff said, unenthusiastic.

"Where's the body?"

Four vehicles were lined up shoulder to shoulder with all of their headlights aimed at the burned cabin. Tubman said, "Guess."

"Can we be professional here?" Skeeter asked.

"Absolutely."

"Then please have your men show me the victim."

Tubman turned to Larry. "Perhaps you could escort the county coroner to the scene."

Larry grunted.

"So what is your first impression?" Skeeter asked.

"Accident."

"We shall see."

Tubman rolled his eyes.

"I hope you don't mind if a reporter from the *Independent Record* comes along," Skeeter said. "Carrie Lowry. I guess she heard the report over the radio."

"I bet," Tubman said sourly. "And I *do* mind. We haven't even secured the scene yet." He turned to Cody. "Put up some crime tape. Make her keep her distance. I don't want her at the cabin taking pictures or getting in the way. Tell her we'll talk to her when we've got something to say."

Cody saluted and said, "Yes, sir!"

Before Tubman turned to follow Skeeter, Bodean, and Larry toward the cabin, he said to Cody, "That'll be more than enough of that shit, mister."

Another set of headlights fanned through the lodgepole pine trunks. Unlike Skeeter, the driver was going slowly, picking through the forest, as if unsure that the road was the correct one. Cody had a six-inch roll of yellow plastic tape that read DO NOT CROSS DO NOT CROSS. He'd tied one end to a tree trunk near the entrance to the parking area and was letting it unwind as he walked toward the other side. He shot glances over his shoulder at the cabin as he unwound the tape. Skeeter was bending over the body while Larry provided the light. Tubman and Bodean stood behind them in the rain looking useless.

The vehicle made the last turn and headlights blinded him. Again. He held up his free forearm to block the light and the vehicle braked to a stop with a squeal.

A woman's voice said, "Oh, come on. You're telling me I can't get any closer than *that*?"

"Sheriff's orders," Cody said.

"You've gotta let me through."

"Sorry."

"Cody," she said, "you are such an asshole."

"Hi, Carrie," he said. "How are you tonight?"

"I thought I was lost," she said. "Then I finally find it and . . . it's *you*."

He shrugged. "Did you bring a poncho or something? It's raining."

"Oh, really?"

He nodded, then continued stripping the tape across the road. She killed the engine and he heard a door slam. He looked over and saw her raise the tape up over her head and start to stride toward the cabin.

"Whoa," he said. "I don't want to have to arrest you and/or torture you until you confess."

She turned toward him, hands on hips. She wore a battered raincoat that bulged near her waistline and a slouch cap that looked like it had been in her trunk for ten years. Her red hair fell on the shoulders of the raincoat and stuck to the wet fabric.

"Nice look," he said. "I hope you didn't dress up just for me."

"Fuck you, Cody," she said.

"Language," he said. "God is listening."

"*Fuck You,* Cody." Then added, "And the horse you rode in on. Skeeter told me I'd have access."

"I'm sure you will," he said, "once the scene is released to him. But that hasn't happened yet. Right now, this is a crime scene under investigation by the sheriff's department. When it gets turned over to the coroner, you'll be the first to know, I'm sure."

She huffed, "What am I supposed to do in the meanwhile?"

"You could help me string this crime-scene tape," he said. "I could use a hand."

"You are *such* an asshole."

"Get back before I shoot you," he said, shining his flashlight on her face so she flinched. But before she did, he got a glimpse of her green eyes, the constellation of freckles across her cheeks and nose, that nice mouth.

"Bastard," she said, wheeling around and stomping back toward her fifteen-year-old Subaru. She climbed back in and slammed the door and he watched her fume until the interior light went out.

He'd met Carrie the year before, shortly after he returned to Montana from Denver. He'd been with the department less than a month, and he sidled up to her bar stool at the Windbag Bar and Grill. He'd watched her fend off rural legislators in town for the session like swatting flies and told her he admired her high opinion of herself. When she didn't swat him away, he bought her another Jack and Coke, even though he explained that by drinking the concoction she was ruining two good drinks.

Over the next three hours he bought her four more. He kept up with her. She told him about growing up in Havre, going to J-school, marrying twice to losers, landing at the *Independent Record*. She covered the police beat, she said. She asked him if he'd be a source. He said sure, if she'd quit talking shop and go home with him.

Somehow, he drove her to his apartment without being picked up by the Helena police, even though he cruised through at least two red lights, maybe more. She never noticed because she was pawing at his belt, fumbling at it, pulling the wrong way on the tongue of his belt but with surprising strength. When he threw her over his shoulder and carried her into his place, she laughed and hit at him until he tossed her on his bed. She was a crazy back-scratching wildcat for ten minutes before he, or she, passed out the first time. He recalled little after that, but he had a vague memory involving him trying to connect the dots of her freckles with a felt-tipped pen, which they both found hilarious at the time.

When she came by the station a week later to interview the sheriff after a Marysville outfitter who had shot his wife twelve times (pausing twice to reload) with a .30-06, their eyes locked for a moment and she tossed her red hair, said, "It was hell getting that ink off of my face," and turned on her heel and clicked away down the hallway.

He knew he wasn't wanted or needed at the cabin so he returned to his Ford and climbed in. The windows steamed again, but it was good to be somewhere dry.

Through the fogged windshield he saw flashlights dancing in the dark at the cabin and figures moving slowly through the black muck. He thought about Hank and something gripped him hard inside like a talon and suddenly he was tearing up. He couldn't believe it. Cody hadn't cried since his dog died when he was twelve. Funerals for his father and mother had been uneventful. But Hank was different. Hank was a tough old bird who wanted to help him solely because he was a kind and good man. Hank was willing to help a fucked-up stranger and show him goodness existed. And Hank was gone.

Cody's hand, as if on its own, crab-walked across the bench seat until it paused near the day pack of the hiker. Cody didn't look over. His hand had a mind of its own. It was out of his control. Then it grabbed the neck of the bottle of Jim Beam.

His other hand, also thinking independently, reached across his body and unscrewed the cap. He took two big gulps, as if it were water and he was thirsty, then he jammed the bottle between his thighs. Something inside him said, *Stop now, while you still can.*

He shrugged the voice away. That had never been difficult, he always won that contest. At first, his belly clutched painfully, as if it were shutting down and rejecting the alcohol. He grunted and leaned forward, doubling up, his forehead on the top of the steering wheel. Then the pain stopped and, as if he were welcoming an old friend, he could feel the familiar warmth radiate through him starting with his chest and spreading out to his arms and legs and head. It was as if he was filling his tank up with rocket fuel.

He sat back and the blackened image of the arm and bloated hand flickered on the inside of the windshield like the screen of a drive-in movie, and he said, "Hank, is this what happened to you? Is this what you did? You opened a bottle again? Tell me I'm wrong because, buddy, I believed in you."

He thought about it. He had another drink.

Then: "Hank, I'm going to find whoever did this to you."

Cody drank fast on an empty stomach. When he put the cap back on the bottle half of it was gone. He wiped his mouth with the back of his hand, turned on the interior light, and looked at himself in the rearview mirror. He remembered that flushed face from scarred mirrors in bar restrooms and from his own bathroom when he got home after closing time.

He said, "Helloooo, handsome. And welcome back."

And he suddenly had a plan.

Then he unwrapped and crammed three sticks of Stride Winterblue gum (every drunk's secret gum) into his mouth and lit a cigarette. The combination would disguise his breath. He knew this from experience. And he opened the SUV door and once again was pelted by rain. If it weren't for the furnace raging through him, he thought, it might feel cold outside.

Cody walked toward the plastic barrier and wriggled his fingers at Carrie as he pushed the crime-scene tape over his head and approached her car on the driver's side. She didn't respond so he leaned his butt against the front fender and drew in deep on his cigarette. He listened to the rain coursing through the pines and heavy drops plunking into surface puddles. Raindrops smacked his cigarette and he felt it important to smoke it to a nub before a lucky drop hit the cherry and drowned it out.

Finally, she rolled her window down. "Yes? Are you here to tell me I can go in?"

"Nope."

"Then get off my car."

He wouldn't tell her he needed to lean against her car for a moment so he wouldn't fall down. Instead, he laughed. "I don't think I can make it look any worse than it does now."

"Jesus," she said. "You are such an—"

"Sticks and stones," he said in a way that even charmed *him*. And he noted she hadn't rolled her window back up.

"Carrie, do you remember when you asked me to be a source? Remember? It was in the Windbag."

She was quiet. Cautious. "Yes."

"I'm ready," he said.

"Are you jerking me around?" Her voice was attractive, kind of husky.

"No, ma'am."

"Are there conditions?" she asked. Her voice had become businesslike. Which for some reason made him want to take her home again, but he'd settle for another cigarette. He slapped his raincoat until he found the pack and matches.

"Those things will kill you," she said.

"Bring it on," he laughed. "Bring it on."

"Cody."

He got the cigarette lit and turned and dropped to his haunches so he was eye-level with her in the car. She didn't draw back away from him, he noticed. He wished he could see her face better.

"Promise me what I tell you will be confidential," he said. "My name can't be in the story and you have to promise you won't even hint at where this comes from."

She hesitated, then said, "Okay. But it's got to be of substance."

"It's of substance. And you can't do one of those 'an unnamed source in the sheriff's department' kinds of things. Or I'll make your life so miserable you'll have to leave Montana."

That made her wince, and she sat back. "Don't threaten me like that."

"No threat," he said. "Just what it is. Are we clear?"

"We're clear."

He looked around. Although he couldn't see everyone at the cabin, he did see flashlight beams bouncing around.

"This isn't an accident, whatever the sheriff or Skeeter tells you. It's a murder."

"Jesus."

"And whoever did it tried to cover his tracks by burning the place down. The victim was a great man named Hank Winters, and we're gonna find who did it."

She shook her head. "Why would the sheriff or Skeeter want to cover that up? I don't understand."

He whispered conspiratorially, "Because it's important to them not to call it a murder. It's political, and it's big. Bigger than hell. This could be the story that gets you on the map if you play it right."

"Oh, Cody," she said, reaching out of her window and touching his arm. Her eyes glistened in the reflection of the flashlights at the scene.

"Look," he said. "The murderer left a clue to his identity. I can't tell you what it was but we're going to follow it to the killer once we get some outside experts up here with some special equipment. And we *will* get him. He's on borrowed time until the analysis comes back."

"What kind of analysis?"

"That I can't tell you yet."

With that, Cody stood and patted her hand back. "Remember," he said, "you didn't hear this from me."

After a beat, she said, "Thank you, Cody. I owe you."

"Just no scratching this time," he said as he turned to walk away.

As he passed under the crime-scene tape he nearly ran into Larry, who stood in the dark with his flashlight off. Cody felt the familiar grip of guilt that came with secret drinking.

"What in the hell are you doing?" Larry said in an urgent whisper. "I heard what you told her, you son of a bitch."

Cody reached out for Larry but Larry backed away. Cody said, "I'm baiting the trap."

"What the fuck are you talking about? What was that about special equipment and analysis?"

Cody found himself grinning maniacally, and couldn't douse it out. He held out his hand to Larry, and said, "I'm pretty sure she bought it."

Larry stared at him, unmoving. They faced off for over a minute with no words.

Finally, Larry said, "You found a bottle, didn't you?"

"Yup."

"And now you're going to self-destruct and try to take me with you."

Cody shrugged. "You don't have to come, Larry."

"You asshole. You stupid jerk."

"I've been hearing that a lot tonight."

Larry said, "What am I going to do with you?"

Cody suddenly felt sober. It happened at the weirdest times, he thought. He said, "Help me find the guy who killed Hank. I'll take it from there."

Larry moaned.

Cody stepped close to Larry and said, "Larry, I'm a drunk but I'm not a joke. You've never seen me unleashed before and believe me, it's a sight to behold. I'll go after this guy like nothing you've ever experienced. And when I find him I'll kill his ass a million times over."

Larry stepped back. "Man, are you okay?"

Cody said, "I've never been okay. But now I've got a *purpose.*" He spat the last word.

Larry's eyes got wide and he shook his head slowly. "You're out of control," Larry whispered.

"Maybe." Cody winked and walked back to his Ford for the bottle. The rest of the night he functioned in a blackout. And he woke up the next morning in his apartment covered with blood. Not his.

5

On the night he shot the coroner, Cody Hoyt was back at Hank Winters's cabin, hiding in a copse of pine trees in the dark. Waiting.

The last twenty hours had been a dense, almost impenetrable fog. He'd called on his reserves to simply stay upright for most of it. As he sipped from the pint bottle of Evan Williams bourbon he'd brought with him to Vigilante Campground, certain disconnected scenes came up to the surface as if for air and he recalled them before they sunk again to be replaced by another. *Whack-a-mole memories!* he thought. Just like the bad old days.

He tried to put them in order.

Driving down from the mountains following Larry's car, Larry pulling over twice to get out and curse at him, saying Cody nearly gave himself away when he was slurring his words to the evidence tech and EMTs as they bagged the body and collected all the evidence they'd tagged. Telling Cody that luckily, the sheriff and undersheriff were back in their vehicles at that point, bitching about Skeeter and not thinking about why one of their lead investigators had to lean on trees or the cabin to keep upright. Noting that Carrie Lowry was long gone, and Skeeter was annoyed about that. Not objecting when Larry pushed him away from the cabin in the dark so no one could hear him talk or see him trying to maintain his balance;

Cutting up the dead cow elk with Larry on their way down the mountain, quartering it with a bone saw Larry had in his gear box, all so Cody could take the meat to the battered women's shelter even though he could barely stand and the huge chunks of raw, still-warm meat had covered his clothes with blood. Ignoring Larry as he bitched and moaned about it, saying those women had plenty to eat as it was and they'd think Cody was crazy;

Hauling the quarters into the walk-in freezer of the shelter after waking up the manager, winking at Larry when she cried and said how grateful she was, how the women and kids staying there would love the meat, offering to clean him up and make some coffee because there was something wrong with his eyes;

Climbing back into the Ford ten minutes after Larry dropped him off at his building, his promises to his partner that he'd go straight to bed and stay off the bottle ringing in his ears, then coming right back out the door when Larry was gone and starting the engine and driving away;

Pounding on the door of a man who ran a roadside liquor store, waking him up because it was four hours past closing, demanding a case of beer and two pints of bourbon, paying for them with a hundred-dollar bill and a pat on the grip of his .40 Sig Sauer to remind the owner to keep quiet about the intrusion;

Calling Jenny, his ex-wife, waking her and making her angry, asking to talk to his son Justin to tell him he could borrow anything he wanted to borrow and to stay away from alcohol and parties, but Justin wasn't there. He was already gone, with Jenny's new rich fiancé, on a goddamned male bonding adventure in the wilderness. Jenny calling him an asshole which made him laugh because he'd been called that so many times that night that *it just might be true,* and her slamming down the phone and refusing to pick up when he called her number three more times until he passed out in his lounge chair with the receiver stuck to his hand by congealing blood;

Waking up covered in stiff brown blood, his pants, shirt, and hands caked with it, dried flakes spackling his hand like cracks in a dry lake bed. Swirls of it in the shower, rich and red and revolting. Kicking at the pink swirls and flakes with bare feet, trying to get them to go down the drain;

Swallowing six ibuprofens to blunt the savage pounding in his head, throwing them up in the kitchen sink, taking six more, finally drinking a beer and a raw egg for breakfast which eased him back into the slipstream and stopped his hands from shaking and made it possible for him to brush his teeth and shave without mutilating himself;

Showing up for the eight thirty staff briefing with the town cops from across the hall, Undersheriff Bodean outlining the circumstances of the death of Hank Winters, sleeping through it with his eyes wide open until the sheriff stormed into the room waving the morning's *Independent Record,* cursing Carrie Lowry and especially that damned Skeeter, who must have been the one who fed her full of lies about the accident being a murder and a lead left at the crime scene that would identify the killer, ordering all of his cops to boycott the local paper until they apologized and ran a front-page retraction;

Feeling Larry's absolutely chilling glare from across the room while Tubman ranted;

Cutting out early after the briefing because he couldn't concentrate and he needed a beer, taking his notes and camera with him;

Spending the afternoon at the Windbag and the Jester, seeing his old friends, laughing at their stories and telling some of his own, feeling like it was a family reunion of sorts for the men and women who drank in the daylight, *his people!*;

Taking the Ford back up the mountain as dusk came, shotgun in the rack and pistol in his holster, hoping to avoid hitting another elk, hoping against hope that whoever did this to Hank would read the paper and be puzzled as hell and return to the scene to try and retrieve whatever it was the cops found;

Knowing it was nuttier than hell but somehow made complete sense;

Parking the vehicle on a road a half mile from Hank's place so it couldn't be seen and hiking through the dark forest still dripping with rain from the storm that afternoon, carrying the shotgun, packing his pistol, and swinging a six-pack of beer by the plastic holder.

He didn't know how long he'd been passed out when the sound of a motor woke him up. Cody moaned and opened his eyes. His head throbbed. He found himself sitting on the damp ground, leaning back against a tree trunk. The cold wet had soaked through his jeans and underwear, and his butt was freezing.

Since it took a few moments to figure out where he was and why he was there, the sound of the tires on gravel and the motor confused him. Then he realized his plan had worked, that the killer had returned to the scene.

He stood up and the waves of dizziness and nausea nearly buckled his knees. He kept his head down, waiting it out, trying to listen to what was going on through the roaring. He heard a man's voice say, "Here it is," and he thought: *There's more than one of them.*

Unless the guy was talking to himself, which was doubtful.

"Here?" A woman's voice.

"There, on that frame that was once a couch. His body was there."

Cody took a deep breath of cold mountain air and it cleared the clouds from his mind a little. The night and his situation started to come into focus. He wished he'd been lucid when they drove up so that he could have seen them before they got out of their car. But that moment had passed.

He left the three full beers and the empty bottle of bourbon in the grass, and took a step toward the back of the cabin. His legs were rubbery, and he lurched to the side, about to fall. Luckily, the trees were close together and his shoulder thumped into a trunk and kept him upright. He inhaled and held the cold air in his lungs, hoping it would sober him up.

"So what are we looking for?" the woman asked.

"I really don't know," the man said. "Whatever was left. If anything."

The unburned part of the cabin was between Cody and the visitors, so he couldn't see them. A shaft of light sliced through the air—a flashlight being turned on—then quickly descended out of view. They were looking for something in the black muck.

He thought, *I have you now, you scumbags.*

"This is sick," she said. "I wished I knew what we were looking for."

"Probably nothing," he said. "It might be the sheriff's idea of a stupid trick to make him look like he's doing something. He may drag this out past the election, is my guess."

The back of the cabin was suddenly in front of him. Cody reached out with his left hand and touched the rounded logs. All he'd need to do was slip along the lengths of the logs until it opened up on the burned section, and they'd be there in the open.

Then he realized he'd left his shotgun back where he'd passed out. Hesitating, he considered feeling his way back to retrieve it. But he'd gotten this far in silence without slipping or stepping on a dead branch to reveal himself. Doing it twice more without making a sound was unlikely at best. He cursed himself and reached up and pinched his cheek so hard he winced. But it helped wake him up. Then he reached down and slowly unsnapped the plastic restraint on his holster and drew his Sig Sauer. As always, there was no safety to worry about and one in the chamber so there'd be no need to rack the slide.

He'd had Trijicon self-luminous sights put on his weapon back in Denver, and he raised it and fitted the front green dot between the twin dots of the back sight. Although he'd never fired at anyone at night on the job, he'd put in hours at the range. He knew if he squeezed the trigger when the three dots were horizontal he should be able to hit what he was pointing at. His only issue was whether or not he'd take out the both of them without warning, or identify himself first. Of course, however it went, in his after-action report he'd say he ordered them to freeze and they didn't, so he had no choice.

Kill the man first, he thought. A double-tap into the thickest part of his torso as fast as he could squeeze the trigger, then swing on the woman and do the same. Then, if necessary, killshots to the head.

Could he kill a woman? The idea sickened him. "There," the man said, his voice rising. "Right *there*. Look."

Had they found it? he wondered.

He saw the pool of their flashlight before he saw them. There was a glint of gold in the muck of the floor.

"It looks like a coin," she said.

"Yes, it does," he said, distressed. "I don't know how I could have missed it."

Because, Cody thought, *I put it there two hours ago.* Gold-foil-wrapped chocolate coins went for $1.89 at Walgreens these days.

And he cleared the edge of the logs and barked, "FREEZE, YOU FUCKERS!"

She screamed and threw her flashlight into the air with the same motion that she covered her mouth.

He blinded Cody with his light but before he did Cody saw a hand reach down and grip a pistol and raise it and there was a star-shaped explosion of fire tinged with blue and a deafening crack. And something white-hot and angry slapped the side of his face.

And that's when Cody shot the county coroner. Double-tap, two loud snaps and two yellow-green tongues of flame. Skeeter went down like a puppet with its strings clipped.

Cody lowered his weapon, the sharp smell of gunpowder and his own blood biting at his nose, and said, "Oh, shit."

Carrie Lowry didn't stop screaming until her sobs and admonitions took over.

6

Cody sat back in an uncomfortable chair across from Sheriff Tubman in his cramped little office. The door was closed, and had been for an hour. There had been no eight thirty briefing that morning. Undersheriff Bodean perched on the corner of Tubman's desk, looking almost straight down at him. On the credenza behind the sheriff was his hat, brim-down, and the morning's *Independent Record* with EYE-WITNESS ACCOUNT: CORONER SHOT BY SHERIFF'S DEPARTMENT blaring across all four columns of the front page. Cody thought, *Carrie got that big story I promised her after all.*

"You really ought to put your hat crown-down when you're not wearing it," Cody said. "You'll ruin the brim that way."

Tubman closed his eyes, to keep from exploding, Cody guessed.

"How you can joke at a time like this is beyond me," Bodean said, shaking his head.

"Really," Cody said, "it'll flatten the brim. Trust me on this."

"Look at my phone," Tubman said. "All the lights are blinking. Everybody wants a statement and they're willing to stay on hold until they get it."

"Sorry," Cody said.

"Yes," Tubman said, "you are."

Bodean cleared his throat and stuck his chin out. "In case you don't know the procedure, Detective Hoyt, this is an officer-involved shooting, so give me your badge and your gun."

Cody shifted in his chair and unclipped the badge and slid it across the desk to Tubman. He pulled his Sig Sauer and handed it grip-first to Bodean. "Careful," he said, "it's loaded."

Bodean walked the weapon over and put it gingerly on top of a metal filing cabinet. He said, "You are officially on administrative leave with pay. We've got a call in to the state to send an outside team to investigate the incident. They're likely to be here tomorrow, so stay in touch with us at all times."

Cody nodded.

"Don't go anywhere for seventy-two hours. That's when we'll take your statement and based on what the state criminal investigation team says, you might be placed under arrest."

Even though he knew it could happen, Cody felt a chill crawl through his scalp.

Said Bodean, "It's my duty to advise you to keep your mouth shut until you give your official statement. At that time, you should be aware that under *Garrity versus New Jersey,* you may be disciplined if you refuse to answer questions about your conduct on the job. You have no Fifth Amendment rights as a cop. In the meantime, the only person you should talk to is a peer counselor we'll assign. Do you understand what I just said?"

"Yeah, but I don't mind talking. And if you send a social worker to my place I'll mace him," Cody growled. "It went down exactly like Carrie Lowry wrote in the paper. Skeeter drew first and fired after I told him to freeze. I shot him in self-defense."

Tubman continued to shake his head, as if he were watching his career slink away.

Bodean said, "She wrote that you didn't identify yourself."

"I didn't get the chance. Skeeter was fast for a ghoul."

"You refused to take a breathalyzer test."

"It's my right. I don't trust those portable things. I took one later here at the station."

"*Hours* later," Bodean said, "after the alcohol in your system had a chance to metabolize. And you still came in a .88. That's barely sober and it was four hours after the shooting. And the officer on the scene said you smelled like a still."

"Dougherty wouldn't know a still if he tripped over it," Cody said.

"You're lucky Skeeter was wearing a vest. Your first slug hit him here," Bodean gestured toward his heart. "The second one was above the armor and really messed up his shoulder. But he should be okay and giving press conferences any time now."

Instinctively, Cody reached up and touched the compress taped over his right ear where Skeeter's round had clipped him. The bullet had taken a half inch of his earlobe and the wound bled like crazy until they got it stopped.

After the emergency room docs had bandaged and released him, he'd tried to talk to the coroner, who was upstairs in the same hospital. He wasn't sure if he wanted to yell at Skeeter or apologize or shoot him again. He didn't get an opportunity to make the choice because a hospital security officer wouldn't let him past his desk until visiting hours.

"Why in God's name was Skeeter wearing a vest and carrying a weapon in the first place?" Cody asked. "He's the *coroner*. And he shouldn't have snuck a reporter into a crime scene just so she could get some photos. That's not right. He was acting suspiciously."

"We'd all like to know that and it'll come out in the investigation," Tubman said. "He might be in as much trouble as you are or more. But in this instance I'm glad he had the vest or we'd have a homicide investigation going and you'd be in our jail."

Cody shrugged. "Speaking of homicide," he said, "I'd still like to help on the Hank Winters murder investigation."

"It wasn't a homicide," Tubman said with force.

"It was," Cody said.

"Stay away from it," Tubman said. "Stay away from this office. Stay away from Larry." He leaned forward on his desk and balled his fists. "And stay the hell away from *me*."

The door opened and Edna stuck her head in. "Sheriff, the governor is on the line. He wants a briefing."

Tubman moaned and sat back. To Cody, he said, "Go away. Go straight out the door and go home. Don't even talk to anyone. And stay by your phone."

Before Cody left the room, he ducked behind the sheriff and turned the offending hat over.

Larry was alone in the detective room, scrolling through digital images of the crime scene Cody had shot two nights before. Although his shoulders tensed when Cody entered the room, he didn't greet him. And when Cody shut the door behind him, Larry seemed to be studying the screen even more intently than before.

"I'll be out of here in a minute," Cody said.

He went to his desk and started filling an empty box he'd grabbed outside the evidence room with his papers, gear, and the nascent murder book he'd begun.

"Next time," Larry said finally, "go for a head shot."

"*Ha.*"

"Man, when you dive in you go *deep*. I'll give that to you."

Cody grunted.

"A gold-wrapped chocolate coin?" Larry laughed.

"It worked, sort of," Cody said. "If the killer thought he'd left one behind . . ."

"You know what's going to happen," Larry said. "Skeeter knows he's in trouble, too. So he's going to try and get out ahead of it with the press and the voters. He's going to start yapping and paint you in the worst light possible and try to taint the investigation."

Cody shrugged.

"So, what happened with the sheriff?"

"I'm suspended until they clear me."

"You are so fucking lucky, Cody. You could have killed the coroner or gotten killed yourself. And I don't doubt for a second that you were hammered at the time."

"I was blitzed," Cody said. "But when I pulled the trigger I felt completely sober. Strange how that happens. Adrenaline trumps alcohol: remember that."

"Are you over it? The binge, I mean?"

Cody said, "I think so. I'm not promising anything, though."

"Yeah," Larry said, finally swiveling around in his chair to face him, "I found out how solid your promises are."

"I'm really sorry about that," Cody said, looking out the window at the lawn in front of the Law Enforcement Center. "And I want to thank you again for covering for me."

"The last time," Larry said. "Ever."

"That's reasonable."

Larry let a beat pass. Then, "I'm rethinking the Winters death."

"You are?" For the first time in forty-eight hours, he felt a little nudge of hope.

"Yeah. While you were partying with your old pals yesterday, I was doing police work."

"And?"

"The preliminary autopsy shows blunt head trauma. Of course, they don't know yet whether it was pre- or postmortem. I mean, the guy was covered with the beams from his roof that fell on his noggin. But there wasn't any smoke in his lungs. Meaning he was likely dead before the fire got out of hand. As you know, it's never the fire that kills 'em. It's the smoke."

"Interesting there was no inhalation."

"And there's another thing good about all that rain and cold weather," Larry said. "According to the lab, there had been too much time between the death and the discovery of the body to find out if there was any alcohol in his bloodstream. Plus, the heat of the fire could have literally burned it out. But because the body was kept fairly cool, they're going to cut his eyes out and test 'em."

Cody winced. "His *eyes*?"

Larry read from his notes. "The vitreous humor can be tested. This is the jellylike substance within the eyeball. Alcohol can be detected there and it lags behind the blood level. That is, it reflects the blood level about two hours prior to death. If it is elevated, the ME can say that the victim was likely intoxicated. They can't get a blood alcohol level, but they can *possibly* say it was there at the time of death."

"When will they call you back?"

Larry shrugged. "Soon, I hope. It's not definitive, but if there's no smoke in the lungs and no sign of alcohol consumption, it will pretty much kill my accident or suicide theory. Because that means somebody opened a bottle and left it to be found with the body, and somebody opened the door of the stove."

Nodding, Cody said, "So our killer bashed him in the head, drank or poured out the bottle, and set the place on fire."

"You're jumping to conclusions," Larry said.

"Well," Cody said, "here's another jump. Whomever did it knew Hank once had problems with alcohol. Since Hank hadn't had a drop in five years, they'd have to know Hank's history. A stranger wouldn't likely know that, would he?"

Larry started to argue but the edges of his mouth turned down and he nodded. "I see where you're going. But who would know, besides you?"

Cody didn't answer. He let Larry figure it out.

"Every other person in your AA group," Larry said. "You people confess everything to each other. *They* would know."

Cody said, "Exactly."

Larry said, "So we need to establish the whereabouts of all of the Helena AA members between the hours of eight and midnight three nights ago."

Cody paused. "How'd you determine the time of death? The ME?"

"Naw. The receipt from when Winters bought the steaks had the exact time on it: 6:03 P.M. It takes almost an hour to drive from the store to his cabin, so let's say he was there by seven. Montana Power and Light said the cabin had a power outage at midnight, which I attribute to the fire. So there's our window."

Cody was impressed. Larry *was* good.

"Back to the alcoholics," Larry said. "Do you know them all?"

Cody nodded.

"Do you have a list?"

"At home," Cody said. "There's thirteen in our little group. Of course, there are groups all over and a hell of a lot more alcoholics in Helena than you'd imagine. But our group is small because of when and where we meet. I can e-mail it to you. I can't officially work on the case, but I can feed *you*."

"Cool," Larry said. Cody could see a light behind his eyes. They were getting somewhere.

"I hate this, though," Cody said. "I'm betraying their trust. This is really a shitty thing to do to them. I mean, you'll be surprised. We're talking doctors, lawyers, a couple politicians. Even somebody in our office."

Larry *was* surprised.

"Edna," Cody said. "But you don't need to question her. She was working dispatch here every night this week."

"Don't worry," Larry said. "I won't even hint at how I got their names. I'll say we're simply following up on everyone we could find who might have known him. I might even fudge it a little and say we recovered an address book and we're just calling all the names in it. I won't mention AA and I won't bring up your name."

"Thank you, Larry. Really."

"But you've got to understand something, you asshole," Larry said. "I'm not being your pal here. I want you to go back. You *need* to go back to AA, or I'll never work with you again. And I'm not blowing smoke."

"I know you're not."

"Oh," Larry said, slapping the tops of his thighs, "I forgot to tell you something else. I sent the hard drive of that fried computer down to some IT guys at MSU. They think they may be able to retrieve the data off it. That surprised the hell out of me because I thought data would, you know, *melt*."

"No shit."

"They're looking at it now. I'll let you know what they come up with."

Cody stroked his chin. "See if they can find any letters or documents he had stored away. That and e-mails, of course. There might be an e-mail exchange with whomever he invited to dinner that night. That would be a hell of a stroke of luck. And the history on his Web browser. Maybe we'll know what he's been looking at lately."

Larry rolled his eyes. "Gee, I hadn't thought of any of that before, Cody. Good thing you're here to straighten me out."

Cody grinned.

The office door opened without a knock. Bodean filled the doorframe, hands on hips. His face was dark.

"I thought I heard your voice," he said to Cody. "Why in the hell are you still here?"

"Larry got all emotional when he heard I'd been suspended," Cody said. "I came in to comfort him and talk him off the ledge."

Larry snorted.

"Get the hell out of here or I'll have you arrested," Bodean said. "You have no authorization to be here. And give me your key card so you can't come back."

Cody handed it over and picked up his box to leave.

"And the keys to your Ford. It's a county vehicle."

Cody said, "I'll leave 'em at the shop when I turn the Ford over to the maintenance guys. Remember—it's kind of wrecked."

Bodean considered that a moment, and nodded. "Sort of like you," he said.

"Wow," Cody said, "that was a good one, Bodean. Clever."

Cody picked up his box to leave.

"It stays," Bodean said. "That's county property, too."

Cody shrugged. Larry simply watched, and raised his eyebrows.

"Go home and stay by your phone," Bodean said.

"Bye, Larry."

"Cody."

"Try not to weep."

"I'll try," Larry said.

The morning was warm and sunny and the sky was achingly blue. Cody shuffled across the lawn toward his vehicle in the parking lot. As he reached it he turned back and looked at the buildings he'd left and wondered when and if he'd be back.

The county courthouse next to the modern brick and glass Law Enforcement Center was a regal old Victorian building built of stone blocks. He saw the DA and his assistant come out holding files. When they saw him they stopped and the DA pointed. He could read his lips even though he couldn't hear him at that distance. The DA said, "There he is."

"Here I am," Cody mumbled.

He patted the keys in his pocket. He was glad Bodean let him keep the vehicle for the time being. His personal pickup hadn't run for months; he needed the Ford to get around.

As he pulled out of the lot onto the corner of Breckenridge and Ewing, he noted faded lettering on the side of an old brick building he'd never even noticed before. BOARDING STABLES was still legible in paint.

He hesitated on the corner. If he turned left he would drive by the Jester Bar. He breathed deeply and closed his eyes. He could use an ice-cold beer. Just one, though. To calm his nerves and maybe take the edge off the nasty jagged edges in his brain. He would leave after just one.

His cell phone burred. Larry.

"The ME called. They sliced his eyeballs open. Winters had *no* alcohol they could detect in his system. You were right."

"We're just getting started," Cody said.

"Wait until I walk down the hall and tell Tubman we might have a homicide after all. With the day he's having, this won't exactly brighten it up much."

"Keep me in the loop," Cody said, turning right toward his place. "I've got a lot to think about. I'll keep feeding you."

7

Even though he was exhausted and stabs of pain pulsed through his ear, Cody refused to take the medication they'd given him because he knew, he just *knew*, that if he let his defenses down even a little he'd start drinking. He knew himself. He'd find a justification to start off on another bender.

His ear hurt;

He was suspended;

Precious hours for finding the killer had been wasted and he'd never get them back;

His dog had died (granted, it was twenty years before, but it was still dead);

He missed his son;

His 401(k) wasn't worth crap anymore.

And that was just off the top of his head. He had to stay as sharp and determined as possible, despite the pain and bone-weariness, so he drank strong coffee and chain-smoked cigarettes and paced and thought.

He lived in a rented duplex with a decent view of Mount Helena from the backyard deck. But the structure was getting tired—old carpets, scarred molding, torn screens, windows that didn't shut tight. It had three bedrooms and two bathrooms, which was too many of each. One bedroom sat completely empty, the other was full of junk and empty moving boxes from a year before, and he had a bed he rarely used except for sex because he always fell asleep on the couch. Books were stacked from floor to ceiling in the living room but he'd never bought a bookcase since his divorce. He kept the downstairs bathroom door closed because it stank of duck. Bringing that wounded mallard drake home and letting it paddle around in the bathtub for weeks had left a stench that wouldn't go away. Stupid duck, he thought. He was glad when it finally flew away.

He went into his basement office and fired up his computer and sent the list of names to Larry. Within seconds, Larry thanked him in a terse e-mail. Then Cody started pacing.

Every time he passed one of his two phones he stared at it, willing it to ring. On the hour, he checked for messages from the sheriff or Larry or anyone. His hands shook and his skin felt twitchy.

He ran through the scenario that best fit the facts and his own speculation. Hank flew back from Salt Lake City and stopped at the supermarket on the way from the airport, buying food for two. He rushed home to cook it.

Cody stopped and smacked his forehead with the palm of his hand. Maybe it was a *woman*. Maybe Hank had a *date*. He hadn't even considered a woman before, but now it made even more sense than a man. But big steaks? That was man food. He shook his head and started pacing again.

So the guest arrived not long after Hank. They hadn't even started the grill yet, so they must have been catching up (man) or who-knows-what (woman). Then, for some reason, the visitor clocked Hank in the head. He didn't even eat first, which said to Cody the attack was likely quick and premeditated and not a crime of passion that arose from whatever transpired in the cabin that night. When Hank was incapacitated, he (she?) took Hank's AA coins and maybe something else—cash?

Drug samples? Gold? A treasure map?—opened a bottle of alcohol, and left it close to the body. The visitor opened the door to the wood-stove, filled it with lengths of pine until it was roaring, and then started the curtains or rug, and left the scene. And it all could have been just about perfect if it hadn't started raining and not stopped for three days.

God, how he hated coming down. It hurt. If he could just have one beer . . .

As the sultry afternoon melded into dusk he went out on the deck with his handset and began his round of telephone calls. This was one of the things he hated most about coming off a bender: apologizing to every-one he'd offended. Sometimes, it went on for hours. Sometimes, he found out friends and relatives never wanted to talk to him again, and he prepared to lose a couple more.

He started with Carrie Lowry, who listened with impatient silence until she interrupted and said she was busy. That her boyfriend Jim didn't like getting awakened like that and blamed it on *her*. Then Skee-ter, who refused to take his call. Then Skeeter's wife Mayjean, who was cold and distant and irritatingly formal. The guy from the liquor store, who said, "No problem, come again any old time and throw hundred-dollar bills at me." Finally, Jenny.

"You were drunk, weren't you?" she said.

"Yes."

"Do you remember denying it? You always deny it and act like you're offended I even asked. That's how I know."

"Yeah, yeah." Cody lit a cigarette off the one he'd been smoking so he wouldn't miss a second of nicotine. He pictured her: long dark hair, blue eyes, pug nose, lush mouth, nice curves. She had a good sense of humor, too, *once,* before he separated her from it. He'd always love her, always want her, and she knew it. She just couldn't live with him the way he was then, and the way he was the last two nights. He didn't hold it against her.

"So this is the apology tour," she said. "Am I the first stop?"

"No, I saved the most important one for last."

"Ahhh," she said, mocking.

He told her about what had happened. She broke in when he mentioned Alcoholics Anonymous.

"I'm so proud of you for going," she said, her voice softening. "Why didn't you tell me?"

"Because if I fell off the wagon I didn't want you to think I was a failure at that, too. Which, by the way, I did. Fall, I mean."

"Then climb back on," she said. "There's no rule against that, is there?"

He thought about the group, how supportive they were. How he was rewarding them for their confidentiality and support by having his partner interview them one by one to determine if any of them might be guilty of murder. Man . . .

"My sponsor was murdered," he said. "That kind of triggered things."

"You're kidding," she said.

"I wish I was." Then: "Oh—did I tell you I shot the county coroner last night?"

Silence.

"He's not dead. And he shot at me first. I'm suspended but it's just procedure. What's killing me is I want to go after the bad guy and take him down—"

"Cody," she interrupted. "You *shot* the coroner?"

He laughed. It sounded funny coming from her. Then he had to tell her how it happened.

It took a while for her to be able to change the subject. He glanced at the sun sliding behind Mount Helena and realized this was the longest conversation they'd had in two and a half years. Then he remembered something from two nights before about her new rich fiancé being gone.

"Where did you say they went? His Richness and Justin?"

"Stop calling him that. I told you all this the other night but you don't remember. He took Justin on a week-long wilderness pack trip. They don't even have cell service, so it's driving me crazy. It's Walt's idea because he wants to get closer to Justin if he can. He feels sort of distant, and . . ."

Cody tuned out. The thought of His Richness and *his* son spending that much time together made him instantly morose. He sort of listened. Something about horses, fly-fishing, all in Wyoming. What a fortune that must cost, he thought.

"Justin called me the other night," Cody said. "He needed to borrow something. I barely talked to him. In fact, I cut him off. I feel bad about that."

His phone clicked—another call coming in.

"I have to go now," he said.

"Call again," she said, surprising him. "Just don't make it part of your next tour."

Larry said, "Dry hole with your fellow alcoholics. Everybody has a decent alibi. That doesn't mean none of them are lying, but three of them were out of town and the other eight gave me names of people who'd vouch for them. Everybody heard about Winters, but since they didn't put any of the info about that bottle we found in the paper, no one connected the dots as to why I was calling."

"That's only eleven," Cody said. "Who couldn't you find?"

"Duh. Hank Winters and Cody Hoyt."

"Oh."

"You need to get some sleep."

"I don't know whether I'm relieved or pissed," Cody said. "Because our best angle just got shut down."

"Yeah, it sucks. My cop radar never went off once talking with any of them. They all were helpful and they sounded sincere."

"Maybe it was Edna," Cody said, his voice dropping into his conspiratorial rhythm. "Maybe she was banging Hank and something went wrong."

"Or maybe it was you," Larry said. "Can you account for your whereabouts that night?"

This is what they did, Cody thought. Cop-talk. But maybe there was a hint of curiosity in Larry's question. In fact, he thought, he had no alibi. He'd been out driving, driving, driving. There was no one to confirm where he'd been.

"Tying flies," Cody said, thinking of what his son was doing.

"You're lying. You need steady hands for that."

"Come and get me, flatfoot," Cody said. Actually, he did tie flies. He'd tied two hundred—caddis, hoppers, Adams, stimulators, tricos, nymphs—in the last two months when he wasn't driving aimlessly around the county. "Did you hear anything from your IT folks?"

"As a matter of fact, yes. They were able to access part of the hard drive but not all of it. The bad news is no e-mails were found. None. So we're screwed on that front. But remember you asked me about the history in his browser? Which Web sites he'd been on?"

Cody said yes. He was starting to feel a tingle just by the way Larry was setting it up.

"They're faxing me printouts and I don't have them yet, but they said most of the sites he visited were from a week before, apparently before he went on his trip to Salt Lake. News, weather, Drudge, ESPN, no porno or weird shit. But the most recent site he visited was at nine on the night he died."

Cody waited. Finally: "Was your guy an outdoorsman?"

"Not really," Cody said. "I remember him talking about hunting, but my impression was it was way back. He didn't fish because I offered to tie him some flies and he didn't want any. Why are you asking?"

"Because the last site he visited was for an outfitter."

Cody heard Larry shuffling papers. "Okay, got it. It was for something called Jed McCarthy's Wilderness Adventures. I don't know what the hell they do, but I'd guess hunting trips. I'm in the cruiser right now going back to the office after dinner so I haven't been able to look it up."

Cody scribbled down the name. "Thanks, man. I'll check 'em out, too."

"Hey, did you hear Skeeter held a press conference from his bed in the hospital?"

"No."

"Called you a 'rogue cop.'" Larry laughed. "The spin has already begun."

"Great."

"In his version, a shadowy creep jumped around the side of the crime scene brandishing a weapon and he fired instinctively to protect himself and the reporter. He said he wants you fired."

Cody said, "You're right. I should have gone for a head shot."

"Next time," Larry said.

The Google search took two seconds and Cody brought the site up: *Jed McCarthy's Wilderness Adventures.* "Wilderness Adventures" was in a bold frontier font and the name of the owner/outfitter was in script across the top at an angle, indicating to Cody the name of the company was a well-established brand if Jed himself was not.

The site was clean and well organized, unlike many of the local productions he'd seen where a fishing guide, dude ranch, or lodge owner hired his granddaughter to throw something up on the Web. The Wilderness Adventures site had a menu including Day Rides, Pack Trips, Multi-Day Adventures, Photos, Fly-Fishing, Rates, Booking, Maps, Virtual Tour, on and on. Even an online booking form. He clicked on "Pack Trips" and read through pages of text accompanied by stunning photos of Yellowstone Park. It turned out Jed McCarthy was one of the few outfitters licensed by the National Park Service to provide long excursions into Yellowstone, and McCarthy took every available opportunity to point it out.

He accessed the calendar page. There were a dozen or so different trips, leaving on different dates. He wished Larry would have told him if the IT guys had isolated Hank's browsing history to a specific trip, or whether Hank was simply looking at the home page.

But it just didn't seem right.

Cody recalled the hours he had spent talking with Hank. They had discussed their failures and their dreams together. He couldn't recall Hank ever saying he wanted to ride a horse into the backcountry, or go on a long wilderness trip, or anything similar. Although Hank obviously liked the mountains—that's why he bought his cabin there—he recalled Hank once saying he'd already spent more than enough time roughing it when he was a marine.

Which led to a new possibility in the murder scenario Cody had put together earlier.

Maybe it wasn't Hank who was going on the trip, he thought. *Maybe it was his guest.* Maybe the guest was showing Hank where he was headed next after leaving Helena. And as Hank read the screen, the visitor slipped behind him and hit him in the head with something . . .

"Shit," Cody said, his mind swimming. Thinking, which trip? There were so many of them . . .

He flashed through them. Snake River. Geysers and Explorers. Slough Creek. Hoodoo Basin Progressive Pack Trip. Lower Falls Adventure. Lamar River. Electric Peak and Beyond.

Then he brought up the calendar again.

"Ah," he said, and it all became clear. Cody had assumed Jed McCarthy had an army of guides and employees and trips going everywhere at once. But the calendar showed only June, July, August, and September. Within those months, three-, four-, five-, and seven-day blocks were marked out and color-coded by which trip was scheduled then. The trips didn't overlap. So what appeared to be the deal was McCarthy and his people took a group out for three or four days and returned to the base camp. A few days later, he led another trip. One after the other from the last week of May through mid-September, the trips bookended by melting snow on one end and flying snow on the other.

He clicked on the link that said "Meet Our Guides." There were two of them. Jed McCarthy wore a big cowboy hat and a silk scarf and in the photo he was striking a manly pose. There was also a nice-looking woman named Dakota Hill, who was pictured with a horse. She looked young enough to be Jed McCarthy's daughter.

His phone rang and he snatched it up. Larry.

"I'm looking at that Web site . . ."

"So am I," Cody said. "I've got a question—did the IT folks fax you the specific page he was looking at? I mean, was it a specific trip?"

"It was the home page," Larry said. "But Hank had been looking at a bunch of the pages previous to that in the last ten minutes before. 'What to Bring,' 'Menus,' 'Interactive Maps.' He was really scoping out this Web site. Which makes me think Hank was either doing some research or planning to go on a trip."

"That doesn't sound right to me," Cody said. "It could be a side of Hank I never saw, but it doesn't ring true. If this was the kind of thing he was into we should have found camping gear, saddles, a sleeping bag, that sort of thing. I don't remember any outdoor gear at all, do you?"

"It could have burned up in the fire," Larry said, but not with much conviction. "And besides, how do we know he wasn't just checking out the site? Maybe thinking about it for some other year? There's nothing we've got that suggests he was planning a trip *this* summer."

Cody shook his head. "I'm not buying. Think about it. He buys dinner to cook, rushes home to greet his guest. He's been gone for days. But instead of unpacking completely or getting dinner ready, he sits in his den and bounces around on the Internet? Does that make sense to you?"

"No."

"But what if it was his guest?" Cody said. "What if the killer was showing Hank where he was going next?"

Silence. "I hadn't thought about that," Larry said.

"Just a second," Cody said, clicking again on the calendar. "What is it, the thirtieth of June today?"

Larry chuckled. "Yes."

"Well, according to the calendar, the biggest and longest trip of the year is this one called 'Back of Beyond: The Ultimate Yellowstone Backcountry Adventure.' A whole bunch of nights in the middle of nowhere." Cody paused. "It leaves tomorrow, July 1."

Said Larry, "So if our man was headed south to Yellowstone to go on a trip with Jed McCarthy, even five nights ago, this would be the only one he could go on now."

"Yeah," Cody said, "because according to this calendar, Jed was finishing up the Hoodoo Basin Trip then. He couldn't have been on that."

"Boy," Larry said, "we're taking a mighty leap here. Just because Hank was looking at a Web site on the night he died, we're saying the killer was headed to Yellowstone. I'm not sure I can buy that one without some kind of corroboration."

Cody groaned his assent. Then: "I wish that damned trip didn't leave tomorrow morning. I wonder if it's possible to get ahold of Jed and find out who's on it? See if Hank's name is on his guest list? Jed probably has a pretty complete manifest or whatever you call it. We can run all the names and see if any of them came from this direction, or if anyone has a record, or if we can link him up with Hank in any way."

"And how do you propose to do *that*?" Larry asked.

"Police work," Cody said.

"Ha ha."

"Don't go anywhere," Cody said, "I'll call you right back."

He punched in the telephone number for Wilderness Adventures. They were based in Bozeman, meaning their headquarters was well outside the northern border of the park. If Jed was leading the trip the next morning, it was unlikely he'd be in Bozeman, but . . .

Cody got a voice mail. An erudite man's voice with a touch of country twang: "You've reached the voice mail of Jed McCarthy's Wilderness Adventures, the home of the only licensed multinight out-fitter in Yellowstone National Park. We're on a pack trip right now so we're unable to take your call. And because of the nature of the trip, I won't be able to check messages for a week. Please go to our Web site and—"

He hung up and called Larry back.

"No one is there," Cody said.

"It's ten at night, Cody. What did you expect? I'm sure there'll be an office manager or somebody there tomorrow."

"Don't be so sure," Cody said. "These outfitter types are generally mom-and-pop operations. Believe me, I know. I grew up with them. My uncle Jeter used to manage his whole outfitting operation from scraps of paper he carried around in his shirt pocket. Jed is probably more sophisticated than that, but what if there isn't anyone to check the files tomorrow and see who is on the trip? We can't wait a week to find out who went. What if our killer is on this backcountry trip?"

"Then he'll still be there when they come back," Larry said. "If any of this pans out we can be waiting for them wherever Jed's base camp is located. That'll give us time to run this all down, see if any of it makes sense. Then we'll need to bring in the state boys and the Park Service rangers. We can't just go charging down there."

"Hmmpf."

"You know we need more time and a hell of a lot more corroboration," Larry said. "We start in Bozeman, at his office. He's got to have someone there answering phones and keeping the business running while he's out on a trip. Probably a receptionist or bookkeeper. We can call down and ask the sheriff or PD in Bozeman to be there when they open tomorrow morning."

Cody moaned. *Tomorrow morning . . .*

Larry said, "This is quite a leap, Cody. Just because that page was on his computer doesn't mean the killer is on the trip."

"I *know* that," Cody said. "But it's the only thing we've got that might indicate where he's going. We have to rule it out first."

Larry said, "If somebody, say Dougherty, brought to you what we've got so far I can hear you laughing your head off."

Cody snorted. "I hate it when you're right."

"I know."

Cody suddenly wanted a tall triple bourbon and water. He said, "If this killer is on the trip, though, how do we know he won't be a danger to everyone else on it? This Web site says the trip is full. So we're talking maybe a dozen people. It would be horrible if this guy is some kind of psycho—like the kind of person who would kill the most gentle man in the world and burn his place down around him. If we don't go at this angle hard we may be putting innocent people in harm's way."

"There's that," Larry said. "But still . . . I mean, I can't spend all night on this and you got yourself suspended."

"I know," Cody said gruffly. "Jeez, I hate being in my house now. Can I ask you a favor?"

Larry sighed. "Man, I'm doing overtime *now*. Bodean put out that memo about no more overtime without his authorization. I mean—"

"We need to play catch-up," Cody said, ignoring him. "Call RMIN and ViCAP, see if there are any other crimes similar to the Winters murder."

RMIN (pronounced "Rimin") was the Rocky Mountain Information Network, a regional clearinghouse of incidents recorded in Idaho, Montana, Wyoming, Colorado, Utah, Nevada, and New Mexico. ViCAP was the Violent Criminal Apprehension Program of the FBI. Both organizations had analysts on staff who could research similar crimes. ViCAP had profilers available as well as a password-protected Web site that could be accessed by law enforcement agencies after hours.

"You're grasping at straws," Larry said. "We can't do much more until tomorrow, Cody. Once we talk to the receptionist and hear back from RMIN and ViCAP, *then* maybe we'll have something to go on."

"I know. But that trip leaves tomorrow morning. Call those guys, Larry. Get things going."

"You owe me so many dinners," Larry said, and slammed down his phone.

While he waited, he did another Google search on the outfitting company, hoping he could find another contact, maybe an after-hours number. He assumed Jed and his people and horses were already in Yellowstone at their base camp, likely out of cell phone range. But surely he would have a way to communicate with his office, Cody thought. Like to check on clients who were late or didn't show up? Although he couldn't find any way to make contact other than the office number, e-mail address, and Web site, he did find an old online article from the Bozeman *Chronicle*: SALE OF PARK OUTFITTING BUSINESS PENDING NPS APPROVAL.

Even though he couldn't see how it would be of much help, Cody read it. It was from February, five years before.

Bozeman newcomer Jedediah McCarthy announced on Wednesday that he was awaiting National Park Service approval to acquire the assets of Wilderness Adventures, the longtime outfitting operation specializing in Yellowstone Park pack trips. McCarthy said he intended to continue the legacy established by Frank "Bull" Mitchell, who ran the company for the past 32 years.

McCarthy stated he planned to maintain the quality of the company and perhaps—with NPS approval—expand the available multiday excursions into the most remote reaches of Yellowstone Park.

"It's time," Mitchell told the *Chronicle*, "Somebody else can put up with all that Park Service BS . . ."

McCarthy aims to emphasize low-impact camping with a

greater emphasis on the unique properties of the Greater Yellowstone Ecosystem, he said . . .

Cody read the rest of the article but found it boring: Jed McCarthy extolling the virtues of his trip and the excellent and professional methodology of the National Park Service. *Stroking bureaucrats in the paper while they considered your application,* Cody thought. *No wonder he got the concession.*

He smiled and jotted down the name "Frank 'Bull' Mitchell."

Then it hit him and he called Jenny again as panic rose inside.

She sounded groggy. "When I said call again, I didn't mean midnight."

"I'm sorry, but I just thought of something. It's nuts, but I have to make sure I'm wrong."

"About what?"

"Justin and His Richness. Where did you say they went?"

"Wyoming. I told you—"

"I know. But where specifically did they go? And did they go on their own? Is His Richness driving them around, or what?"

"Well, he drove them there. But they're going on some kind of long wilderness trip in Yellowstone Park. With some outfitter on horses—"

"Jesus," Cody said.

"What? You're scaring me, Cody."

"Don't be scared," he said to her as well as to himself. "Just find the name of the outfit they're using."

"I think I have a brochure," she said. "But I can't call them. Justin said they'd be out of cell phone range . . ."

"Jenny," he said, "we might have a big problem."

Cody had the Ford backed up to his open garage door and was throwing gear into it—sleeping bag, tent, pad, cooking set, Uncle Jeter's old saddle—when Larry pulled his SUV into the driveway and blocked him.

Larry kept his motor running and his headlights on and swung out. "You didn't answer your phone."

"I was out here," Cody said.

"You can't leave. You know that. You'll give the sheriff a damned good reason to fire you."

Cody said, "Let him."

Larry spun Cody around so they were face to face. "Have you been drinking?" Larry asked.

"Not yet."

Larry leaned forward on the balls of his feet and stared into Cody's eyes. Cody didn't flinch, and said, "Get any closer and I'll clock you."

Larry relaxed a little, apparently content that Cody was sober. "You need to slow down. It's two thirty in the morning. You can't just run away in the middle of the night."

"I'm not running," Cody said. "I'm pursuing a lead."

"You're not a cop right now."

Cody shrugged. "I'm *always* a fucking cop."

"I was afraid you were going to do this," Larry said. "All I can say is it's stupid, and useless, and you're doing more harm than good."

"Sounds like me," Cody said. "Hey, why don't you give me a hand. I was looking for an old pack saddle of my uncle's in that mess of a garage. Maybe you can find it."

"To hell with that," Larry said, squinting past Cody toward the garage. It was piled with junk Cody had never bothered to unpack or organize. His disabled pickup truck took up most of the space.

"Look," Larry said. "I left messages at RMIN and ViCAP, but nobody is working tonight. We should hear back from them first thing in the morning. There's no reason for you to leave tonight and risk your job. And risk *my* job, because if you take off now they'll ask me if I knew you went."

Said Cody, "Tell them the truth, Larry. Tell them you tried to talk me out of it but you couldn't."

Larry shook his head, and his eyes flashed with anger. "Cody, damn you, I can't risk this job. I've got child support payments and no one is hiring. I have to stay in this town to be near my kids. You can't put me in this position. You're such an asshole."

"Yeah, yeah," Cody said, flicking a cigarette butt into the street where it exploded in a shower of little sparks. He lit another. "I know," he said, drawing deep, "but—"

"I found something," Larry cut in. "On the ViCAP Web site."

Cody went silent, squinting at Larry's face through the smoke.

"We won't know for sure if we've got anything until I can talk to an analyst or profiler tomorrow. But since they're on eastern time, I should hear back from them early tomorrow."

"What did you find?" Cody asked.

"I used the national crime database they've got," Larry said, dragging it out like he always did. "I used the keywords *murder, arson, single victim, head injury,* I don't remember what else. Just trying to find out if there were any hits. It isn't an exact science . . ."

Cody felt something red and hot pop behind his eyes and reached out as if he were going to grab Larry's throat. Larry anticipated the move and ducked to the side.

"What did you find, goddamn you?" Cody hissed.

"Four of 'em," Larry said.

Cody's mouth dropped. "Four?"

"One in Virginia a month ago. One in Minnesota two weeks ago. Hank Winters. And another one in Jackson Hole, Wyoming, two nights ago. Three men, one woman. All professional, middle-aged. Alone at the time. No suspects in any of them, and as far as I could tell no one has linked them up yet. They're all classified as still under investigation, although they read like accidents. Just like ours."

"Four?"

Larry nodded. "Of course, we won't know until—"

Cody said, "Justin is on that trip."

Larry rubbed his eyes. "Oh no, man."

"You need to move your rig," Cody said. "I need to get the hell out of here to Bozeman."

Larry sighed and his shoulders slumped.

"Larry, move your truck."

Cody roared down U.S. 287 toward Townsend, the flat south end of Canyon Ferry Lake shimmering with moonlight. The night was warm and he kept his windows open so the rush of air would keep him awake. Synapses in his brain seemed to be firing with the crackling machine-gun rhythm of a spark plug. He shot by the sleeping ranch houses and barns, past the faded wooden archway to the ranch his friend Jack McGuane's parents still ran.

The sight of the ranch brought back a flood of memories both painful and euphoric. A year and a half before, he'd laid it all out there for his friends Jack and Melissa McGuane. In the end he'd lost his boyhood friend Brian Eastman, gutted his own reputation, and lost his stripes in the Denver PD, but it all still felt right to him. Even with the high body count of scumbags, he'd gleefully do it all over again.

That was the thing, he thought. Throughout his life his friends, lovers, and colleagues wondered aloud what made him tick. As if he were like Churchill's description of Russia, a "riddle wrapped in a mystery inside an enigma," when really it was so damned simple. So damned simple. Cody was born damaged. His Maker had flinched when soldering his hard wires together, and they would always short out or overheat at the wrong time. He could probably blame his white-trash family for his criminal tendencies and penchant for self-delusion and self-medication, but he didn't believe in justifying bad behavior with that kind of touchy-feely crap. Cody was not good and he was incapable of being good, but that didn't mean he didn't recognize and revere goodness, and he'd do anything—*anything*—to protect those blessed with clean, unimpeded wiring. Like his friends the McGuanes, whom he'd helped. Like Hank Winters, whom he'd failed. Like Justin, his miracle son, who he *had* to save.

He slowed through Townsend, glancing over his shoulder at a yelp that came from two drunks stumbling out of the Commercial Bar into the street. Thought maybe he might even know them, and smiled bitterly.

Two miles south of Townsend, the inside of the Ford exploded with red and blue light. He glanced into his rearview mirror and squinted at the intensity of the wig-wags on the light bar of the Highway Patrol car.

"Shit," he hissed, noting he was only five miles over the speed limit.

Fuming, he pulled over. He reached for his badge which was no longer there and sat back and closed his eyes. He hoped like hell he knew the trooper and could manage to talk his way out of a ticket so he could get back on the highway as soon as possible. For a second he considered flooring the Ford once the trooper got out of his vehicle, but he knew that wouldn't work for long. No doubt, his plates had already been called in, and there wouldn't be a record of them.

He was caught, unless he could talk his way out of it and get the plate search canceled.

A flashlight blinded him through the driver's window and he looked away.

The trooper, an unfamiliar beefy youngster who looked six months out of the training center, said, "You were aware you only have one operating headlight, mister?"

Cody said, "I'm an investigator for the sheriff's department. I'm in a hurry."

The trooper grinned, his teeth glinting in the secondary light of his flashlight's reflection.

"Well, you'll just have to show me a badge and get the sheriff on the horn," the trooper said. "And in the meanwhile you can follow me back to town until we can get that headlight fixed. What happened, anyway? It looks like you hit something."

"A fucking elk," Cody said, not able to keep the anger out of his voice.

"Yeah," the trooper said, shining his beam on the damage. "I can see some hair and blood. Male or female?"

Cody sighed and covered his face with his hands. "Female," he said.

"Got your cow permit?" The trooper chuckled.

Part Two

Yellowstone National Park

8

Sixteen-year-old Danielle Sullivan was furiously texting her on-again off-again boyfriend Riley as fourteen-year-old Gracie Sullivan looked on. Their father drove the rental car and pointed out bison far below in the valley and two distant elk crossing a river in the early morning sun. Danielle and Gracie were in the backseat.

"I'm surprised he's even up this early," Gracie said to Danielle. She marveled at her sister and the desperate fire in her eyes as she tapped out messages with a blur of her thumbs.

"He's got to get up early for work," Danielle said, not looking over. "Remember—he's got that stupid job with the grounds crew with the schools. They make him show up every morning at eight. They're evil." Gracie nodded and snapped her phone open. She didn't expect any messages although she'd be ridiculously thrilled if there were any. There weren't, so as she often did in the presence of her beautiful, popular, constantly in-demand sister, she tapped out a message to her own phone via her e-mail account:

How are you this morning?

When it came through, she wrote:

Crappy start, but thanks for asking.
I'm sorry.
Don't be. Things are looking up. WE'RE IN YELLOWSTONE
PARK.

Even though Danielle thought Gracie pathetic for spelling out all the words in her texts rather than using text-speak or shorthand, Gracie thought there was no harm done since she was, in effect, talking to herself. It was a scheme she'd come up with to make Danielle think she had admirers in constant contact as well.

You're up early.
I couldn't sleep. I kept thinking I forgot something.
Like what?
Toothbrush. Glasses. I got up at 2:30 to make sure I packed
underwear. I had a nightmare I didn't bring underwear and
I had to borrow a f**king thong from Danielle.

She lowered the phone to her lap with the screen facing away from her sister and looked through the window. There were no buildings, no roads, no power lines. To the south was a vast river valley with tall grass that rippled in the cold morning breeze. A ribbon of river that looked like sheet metal serpentined through the valley floor. To the north the terrain seemed to swell and rise to meet tendrils of pine trees, and above them a dark wall of forest.

"Oh my God," her dad said as the car slowed suddenly. "Look, girls: *wolves.*"

Gracie snapped her phone shut and hurled herself forward. All her life she'd wanted to see a wolf.

Her dad pulled over to the side of the two-lane blacktop and rolled down his window. The small of pine, sage, and cool fresh air wafted in. He pointed toward the river.

"See them, at that bend? Near those big rocks the sun is starting to hit?"

Gracie threw her arms over the front seat and squinted where her father was pointing. Far below, she saw movement.

"They look like dots," she said. "Two little dots."

"They're wolves," her dad said. "Aren't they magnificent?"

Magnificent *dots,* she thought. She wished she could see them closer or figure out what they were doing to make them seem magnificent to her father, who tended toward hyperbole.

"Here," her father said, handing her a pair of binoculars that still had the price tag on them. "You focus using that little wheel in the middle."

While Gracie tried to manipulate the binoculars and frantically rolled the wheel all the way to the left and then to the right and finally realized she was bringing the hood ornament into sharp relief, she heard her dad say to Danielle, "Don't you want to see these fantastic animals, Danny?"

"Maybe in a minute," Danielle said, still texting.

"They may be gone in a minute," he said, trying to disguise the disappointment in his voice.

Gracie finally figured out where to point, and started bringing the animals into focus.

"Dad, it's not like we won't have a chance to see wolves," Danielle said, not looking up from her phone. "Aren't we going to be in the middle of nowhere for five friggin' days? We'll be *sleeping* with wolves. Like that movie."

Gracie mumbled, "*Dancing* with wolves, not sleeping with them," as she brought the animals into sharp detail.

"Whatever," Danielle said sharply.

"I think there's a difference," Gracie whispered, and not too loudly, wishing she'd never said anything at all. To confirm her thought, Danielle drove a sharp fingernail into her ribs that made her jump and lose the animals. She recovered and refocused.

Then she sighed, sat back, and handed the binoculars to her father. "Those are coyotes, not wolves."

"Oh, come on," he said, taking the glasses back.

She waited. She could tell he wanted to turn them into wolves.

Finally, he said, "I'll be damned. I thought they were wolves." He was disappointed they were coyotes and seemed disappointed in Gracie for pointing it out.

Gracie said, "Dad, I *read* those books you sent us. You know, *The Wildlife of Yellowstone, Yellowstone Flora and Fauna, Death in Yellowstone, The Geysers of Yellowstone.* I read them. I studied them," she said, hoping for a grunt of appreciation. "You know," she said, "so Danny wouldn't have to."

That got a smile out of him.

"You suck," Danielle mumbled. "Some of us have lives."

"You read those books?" her dad asked, nodding.

"Some of them more than once," Gracie confessed, and wished she hadn't. She sounded so . . . *without a life.* But the fact was she was captivated with the books about a place on earth that could hold so many fascinating things that weren't made or constructed by man. It had never occurred to her before she read those books that there was an amazing natural location not designed or driven by people. It made her think about how small she was. How small everybody was.

"Don't drive off, Dad," Danielle said.

"Do you want to take a look, then?" her dad asked eagerly, handing the binoculars over his shoulder so Danielle could grab them.

"Naw. I've got a good signal here," she said, deadpan.

"It's gonna get worse," Gracie said. "In fact, we'll lose it for good in a minute."

Danielle looked up, horrified. "Shut *up,*" she said to Gracie. There was terror in her eyes. Then: "Dad, tell me that's not true."

When he realized Danielle didn't want the glasses he lowered them to his seat as if he'd not held them out to her in the first place. Like he was embarrassed, Gracie thought. He said, "I thought I told you,

Danny. There's no cell service where we're going. It's the wilderness. It's the most remote part of the whole country. At least the lower forty-eight states, to be exact. That's the whole *point.*"

Gracie watched Danielle do a slow burn with a whiff of absolute panic.

"*Are you telling me I can't use my phone?*" she said.

"Honey," her dad said, turning around, making his face soft and sympathetic, "it'll be great. You'll forget you even have it. I know I told you all this about how remote it would be."

Danielle's tone was icy. "You didn't say I couldn't use my phone."

"I think I did."

Gracie nodded. "I think he did."

Danielle turned on her. "I don't know why you'd even care, Gracie. Nobody even knows your number."

Gracie looked away, instant tears stinging in her eyes. She should be used to how quickly and ruthlessly Danielle could humiliate her and learn not to tear up. She hated when she let her sister get to her.

"This isn't Yellowstone," Danielle said to her dad, "It's friggin' *hell.*"

"Honey . . ." her dad said, turning in his seat so he could plead with her.

"My friends go to Europe, or Disneyland, or Hawaii, or Mexico for summer vacation," Danielle said. "But no, my dad takes me to friggin' hell."

"Darling . . ." her dad said.

"I should have stayed home," Danielle said, twisting the knife. "I should have stayed with Mom. At least there was civilization and broadband. And my friends. And friggin' cell service."

Her dad turned back around in silence and engaged the transmission and the car eased forward into the lane.

Gracie said, "We can call it Hell-o-stone!"

"Shut the fuck up," Danielle spat.

"Don't say that," Gracie said. "It's against the law to say *fuck* in a national park."

Danielle looked at her suspiciously. "It is?"

Her dad sighed, "Girls, please . . ."

It had been their dad's idea, this trip to Yellowstone National Park. He'd come up with it the previous summer—they stayed with him summers—and he'd announced it suddenly when the sisters returned from an afternoon at the swimming pool at his condo village on the outskirts of St. Paul. Danielle, who'd just broken up with her then-local boyfriend at the pool an hour before and never wanted to see him—or Minnesota—again, said she was all over it.

Anything to get away from Alex and his stupid friends, she'd said, wiping her hands on her pool towel as if rubbing off his disgusting germs.

Gracie, who could never get used to the heat or humidity of the long green summer months compared to where they lived the rest of the year in dry, high-altitude Denver, was thrilled with the idea. Gracie loved animals, hiking, nature, and the idea of a great adventure. But most of all, she wanted to make her dad happy.

It had been obvious for the ten years since the divorce that her dad wasn't really comfortable with them, maybe because they were girls. He'd never outright said he wanted boys instead, but it was clear that at least he'd know what to do with them: take them to baseball games or something. He really wasn't an outdoorsman of any kind even though he'd grown up in Colorado, but Gracie guessed he'd take quicker to learning to hike, fish, or hunt for the sake of his sons than he did ferrying his daughters to movies, the Mall of America, restaurants, or waiting for them to return from the pool. He was dutiful, but there was always something sad about him, she thought. Like he liked the *idea* of having his daughters for the summer more than he actually liked having them there taking over the bathroom or hanging their wet bathing suits from the shower rod to dry.

But this trip really did seem to excite him in a way she'd never seen before. Once he cleared it with their mother—who thought he, and they, were crazy as ticks but acquiesced in the end—he could talk of nothing else for the rest of the year. His eyes sparkled, and his movements seemed more rapid. He fired off e-mails and links about Yellowstone and horses and camping and wildlife. For Christmas he sent them both sleeping bags, flashlights, headlamps, travel fishing rods and reels, new digital cameras, rain ponchos, and *National Geographic* maps of the park.

Gracie read everything he sent, and obsessed over the "What to Bring" list forwarded from the outfitter. Danielle rolled her eyes and said, "What—does he think we're his *boys*, now?"

Gracie suspected there was an ulterior motive to his enthusiasm, but she didn't know yet what it was. She suspected through comments her mother had made over the years that her dad wasn't very happy growing up, that his intensity (he was a software engineer who traveled a lot all over the country and the world) prevented him from ever being loose or carefree. He thought in terms of circuit boards and digital switches, and when the level of drama was high—which it often was with Danielle and sometimes Gracie—that he was "better at hardware than software," as if that explained everything. She thought maybe he was hoping he could go on this wilderness cowboy pack trip and . . . be a *boy* again. She wasn't sure that was something she really wanted to see.

The trip the day before had begun on a jarring note, Gracie thought. It was taking her a while to process what had happened and why it bothered her, other than her natural and annoying propensity to simply worry too much about everything.

They'd kissed their mother good-bye at Denver International Airport in the morning and boarded the United/Frontier flight to Bozeman. Although they'd planned to carry on their luggage—which was ridiculously slight given the weight restrictions Jed McCarthy imposed—because of all the metal and equipment in their duffel bags, they'd had to check the bags through. Gracie thought her mom looked forlorn and vulnerable, as if she wondered if she'd ever see her daughters again. *That* wasn't a good way to start the trip.

Their arrival was slightly delayed—the airplane had to circle Bozeman while early summer thundershowers lashed the airport. Gracie had the window seat and looked out at the mountains in all directions and the black thunderheads on the northern horizon.

"Which way is Yellowstone?" she'd asked her sister.

"Like *I* would know?" Danielle said in a way that was both incredulous and offended.

"That's right," Gracie had said, "how dare I assume you know anything."

Which was met with a hard twist on her ear.

She'd looked out expectantly for their dad in the luggage area because he was scheduled to arrive an hour before from Minneapolis, but he wasn't there.

"His plane must be late," Danielle told her. "I'll check in a minute."

When their bags arrived and the rest of the passengers cleared out, Gracie waited near the outside doors. She knew there was a problem by Danielle's worried face as she came back from the Northwest counter.

"The plane arrived on time but he wasn't on it, they said."

Gracie fought panic. She looked up at the mounted animal heads and stuffed trout on the walls and out at the cold blue mountains to the south. She thought of how miserable it would be to be stuck in Bozeman, Montana, with her sister until they could figure out a way to get back home. And she was worried about what might have happened to their dad. Was he sick? Did he get in a car crash on the way to the airport? She flipped open her phone and powered it up, hoping there would be a message.

"I'm calling Mom," Danielle said, having already opened her cell phone.

That's when their dad bounded into the airport. Not from the area where the planes landed, but from outside on the street.

"*Girls!*" he shouted. His grin and his open arms made Gracie's black dread melt away as if he had touched a flame to a spider's web. He seemed almost too exuberant, she thought. As if he was happy but with a bit of desperation thrown in.

"Come on, the car's out front," he'd said. "Let me help you with your stuff."

Danielle told him they were starting to worry, and what the people at the airline counter had said.

He waved it off, saying, "That's ridiculous. Obviously, I was on the plane. I'm here, aren't I?"

They turned onto a dirt road by a brown National Park Service sign indicating the campsite and trailhead. Her father once again closed his window to prevent the roll of dust from filling the car. Gracie turned off her phone and put it in a side pocket of the door and made a mental note not to forget it when they returned. She watched as Danielle seethed—*no signal at all*—and finally snapped her phone shut.

"Great," her sister said, "I'm completely alone in the world."

"Except for your sister and your father," her dad said with caution.

"Alone in Hell-o-stone," Gracie mocked gently, "Hell-o-stone alone . . ."

Danielle mouthed *Shut the fuck up, Gracie.*

"That's your second offense," Gracie said, deadpan. "We may need to turn you in to the rangers."

"We're here," her dad said with an epic flourish.

Gracie once again bounded forward and hung her arms over the front seat. They'd rounded a corner and could now see that at the end of the road was a very long horse trailer in a parking lot. People stood around the trailer in the sun; a couple were already on horseback. Gracie counted ten or eleven milling about. When she saw the horses her heart seemed to swell to twice its size.

"We're really going to do this, aren't we?" she said, reaching up and putting her hand on her dad's shoulder. He reached across his body and put his hand on hers.

"It'll be the greatest adventure of our lives," he said.

"I'm taking my phone," Danielle said as if talking to herself. "Maybe we'll find a place with a signal somewhere." Then: "Oh my God. Look at all the people! We're going to be stuck for a week with *them*?"

9

Outfitter Jed McCarthy pulled back and tightened the cinch on a mare named Strawberry—she was a strawberry roan—and squinted over the top of a saddle at the car that had just rounded the corner on the side of the hill. It was a blue American-made four-door sedan. Nobody normal drove those, he thought, meaning it must be a rental and therefore the last of his clients to arrive.

"That better be the Sullivans," he said under his breath to Dakota Hill, his wrangler. She was in the process of saddling a stout sorrel a few feet away.

"Is that the party of three?" she asked. "The father and two teenage daughters?"

"Yup."

Dakota blew a strand of hair out of her face. "You know what I think about teenage girls on these trips."

"I know."

"I may have to kill one someday. Push her off a cliff. Damn prima donnas, anyhow."

"I know."

"Or feed her to some bears."

"Keep your voice down," McCarthy said. "Their money's as good as anyone's. And we've got a full boat of paying customers for this one. This keeps up, I can get that new truck. Life is good."

"For you," she said, tight-lipped. "Me, I get the same damned wages no matter what."

"At least you did before you started getting under my skin," he said, smiling his smile that he knew could be interpreted as cruel. "Besides, you got perks. You get to sleep with the boss." He waggled his eyebrows when he said it.

"Some perk," she grumbled.

"I ain't heard any complaints."

"You ain't listening."

Almost twenty-five, she'd grown up on ranches in Montana and drove her father's pickup at eight years old and was breaking horses by the time she was twelve. She had a round open face, thick lips that curved quickly into an unabashed and purely authentic smile, naturally blushed cheeks, and dancing brown eyes. She'd attended a couple of years at MSU, but quit to barrel race and never went back. He'd met her when she delivered some horses to him two summers before. Her barrel horse had come up seriously lame just that day at the local rodeo. The horse would never run again and never earn any more money. She needed a job. He needed a wrangler.

He stepped closer to Strawberry so none of his clients could see him draw a laminated three-by-five index card out of his breast pocket. On it were the names of each of his customers for the trip as well as vital information they'd sent him regarding weight (to match them with a horse), age, riding experience, food allergies, dietary needs, and what they most wanted out of the trip, from fly-fishing opportunities to horseback riding to wildlife viewing to "being one with nature." He made it a point of pride to know the names of everyone on his excursions from the initial introduction, and to constantly surprise his clients with probing questions about their personal needs and to ask them about their lives based on a short questionnaire he'd required them all to fill out and send along with their booking form. People liked that kind of personal attention, he'd found, and he was rewarded for it at the end of the week by the size of the tip. Sometimes they'd rebook a trip because of it. And despite Dakota's grumbling, he knew it was vital to hook the teenage girls early. Usually, it was to match them up with a horse they'd fall in love with. He'd feed the girl some kind of backstory on the horse they were riding—sometimes it was even true—about how the animal was particular and only responded to people who were gentle and special. Then, a few miles up the trail, he'd remark how well-behaved the horse was and compliment the teenage rider for her prowess. Generally, that would do it: the girl would fall in love and never even consider how many other girls before her—and after—would have the same passionate relationship with the same horse.

He'd make sure to send a Christmas card to the girl from the *horse*, telling her how much her horse missed her and that she was the animal's favorite human. Often, it resulted in a customer for life, because he'd found today's parents did not deny their children *anything*. At two thousand dollars a client, it was important to know that.

This particular trip was full. There'd been no cancelations and everybody showed up at the appointed place at the agreed-upon time. With the arrival of the Sullivans, he had everybody.

Before gathering them together for an orientation, he walked along the length of his long horse trailer and looked at a reflection of himself in the passenger window of his pickup. He liked what he saw.

Jed McCarthy was a short, solid fireplug of a man with a gunfighter mustache, trimmed short beard, and blue eyes so pale they were practically opaque. He was a year shy of forty and he'd been running horse pack trips into the Yellowstone wilderness for eight years, one of only two licensed outfitters deemed worthy and compliant by the authorities at the National Park Service. He wore snug Wranglers and lace-up outfitter boots with heels for riding, a sterling silver rancher set for a buckle, and a leather vest with plenty of pockets to hold all the tools and small gear he needed. Around his neck was a red silk kerchief folded over and knotted in the cowboy style. His hair was thinning on top so he rarely took off his droopy brown Resistol hat. He knew from experience his clients spent a lot of time studying him. The women did it because he was interesting and exotic and a damned good-looking cowboy who was also sensitive, manly, humble, and mysterious. They'd likely read on his Web site he was a poet and painter as well as an experienced horseman and man of nature: a wilderness Renaissance man! The men studied him not only as a leader but as a rival. Some of them sucked up to him, trying to get his approval. Others shut up and conceded Jed was the boss because he was a man's man and he was in charge of the outfit.

And he *was* in charge. It didn't matter if his clients were CEOs or actors or millionaire lawyers or doctors or whatever. Once they mounted up and fell in behind his black gelding and his string of three pack mules (Dakota followed up on her horse with a string as well) he was the trail boss. He was the boss of everything. And with the exception of Dakota, he was the only one on the trip who knew where they were going, what to expect, what to watch out for, where they'd camp, what they'd eat, where they'd sleep and relieve themselves. This was his company, his stock, his equipment, his plan, and his permit.

Behind him in the reflection, he saw Dakota slump by. He wished her posture was better as well as her attitude. But she was a hell of a hand, and she was unabashed and enthusiastic in a way that only country girls could be when they zipped their sleeping bags together. Country girls who'd grown up around life and death and sex and birth on the farm or ranch had few inhibitions, he'd found. Plus, she was a quick learner and eager to please. He liked horses and women with that quality. What he didn't like was the way she kept her own counsel at times and the way she vanished for a week here and a week there without telling him where she was going or when she'd be back. He'd have fired her long ago if he could have found a replacement. But it wasn't easy to locate a nice-looking girl twenty years his junior who was not only an experienced wrangler with horses and mules but good in the sack as well. But he never told her that. Sometimes, he hinted there was a long line of eager replacements out there ready to step in if she left. As long as she believed that, he thought, he'd have the advantage.

He pocketed the index card and closed his eyes and repeated their names over and over like a mantra before he turned around, put on his kind but competent expression, and said to the clients milling around near their piles of clothing and gear, "Let's gather here for a few minutes, folks, so we can get to know each other."

He took a few steps into the clearing and stopped. He stuck his thumbs into his jeans pockets and rocked back a little on his boot heels. He'd not go to them. He'd make them come to *him*. This was the all-important first impression, perhaps the single most important half hour of the entire week. He'd learned it could sometimes take days to undo a bad first meeting if he came across as soft, confusing, or incoherent. It was imperative everyone understood the rules, the procedures, and who was who. It started with them all coming to *him*.

And dutifully, in singles and loose groups, they did. Dakota took her place to his right about ten feet away. She led a saddled horse over to use for demonstration purposes.

He waited for the Sullivans to join them. The father looked pale and nervous and had a weak chin and darting eyes. Obviously a desk jockey of some sort, Jed thought. Those types tended to remind him of mice, like this guy did. Whatever Sullivan did for a living—he'd need to check his records but he knew "automation" and "digital" were in the title and he was vice president of development of something—it paid well. Treating his daughters to a trip like this, plus the transportation, was pricey.

The taller girl was striking, Jed thought. Jet-black hair, bangs, blue eyes, nice mouth and figure. Plus, she was looking right at him. That showed attitude and confidence. When he looked back she didn't drop her eyes. He thought: *Arrogant, too*. Then: *Dakota's going to love this one.*

The younger girl was skinny, flat chested, freckle faced, and looked serious and bookish. Freckles *and* braces. His eyes slid right over her and his brain said, *Nothing to see here, folks, move along.*

But he'd have to get to know that tall one . . .

"Folks, I'm Jed McCarthy and this is Dakota Hill. We're your guides, and we're about to embark on the longest, most scenic, and most remote horse packing expedition into the Yellowstone backcountry wilderness available. It's the best trip we do all summer and it's the one we enjoy the most. This is the first and only time we'll do this trip this season, and because the snows last winter were so heavy and have just recently melted away, we're likely to be the *only* people going where we're going. For you, all I can say is I envy you for what you're going to see and experience for the first time. It truly is the trip of a lifetime into the farthest reaches of America's first and best national park.

"I know you all got the materials I sent you and read up on our itinerary and the other info on the Web site, but in a nutshell, we're going to match you up with a horse that will be your horse for the next six days and ninety miles," he said, letting that sink in amidst titters.

Jed continued, "We'll be leaving from here within the hour, so I'd urge you to make sure you've got all your gear out and piled up so we can load it on the mules. This is a progressive trip, meaning we'll be at a new camp every night. Camp One is fifteen miles away along the shore of Yellowstone Lake. Tomorrow, we go into the Thorofare along the river and we follow it upstream to Camp Two. Camp Three is a hell of a climb from the river valley toward the top of the Continental Divide and Two Ocean Pass. We'll ride a few thousand feet up into the mountains, and some of you may experience shortness of breath or maybe a touch of altitude sickness. The best way to ward that off is to keep hydrated. Keep drinking water, folks—it's magic. If you're doing it right, you'll drink two or three times the water you usually drink. That's what we want.

"It's called Two Ocean Pass because the water on the east side of the mountains begins its flow to the Atlantic, and on the west side it's headed for the Pacific. It's high mountain country, and the most re-mote location in the lower forty-eight in terms of its distance from any road or structure. It is true primitive wilderness, but that's what you signed up for, isn't it?

"Keep this in mind, folks: only two percent of Yellowstone's 3,468 square miles is developed in any way. It's the largest remaining nearly intact ecosystem in the Earth's northern temperate zone. What you see around you right now—a road, cars, a parking lot—are the last items of modern civilization you'll see for the next week."

He scanned his clients as he spoke, already putting them into cate-gories. Rarely anymore did anyone truly surprise him. Everyone was a type, and he'd been with all types on his trips. As he looked his cli-ents over he fitted them into slots.

Jed said, "We've all heard the term 'beyond civilization' without really thinking much about it because for most of you, being out of range of cell-phone towers or Wi-Fi isn't something you've thought real hard about. But that's where we're going: the most remote wilder-ness left in our country. We like to call it *Back of Beyond*."

As always, the phrase produced a nice murmur of trepidation.

He'd briefly talked to the lone married couple on the trip, Tristan and Donna Glode. Although in their sixties, they were fit and vigorous. He was a CEO of a manufacturing company in St. Louis and he spoke as if used to being listened to. Tristan seemed clear-eyed if hard-assed—even with that unfortunate name—Jed thought. A guy he could depend on if he didn't cross him or fill him full of bullshit—which he wouldn't. His wife, Donna, was arch and cold. She was one of those fine-boned skeleton women who no doubt did Pilates and had her plastic surgeon's number on her speed dial. She was a horsewoman of a type—the type who stabled her expensive horses and rarely rode them but enjoyed long lunches with the girls and society functions. Jed guessed the two didn't get along all that well with each other anymore. They wouldn't be the first longtime married couple to come on one of his trips with the purpose—either stated or most likely implied—of trying to rekindle a failing or already dead marriage. But when he looked at them, the way they stood apart from each other, he guessed the rekindling would turn out to be unsuccessful. He just hoped neither of them drew any of his other clients into the dispute.

As individuals, these types always wanted to gain sympathetic ears, and gather allies to be on their side. The women were worse than the men in that regard. Already, Jed had noted Donna shooting brief sidelong glances toward the only single woman on the trip, Rachel Mina. She'd already no doubt targeted her as her first and most likely coconspirator.

Jed said to everyone, "We have a method to our madness on the trail, and we'd appreciate your cooperation. First, nobody brought any bear spray, did they?"

No one said yes.

"Good. I know the Park Service advises everyone to have bear spray because we will absolutely see bears, both black and grizzly. But bear spray does the same thing to horses as it does to bears. If there was an accidental discharge while we were riding along, it could set off a panic and a stampede. So I always ask my clients not to bring bear spray. Of course, I won't even ask about firearms because it's illegal to have a gun in a national park. Everybody knows that, right?"

There was general assent.

"Nobody has a gun with them, right?"

Vigorous "Oh, no's" and head shakes all around, except for one man. The single, Wilson. Jed noted it and tucked the impression into his mental "To Do" basket.

He continued, "You may have heard Congress passed a law that it was now legal for individuals to carry firearms in national parks, but that's only half the story. It means if you have a valid concealed-carry permit in the state where the park is located—Wyoming, in our case— you can legally have a gun. It doesn't mean anyone can just show up packing iron. And the releases you signed with us clearly state *no firearms*. Everybody clear on that point?"

General assent. Except for Wilson, who didn't respond either way.

To the left of the Glodes were Walt Franck and his stepson Justin from Denver. Walt was gray haired, short, and he looked soft. He had a kindly unimpressive face and a bulbous nose spiderwebbed with veins, suggesting he was a drinker. He wore a fishing shirt and zip-off pants, and there was a rod tube poking out of his pile of gear. Justin was in his late teens. He was tall, chiseled, and athletic looking. He had long unkempt hair and smoldering dark eyes. As Jed spoke, Justin's eyes were on the dark-haired Sullivan girl who'd just arrived. Jed thought, *This will be interesting.*

As he did with all of his clients, Jed tried to guess the motivation for Walt and Justin to come on the trip. By their age disparity, he guessed Walt was much older than Justin's mother. That fact alone suggested Walt was bringing the stepson along to forge a bond that had been missing between them. Or was it Justin's idea? While Justin looked fit and able, Jed thought, the kid didn't look like an outdoorsman. He was missing all the telltale high-tech outdoor clothing and attitude. No, Jed decided, this was Walt's deal. Take the boy on an adventure, show him how to camp and fish. Show the boy Walt had some skills besides his interest in his mother, after all. Plus, it showed the boy that Walt had serious money that he was willing to spend on *him*.

"I see we have some fishermen with us but according to the registration forms, we also have some wildlife enthusiasts," he said, nodding toward Tristan Glode and the younger Sullivan girl (he couldn't remember her name), "And I can tell you right now you won't be disappointed. I'd suggest you take the strap of your camera and loop it through a button hole and put the camera in a shirt pocket so you can get to it real quick. You don't want to drop your camera or lose it along the trail, that's for sure. The Yellowstone Thorofare is home to all of the major species in the park. We'll see bison, wolves, grizzlies, mountain sheep, mule deer, antelope, black bear, and moose. We'll see smaller species along the way as well—coyotes, beavers, marmots, and dozens of species of birds including bald eagles. We'll see critters in their natural habitat doing things critters do—like kill and eat each other. We won't interfere with them and they won't interfere with us. In all my years of guiding these trips and all the bears we've seen, I've only lost a couple of clients and it was their own fault because they ran slow."

That always got a decent nervous laugh. He glanced over to see Dakota roll her eyes. She'd heard him say that *so* many times.

"Just remember," he said, grinning to show he was kidding, "you don't have to outrun the bear. Bears are fast. You just have to outrun the guy or gal next to you.

"I'm joshing, of course," he said. "Nobody yet has been killed and eaten by a bear." He paused dramatically. "Of course, attacks by wolf packs is another matter."

He soaked in the dark laughter, and clinically noted the exchanges of looks between the father and daughters, between Walt and Justin, between the group of three men, and the absence of sharing between Tristan and Jennifer Glode. Yup, he thought, he had *that* one figured out.

The group of three men in their thirties were the easiest to peg, Jed thought. He knew what they were about when they opened the doors of their rental car and empty beer cans fell out. They were still squinting from high-altitude hangovers. James Knox, Tony D'Amato, and Drey Russell were three gregarious buddies who worked at different firms on Wall Street who went on an annual male-bonding adventure.

They were the cut-ups, the goofballs. Knox, a light-haired man with a long thin nose and brusque East Coast go-get-'em manner, was the organizer. He was maybe a few years older than the other two.

Of all the clients, Jed had been most concerned about the three Wall Streeters. Three men like that could take over a trip and pose a challenge to him if they had the wrong attitude or expectations. But after seeing them emerge from the car and watching them josh with each other and laugh, he was relieved. They were there for the adventure.

Drey Russell—short for André, according to his booking form— was a light-skinned black man with dark kind eyes and a quick smile. Jed didn't get many people of color on his trips, and welcomed Drey so he could get some photos of him in the group to use on his Web site. The National Park Service loved that diversity crap, he knew.

Tony D'Amato looked as dark and Italian as his name, and had a heavy New Jersey accent. He played the part of the perpetually flummoxed big-city boy stuck out in the country, the man who "don't know nothin' about horses except the ones on the carousel," who was the butt of Knox's and Drey's jibes. These three would be no trouble, Jed thought. They were into themselves and their group, and they were there to fill up a sackful of memories to laugh about later when they met after work at the bar. So for them, the tougher, the crazier, the more primitive the trip the better because it would make for better tales to tell. A little high maintenance, maybe, Jed thought, even though they didn't intend to be. Folks raised entirely in cities didn't have perspective when it came to so many outdoor adventures. But they'd try to get along. No doubt they were all used to snappy service at resorts and lodges and probably not the grind of the trail, despite what they might think. He remembered seeing the previous male-bonding trips listed on their applications, including Mexico, Europe, and Scandinavia. Of course, that was before the economic meltdown, back when these guys pulled down seven figures or close to that. Now, as Knox had made it clear on his initial call, the circumstances were

such that the group agreed to keep doing their annual adventure together, even if "they had to slum it for a couple of years." Although Jed
took silent offense to that, he also decided upon seeing them that they
seemed almost normal. Jed would just play to Knox and Drey to get
them on board. They'd keep Tony D'Amato in line. These three could
be Jed's allies, if he played it right. It was always good to establish allies early on.

"You see we have mules as well as horses," Jed said, gesturing behind him to where the animals stood tied abreast along the length of
the horse trailer. "The mules are our pack animals."

Jed paused and smiled slyly. "For our friends from New York City,
the mules are the goofy-looking ones with long ears who are fast
asleep right now."

That got a bit of a laugh and the Wall Streeters enjoyed being high-
lighted. Yup, Jed thought, they'd be all right.

Said Jed, "I'll lead a string of three and Dakota here will follow up
the rest of you with a string of three as well. In those canvas boxes on
the sides of the mules will be all our equipment—tents, food, first-aid
kits, cookstove and kitchen setup, plates and silverware, feedbags,
everything we'll need. That's why I asked all of you to keep your personal gear down to no more than twenty pounds each. We just don't
have the space or animals to take any more. I know it's tough to get all
your possessions down to twenty pounds, but for the sake of the animals and the weight on them, that's what we have to do. You'll learn to
live with and maybe even enjoy not having too many choices of what
to wear each day.

"Even though I sent you a checklist, let me just make sure you all
have what you need, starting with a good sleeping bag . . ."

As he went through the list: sleeping bag, sleeping pad, rain gear, on and
on, he picked out the two remaining clients on the trip, the two singles.
Singles were often a pain in the butt to Jed, since they tended to try to
pal around with him or Dakota if they didn't fit in with any of the

other clients, which was often the case. Singles could sometimes be broody and standoffish, and create dissension. Jed was always relieved when other clients took in the strays so he wouldn't have to.

The singles were a man and a woman. They stood as far away from each other as possible while still being within the group of clients, meaning they had no immediate intention of forming an alliance. The man was named K. W. Wilson. Ken. He was dark and pinched and had provided the least amount of personal information on his registration form of anyone. The only thing Jed knew about him was Ken was from Utah, wanted to fish, and that he couldn't eat cheese. Jed would try to figure the guy out at Camp One so he'd know how to handle him and integrate him into the larger group. If K.W. wouldn't talk, Jed would ask Dakota to sidle up to him. Men liked to talk to Dakota, even if she didn't particularly like talking with them.

Wilson had his camera out and was taking digital photos of everybody and everything. What was odd about it was the man never asked anyone to smile or even permission to click away.

The other single was a woman, Rachel Mina. Aside from the dark-haired Sullivan girl, Mina was the best-looking woman on the trip. She had high cheekbones, white skin, and long auburn hair tied back into a ponytail. She filled out her jeans nicely, Jed thought. And he knew her type the minute the booking form had come through his fax machine: midforties, well-to-do, and recently divorced. The last of the children out of the home, probably, and finally able to do the things she'd never been able to do before, ready for anything, game for anything. Jed could tell Dakota had picked up the same impression right off by the way she glared at her.

It was interesting, Jed thought, that the booking forms for Ted Sullivan and Rachel Mina arrived within days of each other back in November the year before. He assumed they might be together. But Sullivan and Mina hadn't greeted each other or even shared a glance that he'd seen. He chalked the close arrival of the forms to coincidence. Which meant she may be in play after all.

"Any questions?" Jed asked.

Tony D'Amato raised his hand. As he did, Drey and Knox coughed into their hands.

"What do we do if we can't get along with our horse? You know, like we've *never even friggin' ridden one before?*"

Jed said, "Walk." Deadpan. Then he grinned. "You shouldn't have to worry. We'll match you up with the easiest and gentlest horse we've got. The horse knows to follow the horse in front of it. All you'll have to do is keep balanced. The less steering you do the better. These horses know where we're going and who's in charge. They'll fall right into line. We don't allow any cowboy stuff, folks. You're all riding trail horses along a trail. No breaking off from the line, no riding fast. We're into safety and not rodeos. So just sit back and relax. And once we get going, Dakota and I will help you out and give you some tips."

"Maybe you can ride a mule," Drey said to Tony, and both he and Knox broke out laughing.

"I've got a question," said Tristan Glode. His voice was stentorian and without humor.

"Yes, sir?" Jed said. He knew instantly Glode was the kind of man who would expect and appreciate deference and would reward it with a big tip.

"I've been following the weather and the conditions in Yellowstone for the past six months since we signed up for this adventure," he said. Jed noted the Wall Streeters looking at each other and rolling their eyes at his out-front arrogance but looked away before Glode saw him. "It's been unseasonably cold and wet. More rainfall than usual by a large degree. My question is if we'll need to deviate from your established routing because of the high water."

Jed answered quickly, so as not to concern the rest of his clients. "You're absolutely right about the rain, sir," he said. "We've had a hell of a wet spring and early summer. In fact, I had to cancel my first two trips because of it. I didn't want to risk taking folks or these horses through swelled-up creeks and rivers. But the rains finally let up, as you can see. The water levels are going down, and the Park Service gave me the okay. So I don't think there's anything you need to worry about. We can be a little flexible if we need to. If the camp we plan to stay at is washed out, there are plenty of others to choose from. This is a big damned place."

As he said the last part, Jed felt Dakota's probing eyes on the side of his head. He ignored her.

Glode stood perfectly still, absorbing the answer. For a moment, Jed anticipated Glode would say something disastrous, like, "Maybe we should come back another year."

Instead, Glode said, "As long as we get the experience we're paying for, I'm okay with that. I don't want some cheap route because of conditions. I want to take the trip into the back of beyond I paid for."

"That you'll get, sir," Jed said, grinning with relief. "But keep in mind what I said about flexibility."

"What do you think?" Jed whispered to Dakota when they were back at the trailer saddling up the last of the horses.

"Not a bad group overall. Maybe a couple of minor problems."

"Which ones?"

"The older teenage girl looks like trouble but nothing we can't handle," she said, keeping her voice down. "The older couple look like they're spoiling for a knock-down-drag-out with each other any minute. The three Wall Streeters seem okay, but I'd bet they've got more than twenty pounds of gear each on them and most of that is liquor."

Jed nodded. She was getting good at this.

"I like the younger of the two sisters."

"I didn't even notice her."

"You wouldn't," Dakota said. Then: "What was that about using other campsites? You know what the Park Service says about *that*. Why'd you say we might change up the route?"

He shrugged. "You never know. Conditions might dictate a change."

"I thought it was kind of a strange thing to say," she said, trying without success to get him to look back at her.

He changed the subject. "What about the single man? Wilson?"

She looked over. "He's the one who gives me a bad vibe."

He nodded, agreeing. "Maybe you can get him to talk to you a little. Find out what his deal is."

"I knew you were going to ask me to do that."

"He's likely to talk to you before me," Jed said.

Jed finished up on the saddle and leaned into her. He whispered, "If the situation presents itself I may take a look in his duffel to make sure he don't have no gun."

Dakota arched her eyebrows. "And if he does?"

"I'll figure out a way to make it a nonissue."

He could tell his turn of phrase puzzled her but he didn't say more. He liked to leave her hanging, make himself a little mysterious. That was good for a relationship, he thought. Plus, he didn't want her thinking this was their last trip together.

Which it was. Because, Jed thought but didn't say, it was likely to be his last trip back of beyond. And if everything fell into place the way he'd planned it over the long and dark winter, he'd be set for life. Smart-ass girl wranglers like Dakota Hill—and needy clients like the ones who milled around before him—would be things in his past.

Hell, he thought, if things worked out like he planned them, *he'd* be the one getting catered to.

10

Gracie got Strawberry, a light red roan mare with dapples of white on her sides and haunches that had the effect of making her look like a pink horse. After sitting on Strawberry's back for fifteen minutes as the long train of riders wound up out of the parking lot into the trees on the rocky trail, Gracie knew one thing for sure: she was in love.

Already she liked the sounds and rhythm of the ride; the heavy footfalls of the animals, their snorts, the rocking motion, even the smell of them. And she was thrilled with that big-eyed look Strawberry gave her when the old mare turned her head back and seemed to assess Gracie with a practiced eye, apparently satisfied with what she saw.

"I like you, too," Gracie whispered, leaning forward in her saddle to pat Strawberry on the neck. "I like you, too. We're a good team, I think."

"What—are you talking to your horse?" Danielle said over her shoulder as she rode ahead. "Don't be kissing him, now."

"It's a her," Gracie said. "And you *should* talk to your horse. That's one way to get her to like you."

"What's mine?" Danielle said. "I forgot. I know the name is Peanut."

Said Gracie, "You're riding a gelding." She'd overheard Jed the outfitter and Dakota Hill brief her sister on Peanut and his particular tendencies, the worst of which was to take every opportunity available to grab a bite of grass from the side of the trail. "You know what a gelding is, don't you?"

"Of course," Danielle said. "He's a unit."

"A *eunuch,*" Gracie corrected.

"Right," Danielle said, "a horse with no balls. A Peanut with a limp penis. Just great."

"You wouldn't want a stallion," Gracie said. "They have only one thing on their minds."

"I'm used to boys like that."

"I know you are."

"*Shut up,*" Danielle said. "Just because you took some lessons you act like you're an expert."

"I'm not," Gracie said. "But I wish you would have gone to those lessons with me like I asked you. I learned a lot, and you would have, too. If nothing else, you could have listened to Jed and Dakota tell you about him. I don't know how you get by never listening to anyone."

"Yet somehow I do," Danielle said, looking over her shoulder, smiling seductively, and batting her eyelashes.

Gracie rolled her eyes.

From behind her, Gracie heard Dakota Hill say, "S'cuse me while I puke."

Gracie giggled and looked around. Dakota was leading her three mules and mumbling to herself, and acted embarrassed that Gracie had heard her. Gracie winked. Dakota grinned and winked back, obviously relieved they had something in common.

Gracie wondered what the deal was with Jed and Dakota, if they were an item. She'd seen how they talked with each other at the horse trailer.

Yes, she decided. They were a couple, even if Jed was too old for her. Maybe, Gracie thought, there weren't many choices of men in Montana.

The order of the riders, horses, and mules was established in the parking lot by Jed. Once everyone was mounted, he'd explained that the reason for the order of riders was not based on merit or preference, but by how the horses behaved with each other.

"If you want to change the order," he said, "we can maybe work it out at some point. We may find we want to change things up as well to keep the peace. But right now, just memorize the look of the rider's butt and the horse's butt ahead of you and follow those butts. Horses have an established pecking order. They also have friends and enemies. We know these horses better than we know you folks at this point, so trust us on this. Safety first, folks. If you change up the order you increase the chance of a wreck."

Gracie rode next to last on Strawberry. When Jed handed her the reins of the pink horse, he told Gracie the animal was a sweetheart and "Don't have an ounce of mean in her anymore if she ever did." Strawberry was older than Gracie, he said, and this may be her last trip before she was retired to be a brood mare. All Strawberry required, Jed said, was kindness and she'd pay Gracie back with loyalty and predictability. "You look like a nice girl," Jed had said.

"Most of the time," Gracie answered.

"You've ridden a little?"

"Quite a bit, actually," she said.

He gave her a paternalistic smile. "We'll see," he said.

11

Cody Hoyt said, "So, do you have a headlight that will work?"

It was ten thirty in the morning and the mechanic leaned against a rolling, red-metal standing tool chest and drank a cup of coffee. Above his head was a Snap-On Tools calendar featuring a blonde winking while holding a wrench. The little garage was dark and close and smelled of oil and gasoline. Dust motes floated through the shafts of light from the cloudy windows. The mechanic wore gray coveralls and a Rocky Mountain Elk Foundation cap. He was short and wiry with deep-set eyes and short-cropped salt-and-pepper hair. He'd shaved but had missed a triangle of whiskers above his Adam's apple. Cody had waited for him outside the shop for an hour while the mechanic had leisurely morning coffee with other locals at the diner next door.

"I might have one," the mechanic said, "depending on your attitude."

Cody nearly launched himself across the floor at the guy, but managed to take a deep breath and look away. Orange spangles danced around the edges of his vision. He wanted to flash his badge or show his gun. He wanted to put the mechanic in a sleeper hold and threaten his eyes with pepper spray—anything to get the guy moving. He *hated* being a civilian. And he hated the fact that he had to operate below the radar and on his own. If he'd told the trooper the night before where he was going and why, the patrolman would have been duty bound to call it in and check the story. Cody couldn't afford to have the sheriff know he was gone, and Townsend was close enough to Helena Bodean that she might send someone to get him and bring him back. So, gritting his teeth against his nature, he'd followed the trooper back to town and nodded meekly when ordered to "Park it."

If he leaned on the mechanic the trooper would come back and he might never get out of Townsend, Montana, population 1,898.

"Look," Cody said, "just please put your other jobs aside long enough to wire in a new headlight."

The mechanic eyed Cody with a squint, sizing him up. Waiting for more groveling, Cody imagined.

"I've been here all night," Cody said. "The trooper said you're the only mechanic in town right now. I'm really desperate to get on the road and he won't let me go until I've got a headlight that works."

Finally, the mechanic said, "I doubt I can match the headlight. I might have to order one out of Helena or White Sulpher Springs—"

Cody broke in, "It doesn't have to look pretty. It doesn't even have to *fit*. It just has to light up."

The morning was cool and sunny and there were no pedestrians on the street. The Commercial Bar across the road was open, as it always was. Cody watched as a ranch truck parked at the curb and a beat-up old cowboy got out and went in for his breakfast beer. He wore irrigation boots and a sweat-stained straw hat. *Jesus,* he thought, *a breakfast beer.*

As he walked he thought of Justin, and his stomach turned sour. Therefore, he *had* to keep it going. He *had* to find his son and keep that going. He owed the world the favor.

He pulled out his cell and speed-dialed Larry's extension.

"Olson."

"Larry, it's me."

There was a beat before Larry cleared his throat and said, "Excuse me, what did you say your name was?"

"Come on, Larry."

"And you're with what company again?"

"Ah," Cody said, "Bodean's in the room. Got it."

"Yes," Larry said, clipped.

"Can't talk?"

"No. How did you get this number?"

"I'll call back on your cell, then."

Larry said, "I don't purchase toner or anything else for the office, lady. I'm a detective for the sheriff's department, for crying out loud. I've got important work to do." And slammed his phone down.

Cody called back three minutes later to find out Larry's cell phone had been turned off.

Cody closed his phone, puzzled. Larry *never* turned off his phone. So either Bodean was still in the room or something else was going on. What?

Cody's phone went off. He looked at the display. It was an unknown number but had the Montana 406 area code.

"Yes," Cody said.

"Me," Larry said. By the background traffic noises from Larry's cell, Cody guessed his partner had taken a walk outside.

"Don't call me on my cell or the office number again," Larry said. "They don't know you're gone. There can't be a record of calls between us on either phone. And if they ask me if I've heard from you, I'll tell them the truth. I can't lie for you, Cody."

"I understand. So what is this phone you're using?"

"You know, it's one I borrowed," Larry stammered.

"You're learning." Cody smiled to himself. He remembered the afternoon when he showed Larry how many phones there were in the evidence room, each tagged for specific cases. Some still had a battery charge left. He'd told Larry how, down in Denver, he'd used confiscated phones to make calls that couldn't be traced back to him and sometimes, to aggravate a criminal, he'd call random numbers in Bolivia and Ecuador just to run up astronomical phone charges.

"So, where are you?" Larry asked.

Cody sighed. "I made it as far as Townsend and an HP trooper picked me up and marched me back to town for that fucking missing headlight."

Larry laughed. "Townsend? That's as far as you got? You're *kidding*."

"So I spent the night bouncing off the walls of the Lariat Motor Lodge. I'd recommend it only because it's probably the last place in America that still has black-and-white TVs in the rooms and bedspreads that remind you of your grandmother's house."

"You should have stayed home," Larry said.

Cody grunted, "No way. I'll be back on the road in a few minutes."

Larry sighed.

"Have you heard anything back from ViCAP or RMIN?"

"Sort of," Larry said. "RMIN is running the police reports from the most recent victim in Jackson Hole and they'll be getting back to me. The case was classified as an accident but it sounds, well, real familiar. A woman named Karen Anthony, forty-six, divorced and living alone, was found dead in her home outside of Wilson. Same deal, Cody. Her place was burned down around her and she was found the next day underneath the debris. Head injuries the likely cause of death."

Cody said, "Anything like what we've got in terms of an open stove, or the bottle?"

"Nope. The evidence so far doesn't match up to ours. But the circumstances of the death ring true."

Cody walked down the empty sidewalk, pacing. He noticed a face watching him from the window of the Commercial Bar. It was the cowboy he'd seen enter earlier. The man tipped his hat and took a deep drink from a beer mug as if to taunt him. The cowboy was drinking a red beer—spiced tomato juice and Bud Light. Cody used to start the day with one. Its properties were magical.

"Bastard," Cody said.

"What?" Larry asked.

"Not you. What did Karen Anthony do? What was her job?"

"Let's see," Larry said. "Okay, here. She was an independent hospital consultant. Had her own firm, and apparently a pretty successful one. She had an office in Jackson and one in Denver, Minneapolis, and Omaha."

Cody rubbed his face. "One of the victims was from Minnesota, right? Is there a connection there?"

"I don't know. We're too early in this thing. I've got a telephone meeting scheduled with an analyst at ViCAP later today so maybe we'll be able to establish a link of some kind. The only thing I can figure, obviously, is Winters was a pharma guy and Karen Anthony was a hospital consultant. So maybe they worked together somehow or knew each other. But it'll take a hell of a lot more digging."

"Yeah," Cody said. "We still don't know anything about the Minnesota and Virginia deaths. They could be connected to these two or not. ViCAP might be able to help with that."

Larry said, "And Cody, nothing really connects Winters and Anthony yet except for the burned-down houses and the proximity of the dates. This thread is so thin. . . ."

"I know," Cody said. "Keep me posted, okay? My cell should work all day until I get to Yellowstone."

"So you're still going," Larry said.

"Damn right. Hey—did you get in touch with Jed McCarthy's office yet?"

Larry paused while a diesel vehicle passed him, the engine hammering away. Then: "I've left two more messages to call me."

Cody stopped. "You haven't asked the Bozeman PD to roust it? Come on, Larry!"

Silence. Then it dawned on Cody but Larry spoke before he had a chance to apologize.

"You asshole," Larry said. "You were supposed to be at that office when it opened. You weren't supposed to be playing with yourself in fucking Townsend, Montana. And how would it have been for you if you showed up at Wilderness Adventures at the same time as the local cops? Don't you think they'd ask questions? Don't you think they'd figure out real damned quick you were a suspended detective and call up here and talk to Tub?"

"I know," Cody said, "I'm sorry. You're thinking clearly and I'm not. Thank you, Larry."

"I'm tired of doing you favors," Larry said.

"I know. I don't blame you."

"You are an unthinking prick sometimes," Larry said.

"*Okay,*" Cody hissed, "I've got the point."

"Good," Larry said with finality.

Cody heard the rolling-thunder sound of the garage door being opened up. He turned to see the mechanic backing out his SUV. There was a headlight there, all right. It didn't fit into the damaged fender but was wired and taped around the dented hole. It looked like a detached eyeball.

"I'm ready to roll," Cody said. "Keep me posted on what you find out from ViCAP and RMIN."

Larry sighed.

"You call me, I won't call you," Cody said, "but keep that burner phone handy and hidden, okay? In case I find something out from the office in Bozeman."

"Gotcha," Larry said.

"Thanks, buddy."

Cody waved and took a deep breath as he drove by the highway patrol car pulled over on the side of the highway a mile out of Townsend. The trooper whooped on his siren and gestured for him to pull over.

Cody sat seething while the trooper slowly got out of his car and slowly walked up along the driver's side. He powered the window down.

"Now what?" Cody said.

"I see you got a headlight. It doesn't look so good, though," the trooper said. "I hope you'll get that front end fixed and get a new light as soon as you can."

"I will."

"I've got a question for you," the trooper said, tipping his hat back and watching Cody's face carefully for tics or tells. Cody knew the drill. He was about to be asked a question he wouldn't want to answer, and the trooper hoped to catch him in a lie. "I ran your plates. According to the Department of Motor Vehicles, this vehicle doesn't exist. Your number doesn't correspond with a name, in other words."

"That doesn't surprise me," Cody said quickly. "I bought it at a county auction up in Helena. They used to use it for undercover surveillance, the auctioneer told me. He said the sheriff's department uses some dummy plates so the bad guys don't know who they are. I guess they just kept the plates on."

The trooper rubbed his chin, thinking that over.

"I'll get some new plates as soon as I get home to Bozeman," Cody said. "I promise you. I'll send you the receipt to prove it."

At that moment, the trooper's handheld squawked. Cody heard the dispatcher reporting a one-car rollover five miles north of Townsend.

"Guess you better go," Cody said.

The trooper hesitated for a moment, then said, "Send me that receipt. But something about that story of yours is fishy."

"Check it out," Cody said. "You'll see."

The trooper waved at him dismissively and started back to his car. Cody silently thanked whomever had lost control of their car north of town, and eased back out onto the road.

The headquarters for Wilderness Adventures was located south of Bozeman on U.S. 191 near the Gallatin Gateway Inn on the road to West Yellowstone and Yellowstone Park. Cody arrived at 1:30 P.M., cursing himself yet again for the debacle in Townsend that put him twelve hours behind where he wanted to be.

The office was a converted old home shaded by ancient cottonwoods and surrounded by rolling pasture and outbuildings and corrals in decent repair. Six or seven horses grazed and twitched their tails against the flies and didn't look up to greet him. It wasn't the kind of office guests were likely to visit, he thought, but no doubt it made for a good staging area for large-scale horse operations. The pasture fed the horses when they weren't on a pack trip. The sign for Wilderness Adventures was homemade; a modern swooping logo painted on a frame made of old barnwood. There was an older blue sedan parked on the side of the building.

He killed the engine, vaulted up the wooden steps to the porch, and banged on the frame of the screen door.

"Yes?" A woman's voice. She sounded startled.

"My name's Cody Hoyt," he said. "I need to talk to someone who knows something about the pack trip in Yellowstone."

"Oh my," said a plump older woman who suddenly came into view through the screen. "You weren't booked on the trip, were you? Because it left this morning."

Her name was Margaret Kerley and she was the sole office employee of Wilderness Adventures and had been for twenty-five years, she said. She wore thick glasses and her hair was tightly curled and looked like steel wool. She wore jeans, a white shirt that bulged in the middle, and a Western pattern vest embroidered with cowgirls and lariats. The lobby of the office was filled with large cardboard boxes reading DELL.

"We're in the process of computerizing," she said, shaking her head sadly. "Jed is making me learn how to run one of those things. He says it will make us more efficient, but I think it's, you know, a *fad*. This old dog doesn't need new tricks. I've been running the business part of the company all these years and I don't need a machine. I've got everything I need in there," she said, and gestured toward a bank of old metal filing cabinets. "I'm supposed to put all that information back there into the machine, and Jed says he wants me to update the Web site so he doesn't have to do it from home. Can you imagine that? The World Wide Web? I want no part of it."

Cody nodded curtly. He noticed the telephone on her desk was blinking with messages.

"Don't you answer your phone?" he asked. "My colleague was calling you all morning."

"Of course I answer the phone," she said, her eyes flashing behind those thick lenses. "But it's a little hard to do when you're sitting in a computer class the entire morning learning how to work a program called Excella."

"Excel," Cody said. "So you haven't been in until now?"

"I just got here a half hour ago," she said, still miffed at him. "I was working. I just wasn't here. Jed insisted I take that class once a week and today is the day."

Cody said, "Do you have the list of clients on the current trip? I need to look at it."

"Of course I have it," she said. "But can you tell me why you want to see who is on it? Isn't this kind of an invasion of privacy?"

Cody caught himself before he rolled his eyes. "I don't see how it could be," he said. "Look, I need to know if my son is on this trip. It's important. There's an emergency in the family."

"You won't be able to contact him," she said, shaking her head. "There's no way to communicate with a pack trip once they've left into the park. There are no cell things."

"Towers," he said. "Look, I know that. But if he's on it I need to know. I'll figure the rest out."

She squinted at him and pursed her lips. "Your manner is very brusque."

"Sorry," he said, stepping toward her. "But show me the *list*."

She made a show of sighing dramatically, then turned around and approached the filing cabinets. "I know where everything is," she said. "I have my own filing system. Apparently, it aggravates Jed that he can't find anything, even though I've tried to explain to him how it works. Let's see, today is July first, so 07/01. Seven corresponds with G in the alphabet, the seventh letter. One corresponds with A . . ." She reached for a middle drawer and pulled it out and started fingering through tabs marked by handwritten letters.

Cody tried to remain calm.

"Here it is," she said, pulling a file. "All the applications and signed releases of liability. And here," she said, slipping a single handwritten sheet out of the file, "is the complete list in the order they came in."

He snatched it out of her hand and read down the list.

1. Anthony D'Amato
2. Walt Franck

"His Richness," Cody mumbled. "Damn it."

3. Justin Hoyt

"*Damn it*," Cody whispered. "He's on it."
Cody scanned the rest of the list:

4. James Knox
5. Rachel Mina
6. Tristan Glode
7. Donna Glode
8. André Russell
9. Ted Sullivan
10. Gracie Sullivan
11. Danielle Sullivan
12. K. W. Wilson

None of the other names rang a bell. But he thought one of them might produce a ViCAP hit.

"I'll need that back," she said.

"In a minute," he said, shuffling through the applications. Here, in the folder he held in his hand, were the names, addresses, physical descriptions, and details of each client on the trip. He was ecstatic. "Where's your fax machine?"

"Is it long distance?" she asked. "You know, each fax is just like a long-distance phone call."

Cody dug in his pocket and threw her a twenty-dollar bill. "That should cover it."

"Where are you faxing the pages?" she asked.

"Just tell me where the goddamn machine is," he said.

"No need to be like that," she said, pointing to a supply room behind her.

While Cody fed in each page and transmitted it to Larry, he turned on the copy machine next to the fax. After each application was sent he made a copy for himself. Margaret Kerley was at her desk retrieving telephone messages, and had left him alone. He hoped she wouldn't object to him making copies but it didn't matter—he was taking the applications with him. Because one of these people, he thought, killed Hank Winters and was near his son.

When he was through he returned all the original documents to the folder and stuffed the copies in under his shirt.

He handed the folder to her at her desk.

"Why do you suppose a detective is calling me?" she asked him. "Is this your colleague? Are you a policeman?"

He nodded.

"Why didn't you tell me?" she said, suddenly sitting up straighter.

"Undercover," he said. "And this matter is confidential. Please tell no one I was here. Do you understand?"

She nodded furiously.

"Now I need you to think for a minute," he said. "What is the best way to catch up to the pack trip? Don't tell me the outfitter doesn't have a satellite phone or some way to get in touch with the outside world."

She shook her head. "I'm sorry, but he doesn't."

"How can that be in this day and age?" Cody spat. "What if the Park Service needs to contact him? What if he's got an emergency, like a client has a heart attack or something?"

She smiled sympathetically. "Then he's to locate a park ranger and the park ranger places the call. You don't understand how they can be. The Park Service, I mean. Such bureaucracy! They're the reason Bull Mitchell finally sold the business. I wish he never had. I know *he* wouldn't be making me learn how to work a computer."

Cody took a deep breath. "Okay, so I can't call them. So how would I find them? Is there a designated route? Doesn't the Web site indicate they stay at a specific camp every night of the trip?"

She nodded her head. "Unless they camp somewhere else," she said. "Things happen out there. Sometimes they'll camp in other places, or even on a different trail if the trail is washed out or trees fall over it or something. All I ever know is where they start and where they end. The middle is kind of . . . random."

He slapped the desk in frustration. Then he said, "Where can I find Bull Mitchell?" Thinking: *Does he even live in Bozeman? Is he alive?*

She looked at her watch.

"It's nearly two," she said. "That means he'll be at the library."

"The *library*?"

A misty look came over her eyes. "You'll see," she said.

12

Gracie didn't mind being so far back in the string at all. She liked being able to observe the riders ahead of her, something she couldn't have done if her horse was higher in the pecking order.

Jed was first, trailing three mules strapped with massive pack-boxes of gear and food. He constantly turned in his saddle to make sure everyone was behind him and in the order he'd set for them.

Behind the mules was the older couple, Tristan and Donna Glode. Gracie hadn't heard Tristan say much so far on the trip, but he had a kind of serious and businesslike bearing, she thought. His wife seemed cold and aloof, but Gracie noted how gracefully she'd climbed on the saddle and how elegantly she rode. She was the only guest wearing honest-to-God English riding boots. Gracie tried to model her riding style—relaxed, not slumping, head up, reins loose in her left hand—after Donna Glode. But that's the only thing about Donna Glode Gracie wanted to learn.

Walt and Justin were next. Gracie noted how often Walt turned in his saddle and sized up his soon-to-be stepson and then nodded approvingly at what he saw. She wondered what it was Justin was doing that was worthy of the head nods since it seemed to her the only thing Justin wanted to do was bump along and steal looks at Danielle. Justin rode well, Gracie thought, the way a natural athlete would ride. He wasn't smooth but he looked strong and well balanced. He had a certain style about him, an attitude: confident, cocky, maybe a little full of himself. He knew he was the only young buck on the trip. He apparently saw no reason to put his feet in the stirrups, for example, and they dangled on the sides of his horse.

Rachel, the divorcée or widow or whatever she was, rode behind Justin on a slick jet-black gelding. Gracie thought the horse, named Midnight, was by far the best-looking of the herd. Midnight's coat was so black it shined dark blue, like Superman's hair, Gracie thought. And Rachel Mina looked good on him. She wasn't as self-consciously slick as Donna Glode, but she'd obviously ridden before. Her posture was good, Gracie thought, as she found herself sitting more upright in Strawberry's saddle. Gracie thought it would be interesting to talk to Rachel Mina to find out why she'd come alone on a trip like this. She had a feeling the woman was interesting, or had a good story, at least. And was she mistaken, or did Rachel Mina smile at her earlier in an almost familiar way? Like they'd met before, which Gracie was certain hadn't happened.

The three Wall Streeters rode behind Rachel Mina; James Knox, Drey Russell, and Tony D'Amato. Gracie guessed that *maybe* Knox had been on a horse before, and possibly Drey. But certainly not Tony, who kept saying things like, "Where is the brake on this thing?" and "What good is a saddle horn that doesn't honk?" Tony kept the other two laughing with his stupid asides and observations, and Gracie guessed it was kind of an act. Tony pointed out each time Knox's gelding's long penis unfurled and swung loose from side to side as the horse walked, saying, "Look who's relaxed," or "He reminds me of *me* when he does that." The three men together were interesting, she thought. She'd seen very few male friendships up close in her life and the way they chided and insulted each other was a way of showing affection, she guessed. If women talked like that to each other there would soon be scratching and blood. She also thought how quickly boring it would become if every other statement was about their sexual organs, as it was with the male Wall Streeters. Despite their goofiness, though, Gracie liked having the three men around. They seemed solid and anchored. Better than three women, she thought. Especially on a trip like this.

The strange man, K. W. Wilson, rode behind them on a pale gray gelding. Although he wasn't wearing a black hat or shirt, there was something dark about him. Brooding but at times kind of smiling to himself. Like he had a secret or found his thoughts amusing. The ghostly pallor of his horse only added to the image. He was thin and his face was made of sharp planes shoved together, as if he'd once had a normal face but somebody crumpled it in from the sides where it bent like sheet metal. His eyes were mounted close over the sharp bridge of a hatchetlike nose. He needed a shave and the trip had barely even started. He didn't seem to laugh at the jokes of the Wall Streeters, not at all. Gracie was wary of him, and unlike Rachel Mina, had zero desire to get to know him at all.

Her dad rode behind Wilson, and Danielle was just ahead. Danielle rode well even though she didn't have a clue as to what she was doing. Gracie wished *she* filled her saddle as well as Danielle, and wondered if and when her own butt wouldn't be skinny and bony like a boy's. Already it hurt. She could use some of Danielle's padding, she thought.

"How's that horse ridin'?" Dakota Hill asked in a tone Gracie could hear but low enough the others couldn't.

"Good," Gracie said. "I really like her."

"Strawberry's a good little horse. You can depend on her. Just don't get her too close to those horses up front if you can help it, especially that black one, Midnight. Midnight don't like Strawberry."

"That's too bad," Gracie said, again leaning forward and patting Strawberry's neck, " 'cause she's such a sweet girl."

"Yup."

Gracie thought Dakota Hill looked like a natural cowgirl in a way that Jed didn't look like a natural cowboy. She was the type of woman, Gracie thought, who would be almost beautiful if she wore makeup. But Dakota seemed determined to fight against type by playing at being gruff and no-nonsense. What kind of woman wanted to be known as a "mule-skinner"? Gracie was puzzled by her but oddly fascinated at the same time.

When she turned back around in the saddle with the smile still on her face, she was jarred by two sets of eyes directly on her. From the front, Jed McCarthy looked on in what seemed like disapproval. And from a few horses away, K. W. Wilson smirked.

They were walking their mounts through the middle of a large green saddle slope rimmed by trees on all four sides. The air smelled slightly of sulfur. Jed had walked his string off the trail and let the others pass by. Gracie could see him talking to each rider in turn as they rode past him.

As she rode up next to him he asked, "You and that horse getting along?"

"Yes."

"You sit a nice horse," he said, nudging his horse into a walk until they rode side by side.

"I've been telling everyone to make sure to stay on the trail," he said. "It's more important here in Yellowstone than anywhere else." He gestured toward a large white patch of ground to their right about a hundred feet away. "See that there?"

"Yes."

"See anything unusual about it?"

"There's no grass on it, I guess."

"Look closer. Look at it about an inch above the ground."

She squinted and noticed how the air seemed to undulate slightly, as if it were underwater. In the center of the white patch, a slight wisp of steam or smoke curled out of a hole the size of a quarter.

"What is it?"

"This is the thing about this place," he said. "That's a fumarole, or steam vent. The white is a dried mineral crust that's covering a place where superheated water comes up out of the ground. The hole there releases some of the steam. Otherwise, it might build up too much pressure and erupt."

"Wow," she said, shaking her head.

"The crust is brittle," he said. "If you walked over the top of it or took your horse over there you'd break right through. The water underneath would scald the hell out of you or your horse. Might even kill you if you got bucked off in it."

"Really?"

"Really. It's the reason we have to stay together on the trail and not ride off. Those things are everywhere, and some are much worse," he said. "There's a little canyon in the park where so much methane gas is produced naturally out of the ground that any living thing that wanders into it will die within minutes. The floor of the canyon is covered in elk and bison bones, and maybe even some old Indian bones."

He'd softened his voice and she found it oddly rhythmic. She felt a chill ripple through her.

"But when you look at that white patch," he said, "I want you to imagine something else. Imagine most of Yellowstone Park itself is that white patch. There's a real thin crust covering hell itself, which is trying to boil over. That *wants* to boil over. And someday, it will. It's known as the Yellowstone Caldera. In fact, darlin', when it blows it'll take two million people with it. It's blown a few times through history, and we're sixty thousand years overdue."

"Why are you telling me this?" she asked.

"To heighten your awareness," he said. "I want every one of my clients to be awake."

"I'm awake," she said.

13

Although it once seemed like he lived in one, Cody Hoyt had not been in a public library for years. And as soon as he entered the Bozeman Public Library on East Main Street, he felt like he was being hurled back in time to when he rode his bike to the Helena library after telling his buddies he was going home. He loved the library, although he kept it in absolute confidence. Only the librarians knew, and they gave him his space and not-so-secretly delighted in the fact that a Hoyt of the violent and rough-hewn Hoyts was actually in their sanctuary of civilization. Often, a librarian would give him a sandwich because he was obviously missing dinner and he'd eat it at his own private table in the back.

He read everything; newspapers, magazines, hunting and fishing books, crime novels, biographies of American presidents, anything he could find on World War Two. He read reference books and *Ripley's Believe It or Not* and sex manuals that got him all worked up. Not once did he check out a book and take it with him, because he didn't dare take a chance that his dad would see it and tease him. And as far as his father knew, he wasn't home because he was at football or wrestling practice. Since his dad never went to any games anyway, he never found out Cody didn't participate in the sports he claimed he did.

Lying to his friends about going home and lying to his dad about staying at school started a prominent pattern in his life, he realized later. Leading parallel lives and telling serial lies helped prepare him for the trials and rigors of full-blown alcoholism, which, in itself, was like a second full-time—although secret—career. He'd learned early how to multitask.

Cody learned nothing in school and everything he knew in the library. He still read widely and constantly, and was never without a book in his glove compartment (along with a pint of bourbon). For the past year, he'd been alternating among Jim Harrison's novels, John McPhee's nonfiction, Flannery O'Connor's short stories, and the crime novels of John Sandford, Ken Bruen, and T. Jefferson Parker. His books were stacked like Greek columns in his living room and basement. Once he finally built those bookshelves, he could showcase an impressive collection. But he never got around to it.

He was mildly surprised by the banks of computers and the teens and twenty-somethings at each terminal. As he walked past, he noted a familiarity in what they were doing—updating their Facebook pages. He thought, *Some people used to go to libraries to gather information. Now they come to write about themselves.*

He approached the information counter and a slim girl with bangs and a nose ring swiveled his direction and arched her eyebrows as if to say *Yes?*

"Someone told me Bull Mitchell would be here," he said. "Do you have any idea where to find him?"

She pointed across her body past the reference book aisle. There was an archway painted with Mother Goose and Dr. Seuss characters and a sign that read *children's room.*

"No," Cody said, "I'm looking for an old guy named Bull Mitchell."

She said, "Yes, and I'm telling you where to find him."

Cody checked his wristwatch as he entered the children's section, wondering how much time he was wasting when he should be coursing down the highway toward Yellowstone. But since he was here, he entered the room and walked toward the back where he could hear a gruff deep voice.

It's me again, Hank the Cowdog.

I just got some terrible news. There's been a murder on the ranch . . .

"Jesus Christ," Cody grumbled.

Two young mothers were standing in the aisle and they turned when they heard him, and one of them lifted a finger to her lips to shush him. She was wearing a track suit and her blond hair was pulled back in a ponytail. She was vaguely attractive but already angry with him, so he looked to the other one. She was tall and slim with auburn hair and kind brown eyes and a nice mouth. Her face was wide open. She was pretty in a natural, athletic way.

He shrugged his apology and sidled up to them. He noted other mothers gathered along the windows on the side of the room.

"I'm looking for Bull Mitchell," he said. "Do you know him?"

"Of course," the tall woman whispered. "That's him reading."

Well, you know me. I'm no dummy. There's a thin line between heroism and stupidity, and I try to stay on the south side of it . . .

"That's Bull Mitchell?" Cody asked. "I can't see him."

"Here," the tall woman said, stepping aside.

Cody nodded his thanks.

There, in the middle of twelve or thirteen kids gathered on the floor, was a big man sitting in a comically undersized chair wearing a heavy wool work shirt, jeans, and cowboy boots. His head was a cinder block mounted on wide powerful shoulders and his huge hands held *The Original Adventures of Hank the Cowdog* indelicately, like a grizzly cradling a candy cane. He had silver-white hair but jet-black crazy eyebrows that looked like smudges of soot. He was an unpracticed and halting reader, Cody thought, but when his voice boomed for exclamations like *Good dog!* and *Will you please shut up?* the walls seemed to shake and he likely scared the bejesus out of the kids.

That's when he noticed a tiny white-haired woman in a wheelchair next to the seated children. She had a wool Pendleton trapper's blanket over her lap and she leaned forward to listen with a gauzy smile of pure enchantment.

"What's with the old lady?" Cody asked the tall woman. "What's she doing here?"

She reacted as if he'd slapped her. The blond woman rolled her eyes and snorted in contempt.

"What?" Cody said, genuinely surprised and puzzled.

Oh Hank, there's been a killing right here on the ranch and we slept through it! . . .

The tall woman said, "He's my father and 'the old lady' is my mother. She's in the advanced stages of Alzheimer's, and this is the only way he can connect with her these days, by reading children's stories."

Cody slumped and sighed. "I'm such an asshole," he said.

"Yes, you are," the tall woman said. "But I can see you didn't know."

The blond mother shushed them both.

Cody said to the tall woman, "When he's done will you introduce me to him?"

She almost smiled. "How can I introduce you when I don't know your name?"

"Cody Hoyt," he said. "I'm a cop."

She eyed him suspiciously. "Is this official business? You don't seem to have a badge."

Cody said, "It's more important than that. Give me a few minutes and I'll lay it out."

"Angela Mitchell," she said, extending her hand. "I'm the proud daughter."

Cody thought, *In other circumstances I would like to get to know this woman.*

The blond mother leaned toward them hissing, "*Shhhhhh.*"

And Bull Mitchell read:

. . . Being Head of Ranch Security is learning to ignore that kind of emotion. I mean, to hold down this job, you have to be cold and hard . . .

Cody hovered behind Angela and Bull Mitchell as Bull pushed his wife through the aisles in her wheelchair to the van to return her to the nursing home. The children had joined up with their mothers or nannies and dispersed. Bull said to Angela in a flat, declaratory tone not unlike his reading, "So who's the guy?"

"He says his name is Cody Hoyt. He wants to meet you."

"Hoyt?" Bull barked.

"Yes."

"I knew a couple guys named Hoyt. One was a drunk and the other one was a criminal. Why does he want to meet me?"

"Hey," Cody said, "I'm right here. I can speak for myself."

Bull paused and twisted slightly to a quarter profile, as if he wasn't sure turning around to talk to Cody was worth more than that. He looked Cody up and down, said nothing, and said to his daughter, "Tell him not to interrupt my stories, goddammit."

"I apologize," Cody said. "I just wasn't expecting a guy named Bull in the children's room."

Bull kept his back to him and guided his wife's wheelchair out the front doors of the library. The attendant in the van climbed out to help position her chair on the lift. Cody saw she was still smiling and her eyes were wistful. She was small and reed thin and her body seemed to be drawing inward as if to fold up on itself. Her back was hunched, which made her head stick out forward rather than up. A baby bird, Cody thought, she's turning into a baby bird in the nest, stretching out on a long neck. He felt sorry for her, for Bull, for Angela, and for him being there at that moment.

In a wavery voice as light as mist she said to her husband, "That was a wonderful story, Mr. Bull. One of my favorites. I wish I could have read it to my daughter Angela, you know."

"I know," he said softly.

Cody noted how Angela flinched when she heard what her mother said. She didn't say *I'm right here, Mom.* No point.

Bull dropped to his haunches so he was eye level with his wife. She smiled at him with big teeth stained by decades of coffee.

"Good-bye honey," he said, and bent forward and kissed her on the forehead. "I'll read to you in a week."

Her waxen face flushed pink and she giggled and batted her eyes, admonishing him, "Mr. *Bull* . . ."

He leaned forward and whispered something in her ear and she blushed further and windmilled her tiny hands as if naughtily delighted by the words. Cody looked away.

The van driver activated the hydraulic lift and secured her in the van and drove away.

Angela said, "She was happy."

Bull grunted.

"I think she's falling for you," Angela said.

"Who wouldn't?" Bull said. Then he focused on Cody. His tone was gruff. "Now what do you want?"

Cody said, "Can I buy you and Angela a cup of coffee? I need your help."

"You can buy me a beer," Bull said. "Come on, I know a place a few blocks down."

———————

In the gloom of the Crystal Bar, the kind of old dive Cody loved with its dim lighting and the midafternoon musical clicking of pool balls from a table in back, Bull said to the waitress, "I'll have a PBR."

Cody hesitated a moment, then ordered a tonic water. Angela asked for coffee.

Bull eyed him across the table for an uncomfortable length of time, then said, "You don't like Pabst Blue Ribbon or are you an alky?"

"Why do you ask?"

"Because only alkies drink tonic water. It kind of reminds 'em of a real drink. Or so I've been told."

"Guilty," Cody said.

"Thought so," Bull said. "You have that look about you. Believe me, in this country I see that look you got a lot."

Cody looked to Angela for help. She shrugged back with a *that's-the-way-he-is* kind of look.

"So," Bull Mitchell said, "why are we here?"

Cody shot a quick glance to Angela, then told the entire story, leaving nothing out. Hank Winters, his binge, the coroner, his suspension. Bull listened wordlessly. Angela squirmed toward the end, getting more and more alarmed.

"So that's the deal," Cody said. "I need to find that pack trip as fast as I can but I don't know the park well enough and I've got to keep quiet about it or I'll lose my job at the very least. You're the only guy I can think of who is familiar with Jed McCarthy and 'Back of Beyond: the Ultimate Yellowstone Backcountry Adventure.'"

Bull scowled, "I didn't name it that. That was Jed's deal. He thinks he's a wizard with words."

"And women," Angela added acidly.

Cody waited for more but it didn't come and she obviously wished she'd said nothing by the way she shifted her weight in the booth.

To Bull, Cody said, "You've done it, this trip I'm talking about, right?"

"Dozens of times," Bull said. "I blazed the trail in the first place after the park rangers at the time said there was no realistic way to take packhorses where I told them I wanted to go. So I had to prove them wrong. I goddamn *invented* that trip."

Cody tried to keep himself low-key and persuasive when what he really wanted to do was get going. He said, "Can you tell me how to find them? Where they left from, which trail they took? Where they'd likely be right now as we're talking?"

Bull nodded. "Pretty close. But what are you going to do? *Hike* after them?" he said with sarcasm.

"Dad," Angela said with alarm, "he wants you to guide him."

Cody kept quiet.

Bull said, "I don't do that kind of stuff anymore. I haven't in years."

"I'll pay you," Cody said, trying not to let Angela's glare penetrate him.

"How much?" Bull said, gesturing to the waitress for another beer. "Jed McCarthy charges more than two grand a head."

"I'll pay you four," Cody said, thinking he had barely eighteen hundred dollars between his checking and savings accounts and he could maybe get another thousand if he got his pickup running and sold it. Maybe he could get a thousand from Jenny, who could dip into the bottomless coffers of His Richness . . .

Bull scratched his chin, thinking about it.

"Dad," Angela said, "this is crazy. It could be really dangerous. You said yourself horse packing like that is a young man's game— that's why you sold the business, remember?"

"I sold it because I couldn't take dealing with the Feds anymore," Bull said, flashing a look at Cody to gauge his reaction.

Angela put her hand on her father's arm. "Dad, if you find them you're finding a potential killer. Think of Mom."

He just looked at her. His voice dropped. "Your mother is all I think about and you should know that by now. Do you have any idea how much that facility she's in costs? Thirty-five hundred a *month*. A *month*. I'm burning through the savings."

Angela didn't back down. "Dad—if you'd get some help . . ."

"I don't want any goddamn help," he said flatly. "I never asked for it and I don't want it now."

She said as an aside to Cody, "We've had this discussion many times before. There are federal programs my parents qualify for but he won't take the money. In fact, he sends it back with mean notes attached. I've read some of them and they'd curl your hair."

Bull nodded. "If everybody did that we wouldn't be in the shithouse like we are now."

She said, "And you won't let me help you, either."

"Nope," he said. "Taking charity from my daughter is the last thing I'd ever do. Might as well just shoot me in the head and leave me there if it comes to that."

Angela said to him, "But you wouldn't have to be seriously thinking about going back to the park right now. Like I said, think of Mom."

"Your mother," Bull said to her, "she don't know me from week to week, Angela."

"Then think of *me*."

Bull placed his own massive hand on top of hers.

Cody said, "Five thousand just for trying. And two thousand bonus for finding them." He'd get His Richness to kick in more. "That's more than two months of care."

Angela shot him a look that was designed to freeze him into silence.

Bull took the second beer and drank half of it in two long pulls.

Angela said to Cody, "With all due respect, you should be talking to the park rangers, not my dad. It's their job to do this kind of thing in Yellowstone. And if you didn't get yourself in trouble, you could be doing this all legitimate."

Bull said, "Talk to the bureaucrats? The time it would take you to lay this all out to the Park Service and for them to have meetings and come up with a budget . . . hell, you don't have that kind of time. And I doubt any of 'em really know the backcountry well enough to find that trip. They'd probably have to hire me anyway, as much as they'd hate that."

"Exactly," Cody said.

Bull leaned forward and his daughter's hand dropped away from his arm. He said to Cody, "It'll take me some time to put everything together. I haven't used any of my equipment for a while."

Cody nodded.

Bull said, "And we need to go in and get back within a week. One week, because I can't miss the storytime. You got me? I can't miss it. And I'll tag a three-thousand-dollar-a-day penalty on you if we do."

"Okay," Cody said, refusing to even consider the ramifications. He could tell by Bull Mitchell's eyes that it was a deal kill should Cody balk or want to negotiate further.

"I don't suppose Margaret will mind us taking some of Jed's horses and panniers," Bull said to himself.

"Dad, you can't be really thinking about this," Angela said. "Just do the smart thing—both of you—and call the park rangers."

"They'll fuck it up," Bull said, growling. "We can't risk lives while they screw around."

Angela left the booth and stomped toward the bathroom.

"She's upset," Bull Mitchell said. "In her mind, I've been out of the game for a long time."

Cody said, "What you do at the library, man. It's, you know, pretty dedicated."

Bull shook the compliment off. "Gotta do something. She was there for me for forty-five years and believe it or not, being with me ain't a sweet picnic all the time."

"Somehow," Cody said, "I can believe that."

Bull stifled a smile.

Cody said, "You knew my dad and my uncle Jeter, then?"

"Yeah," Bull said, his face contorting as if he'd bitten into something sour. "I turned in your uncle for poaching elk in Yellowstone, and he threatened to kill me for it. I said, 'Come on down to Bozeman, Jeter Hoyt.' I think he was on his way when the judge sent him to Deer Lodge the first time. I've been kind of looking out for him ever since. Is he still around?"

Cody looked away. "We can talk about it later." Then: "Why are you called Bull?"

" 'Cause I'm hung like one," he said, and finished his beer.

As Angela came back to the booth, Bull said to Cody, "I'll meet you at Jed's place at four thirty tomorrow morning. Get some good boots and clothes and put your personal crap together in a duffel bag weighing no more than twenty pounds."

Cody nodded. He was seeing Bull Mitchell the outfitter reemerge. "Any way we could get going sooner?" Cody asked. "I mean, I've already wasted a day."

"That's your problem, not mine," Bull said. "I got things to get ready and business to put in order."

Angela said, "I guess there's no point in talking about it anymore."

Bull said, "Nope. Sorry, sweetie. We've got to go get this young man's boy."

She said to her dad, "This has nothing to do with his boy. This has to do with you acting like one."

Bull clapped his hand over his breast, and said, "Straight to the heart."

Cody was outside the door of the Crystal Bar when Angela chased him down and grabbed his shoulder.

Her face was set. She said, "If my dad gets hurt on this trip, I'll be your worst nightmare."

Cody said, "I understand."

"I don't think you do," she said. "I think you're just focused on your son. But if my dad gets hurt or doesn't come back—it's on you.

And if you think getting suspended from the sheriff's department is a big deal, just wait to find out what it's like to find me on the other side of the table."

Cody said, fingering her card, which read ANGELA MITCHELL, ATTORNEY AT LAW, "I was kind of hoping we could be friends. But I've never gotten along real well with lawyers."

"I'm shocked," she said, her eyes flashing. She said, "I'm going to open a case file this afternoon with a tab that reads 'Cody Hoyt.' By the time I see you next I'll know everything there is to know about you. And I have the feeling it'll be a real thick file."

He nodded. "You're probably right."

She said, "The only way you're going to skate is if you bring him back better than he left and you do it within a week. Otherwise, I'm calling your sheriff and every cop I can find to come after you."

"Got it," he said, sliding the card in his pocket.

"Good," she said. "Now if you'll excuse me, I've got to go help my dad get ready."

He watched her storm back into the bar. He thought she looked pretty good doing that. He tried to imagine what her face would look like when she started researching his record.

"Another reason to get the hell out of here," he said aloud to himself.

14

After Jed the outfitter peeled off the trail into the trees and called out "Welcome to Camp One, folks!" the long line of horses followed his lead, glad to be done working for the day. It was almost comical, Gracie thought, the way the animals just turned off the trail and at the same time they broke the psychic connection with their riders. They *knew* their shifts were done. Jed and Dakota led the mounts one by one to a makeshift corral designated by a single strand of white electric fence wire Jed had strung through the trees.

"Hey Jed," D'Amato called out. "What—are these union horses?"

Which made most of the riders smile or laugh.

Gracie waited her turn to dismount behind Danielle, who was squirming in her saddle.

Gracie said, "What's the problem?"

Danielle turned to Gracie. In an urgent whisper, said, "I have to pee. Where do I *do* that? In the woods like an animal?"

Gracie shrugged. That's what *she'd* done earlier when nobody was looking.

It was late afternoon and to the east the sun shimmered across the surface of the southeast arm of Yellowstone Lake. Small lazy waves lapped against pink football-sized rocks on the shoreline, making background music like a cool jazz soundtrack. Far across the lake, dark timbered mountains plunged sharply into the water. The sultry warm afternoon was being penetrated by slight currents of colder air washing down through the trees from the mountains to the west.

Gracie was tired, sore, hungry, and mentally overwhelmed with the sights, sounds, and smells of the trip so far. She'd not only fallen in love with Strawberry, she was falling in love with the park itself. They'd seen a bull and a cow moose in the willows, five bison grazing on a treeless sagebrush hillside, and a bald eagle feeding on a fish. The national symbol stood on the bank of the river, tearing bloodred fillets off the sides of the trout and eying the riders as they passed. When they rode over the ridge, the Yellowstone River valley sprawled out before them. The vista was made up of endless mountains, lakes, clouds, and trees as far as she could see. All of it was lit in golden afternoon sunlight. The vastness and altitude made her slightly out of breath, and exhausted her.

It was another world and she'd willingly given herself up to it, holding back little.

"How's it going?" Jed asked Gracie gruffly, taking the reins from her and guiding her horse toward the others.

"I'm blown away," she whispered. "Dad told me it would be beautiful, but this is amazing."

He smiled in a perfunctory way—his eyes were elsewhere as Danielle walked past after dismounting—and said, "It'll get better tomorrow."

"Better than blown away?" she said, realizing he hadn't heard a word she'd said.

She waited with Danielle for their dad. Danielle shifted from foot to foot and grimaced. Most seemed to hurt already from the ride, Gracie observed. The Wall Streeters were moaning comically, with D'Amato flopping on his back in the grass and stretching out as if making snow angels. Walt had already broken out his fly rod near the water and was stringing line on it while Justin stood by him and watched and asked quiet fishing questions. She looked at her wristwatch: only five hours from the parking lot, but it was a completely different planet.

Gracie watched as Jed and Dakota led each unsaddled horse from the makeshift corral out through the trees to a sunlit grassy meadow. Strawberry, like the others, had a wet square of sweat on her back from where the saddle blanket had been. Dakota buckled some kind of straps on Strawberry's fetlocks and returned for the next horse.

"Those must be hobbles," Gracie said. "So the horses can move and graze but so they can't run off. I've read about them."

"So, are you going to find out?" Danielle asked Gracie impatiently.

"You're the one who officially has to pee."

"You'll have to eventually. You can't hold it in for five days."

"I can," Gracie said, deadpan, "I've been practicing."

"You are so full of shit sometimes, girlie."

Gracie shot a glance at her sister to see if she was making an intentional pun. Nope.

"Maybe we can get Dad to ask them," Danielle said. "It's sort of embarrassing. It's like we're just supposed to know everything even though none of us have been out here before."

Their dad was obviously feeling the effects of the first day of riding as well, the way he limped toward them. Despite the apparent pain, though, he was beaming.

"Look at him," Gracie said. "Look at his face."

"What about it?"

"I've never seen him look so happy," she said. "Look at that smile."

Danielle studied him as he approached. "My God, you're right. Who took our dad and switched him with this guy? He looks friggin' *goofy*."

Gracie giggled at that.

"What did I tell you, girls?" her dad said, shaking his head with pleasure. "Didn't I tell you it would be great? I mean, look at this! It's like we're the first explorers in the Garden of Eden or something.

Look," he said, squeezing between them and pointing across the lake toward the trees. "You can see steam from a fumarole coming out from the trees over there."

"A what?" Danielle asked.

"A fumarole. A steam vent. There are three kinds of thermal features in the world and all of them are in Yellowstone: geysers, mudpots, and fumaroles. That's a fumarole. So we not only have this spectacular wilderness around us, we are also in one of the world's most active thermal areas. Jed said there were over ten thousand thermal features in the park. It's just amazing." As he talked, he reached out and pulled both girls in to him. He said, "And there's nobody on earth I'd rather share this with than my two girls." Gracie smiled and felt a tiny sting of tears in the corners of her eyes.

"I have to pee," Danielle said. "Do you know where the bathroom is, or do we just wander off into the trees like cavewomen?"

Gracie watched her dad flush. He said, "There aren't any *bathrooms*."

"It's just an expression, Dad," Danielle said, rolling her eyes and hopping from foot to foot. "Could you go ask them?"

Her dad made a face, but he said, "Sure," and started off for Dakota and Jed, who were carrying stacks of rolled-up tents toward a grassy shelf that overlooked the lake. Gracie glared at her sister.

"I'm sorry," Danielle said, her eyes flashing. "I know it was a lovely family moment, but . . ."

While their dad talked with Jed, Gracie surveyed the group. Walt and Justin were still rigging up to fish. James Knox, Tony D'Amato, and Drey Russell stretched out on rocks and downed logs near them, listening to Walt explain the parts of his fly rod and the line to Justin, who stood by, feigning patience. It was obvious he was ready to take the rod from his stepfather and start casting. Tristan Glode stood quietly farther down the shoreline smoking a cigar and looking out over the water as if he owned it. Donna Glode had stripped to tight bicycle shorts and a tank top and was doing some kind of yoga or exercises in the middle of a clearing in the trees where Gracie guessed the cooking stove and eating area would be set up. Although the woman was isolated from the others, Gracie had the impression Donna wanted to be watched as she stretched her long limbs and bent over so her chiseled butt was in the air.

Over on the grassy bench where their dad had walked, Rachel Mina hovered near Jed and Dakota holding her duffel bag, looking like she couldn't wait to get into her tent when it was set up.

Gracie narrowed her eyes and swept the area a second time. K. W. Wilson was nowhere to be seen. Maybe, she thought, he didn't need instructions from Jed and Dakota where to relieve himself.

"You're not going to like this very much," her dad said to Danielle as he walked back to them. Gracie could tell he was suppressing a smile.

Said Danielle, "What?"

"There's a little portable toilet up the mountain," he said, pointing into the trees away from the lakefront. "Dakota said the trail goes up from the eating area over there where that lady is making a spectacle of herself. It's about a quarter mile up the mountain, Dakota said."

"A *quarter mile*?" Danielle cried.

"Park Service regulations, is what they told me," her dad said, still controlling the grin. "Anyway, Dakota said she set it up first thing so you're the inaugural user. There's a roll of toilet paper in a Ziploc bag near the firepit."

Danielle nodded and started for the trees.

"One more thing," he said, winking at Gracie so Danielle couldn't see him. "The Park Service has a regulation about the paper. After you're done with it you need to bring it back down and throw it in the firepit. It has to be burned so there's no trace."

"What?" She was outraged. "I have to wipe myself and bring the paper back down? In my *hand*?"

He shrugged. "It's the rules."

Danielle turned to Gracie. "You're coming with me."

"I don't have to go."

Danielle narrowed her eyes. "You need to help me find it."

"*I don't have to go.*"

Her dad said, "Gracie, it would be nice if you went with her."

"Let's go *now*," Danielle hissed.

Gracie said, "Ugh."

"I'll wait for you here," their dad said. "I'll figure out which tents we get in case you girls want to take a rest or change clothes or anything."

It was striking, Gracie thought, how cool the temperature was in the shadows of the trees away from the lake and the clearings near the shore. She trudged along behind her sister's long strides beneath the high canopy of the trees. They pushed their way up the hillside through knee-high ferns. At one point, Gracie turned and could see the sun-fused lake through an opening of branches and a glimpse of a yellow dome tent being set up on the grassy bench. Her dad stood near the yellow tent talking to Rachel Mina. Their conversation looked comfortable—even animated. Gracie was fascinated because she so rarely saw her father in the context of other people. Especially single women around his own age. She wondered if her dad was different with Rachel Mina. Maybe not so uptight and stiff as he was with them. And she wondered what Rachel Mina thought of him.

"Hmmm," Gracie said.

"Come on," Danielle said, "quit stopping." Then: "My God—we have to have hiked a quarter of a mile so far. I wonder if we passed it?"

"We didn't pass it," Gracie said. "Keep going."

"I might just drop my jeans and go right here."

"Go ahead," Gracie said, "I'm not stopping you."

"Maybe a little farther," Danielle said. "But if they think I'm carrying down the paper in my hands they're out of their fucking minds. Jed can come up here and *get* it."

"Sure, okay," Gracie said, "let's piss off the outfitter the very first night of the trip. That's good thinking, Danielle."

Her sister pushed her way through pine boughs and suddenly came to an abrupt stop before a small portable toilet with four metal legs and a square of plywood with a hole in the middle of it. A dark plastic bag hung down beneath the seat, the bottom of the bag inches from the pine-needle carpet. There were stunted pines near the apparatus, but basically it was in the open.

"*Oh. My. God,*" Danielle said, looking around as if trying to find the missing walls of the outhouse.

"Not a lot of privacy, is there?" Gracie said, needling her sister. "It's like anybody could be hiding in the trees out there watching you. Or like a bear could come out of the woods and bite you on your naked white butt.

"Or ravens," Gracie said, reveling in it, recalling when Danielle had once confessed her fear of the black birds. "Maybe ravens will fly down while you're squatting and take a big old chunk out of your right cheek! You'll be scarred! You'll need surgery. You can never wear bikini bottoms again without people pointing and laughing at the girl with one ugly cheek!"

"Sometimes," Danielle said, lowering her pants and shooting dagger eyes at her little sister while she squatted over the seat, "I could just kill you."

Gracie turned away. It would be funnier, she thought, if *she* wouldn't have to use the little toilet later.

And if she hadn't just heard the muffled crack of a branch from someone coming up the trail toward them.

"What was that?" Danielle whispered. "I heard a sound. And don't tell me it was bears or ravens."

Gracie held her finger up to her lips to indicate to Danielle to be quiet, that she'd heard it too. Danielle's eyes got wide and she mouthed, *Who is it?*

Gracie shrugged and stared into the forest below them. It was so green, wet, and dark up there, so different from the camp and the lake. So much foliage. So many places for a man or animal to hide.

"Keep them from coming up here until I'm through," Danielle said.

Gracie put her hands on her hips and shouted, "Hey—whoever you are—give us a minute. We're up here right now. Wait your turn, please."

There was no response, which was disconcerting. Behind her, she could hear a hard stream of liquid strumming against the inside of the plastic toilet bag. Danielle was hurrying the best she could.

Then, after a beat, there was the sharp crack of a twig. Only this time, it wasn't from below on the trail but to the side of them on the slope of the mountain. Whoever—or whatever—it was had deliberately left the trail and bushwhacked into the wet brush. For what reason, Gracie wondered—a better view?

"Hey," Gracie called, "who's out there?"

No response. She wished she had bear spray with her. Or a knife or club or some kind of weapon. She looked around and saw nothing she could really arm herself with. There was an old dry stick a couple of inches thick on the ground near her feet and she bent over to grab it, but it was rotten and broke apart as she lifted it.

Finally, Danielle was done. It had been only a few seconds but it seemed like forever to Gracie. Danielle cursed as she stood and fumbled for her thong and long pants. While she cinched her belt, she yelled, "This isn't funny, pervert. Not funny at all. Hear me? *Not funny.*"

"Always the diplomat," Gracie said under her breath.

Then there was a deep cough from the brush. It sounded closer than Gracie would have thought possible since she still couldn't see anyone.

The cough did it. Gracie and Danielle exchanged terrified glances, then broke for the trail, their boots thumping the ground. Gracie thought about screaming, but didn't.

Danielle passed her on the way down as Gracie paused to look over her shoulder to see if anyone was coming after them. She could see no one, although she thought she might have heard a chuckle.

"Did you hear that?" Gracie said to her sister as Danielle went by.

"What?"

"Somebody laughed."

"Fucking pervert!" Danielle said over her shoulder before continuing down the switchback trail. Gracie followed. They ran down the trail for twenty feet before Danielle veered off, choosing to cut the corner for a more direct route through the brush. Danielle shoved branches aside that whipped back and hit Gracie in the face until she learned to duck under them.

Danielle led them into an impassible tangle of downed logs. The logs were old and gray, and blue-green lichen clung in clawlike pods in the elbows of branches. Something small, long, and dark scuttled out of the tangle away from them, rustling through the tall grass. Gracie couldn't see what kind of animal it was.

"Shit," Danielle said. "I don't know if we can climb over this. It's like we're trapped here."

"You trapped us," Gracie said, letting her annoyance come through. "I thought you knew where you were going."

Danielle turned on her and said with perfect logic, "So when have I *ever* known that?"

"You're right. You're off the hook."

Danielle nodded triumphantly.

Said Gracie, "We'll need to go back and find the trail. Then we can get back to camp. Whoever isn't down *there* was up *here*. We'll know who it was spying on you."

Danielle said, "Which one of them do you think is the pervert?"

Gracie shrugged and led the way back until she broke through the foliage and found herself back on the trail. At least, she thought it was the right trail. For a second, she was confused which way to turn.

"Go right," Danielle said, and Gracie did, even though she wasn't any more confident of Danielle's sense of direction than she was of her own. She made a promise to herself right then to wake up and pay more attention to her surroundings. She couldn't just blindly follow Danielle, or Jed or Dakota or even her dad. She never wanted to feel lost like this again. Her stride lengthened and she picked up speed. The slope and the trees started to look familiar again. She almost ran through a mud bog but managed to skirt around it. The bog was the result of a thin trickle of water that came down from a spring somewhere higher on the mountain. She remembered the spot from the way up and felt a warm wave of relief because now she was sure they were going the right direction. But as she ran past it she noticed something different and stopped. Danielle practically ran over her.

"What?" her sister asked.

Gracie pointed toward the mud. "Look."

There was half of a large fresh boot print on the edge of the mud, as if whomever had made it had tried to avoid stepping into the mud at the last second and almost succeeded.

Gracie wished she knew more about men's boot sizes. But she could tell it was maybe a size ten or twelve since her dad wore size eight and these were bigger. The print had sharp lugs pressed into the dirt, a deep heel imprint, and a little diamond brand where the wearer's arch was. The print was pointed up the trail.

"I don't remember seeing that on the way, do you?" she said.

"No, but I didn't look."

Gracie nodded. "Memorize it. We may see who wears that boot later."

When they broke through the trees into the sunshine Danielle passed Gracie again and they ran toward their dad. He was still standing next to Rachel Mina. All the tents were up and Dakota was shoving the last of the tent stakes into the soft ground. Gracie noticed an amused look on her father's face as they approached.

"That go all right?" he asked.

Danielle answered with a rush of words. "Somebody up there was *spying* on me. He scared the *shit* out of us."

Rather than concern, her dad suppressed a grin. "Come on, girls," he said. "Who would do something like that?"

Gracie ignored him and concentrated on doing inventory of the

BACK OF BEYOND   159

camp. Not a lot had changed, although she noticed there were four men missing: Wilson, Tony, Knox, and Jed.

Her dad said, "Don't let your imaginations get the best of you. Do you know how many animals there are up here?" It was obvious he didn't want to believe them, didn't want the trip to take this kind of unpleasant detour on the first day. Her dad didn't like detours, or surprises, or events wrought with emotion. No matter what the situation or the crisis, his first words were generally *I wish I would have known about this sooner,* as if it were possible to know everything in advance and avert every problem if he just had the foreknowledge. It was a trait that annoyed Gracie because it always put the burden on *her.* Danielle was never expected to know anything in advance.

Her dad looked at both of them. Neither budged.

Gracie said, "Animals don't wear boots."

He sighed, said, "Okay, let's go take a look."

Gracie nodded and turned to lead the way.

"Mind if I come along?" Rachel Mina said to them as they started toward the trailhead up the mountain. "I overheard and I don't like the idea of being spied on, either."

Her dad said, "We're not exactly sure what happened." To Danielle, he asked, "Did the guy say anything at all?"

"No. He just coughed and laughed."

"He *laughed*?"

Gracie and Danielle exchanged guilty looks.

"Gracie thought he did," Danielle said.

"Did you feel threatened?" Rachel Mina asked them both.

"Pretty much, yeah," Danielle said.

Said Gracie, "They should let us carry bear spray."

"Or they should build a real fucking toilet," Danielle mumbled.

"Language," their dad said, and Gracie caught him shooting a quick glance to Rachel Mina to see her reaction to the profanity.

"Sorry."

Her dad said, "Did you consider maybe he was as embarrassed to find you girls as you were? I mean, I've stumbled into a bathroom before and found somebody in it. It's always a shock and I've been embarrassed. I remember opening the door on a stall once in a gas station and seeing this fat guy on the toilet looking at me. We were both kind of horrified."

Rachel Mina laughed politely.

Her dad continued, "I remember I didn't say anything—I was too red-faced. I just shut the door and went outside the station. When the guy finally came out neither one of us looked at each other. He went on his way, I went on mine. We both sort of pretended it didn't happen, you know?"

Gracie hadn't thought about it that way and she felt a needle of doubt creep in. Maybe they *had* overreacted with their shouting and Danielle calling him a pervert and all. Who would want to respond after being called a pervert? And much of the panic she'd felt earlier was more as a result of thinking she was lost in the forest than anything anyone did.

Still . . .

As they entered the trees Gracie did a 360-degree pivot to see if anyone was watching them carefully. Dakota waved from near the firepit where she was breaking sticks into kindling. No one else met her eyes.

Within five minutes she found the bog. The footprint was gone, obscured in the mud by a gnarled knot of pitchwood that had been dropped on top of it. Whoever had left the print had crushed it out of existence.

"It was here," she said to her dad and Rachel.

"I'm sure it was," he said, waggling his eyebrows in a way of saying maybe they'd been mistaken.

"It was," Gracie said with less assurance.

"Who knows what we thought we saw?" Danielle said. "You know how you get. Remember when you used to say there was a werewolf under your bed?"

Her dad stifled a smile. Rachel looked away.

Gracie hated her sister at that moment.

When they returned to the camp, Jed was setting up the aluminum cooking station—a series of interconnected boxes that became a counter, sink, and chuck box—and Dakota set a coffeepot over the fire. James Knox, Drey Russell, and K. W. Wilson sat on separate logs watching the fire burn. All of them looked up as the Sullivans and Rachel entered the camp from the trees.

"Everything all right?" Jed asked.

"Fine," Gracie's dad said quickly. He wanted to preempt either of his daughters. To say something now, Gracie thought, would seem silly. She collapsed on a log bench to watch the fire across from her dad and Danielle, who chose another log. Rachel sat next to Gracie, saying nothing but sitting close enough that Gracie felt the woman was sympathizing with her. That was nice.

"You folks might want to get your stuff all laid out in your tents," Dakota said. "We'll have dinner ready in about an hour and it'll get dark fast. This way, you won't have to try to unpack everything by flashlight."

Her dad slapped his knees and stood up. "Makes sense."

As Gracie rose she noticed Wilson had changed into moccasins. Maybe, she thought, so they wouldn't see that his boots had been muddy.

15

Cody chain-smoked cigarettes in his room at the Gallatin Gateway Inn, breaking the filters off each stick and lighting the new one from the cherry stub of the old one. It had only taken him two minutes to dismantle the smoke detector on the ceiling by unscrewing the faceplate and disconnecting the white and red wires. He hoped he'd remember to put it all right before he checked out in the morning.

He paced and surveyed his new gear piled on the bed. Before the stores closed, he'd found Ariat cowboy boots that didn't hurt his feet at Powder Horn Sportsman's Supply on Main as well as a straw cowboy hat, chaps, jeans, two sets of nylon saddlebags, and denim jacket. He'd felt foolish buying Western wear, but Bull Mitchell had insisted. Everything else he needed—sleeping bag, pad, water filter, daypack, .40 caliber Smith & Wesson cartridges, .223 rounds for his scoped departmental AR-15, a saddle sheath for the rifle, Steiner binoculars—he found at Bob Ward Sporting Goods on Max Avenue. Rounding out his purchases was a plastic grocery bag packed with two cartons of cigarettes, a long sleeve of Stride gum packets, plastic bottles of tonic water, and instant coffee. He'd spent five agonizing minutes staring at a pint of Wild Turkey behind the clerk's head—*Just one pint, just one, what could it hurt?* Hell, he thought, he'd save it until he had Justin with him and the killer in cuffs or in the ground. It would be his *reward*.

While he argued with himself he tried to conjure up the image of Hank Winters saying, "Once you start you cannot stop. That is our curse." Instead, the image of Hank was of a roasted and bloated arm reaching up from the black muck in the rain. And when the eager young clerk behind the counter asked, "May I help you?" Cody snapped, "Go to hell," and stomped out of the place.

He felt guilty for that now.

He was pleased to find out they had available rooms at the Gallatin Gateway Inn—a restored grand hotel from the early railroad days—because it was less than a half mile from the headquarters of Wilderness Adventures. The female receptionist wore a crisp white shirt and sniffed at him, saying, "Please keep in mind we have a strict no-smoking policy here."

"I thought this was a railroad hotel," Cody said. "Railroaders *smoked*."

"At one time," the clerk said. "Many many years ago. And there aren't any railroaders around here anymore, if you noticed."

"So this is a snooty place," he said.

"Not at all," she said crisply.

He winked at her and gave her his credit card. After she took the imprint, he hauled all his gear to his room to unwrap his purchases, clip off the price tags, and fill his new nylon saddlebag. To hell with Bull Mitchell's twenty-pound limit, he thought.

It was dark by the time he had everything packed. He'd made several trips to and from his Ford. There were things in the tool box and investigations lockers he wanted to take with him, including his rain gear. He was pleased he remembered to bring the Motorola Iridium

9505A handheld satellite phone. He'd stashed it in his SUV a few months ago after he stole it from the evidence room. Drug runners had used the phone so they wouldn't be tracked via their cell phone calls by law enforcement, and the case was a slam dunk because the bad guys turned on each other so the phone was never introduced in court. The phone was small for a sat phone, less than a pound, and cost sixteen hundred dollars retail. It had three and a half hours of talk time without recharging and thirty-eight hours of stand-by time. He stuffed it in a saddlebag.

Then he sat at the small desk in the room, turned on the ancient banker's lamp, and placed his cell phone within reach, waiting for Larry to call. It had been way too long not to have heard from him since he faxed the material, he thought. His partner must know something by now—he'd had the sheets all afternoon. Cody vowed to himself that if Larry didn't call him by midnight he'd break his pledge and track Larry down like a dog.

He poured a glass of tonic over ice and lit yet another cigarette, and opened the file he'd taken from Margaret Kerley. He looked at his list of suspects:

1. Anthony D'Amato
2. Walt Franck
3. Justin Hoyt
4. James Knox
5. Rachel Mina
6. Tristan Glode
7. Donna Glode
8. André Russell
9. Ted Sullivan
10. Gracie Sullivan
11. Danielle Sullivan
12. K. W. Wilson

On the bottom of the page he scrawled,

13. Jed McCarthy
14. Dakota Hill

He thought, *Everyone on the list could be the killer.* Except Justin, of course.

The applications had arrived in Jed McCarthy's office throughout the past year. They were designed to elicit information Jed needed to know to plan the trip and to match up horses with riders. There was a short questionnaire about dietary restrictions, riding ability, allergies, medical issues, and emergency contact information. The last item on the application was "What do you hope to gain from this backcountry wilderness experience?" Cody wished there were more questions and information but he was grateful he had what he had. He hoped Larry was running the whole lot of them through every criminal background database he could access.

Anthony D'Amato, thirty-four, was from Brooklyn, New York, and worked for Goldman Sachs. He was married, no children. He weighed 185 pounds and listed his wife Lisa as his emergency contact. He'd ridden a horse once, at the Iowa State Fair when he was visiting relatives as a teenager. He answered the last question, "To not be eaten by a wild animal."

Walt Franck, fifty-four, listed his home locations as Aspen and Fort Collins, Colorado, as well as Omaha. He was a commercial Realtor and developer of strip malls in the Mountain West and Midwest. He was soon to be married to Jenny, Cody's ex, and listed her as his emergency contact. Cody snorted derisively when he saw His Richness listed his weight as 220 pounds, and he planned hereafter to refer to him as "His Fat Richness." Walt was a novice rider, and he hoped the trip would "provide unique fly-fishing locations and bonding opportunities for me and my future stepson." Cody snorted again.

Justin Hoyt, seventeen, Fort Collins, 165 pounds, stepson of His Fat Richness, was next. Cody recognized the handwriting on the application as Jenny's, and it elicited a sudden desire for her again that had been rekindled the night before. He shook it off and continued reading. She said Justin wanted to experience "nature and outdoor skills."

"Shit," Cody said. "Send him to me in Montana. I could do *that*." But he doubted Justin had even seen the application, much less discussed it with his mother.

James Knox, thirty-seven, Manhattan. Not married but had a partner named Martha, who was also his emergency contact. Worked as an executive with Millennium Capital Advisors and weighed 180 pounds. He had no experience with horses, and wrote that he and his two friends wanted to experience "the nature and diversity of Yellowstone while waiting for the market to come back."

Cody smiled at that, and skipped ahead in the stack to find the third of the buddies.

André Russell, thirty-nine, of Manhattan. Married, two children, a boy and a girl, ages twelve and nine. Wife and emergency contact was named Danika. A VP with J. P. Morgan and had ridden horses at stables in Central Park to prepare for the trip. Cody was impressed by that. For his ambition for the trip he wrote, "To try and keep Tony D'Amato from being eaten by wild animals."

Cut-ups, Cody thought. Or liars. A three-man team of killers from the East? He shook his head. The idea didn't grab him, and seemed much too cinematic and far-fetched. He moved on.

Rachel Mina was single. She didn't indicate whether she was divorced, widowed, or never married. A hospital administrator on leave from Chicago. She was thirty-seven and weighed 115 pounds. In Cody's experience, that meant he should add a few years and at least ten pounds, so he scratched in "40" and "125" on the page. Mina indicated she was a vegetarian (fish was okay) and intermediate rider. She wrote: "Discovery tour."

He wondered what "on leave" meant. His first thought was she seemed to be the only one of the clients thus far who might have had the free time—and means—to visit homes in four states and leave bodies and ashes behind. But a woman, and a single one at that?

Discovery tour, Cody mouthed, squinting through smoke at the page. It sounded phony and new-agey, he thought. Or facetious. And an interaction between a hospital administrator and Hank Winters seemed possible.

He placed her application aside from the others into what he thought of as the hot stack.

Tristan Glode was the president and CEO of The Glode Company of St. Louis. Cody didn't know what the company did but planned to find out. Glode was sixty-one and claimed to be an expert rider. He'd indicated he weighed 211 pounds and had written in the margin that he had bad knees and would prefer a Tennessee walker for a horse. In the margin, someone (Jed?) had scribbled, "Call Pat." Cody guessed Pat, whomever he or she was, knew of a walker that could be leased for the trip.

In the space for what Tristan was seeking, he wrote, "TBD." To be determined.

"What the hell does that mean?" Cody grumbled, thinking the man sounded arrogant. Asking for a specifically gaited horse, claiming to be an expert rider, listing his weight at 211 pounds. Anyone normal would write "210," Cody thought.

He put Glode's application in the hot stack with Mina's. Now he had two prime suspects.

Then he read the next application: Donna Glode, sixty, St. Louis, 130 pounds. Another expert rider. For what she was seeking she wrote, "Yellowstone by horseback. A peaceful journey."

So, husband and wife. Cody reached over and pulled Tristan's application and put it on the cold pile along with his wife's.

Ted Sullivan, forty-five, was divorced and lived in Minneapolis. He was a 185-pound software engineer with a firm called Anderson/Sullivan/Hart. He'd scratched an "X" between beginner and intermediate, slightly closer to beginner. Very precise and engineerlike,

Cody thought. He listed his emergency contact as his ex-wife. And in carefully printed handwriting, Sullivan said, "I hope to gain a closer and more intimate relationship with my daughters, Gracie and Danielle. I hope it will be the greatest shared experience of our lives."

Nice, Cody thought. Heartfelt. He skimmed over the applications for Sullivan's daughters, ruling them out immediately.

He started to toss the three documents on the cold pile, then stopped himself. He retained Ted's app and looked it over again. At first, he'd thought there would be no way for the father to have done the crimes with teenage girls around, and based out of Minneapolis. But because the man was divorced, that meant it was possible the girls hadn't been with him until recently. Cody had never heard of Anderson/Sullivan/Hart but the fact that it was simply a string of surnames and that they apparently felt no need to add "software" or "consulting" or "business solutions" to the end of it indicated that they either wanted to be thought of highly or they *were* prestigious. Meaning it was a good likelihood Sullivan traveled. Cody often saw men like Sullivan in airports; road warriors who were constantly on their Bluetooth cell phones and computers, those things hanging out of their ears, talking to clients all over the country and checking in with their colleagues to form strategies and solutions.

But would a cold-blooded killer pause to take his daughters on a wilderness pack trip? Cody asked himself. His answer was, not likely. Still, though, he couldn't rule him out and he put the application between the hot and cold stacks.

Cody looked at the last application and whistled. As he read over it he started to nod. Jesus:

K. W. Wilson, fifty-eight, Salt Lake City, Utah. No marital status indicated. No occupation listed except "transportation." One hundred seventy pounds and an intermediate rider. Under dietary restrictions Wilson had scrawled, "No cheese." For what he was seeking, Wilson had written, "Fishing and adventure."

Cody said to the application, "Congratulations, you're now number one," and placed it on the hot stack.

Doubts remained, however, if he was even on the right track.

Cody remembered seeing a business center in the lobby with two computers for guests. He gathered the applications back into the file to take them downstairs. He'd find more about all of the names, as well as get some background on The Glode Company, Anderson/Sullivan/Hart, Rachel Mina's hospital, and anything he could locate on K. W. Wilson.

His cell went off and danced across the surface of the desk since he'd set it to ring and vibrate.

He checked the display: Larry.

"About time," he said.

"Are you sitting down?" Larry asked.

16

Gracie wished she'd unpacked her heavier jacket because when the sun doused behind the mountains the temperature dropped a quick twenty degrees or more within minutes, as if the thin mountain air was incapable of retaining the afternoon heat. She thought about going back to her tent to dig out her hoodie, but the instant darkness didn't encourage a trip and the warmth and light of the campfire held her in place as if it had strong gravitational pull.

She was sitting on a smooth downed log with Danielle and Justin. She couldn't stop staring into the fire, which was mesmerizing. The meal had been huge and consisted of things she normally didn't like that much: steak, baked potatoes, baked beans, half a cob of corn dripping with butter. She'd wolfed most of it down, leaving only a quarter of the steak. She had no idea why she'd felt so hungry, or how the food possibly tasted so good. The apple cobbler baked in a jet-black Dutch oven was one of the best things she'd ever eaten, and she'd had two helpings of it. Her mouth still tasted of cinnamon from the cobbler and hot fat from the meat. Now, the entire meal sat in her stomach as heavy as a rock, and it made her sleepy and uncomfortable.

Normally, Gracie hated it when portions of food touched each other on her plate. This time, though, she didn't care that the steak tasted of bean juice and the potato turned pink because it sat in pooled grease. It was all so wonderful she'd nearly forgotten about what had happened earlier. But not completely.

Earlier, when Dakota had twirled an iron bar around on the inside of a battered metal triangle to signal dinner, they'd all stopped whatever it was they were doing and lined up at the portable aluminum kitchen station holding empty tin plates. One by one, they presented their plates so Jed McCarthy and Dakota could serve the slabs of meat and plop down the sides. The line was interrupted once when Tony D'Amato whooped—and jumped back—when he saw a snake slither through the grass between his feet.

"Damn," he shouted, his voice high-pitched. "It went over my *boot*."

Dakota reacted quickly and tossed her spoon aside and chased down the snake. She grabbed it behind its head and held it up, asking if anyone wanted it for dinner. D'Amato and his friends laughed at that, and he seemed embarrassed by his outcry. Danielle, who was standing in line in front of Gracie, had turned and said, "Great. Snakes, too. This place *sucks*."

"It's harmless," Gracie said. "It's just a snake. Maybe we should try it."

"Just a snake," Danielle said. "Jesus, you're weird."

Gracie sat quietly while Justin and Danielle talked. She eavesdropped halfheartedly, absorbed with re-creating the incident up at the latrine that Danielle seemed to have already forgotten. Something had happened up there that bothered her, because it suggested someone on the trip had an agenda besides the adventure itself. It reminded her that people could be evil, something she believed more and more the older she got.

Danielle, however, was at her charming best. Subjects ranged from their schools to Facebook pages to sports, television shows, and bands. Gracie found herself rolling her eyes each time Danielle and Justin discovered more and more common bonds. When Danielle mentioned their parents were divorced, Justin said, "Shit, mine too."

Justin was handsome and well built but shallow, Gracie thought. Exactly Danielle's type. Gracie wanted to warn him now, before it was too late. But she didn't think he wanted to know what her sister could be like, how she collected and discarded boys like him. And, Gracie thought, maybe he wouldn't even care. It wasn't like he was on the trip to establish a meaningful relationship, was it?

The more Gracie stared at the fire, the more interesting it was. Unlike her sister and Justin.

"So your dad has you for the summer?" Justin asked Danielle.

"Sort of," her sister said, keeping her voice low so only Justin—and Gracie, unfortunately—could hear her. "My dad's had a bug up his butt about this trip for a year. It's like a father–daughter bonding thing, I guess."

Justin said, "Same here, only Walt is my stepdad. He thinks we'll become lifelong buds after this or something. He thinks fly-fishing is, you know, *religious* or something. And it's all right, I like it and all, but Walt is kind of old and everything. So I don't know."

"What's your real dad like?" Danielle asked, leaning closer to him. "Is he around, I mean?"

Justin hesitated, then shook his head. "He's okay. He's a cop. He's tough to figure out. Sometimes he's a great guy, and sometimes he's just an asshole."

Danielle acted like that was the funniest thing she'd ever heard, and covered her mouth while she leaned back and laughed, making sure to grasp Justin's thigh to keep her balance.

"He's in Montana," Justin said, "but he calls me and stuff. He never knows what to say and neither do I. He sends me stuff—fishing rods, computer games, CDs, things he thinks I'll like. But," he said, leaning even closer to her and lowering his voice, "sometimes he forgets to take the evidence tags off. I mean, I'll get a set of walkie-talkies with a piece of tape on 'em that says 'Exhibit A' or some damned thing."

Which made Danielle squeal with laughter. Gracie tried to tune her out.

After a few minutes, Danielle shoved her and nearly knocked her off the log. Justin chuckled.

"*What?*" Gracie said.

"I was talking to you," her sister said softly, not wanting the others to overhear.

"I thought you were talking to Jason."

"Justin," she corrected. "And I was. I was telling him about what happened earlier up on the mountain and I said you were there as my witness."

Gracie looked over. Their faces were lit with firelight. Justin *was* good-looking, but the way his eyes reflected the fire made him look kind of creepy. And, she wondered, was it him? Then she dismissed it because he'd been fishing with Walt at the time.

Justin leaned toward her, resting his hand on Danielle's knee. Her sister didn't seem to mind.

"So you think it was that Wilson guy?" Justin whispered.

"I don't know," Gracie said. "But I noticed he's wearing moccasins tonight so we can't see his boots."

Justin started to turn his head to confirm it but Danielle clasped her hands on both sides of his face and said, "Don't look, silly. He'll know we're onto him."

Then she stood up. "Now just keep an eye on him. I've got to go pee."

"Again?" Gracie said.

Danielle narrowed her eyes at her sister and said, "This time I'm not going up to that stupid toilet. I'll be back in a second. Don't try to steal Justin away, as if you could."

After she was gone, Gracie and Justin sat together uncomfortably. Or at least Gracie did.

Justin said, "Your sister seems nice."

"She isn't."

Justin chuckled. "I guess what I mean is she could be nice, if she tried."

"Don't count on it," Gracie said, warming to him. "I know her."

"There's good in everybody, Gracie."

She looked over to see if he was serious. He was. He said, "I always expect the best out of people. I think when you do that, you get the best most of the time. I just kind of bump along, expecting the best, and good things just happen. That's my secret."

She said, "Why are you telling me your secret?" She was flattered. She thought a strapping, good-looking guy like Justin would be unapproachable in every instance. He was too handsome, too confident, and too cool.

"I'll tell anyone who will listen," he said softly. "What I can't figure out is why everybody doesn't do it. Look for the best, I mean. It's easy, and it makes life go easier."

Gracie just stared. He was too good to be true, she thought. Her instincts were not to trust him.

"That's a nice thing, I guess," she said to her shoes.

"Sure it is. Just accept yourself and look for the good in others. It's not complicated."

"Do you see good in me?" Gracie asked.

He smiled. He even had a nice smile. "Of course. You watch out for your sister and your dad, I think."

"So who watches out for me?"

"I will, if you want," he said sincerely.

Gracie shook her head. She'd never met someone so comfortable in their own skin. It weirded her out. There must be more to him, she thought. A dark side. But when she looked into his open face and that impossible smile, she couldn't see it. No one was that good. Maybe he was a *sociopath*. And she felt immediately guilty for thinking it.

"See how it works?" he said, as if reading her mind.

Gracie was grateful when Danielle suddenly reappeared and grasped Justin's face between her hands before sitting back down.

Justin didn't pull his face away, and smiled at Danielle sloppily. He liked it. Gracie rolled her eyes again and looked back to the fire. "Hey, look," Justin said to Danielle, "out on the lake. Can you see what's going on?"

"What?" her sister asked.

"The fish are rising."

Gracie followed his outstretched arm. The moon lit the still surface of the lake in light blue and sure enough, ringlets were appearing everywhere, as if it were raining upside down.

Justin said, "Want to go down to the shore with me and see if we can catch one?"

Danielle was up like a shot. She stood in front of Gracie and blocked the light and heat, and Gracie felt as if she'd been plunged into cold. She started to stand but Danielle reached back and put a hand on her shoulder, preventing her from rising. Danielle turned and bent over close to her ear, and said, "Not you."

Justin winked and asked Gracie, "Do you want to come along?"

"No," Danielle said. "She doesn't."

And Gracie thought, *She doesn't deserve him*.

After they'd left, Gracie considered asking Dakota to help her find that snake so she could put it into the bottom of her sister's sleeping bag.

She hugged herself against the chill, now that her sister had abandoned her. It seemed very late but it wasn't even ten yet. The sky was a bright smear of stars she'd never known existed before, and the busy sky above and the absolute darkness of everything beyond the fire made her feel smaller than she'd ever felt.

The campfire was the hub that held everyone in place. When it started to die Dakota or Jeb would leave their place behind the cooking station where they were washing dishes and toss another piece of wood on it.

She observed the others without staring at them.

The Glodes kept to themselves. They were the farthest away from Gracie, on the opposite side of the fire. Tristan Glode smoked a big black cigar, and the glow danced in the darkness. Donna stared into the fire as if she were comatose. Gracie thought that although they were by themselves they weren't really with each other. It was as if there were a wall between them even though they were a couple of feet apart. How sad, she thought.

Two of the three Wall Streeters, Tony D'Amato and Drey Russell, were whittling on sticks and joking about it. Everything, it seemed, was a joke to them. Little light-colored piles of shavings gathered on their boots, and the blades from their pocketknives flashed in the firelight.

"A year ago," D'Amato said in a singsong, bluesy cadence, "I was looking out over the Sea of Cortez from my air-conditioned bungalow in Baja. Now here I am in the freezing mountains, sittin' on a log. Whittlin'."

"You a whittlin' man," Russell sang along.

"I'm a whittlin' man," D'Amato sang back. "Whittlin' 'til I ain't got no stick left."

"You a whittlin' man . . ."

"Think I'll whittle me a boat and float on out of here back to Baja . . ."

"He a whittlin' man who ain't a-scared of no snakes!" Russell laughed, and the two of them collapsed in on each other. Luckily, they held their knives out to the side.

"You guys are embarrassing me," James Knox said from the cooking station.

Gracie found herself staring at them with more than a little awe. Knox caught her, smiled, and said, "Do you find us strange?"

Embarrassed, she said, "I've never met any New Yorkers before. I've heard about you and read about you and you're on all the television shows, but . . ."

D'Amato laughed. "But you've never met any of us in real life. You make me feel like a zoo animal or something."

"Sorry," she said, and looked down. It was just that they were exactly how they were portrayed, and she'd always thought they couldn't possibly really be like that: fast-talking, ethnic, animated. Like they were playing the roles of New Yorkers according to the script. Just like TV. But she didn't say it.

To the right, Gracie's dad was perched on a large rock next to Rachel Mina, who sat in the grass with her plate in her lap, finishing her dinner. Gracie had noted how Rachel had waited patiently for everyone else to be served steaks before getting her dinner—panfried fish and the last of the beans and corn. She admired the fact that Rachel hadn't made a fuss but simply waited for her nonmeat meal. Too many of Gracie's vegetarian friends went on and on about their preferences in the lunchroom, she thought. On and on about what they could eat and what they wouldn't. They could learn something from Rachel Mina. The clicking of her utensils on the tin plate was rhythmic and delicate and Gracie hoped that someday she could be as graceful and feminine when she ate.

Then, obviously thinking no one was paying attention, her dad reached down and snatched a small piece of fish off Rachel's plate and popped it in his mouth. She looked back but rather than object, she smiled at him. Her dad raised his eyebrows in an *It's actually good* gesture. Rachel turned back around and finished her plate.

It had happened quickly, and without a sound. But Gracie sat transfixed as if a thunderbolt had hit her in the chest.

They knew each other, she thought. The scene had a kind of sweet intimacy about it, like it had happened often before and had become a shared joke.

They knew each other. Really well.

She felt bushwhacked. Her eyes misted and she looked away.

When she opened them she saw Wilson, who'd suddenly appeared from the direction of the tents. Standing there, staring at her, his face lit orange with firelight.

"What do *you* want?" she asked, too loudly.

The others around the campfire stopped talking or doing what they were doing. Jed and Dakota peered over the top of the cooking station, washcloths poised and still.

"Goodness, little girl," Wilson said. "What is *your* problem?" He looked at the others with his palms open and held up. "All I did was walk up here to get warm. I didn't do anything."

No one said a word. A beat passed, and she was glad no one could see her face flush red. She wiped angrily at the tears in her eyes with the back of her sleeve.

From the right, her dad said, "Gracie, are you okay?"

She stood up and refused to look at him. "I'm going to bed," she said, and started for the tents.

She was gone before her eyes could adjust from the fire to the total darkness, and she tripped over a root or rock and she sprawled forward. She landed spread-eagle, grass in her mouth.

Somebody—D'Amato or Russell or Jed—barked a laugh. Someone else said, "Cool it, that's rude."

"Sorry."

She scrambled to her feet spitting grass and dried weed buds and stomped toward the tents. D'Amato called out to her, "Sorry, darlin', I didn't mean to laugh at you. Come on back and join us."

And her dad followed her, saying, "Gracie, what's going on? Are you all right, Gracie?"

She kept going until she approached the collection of tents. She wasn't sure at first which was hers—they all looked alike. Nine lightweight dome tents, looking in the soft moonlight like plump pillows.

"Gracie," her dad said, finally grasping her hand.

She pulled away. The third one, she thought. Her stuff was in the third one from the top.

He grabbed her again, said, "Honey . . ."

She wheeled on him. "When were you going to tell us?" she asked, her voice catching like ratchets on sobs. "Is this why you brought us with you? So you could be with your secret *girlfriend*?"

Her dad just stood there. She could see his stupid face in the moonlight. His mouth was moving but nothing was coming out. He finally said, "Gracie . . . really . . ."

But what she heard was his lack of denial.

"Stay away from me!" she said, and she dove into the opening of her tent. It was small inside but the sleeping bags cushioned her dive. She spun and zipped the opening closed. As she did, her last glimpse of her dad was of him standing there like an idiot with a swarm of stars around his head, trying to come up with the right words—as if there were any. She said, "Go away. This is the worst fucking trip of my life."

Inside, she could hear him. For five minutes, he stood there, breathing shallow breaths. Then he moaned and said, "I was waiting for the right time to talk with you girls. Really, honey."

She didn't respond.

Finally, he turned and trudged away back toward the fire.

An hour later, Gracie heard footfalls approaching the tent and she opened her eyes. She hoped it wasn't her dad coming back, and if so she planned to feign sleep.

The door zipper hummed and she sat up, alert.

Danielle said, "Oh my God, I *love* him."

Gracie flopped back down.

"He's so damned cute I want to eat him up," Danielle said. "He tried to help me cast to the fish but I couldn't get past how he put his arms around me. Damn, he's hot and I love him."

Gracie said, "Did you think for a second I might be asleep?"

Danielle hesitated, said, "No." Then went on, "Before I came back here he gave me just a little kiss—nothing major—and said, 'To be continued.' Is that classy and cool, or what? Is that awesome, or what?"

Gracie rolled away from her.

"What's your problem?" Danielle asked.

Gracie told her sister about their dad and Rachel Mina.

"You're kidding," Danielle said, finally.

"I'm not."

Danielle shook her head back and forth. "That just doesn't seem right," she said.

Before Gracie could agree, Danielle said, "She's much too awesome for *him*. What does she see in the guy?"

In the dark, Gracie covered her face with her hands and moaned.

"They're all still out there," Danielle said, regaining her stride, pushing the news aside. "Except for Justin, I mean. He went to his tent, too. Gee, I wonder what he's doing in there all alone?" she giggled.

Gracie said nothing.

"I saw one of the Wall Streeters open a bottle," she said. "I think they're all going to pass it around and tell stories or something. I hope they don't stay up too late or get too loud, 'cause we need to get some sleep."

"You think?" Gracie said.

"Yeah, there's a big day tomorrow," Danielle said, slipping out of her clothing to her sports bra and wriggling into a pair of light sweatpants. "At least it'll be a big day for *me*."

"That's what's important," Gracie mumbled.

"Are you being sarcastic?"

"Never."

"Well, don't," Danielle said, sliding into her sleeping bag and pulling the zipper up. "It's boring."

"Justin is too good to be true," Gracie said.

"He is, isn't he?"

Gracie thought any more conversation would lead to an argument. "Good night."

"Good night, Gracie."

———

She lay brooding in the dark for hours. Occasionally, she could hear a whoop or laugh from the direction of the campfire. Danielle's breathing got deeper and she slept the sleep of the dead and Gracie wished she'd gotten that snake from Dakota.

She'd never hated her father before.

17

Larry said to Cody, "A pattern is emerging in these cases."

Cody felt his scalp tighten. He stood. "You mean besides the method of death, right?"

"Yeah."

"Where are you now?"

"At the office. Unauthorized overtime, as usual."

"Good," Cody said, standing and gathering his files under an arm while holding the phone with the other. He snuffed out his cigarette, pocketed the keycard, and pushed his way out into the hallway. "I'm at a hotel and I saw a business center downstairs. I'll go down there and fire up one of the computers so we can both be online."

"Want me to call you back?"

"No way," Cody said. "I've been waiting all night to hear from you. Don't worry, I can walk and talk at the same time."

The hallway was shadowed and cavernous and he padded down the carpeting toward a curving staircase at the end. As he approached he could hear a swell of conversation and laughter from the lounge on the first floor.

Cody descended the stairs. Across the lobby the receptionist saw him and nodded. He nodded back, gestured toward the closed door of the business center, and the receptionist indicated it was open for use. He sat at a PC beneath a window that looked out into the lobby. The doorway to the lounge was straight ahead, and he could make out bodies inside lining a bar. The men and women were well dressed with the women in dresses and men in suit jackets with no ties, about as formal as Montanans were likely to get. The crowd looked young and elite; professionals out after a concert or fundraiser. The kind he usually made a point to avoid.

"So what's the connection?" Cody asked Larry as he placed the files on the counter next to the computer.

Larry said, "Before I spill it, let me say this is pure speculation at this point."

Cody sighed. "Of course."

"And it's just me right now. I don't have anyone else on the case to confirm what I'm saying or poke holes in it."

"Yes, Larry," Cody said impatiently.

"Let me walk you through it," Larry said. "Got a pen?"

"Sure," Cody said, firing up the PC and waiting for it to boot. He opened one of the files to take notes on the front inside cover.

"First," Larry said, "we've got nothing new on our end. The arson tech is still sifting through the burned-out cabin and they've confirmed everything we thought. I talked to one of them today and he said there was no sign of accelerants, which tilts it toward an accident rather than a homicide, but in my mind it isn't convincing. The place was old and dry to begin with and built with logs. Those kinds of buildings go up like a box of matches, especially when there is spilled alcohol on the floor to help it along. The guy said the fire spread normally from right in front of the open woodstove throughout the room."

Cody said, "Has anything else been found by the crime-scene techs? Hair, fiber, anything like that?"

"Nope. It looks like whoever did it literally left no fingerprints. But more likely, he spent the whole evening in the living area and didn't venture into the kitchen. There are some latents in the bedroom, as you know, but we don't have any hits on them yet."

"Damn," Cody said. "Call me if anything comes of that."

"Yeah," Larry said. "I'm thinking the bad guy knew the best way to cover his tracks was to burn everything down around him when he was through."

Cody nodded. "I agree. It accomplishes a couple of things. The fire not only destroyed any latent evidence, the fire itself points us away from homicide."

"Speaking of," Larry said, "the three victims other than Hank Winters I found through ViCAP all died within the last month. There might be more and there could be other methods of death, but for now that's our universe, okay?"

Cody nodded as if Larry could see him. He could hear Larry shuffling papers.

"The first was a William Geraghty, sixty-three, of Falls Church, Virginia. The police report on him says he was a midlevel Democratic political consultant. He was found at his beach house three and a half weeks ago. His cottage was burned down and his body was found in the wreckage. The police there initially called it an accident but a few days later a witness said they saw a vehicle coming from the place in the dark shortly after it was established the blaze took off. No good description of the vehicle or driver, but because the cottage was located on a dead-end road and it was the middle of the night, the car was considered suspicious. The autopsy of Geraghty sounds real similar: blunt-force head injuries and lack of smoke in his lungs. The cops there list it as a possible homicide and the case is open. I spoke to the lead detective in Falls Church and he basically said there has been no progress in the case; no further leads at all."

"Sounds familiar," Cody said.

"Yes. But in this case the fire damage was total. They didn't have rain to stop it. Which means no hair or fiber, and no DNA to run."

While Larry talked, Cody Googled the name "William Geraghty" and found items including his death notice in the local paper and older references to his involvement in political campaigns throughout the country. He would study the items later, when Larry was done.

"What do we know about him besides his job and his death?" Cody asked.

"I'm getting to that, but let me do this in my own way."

Cody knew better than to try and get Larry to cut to the chase.

Larry said, "The second victim identified by ViCAP is Gary Shulze, fifty-nine, Minneapolis. This was two weeks ago. He was a professor of literature at the University of Minnesota in Minneapolis. His body was found at his cabin near a place called Deer River in the northeast corner of the state on Lake Winnibigoshish. Same thing we're getting used to: burned cabin, body inside, head injuries. The difference here is it appears there was a deep puncture wound into his brain as opposed to bludgeoning. The wound was initially explained away as a postmortem injury caused by glass shards driven into his body by falling timbers, but the coroner doesn't rule out the possibility it was caused by a knife blade driven into his skull and withdrawn. Obviously, the locals initially thought it was a suicide or accident, but Shulze's wife Pat convinced them her husband had recently cleaned up his act and had undergone some kind of conversion. She said he was loving life. There was no way he'd do himself in, she said. Of course, we've heard that kind of thing before from loved ones, but the detective told me she was so convincing that they listed the case as open even though they have their doubts."

Cody opened another window on the browser and Googled the name "Gary Shulze." In addition to his participation on various literature councils and a personnel listing for the U of M faculty, there were death notices in both the Minneapolis *Star Tribune* and the *Western Itasca Review*.

"Same total crime scene devastation as Geraghty," Larry said. "No traces of evidence have been found that point to anything other than an accident involving a single victim."

Larry sighed. "The last one before Hank Winters is the one we know about, the close one in terms of time and mileage."

Cody said, "Karen Anthony."

"Yeah, her," Larry said. "Forty-six-year-old hospital consultant living in Jackson Hole and Boise. She's a little different because her place in Jackson—actually Wilson, Wyoming, outside of town—was some kind of historic home she'd refurbished. Like Geraghty's, the place is pretty remote and only accessible by a two-track through the trees. A neighbor saw a vehicle come down their shared road about a half hour before he noticed the flames up on the hill and called the fire department. The Teton County Sheriff told me they got a partial on the vehicle: dark blue or black SUV, single driver, light-colored license plates, which apparently means out-of-state but the witness couldn't tell which."

"That's no help," Cody said. "Finding an SUV in Wyoming is like looking for a fly at the dump—they're everywhere."

"I know," Larry said.

"So," Cody said, opening another window and typing in Karen Anthony's name, "we've got three victims who basically died the same way, burned in their homes long before the fire could be put out. And the victims are all roughly middle-aged and professional. And alone. That's a string of similarities but really not much to build on."

"Exactly," Larry said. "I spent half the day reading and rereading all of the police reports, trying to find something that linked them beyond the obvious and trying to find a connection to Hank Winters."

"And?" Cody said.

"Nada," Larry said. "The cops I talked to couldn't come up with anything either. When I told them about the other cases, they were surprised there were similar incidents. So nobody has been looking into this as a pattern, including the FBI.

"So," Larry said, "I took a flyer and called Geraghty's wife in Falls Church. I told her who I was and what I was investigating, and you know how that goes. She was falling all over herself trying to help. My guess is she hadn't heard from the locals since shortly after the fire because they didn't have anything to tell her. So she was excited I was working it."

Cody nodded, then said, "Hmmm," so Larry would know he was listening.

"I asked the usual. Any enemies, ex-wives, business problems or rivals, financial problems, et cetera."

"Hmmm."

Larry said, "What she told me was almost too good to be true. She said they'd had some real rough patches in their marriage but that Geraghty had straightened up in the last few years and everything was fucking wonderful. She said that was the worst part about it all—that things were going so well when it happened."

Cody felt a jangle in his chest. He said, "Didn't Shulze's wife say kind of the same thing?"

"That hit me, too," Larry said. "So I kept asking Mrs. Geraghty questions. She was a little reluctant at first, but she finally spilled the beans. Geraghty was a big drinker for a long time. A good-time-Charlie type who spent a lot of time on the road with other political types. Between the lines, I got the vibe he was abusive to her when he was on a toot. But she said after he got a DUI he finally entered a twelve-step program and cleaned up his act. She said he's been stone-cold sober for the last two and a half years.

"So I called Pat Shulze," Larry said. "After a while, I got the same story. Shulze had checked himself into rehab three years before because the university made him, and it took. She said it was like having the guy she married back. He was writing a book about his recovery and doing speaking engagements at faculty association meetings around the country, I guess. He even had a Web site on recovery where he answered questions and such."

"Damn," Cody said. "So what about Karen Anthony?"

Larry said, "I called her sister in Omaha. Same deal. She said Anthony was a hard partier all her life until the last five years, when she found Jesus and AA. So it looks like our guy is targeting ex-alcoholics."

"Christ," Cody said, thinking of Hank. "That's just *wrong*." Then: "For the record, there's no such thing. But we can talk about that later."

"Yeah, yeah," Larry said.

Cody paused. "I'm trying to wrap my mind around this. So we've got a guy traveling the country and setting up rendezvous with recovering alcoholics, then bushwhacking them in their homes. I see a pattern but not a motive."

"Me neither," Larry said. "I've been racking my brain. Who would want to go after people who'd straightened out their lives? What's the point of that?"

Cody grumbled that he didn't know, then thought of something. "Larry, did any of the locals in Virginia, Minnesota, or Wyoming find any AA coins at the scenes?"

He could hear Larry shuffling through papers. "No mention of them anywhere," he said. "But that doesn't mean anything for sure. They didn't catalog every item they found at the scene. No reason to."

"Unless," Cody said, "the bad guy is taking the coins with him like he did with Hank. That way the locals wouldn't even have a reason to bring the AA angle into the picture. Hell, we wouldn't have gone down that road if I didn't know Hank took his coins with him everywhere he went."

"I didn't think of that, dammit," Larry said. "Or I would have asked the detectives."

"Find out," Cody said.

"I will tomorrow," Larry said. "But we still don't know why our bad guy even knew them at all."

"I don't know," Cody said, "unless maybe the victims did something to the guy before they sobered up. Maybe, I don't know," he said. "I can't come up with a scenario that makes any sense. Not without knowing if the victims even knew each other or were ever in the same place."

Larry agreed. "We've got four different locations thousands of miles apart. Four different lines of work. I can't see where they possibly intersect."

"This is going to take some fine police work," Cody said. "Can you pull in the cops in all those states to help?"

"Some," Larry said, his voice dropping. "But you know how it goes. They're all up to their asses in alligators. They'll probably all agree to help, but no one is going to make this top priority. I can't blame them. I'd do the same thing if one of them asked me. I'd put it on the back burner and concentrate on my local caseload. I wouldn't drop everything to go investigate this based on my speculation."

"What about the Feds?" Cody asked.

"I've got a call in to them," Larry said. "Which means I had to clear it with the sheriff and Bodean. Luckily, I asked Tubman in the middle of another blowup with the coroner who, by the way, announced his intention to run for sheriff next year."

"Did Tubman ask about me?" Cody asked.

"Not yet. But Bodean hit the roof. I walked him through what I had so far thinking he'd ease off, but he came unglued. He said if I heard from you I was to tell you to get your ass back here ASAP."

Cody exhaled deeply. "Duly noted."

"I wouldn't be surprised to see Bodean throw his hat in the ring for sheriff," Larry said. "He seems to suddenly be doing damage control."

Cody's mind was elsewhere. He said, "Larry, this seems like the right track, but I can't see things coming together fast. I need them to come together fast."

"I need a lot of things I can't get," Larry huffed. "Like a raise and some hair."

"Sorry," Cody said. "I've got to think about all this. We have to be able to connect the victims with somebody or someplace. Then we can get the other agencies and departments moving, once we've done that."

"Agreed. But it's that first part that seems impossible," Larry said, gloomy.

"You can do it," Cody said. "If anyone can."

"Yeah," Larry said, "I know."

"I'm still going after Justin tomorrow," Cody said. "I'll turn on that satellite phone. Call me with anything else, and I'll do the same."

After a beat, Larry said, "Are you going to alert the Park Service that you're entering their sacred domain?"

"Hell no."

"Cody . . ."

"They'll just muck it up. I don't have the time for them to have a bunch of meetings and go up the chain of command. I have to find my boy and put this bad guy on ice."

Larry was exasperated. "How many violations are you going to break on this deal? I can't even keep track."

Cody shrugged. "I don't care," he said.

"Look," Larry said, "you may not care but I'm complicit in every stupid thing you do. So I'm going to cover my ass a little. I've already figured out that the sheriff is so distracted by Skeeter I can claim I told him everything at some point and he'll probably believe me. He won't know the difference. Of course, Bodean is a different animal. I'll have to figure out how to bypass him."

Cody agreed.

Larry said, "And tomorrow I'm going to call a buddy of mine named Rick Doerring with the Park Service. He's the ranger I met last year."

Cody shook his head, not liking where this was headed. "Last year?"

"Yeah, remember when someone from Bozeman called in that they saw a small plane headed toward Yellowstone? Remember, the citizen said the plane looked damaged and it was flying real low toward the park."

Cody vaguely remembered the incident. From what he could recall, the FAA had no record of the aircraft and there were no reports of a missing plane. Since Larry and Bodean were the departmental assignees to an interagency Homeland Security Task Force, they'd had to scramble because unknown airplanes headed for federal land were a big deal these days. Rick Doerring was on the task force as well. The plane was never found, and no one ever reported it missing. The incident faded away quickly.

"Rick is a good guy," Larry said. "Almost normal, for a Fed. I may run this by him on the sly and see what he says."

"I can't stop you," Cody said. "But at least give it until the afternoon. By then, I should be deep into the park where he—or you—can never find me. I don't want their help with this unless it's on my terms."

Larry didn't agree, but he didn't argue.

"Look at the bright side," Larry said. "Your son is likely not a recovering alcoholic." It was meant to be funny.

"No," Cody said, "but why is our guy on this particular trip? What is he after, or is it his way of hiding out after his spree? No matter how you cut it, the guy must be a little desperate after all he's done. I wouldn't think anyone around him would be very safe," he said, tapping the file of Jed McCarthy's clients.

"We still don't know if he's on the trip," Larry said.

"I *know*," Cody replied. "Don't remind me how much of a leap this is."

"So where are you now?" Larry asked.

Cody said, "Close to the park."

There was a beat of silence. Larry said, "You're not going to say, then?"

"Nope."

"Don't you trust me?"

Cody said, "Larry, you're the only guy I trust. But the less you know, the better for both of us. As you said, you're complicit in every stupid thing I do."

Larry snorted. "I see your point. But answer me this, cowboy. How in the hell are you going to find this pack trip in the middle of the wilderness?"

Cody said, "I've got a plan."

"I hope it's a good one."

Cody said, "Me, too."

He showered and left his clothes in a pile on the bathroom floor, and slipped into bed naked. He set his alarm for 3:30 A.M. and called the front desk and requested a wake-up call for the same time.

He knew he wouldn't sleep. Couldn't. The things Larry had told him swirled around the dark ceiling, darting in and out of his consciousness. He hoped strands of what he knew would somehow miraculously connect and he'd sit bolt upright with an epiphany and suddenly know the connections as well as the answers.

Didn't happen.

What did happen, two hours later, was the slight creak of old flooring outside in the hallway. He turned his head in bed and glanced at the digital clock that showed 2:23 A.M. glowing in red.

When he smelled a sharp odor he thought it must be his breath. Then he recognized it as lighter fluid.

Cody propped up on an elbow and stared at the yellow bar of light beneath the door to his room. He rubbed his eyes and tried to convince himself what was happening was not his imagination. Two shadows of feet were evenly spaced within the bar. Someone was standing just outside. And there was a growing pool of liquid that streamed from under it across the tile floor, rivulets reaching out toward his bed like grasping fingers.

Then the distinct sound of a match being struck.

18

Jed McCarthy liked the way the situation was shaping up. He considered himself a kind of master of managing group dynamics, and he had once again proved himself right. He tried not to act too smug or vainglorious about it, although it wasn't easy.

It had started out with an hour or so of stories after dinner, after Ted Sullivan had come back from the tents. After he'd had some kind of scene with the youngest daughter. Sullivan had settled back on the log next to Rachel Mina and they shared a long, sad look that told Jed as much as he needed to know about them. Sullivan sat with his head down and his arms hanging between his legs, as if he'd received a slip of paper in a game of charades that said *Dejected.* Jed had left his place with Dakota behind the cooking station and conspicuously walked around the fire. All the voices quieted and faces turned toward him. He handed Sullivan a bottle of Jim Beam. Sullivan took it, both surprised and grateful for the gesture, and took a long drink that made his eyes water and sparkle from the fire. Sullivan offered the bottle to Rachel, who said, "No thanks." The man tried to give the bottle back, and Jed said, "Keep it. Have another drink, then pass it around."

From that moment on, Jed knew he had Sullivan on his side. A gesture was all it took with weak men like Sullivan who weren't used to them from men who weren't weak, like Jed. It elevated Sullivan in the eyes of the others that Jed had sought him out like that. The only person who didn't appear impressed was Rachel Mina, who eyed Jed with caution. Jed pretended not to notice.

He returned to the cooking station and monitored the progress of the bottle as it made its way around the campfire, and soon there were other bottles as well.

Inhibitions lowered as voices rose, and Jed made it a point to keep the fire going but not too brightly. Just bright enough he could see their faces and expressions and confirm they were all on the tracks he wanted them to be on.

He felt Dakota's eyes on him. She was standing beside him at the cooking station, washing dishes and the pots and pans.

Finally, he glanced over at her and mouthed, *What*?

She whispered, "What in the hell are you thinking?"

He grinned and looked away.

"Why are you doing this?" she asked. "You've always told me to keep our alcohol packed away for later, in the tent. You've never brought it out before, and you sure as hell haven't passed it around."

He thought her whisper was getting loud enough to be overheard, so he did a quick survey of his guests to see if anyone was looking up. Nope.

"I know what I'm doing," he said. "Don't question me with the guests present."

She grunted her assent.

He said, sotto voce, "And don't forget you've got a mission tonight."

"Which tent is his?" she asked softly. That meant she was still with him, even though she was angry. But she still wouldn't meet his eyes.

"The blue and green Mountain Hardwear."

"The one with the stain on the side of it?"

"That's the one."

She nodded that she understood.

He again reached out for her and she jerked away again and he left her there fuming.

"Hope you don't mind if I join you," Jed said to his guests, taking the sitting log used earlier by the Sullivan girls and Walt's soon-to-be stepson.

"Cool," James Knox said, "please do."

"And to what do we owe this pleasure?" Tristan Glode asked.

"I've got a proposition for you folks a little later," Jed said. "But first I'd like to have a drink."

"Try this," Walt Franck said, offering the single malt.

Jed raised his eyebrows in false trepidation, getting a couple of laughs, then sipped the smooth liquor. It burned nicely on the way down. He said, "It's not Jim Beam, but it's pretty good," to more laughs.

Jed let them ask him to expound about Yellowstone, wildlife, horses, and outfitting. He did, but not at great length. He wanted them wanting more.

He did a quick inventory. The Sullivan girls and Walt's stepson Justin had gone to their tents. Perfect, he thought. He didn't want the young ones to weigh in. Sullivan Senior sat by Rachel, Sullivan still moping over whatever it was his daughter was worked up about, but coming out of it. The alcohol helped. Rachel looked on at Sullivan as if sizing him up, as if unsure of her conclusion. Women only *thought* they liked weak men, Jed surmised. Jed wondered what she'd be like with a strong one. Probably a pain in the ass, he thought.

The three Wall Streeters sat on the ground on a tarp with their backs to a downed log and their feet splayed before the fire. They passed their bottles back and forth. They were tired and getting pleasantly drunk. He doubted they'd make a late night of it, but he didn't want things to get too wild before he made his proposition. Drey Russell had been quiet a long time and wasn't as boisterous as Knox or D'Amato. Jed wondered if Russell was having a good time, or doing his best to pretend he was. Russell seemed introspective. Jed wondered if Russell had camped much in his youth, or been in the mountains in such a raw state before.

Tristan and Donna Glode sat on separate stumps to the left of the Wall Streeters. Tristan did take a sip of the single malt but declined the Jim Beam, which didn't surprise Jed. Donna gulped both, to hoots from D'Amato and Knox, and Jed stifled a smile. This woman was a *drinker*. And a looker, in her day. Too bad her day had passed. Jed had a feeling Donna was grinning a bit too much at D'Amato and Russell. D'Amato seemed to respond, but Russell had none of it. When he saw her lean over and touch D'Amato on the knee to ask for a sip of his tequila, he saw potential trouble brewing for Tristan.

Jed focused on Tristan, and thought he had the man figured out. He seemed uncomfortable, but not because of Donna. Jed got the impression Tristan was a man used to being catered to and he fancied himself an outdoorsman but he didn't necessarily enjoy being with other clients not in his social strata. The joshing and passing of the bottles didn't amuse him but he knew enough about human nature to know if he got up and left he'd be talked about and made the butt of jokes. So he stayed and endured and simply hoped the night would break up early. Tristan had made it clear to Jed he'd studied their route in advance and was as familiar with it as anyone could be.

For that reason, Jed saw Tristan as a challenge. He hoped he'd be able to turn him. And now that he saw Donna flirting with D'Amato, he knew he had leverage he hadn't before.

K. W. Wilson sat alone. He was dark and quiet. When Walt Franck offered him a sip of Scotch, he started to reach out for it, then declined. Jed found that interesting, and wondered why Wilson wasn't drinking. He *looked* like a drinker. His haunted eyes and hollow cheeks practically told drinking stories of their own. But he didn't take a sip, meaning he was choosing to be antisocial or he had a problem. Or an agenda, something he wanted to keep sharp for. Jed shot a quick look over his shoulder. Dakota was gone. He smiled to himself. It wouldn't be long before he knew a lot more about K. W. Wilson. Not that it would matter all that much in his strategy, which was to use Wilson's sour personality as a tool to isolate him and to make his opinion irrelevant, whatever it would turn out to be.

Walt Franck was simply affable. He was slightly younger than Tristan, Donna, and Wilson, but older than the rest. He laughed politely at jokes but told none of his own. Jed thought he might be concerned that his son Justin had suddenly found a new interest—Danielle Sullivan—that might change the purpose of the trip from stepfather/stepson bonding to the blind pursuit of a hot little chick. Surely, Walt wouldn't really welcome that development, even though there was next to nothing he could do about it. Jed knew that trying to stand between a hormone-fueled teenager and his love interest was akin to walking between a grizzly sow and her cubs, and Walt didn't look dumb enough to do either. Walt's distraction would help Jed, though, and that's all that mattered.

After a few minutes, Rachel Mina stood up and announced she was going to her tent for the night. She said it in a way that made it obvious she expected Ted Sullivan to go with her. Obvious, that is, for everyone except Ted Sullivan, who took a bottle from Knox and took another swig.

"Before you go," Jed said, "I wanted to float a proposition. I'll go with whatever you all decide. This is a simple majority rule deal, and I'll go with the majority because it's your trip."

She still eyed him with doubt and put her hands on her hips, waiting. He decided right then he'd need to either win her over or isolate her if she didn't fall in line. It would be her choice either way it went.

Jed gathered himself to his feet and cleared his throat. "What I'm wondering about," he said, "is how married everyone is to the route and the trail we talked about this morning to get to our next camp tomorrow night."

He let that settle in a moment before continuing. "Here's what I'm thinking. We've had a boatload of rain up here this summer, much more than usual. I mentioned it this morning to Tristan," he said, nodding toward Glode. "See, the trail down along the Yellowstone River is pretty swampy, even in a good year. As I mentioned before we left, the snowpack took a long time to melt this year because there was so much of it and the temperatures have been so cool, plus all the rain we've had. I'm concerned if we go down there the regular way we might be walking our horses through miles and miles of gunk. That's no fun and it slows us way down. It's hard going for the animals, plus it means mosquitoes. There's also the possibility the trail is washed out enough that we might lose quite a bit of time finding work-arounds."

Jed presented his left palm to the group and pointed to it with his right index finger.

"If my palm here is a map, think of the lifeline as the Yellowstone River," he said, tracing it from top to bottom. "The trail parallels the river pretty much, going north to south. Normally when we get almost to the southern border of the park," he jabbed the heel of his hand with his finger, "we take the fork by South Boundary Creek and leave the river valley and cut due west into the mountains up toward the Continental Divide and Two Ocean Pass. That's where we've got our camp for tomorrow night, up on Two Ocean."

He looked up to make sure everyone was paying attention. They were, although only Tristan Glode and K. W. Wilson seemed rapt. The rest looked pliable.

He continued, moving his finger up an inch on his palm. "So what I'm proposing we do tomorrow is leave the trail earlier than we'd normally turn west. That means cutting to the west between Phlox Creek and Chipmunk Creek. I've been studying my topo map and it looks doable. We still have to climb up into the mountains and we should still be able to get to our camp, it's just that we're arriving an unconventional way through country that probably hasn't seen ten people in a hundred years."

Somebody, likely D'Amato, whistled.

"Excuse me," Tristan cut in, "but I remember asking you about the trail this morning. You didn't indicate then we may have trouble."

Jed said patiently, "Mr. Glode, I believe I did. I said it was possible the trail might be washed out in places. This is the first time I've been up this way this year, so there was no way to know for sure. Even the Park Service doesn't send many rangers down where we're going until hunting season when they try to guard against poachers coming up from Wyoming. There were really heavy snows last winter and big runoff this spring and the rain this summer. I don't think there's been anyone down that direction yet this season to provide a report."

"So what changed your mind?" Tristan asked. There was an edge to his voice.

19

The ignition of the lighter fluid had been instant, less than a second after Cody heard the match strike. There was a *whump* that sucked most of the air out of the room and his lungs, which left him gasping. Bitter smoke lit hellishly with the orange and blue tongues of flame. His eyes filled with water and his lungs screamed from smoke he inhaled rather than air and he thought he knew how Hank Winters and the others must have felt if they were conscious in their last moments.

Outside the door, he heard footfalls thumping down the hallway so quickly he knew he'd never be able to catch who did it.

The flame seemed to burn away his sense of time as well. He had no idea if it was seconds or minutes before he scrambled out of the bed and stood naked. Since it was pushed against the wall, the only way he could get out was toward the fire. It had likely been a few seconds since the *whump*; he felt sluggish and cloudy-headed and blind due to the thick smoke. He felt around his feet for the saddlebags because he needed to save them. As he reached toward one of them it ignited, the fire eating up the nylon exterior as if starving for it. He managed to snatch the other one off the floor before it went up, too, and he backed around the foot of the bed into the bathroom. He stood trembling, his back against the sink, gasping, looking through the doorframe at the violent orange glow in the bedroom. He squatted to his haunches and he was able to get below the roiling bank of black smoke. He sucked in the superheated air and was thankful his lungs didn't explode. The fire had consumed the rug near the door and was curling the flooring. It spread to the sheets and comforter of his bed. He gathered his loose clothes in his arms.

Then he remembered why the smoke detector didn't trigger an alarm or activate the sprinkler system, and thought, *Shit!*

He reached behind him into the bank of smoke for the sink. When he found it he turned on both taps, then stood and jammed down the stopper with the heel of his hand so the sink filled. While the fire in the bedroom was snapping angrily, grabbed two towels off the rack and plunged them into the water to soak it up.

His riding boots were within reach in the bedroom near the bed and he found them and pulled them on. The soles were hot. He shoved his arms into a hotel bathrobe that was hanging from a hook behind the door and cinched the tie. Then he dropped down toward the floor again to get a gulp of air. Retrieving the wet towels from the sink, he wrapped one around his head and the other around his hands and ran toward the door using the bag out in front to help block the heat. As he bolted through the flames he felt the hairs on his legs and forearms burn down to the skin and the soles of his boots melt into gel. He could smell the awful acrid smell of his own burning hair.

Cody prayed that whomever had set the fire hadn't blocked the door so he couldn't get out, then remembered it was unlikely since the door opened in. In the time it took him to run from the bathroom across the bedroom the heavy water in the towels heated up.

He hit the door hard with the bag out in front of him to cushion the impact. He couldn't see through the smoke but he reached around the bag for the handle. When he turned it the deadbolt rescinded and he threw himself out into the hallway. The rush of fresh air flowed into the room and fed the fire and the heat from it on his back and neck was instant and intense. Particularly, he felt it on his buttocks.

The hallway was empty except for the round bland face of a disoriented woman who'd just opened her door to peek out. Her eyes fixed above him at the roll of dark brown and yellow smoke that was advancing across the ceiling.

"Get out," he said to her, "there's a fire."

"My things!" she said, her eyes welling with tears.

"Buy new ones," he said, grasping her hand and pulling her out her door. "Is there anyone in there with you?"

"Sam!" she cried, and turned and tried to wrench her hand free.

Cody shouldered her aside and thumped into the room. Sam, who, like her, was in his midseventies, was sitting up in bed in a pair of boxers and a threadbare wife-beater, rubbing his face.

"Who are you?" Sam asked.

Cody didn't take the time to answer, but jerked Sam to his feet and pushed him toward the door.

"Let's get out of here," he said, herding Sam and Mrs. Sam out ahead of him like stubborn steers. As they went down the hallway he slammed his fist on every door and wished he knew which ones were occupied and which ones were empty, but at each one he yelled, "Get the hell out now! The place is on fire!"

The three of them descended the stairs and were suddenly joined by guests from the other wing and Cody realized that the ringing in his head was from the fire alarms. The alarms bleated and emergency lights flashed in staccato everywhere. Overhead sprinklers suddenly hissed to life making flower-shaped showers that streamed down the walls and pattered on the carpets. The guests covered their heads against the water, and one woman said she was going back for her umbrella but her husband put a quick stop to *that*.

Cody was impressed by the lack of shouting or panic as barely clothed people of all ages streamed across the lobby. There were several sharp shouted curses, but most delivered by him.

As the people were herded toward the massive front doors, the hotel staff shouted and gestured for them to keep moving. From outside, sirens were whooping and Cody thought, *Man, that was fast.* Too fast. And he guessed whoever had lit up his room had called it in so there would be only one fatality.

In the river of guests headed toward the doors, under the interior lights that strobed in rhythm with the honking fire alarms, he searched for anyone who looked out of place. He didn't remember kicking or seeing an empty can of lighter fluid in the hallway, so he searched the throng for anyone who might be holding a can or trying to hide one or someone fully clothed booking it toward a side exit. He saw no one that made *his* alarm bells go off.

He was outside in the instant chill before he thought to check out the hotel staff and emergency responders to see if one of them might be the guy who did it. There was already a fire truck in front of the hotel with firefighters pouring off it, and another coming down the drive.

When he turned to go back inside, a firefighter in heavy gear blocked his path and shooed him away.

"Let me back in," Cody shouted at him, "I can help get people out."

The firefighter, who had a wispy blond mustache and pale blue eyes under his helmet, said, "Now why would you want to do that? Now turn back around and go with the others. You're blocking the door."

"Let me by," Cody said.

The firefighter shook his head. "Get back, sir. We've got this under control."

Cody thought about guests who might have slept through the alarms who were now unable or unwilling to get out, and he thought of his burning saddlebag of gear in his room.

"Let me in," he said, trying to squeeze by the fireman in the doorway. "Look, I'm a cop. I can help in there."

"Get with the others, now," the fireman barked, inadvertently whacking Cody on his injured ear. The blow stunned him, froze him, the pain sharp and furious. His eyes teared again.

"Sorry," the fireman said, "but I mean it. Get back with the others."

The door filled with two other firefighters and a staggering night manager. Cody assumed they'd entered through the rear entrance, meaning there was another truck back there. The firemen were quizzing the manager: "Is that everyone? We need a count. We need to know if anyone's still inside."

The manager said, "I think so, I think so . . ."

"You better be right," one of the firemen said.

The man who'd hit Cody gestured toward him, telling his colleagues, "This guy is a problem. He says he wants back in."

Cody backed off.

He'd fought against his instinct to badge the guy and demand his way back in, but he remembered it had been taken away. And now that he was outside, he knew why his butt had felt the heat so much when he reached back and found the basketball-sized burned hole in his robe. He melded into the crowd, sidling around them so they wouldn't look at his singed butt, and the more he thought about it the more he realized he was glad he hadn't had access to his badge.

20

"The water levels," Jed said quickly in response to Tristan's question. "I've been noticing every stream we've crossed is quite a bit higher than normal, almost like May or early June flows. The lake is higher than I've ever seen it this time of year as well. So if the water is high where we're at, it'll be a hell of a lot higher lower down in the Thorofare valley."

Rachel Mina said, "Have you ever taken this new route before, Jed?"

Jed shook his head. "No, ma'am. We'll be seeing and riding through country very few people have ever seen, including me. But according to my topo maps, the elevation rise isn't much more severe than what we were going to do anyway, so I'm not worried about *that*. What I can't guarantee is that we won't have to stop from time to time and scout out ahead, which is something we haven't had to do today. We'll want to avoid black timber that may have trees down in it our horses can't navigate through. And I'll want to ride ahead from time to time to make sure we don't get into a situation where we get rim-rocked."

"Rim-rocked?" she asked.

"It means riding or climbing up into rocks and boulders but not being able to get back down," he said.

"Great," D'Amato said.

"But there's an upside," Jed said. "We may discover some thermal activity and see vistas and wildlife we'd never experience any other way. There are over ten thousand thermal features up here in this park, and who knows what we might find in the kind of virgin territory I'm talking about."

"I'm from Brooklyn," D'Amato said. "I do not know of this virgin territory."

Which got a laugh out of Donna Glode, if no one else.

"The other thing," Jed said, "is we're likely to get to our next camp even earlier than the normal route, since we're kind of cutting the corner. We might even discover a shortcut."

"Of course," he said, "we don't have to try this new route at all. We can stay on our trail and give it our best shot despite the mud and the potential of washouts. I just want you all to know there is an option available."

He stopped talking. Jed knew one sure way of killing a sale was to oversell it. He wanted the group to come to their own consensus without him appearing to force it.

No one, it seemed, wanted to speak first.

Then Russell said, "We'd be like the Lewis and Clark Expedition. We'd be going through a part of Yellowstone Park practically no one has ever been through. That appeals to me, at least. I like being an explorer."

D'Amato cracked in a bad pirate voice, *"Beware, there be monsters."*

Knox said, " 'Back of back of beyond,' we'll call it. I like the sound of that."

"Me too," Donna Glode said. "Bring on the adventure!" She rubbed her hands together in what Jed thought was an overplay designed to show the Wall Streeters—D'Amato in particular—she was with them.

Walt said, "Is there still good fishing this new route?"

Jed said, "It looks like it, anyway. Those creeks I mentioned earlier,

Phlox and Chipmunk, plus Badger Creek. One thing for sure, they haven't been fished much. So you and Justin might be in for a rare treat—native cutthroat trout that've never seen an artificial fly."

Walt nodded and smiled. "I like that idea," he said.

"I think I'm in," Sullivan said. "I think my girls would like the idea of seeing country no one has seen for a long time. I know I would. Go big or go home, I say."

Jed noticed that Rachel Mina shot Sullivan an approving look.

Tristan stood up, and turned away from Jed to address the group. "I feel it's my obligation to bring something up," he said, the back of his shoulder to Jed. "What Jed is suggesting is kind of radical. We don't have radios or cell phones. The only thing the Park Service knows about us—or our families at home—is where we're *supposed* to be from day to day. So if we don't show up at the end they know where to look. If we deviate from the trail and get lost or 'rim-rocked,' no one will know where to find us."

Tristan said, "I've had a lot of success in my life by determining where I want to get to and staying the course. It's when my partners convinced me to deviate from the plan that I failed. What Jed is suggesting here is trading in a sure thing—even though it might be unpleasant for a while—for a flier filled with unknown variables. I'd rather stay the course. It's what I—and all of you—paid for."

Even Jed conceded to himself Tristan was persuasive.

"Oh for Christ's sake, Tristan," Donna said, "didn't you just hear him? You are *such* a tight-ass. This isn't a product launch. I thought the purpose of this trip was for us to experience high adventure. Isn't that what you said?"

Tristan didn't answer her, but even in the firelight Jed could tell his face flushed red. She had embarrassed him, cut his feet out from under him. And his argument. Jed felt the momentum shift back.

"I'm in," Knox said. "The worst that could happen is I never make it back to the firm to be at my desk when I get laid off."

"Damn right," Russell said. "Me, too."

D'Amato covered his face with his hands as if horrified, then squeaked, "Me, three."

Jed looked around. All in favor, one opposed, one not heard from.

"Mr. Wilson?" he asked, expecting it to go five–two.

Wilson said nothing, but his glare was intense.

Jed tried to read Wilson's eyes, and what he saw was genuine surprise. As if *he'd* had his feet cut out from him, too. Finally, because all the attention had turned toward him, Wilson said, "That's fine. I'll go with the majority."

Tristan looked around, and said, "I'll have to decide tomorrow if we'll even stay with this expedition."

His words fell heavily, until Donna said, "Speak for yourself, kemosabe."

Humiliated again, Tristan Glode stormed past Jed, headed for the tents. Over his shoulder, he said, "Democracy is no way to run a business, Jed. You'll need to learn that."

After a beat, Knox said, "I don't think he likes losing arguments."

"You think?" D'Amato said. "Man, what a buzz kill."

"Welcome to my life," Donna said, sliding across the ground toward D'Amato and taking the bottle of tequila from his hands.

Rachel Mina was curt: "Good night, everyone." She strode away from the fire, followed by Sullivan.

"Okay then," Jed said, taking the rest of his bottle from Walt, who'd gotten stuck with it. "We've got a decision. That means it's going to be a real interesting day tomorrow, and we'll be getting up early."

"Interesting," D'Amato said, repeating the word and getting up. "As if today was boring."

"That's what I like to hear," Jed said, smiling.

Jed turned to the sound of Rachel and Sullivan arguing in the dark near the tents. He saw Dakota standing there, glaring at him. He wondered how much she'd heard.

That question was answered when she slowly shook her head, as if she couldn't believe what was happening.

21

Framed by the pulsing wig-wag lights that painted the stone walls and arched windows of the front of the Gallatin Gateway Inn in vivid reds and blues, Cody Hoyt tossed the bag he'd saved into the back of his Ford. He had trouble breathing due to the smoke inhalation and he coughed violently and spattered the back windows with globules of black sputum.

Behind him, guests gathered in knots in the front yard. The staff who'd helped evacuate them formed a perimeter with several firemen and now a few deputies who'd just arrived. Cody had slipped away while they all watched a bucket truck back across the lawn toward the hotel. He paused to take it all in before entering the Ford. His room on the second floor was easy to spot because of the bright orange glow of flames from inside. Several firefighters had climbed into the bucket and were now being raised toward the second level. When they were even with the orange window, the bucket paused and swayed a bit while a horizontal column of water blasted through the window. When the glass broke a ball of flame shot out of the frame accompanied by gasps from the guests on the lawn.

He noted the fire seemed to have stayed within his room and not spread to any others, no doubt due to the sprinkler system. Cody guessed it would be short work now to put it out and gain control of the building. It wouldn't be long before the investigators figured out who had been staying in the room and would want to question him.

He swung inside the Ford and it was immediately filled with the acrid smell of the smoke from his clothes and hair. His bare skin stung from exposure to the fire, and when he brushed his forearm with his other hand the singed hair on it broke and fell off.

Thumping the steering wheel with the heel of his hand hard enough to crack the plastic, he cursed and spat and started the engine and rolled away.

The lights and sirens faded as he turned from the inn grounds onto U.S. 191 South. It didn't take long before he was engulfed in darkness and safely away from the scene. He wheeled the Ford into a pullout and killed the engine.

Someone had found him and tried to burn him alive.

He found a half-full pack of cigarettes in the console and lit one. He inhaled deeply—smoke on smoke—then coughed. Jesus, he thought, it was like he was trying to burn *himself* up from the inside out. He tossed the cigarette out onto the gravel.

There was a bright side to the fire, he thought. Now he knew he was on the right track, because someone was trying to kill him.

The more he thought about what had happened and what had almost happened, the more his skewed world tilted even farther off plumb.

He was glad he hadn't gone cop on the fireman or spoken to anyone on his way out, even though possibly they could have found whoever did it through the process of elimination. But his story would sound preposterous at first, he realized. The firefighters would quickly discover he'd dismantled his smoke detector and they'd find the small mountain of cigarette butts in his room. The conclusion they'd reach immediately was he was smoking in bed and started the fire and had come up with a story about lighter fluid to cover himself. Or they'd accuse him of accidentally—or intentionally—spilling the accelerant on the floor and it went up. Hell, he thought, given the facts on the ground he'd come to the same conclusion. Within minutes they'd have his ID and call it in, discover who he was and where he was supposed to be, and he'd likely spend the rest of the night in the Bozeman jail waiting for a Helena deputy to come get him and take him back. No doubt the damage to the hotel caused by the fire and water would cost millions to repair. He thanked God all the guests had been accounted for, or there would be a murder charge as well.

He couldn't risk *that*.

Since the attempted method of getting rid of him had been fire, he wondered if the murderer he was tracking wasn't on the pack trip after all, but had stayed around Bozeman. But how would the killer know he was in town, or what he was up to? And how could he possibly know he was spending the night at the Gallatin Gateway Inn, or which room? It made no sense.

Did this mean he was next on the killer's list? Cody dismissed it, since the other victims had been clean and sober for years and he hadn't. Unless, of course, the killer knew Cody was getting close and had decided to try a preemptive strike.

In many ways, Cody thought, the crime could have been almost perfect. The flames had moved so fast that if he hadn't been awake at the time the match was struck, he might have been incinerated in the bed. A little digging would bring forth stories of the recent incident with the coroner in Helena, his suspension from the Denver Police Department a year ago, and his infamous alcohol-related binges.

Which meant that whoever had done it knew him well enough to know they might get away with it.

He thought about the few people he'd been in contact with who knew where he was or what he was doing. Larry, obviously, but he'd withheld crucial info from him, like his location.

Cody retraced his steps that day. Other than Kerley and the Mitchells, he'd encountered a half-dozen sales people and the hotel staff.

There had also been the state trooper and the mechanic in Townsend. While each may have known a very small piece of what he was up to, no one could have realistically put it all together, he thought.

This was the kind of puzzle he liked to bounce off his partner, because the two of them could usually brainstorm their way to a plausible answer.

His cell phone had a good signal and he scrolled through his contacts until he found Larry's home phone, but something stopped him before he speed-dialed. He sat in silence, staring at the lit screen, then closed the phone and turned it off. He opened the driver's door and let the phone drop to the gravel, then smashed it into pieces with the heel of his boot.

Whether they'd followed him from Helena or called ahead he wasn't sure. If they were keeping tabs on him through the GPS embedded in his cell, that would be the end of that.

Then it hit him with a force that took his breath away.

The stop in Townsend, the overnight there that slowed him down. The long delay that held him in place until tonight. Had the trooper been tipped to keep an eye out for him?

He climbed back into the Ford and covered his face with his hands. Only two people could possibly know the entire story, every part of it. Only two people knew where he was going, why he was going there, and what he planned to do.

One of them was the killer. The other . . .

He said aloud, "Larry, you treacherous son of a bitch. Why?"

22

By the light of a headlamp, Jed McCarthy stripped down to his T-shirt and underwear in his tent and jammed his outside clothing into a stuff sack he'd use for a pillow, then checked his watch. Getting late. Dakota should be back any second.

He'd left some clients at the fire. Two of the three Wall Streeters were still there, Knox and D'Amato. So was Donna Glode. And K. W. Wilson. Ted Sullivan had left a half hour after he had words with Rachel Mina, saying, "Better go try to patch things up." Walt Franck had also gone to his tent.

His tooled leather business backpack was stored where it always was, near the head of the tent. He retrieved it and unzipped the front flap, then reached down through his files, canisters of bear spray, the new portable GPS unit, and his loaded .44 Magnum secured in an Uncle Mike's Cordura holster by an interior zipper that was hidden by design. The light from his headlamp bobbed around while he did it. He kept his ears open for Dakota's boots swishing through the tall grass toward the tent.

He withdrew a thin brown envelope made stiff by the eight-and-a-half-by-twelve-inch piece of cardboard inside and dumped the contents on the top of his sleeping bag. Newspaper clippings, GPS coordinates, and most important, the Google Earth maps he'd printed off on high-grade photographic paper while Margaret Kerley was choking back tears out in the reception area as she read (out loud) the instructions on how to operate Windows Vista. She'd had no idea what he was doing.

The photographic images were precise. He found the location of Camp One, where they were now, and traced the trail south along the shoreline of the lake with the tip of his finger. He reviewed the place he'd marked with an X at the natural junction where they'd cut west toward Two Ocean Plateau as he described it to his clients around the campfire. Although the terrain and the creeks were burned into his memory from endless hours with the maps, he wanted to reassure himself for the hundredth time that it looked passable, that he could lead the group up and away from the Thorofare on terrain they could handle, that the horses and mules could navigate.

He hoped the new route from the Thorofare to Two Ocean was as clear and unencumbered as the photographs showed. He wished he knew how old the images Google had posted were. If they were a couple of years old, he prayed there'd been no severe timber blowdowns or microbursts in the meanwhile. In the back of his mind was his memory of seeing an entire mountainside in Yellowstone leveled by a nighttime weather phenomenon that scattered hundreds of acres of lodgepole pines like so many pick-up sticks. No one had seen it happen, and the Park Service, being the Park Service, refused to acknowledge that it did. But Yellowstone was a world of its own, as Jed knew better than anyone, and the physical landscape could change literally overnight as geysers shot through the thin crust or earthquakes rattled the ground or unspeakably violent storms blew through. Fires would be okay because they'd help open up the undergrowth, and he knew there had been a dozen lightning-caused blazes in the area the previous fall.

But he knew that no matter how carefully he'd planned things they'd never go exactly right in Yellowstone. The place seemed designed to foil human plans and aspirations. Conditions within the Yellowstone ecosystem were ramped up and exaggerated compared to the world around it. Every natural phenomenon—storms, fires, temperatures, thermal activity, wildlife, geography, weather in general—always seemed pushed to extremes. The more time he spent in the park the smaller he felt, and the less in control of the world around him. All he could do at times was point himself in the general direction of where he wanted to go—both figuratively and literally—and hope he'd get there. He remembered Bull Mitchell telling him something like that when he bought his company, but Jed discounted the statement and credited Bull's advancing age. Now he knew it to be true.

He jumped when Dakota suddenly entered the tent. He hadn't heard her coming, and she hadn't signaled him in any way like she sometimes did with a whistle or a finger-drum on the taut tent wall. It was simple camp etiquette to do so and he'd taught her that. She'd disregarded it, though, and he scrambled to stuff the maps back into the envelope before she saw what he was doing.

She winced when he looked up at her and shined his headlamp directly into her eyes, pretending it was inadvertent.

"Jeez, Jed," she said, waving her hand at him, "you're blinding me."

"Sorry."

"I bet."

Once the papers were back in the envelope and the envelope slipped under his sleeping bag, he turned his head and the beam of light. *That was too close,* he thought.

She didn't unzip her jacket or remove her boots, but sat Indian style on the foot of her sleeping bag.

He pulled the headlamp off and hung it from a loop so the light hit the inside tent wall and was diffused. "Horses okay?" he asked.

"Yup."

"Food hung up?"

She nodded.

"Kitchen wiped down and locked up?"

"Like always," she said.

"Anyone left at the camp?"

Dakota said, "Donna Glode is still there with Tony D'Amato and James Knox. Knox is trying to protect his friend from her, I guess."

"Donna will be easy to track if she gets lost," Jed said. "We'll just have to follow the cougar tracks."

Dakota didn't even smile as she fixed her eyes on him. "Jed, what the *fuck* is going on?"

"Keep your voice down," Jed said. Even though their tent was two hundred yards from the other tents and closer to the horses than the camp itself, he always worried about being overheard by any guests, since the topic of conversation was generally them.

Her eyes blazed in the semidarkness. "You're breaking every damn rule you've ever told me about," she said. "You've got something going on here or else you've just lost your damn mind."

He started to speak but she cut him off.

"*Never* leave the guests to tend the fire at night," she said. She lowered her voice and added a low drawl to mimic his cadence as much as possible. "Gently encourage the guests to take their socializing to the tents and wait them out if necessary so you can secure the camp and make sure there's no food or anything around to draw animals in, then put the fire out with water. Then do a walk-around to double-check the night checklist. Last, make sure the animals are fine."

He hated when she mocked him.

Which didn't stop her. She said, "*Never* encourage alcohol consumption. We may want a nightcap of our own in the tent before we turn in, Dakota, but *never* drink in front of the clients or encourage them to do so.

"*Never* antagonize a paying guest and promote rancor among the group, Dakota," she said. "Be the facilitator to smooth out any disagreements. Be on everyone's side, or lead them to think you are. Be a benevolent dictator, but more the former than the latter. The whole experience gets poisoned if resentment is left to linger."

He held up a hand to interrupt her but she was on a roll.

"*Never* fraternize with the guests until the last night, Dakota. Keep a professional distance so they respect you. You are the captain of the ship. Maintain a little mystery about you, so they'll listen when you tell them something. Be professional at all times. Don't become one of them, Dakota. Never let your guard down to the clients, Dakota," she said, angry.

Then she leaned forward and backhanded him on his shoulder. Before he could react, she said, "So what do you do, you hand them a bottle! Then you sit with them and get them all stirred up about taking a new route. And what is this about water levels bein' up so we can't stay on the trail, Jed? Where in the *hell* did *that* come from?"

He sat back and glared at her although he was a little taken aback. "Keep your voice down," he said through clenched teeth. "And where do you get off talking to me like that?"

"I'm using your own words," she said.

He said, "This is my trip and my company. I've been keeping a close eye on the creeks we crossed and the level of the lake all day while you emptied your head and tugged your mules along. You would have seen the same thing I did if you'd been looking. And keep the hell in mind I don't need to clear every decision with you. Keep the hell in mind this is my outfit and my risk and you're the hired help."

She reacted as if he'd slapped her. She said in her own voice, "Is that all I am to you?"

He was sorry he said it because he still needed her. But he didn't take it back. He could tell she was trying not to tear up. No matter how tough she talked or acted, he thought, she was still just a damned girl.

He knew what her next move would be. Furiously, she started clawing at her sleeping bag, gathering it into a ball she could carry away.

This wasn't their first fight, but he sensed the cold edge of finality creeping in unless he headed it off.

"You can still sleep here," he said calmly.

"Bullshit," she hissed, backing away on her hands and knees toward the door of the tent. "You can sleep alone. I don't even want to breathe the same air as you tonight."

It was the word *tonight* that made his shoulders relax and his stomach unclench. *Tonight* meant she didn't consider the rift permanent.

He chuckled, then said, "Do whatever you have to do, darlin'. Just don't let any of the guests see you."

"Fuck you, Jed."

He quickly sat up and reached over and cupped her chin in his palm, forcing her to stop and look at him. "Don't escalate things out of proportion," he said. "I know what I'm doing. Trust me a little bit."

"Why should I?" she said, but he knew she was softening.

"Have I steered us wrong before?"

She paused, then said, "Not much up to now."

He laughed, and felt the tension in her dissipate a little. He said, "Before you go, did you complete your job tonight?"

He knew her slavish obligation to her duties would further override her anger. She was like that.

Dakota jerked her face away from his hand, sat back on her haunches, and dug into her coat pocket. He figured she was as angry now at her own caving in as she was at him.

She threw a handful of cartridges in his lap. They landed heavily and he picked one up. He said, "Three-fifty-seven Magnum. Did you find any more? A box of shells?"

She shook her head.

"And you left the gun, of course," he said. "So he might not even know you unloaded it."

She just glared at him.

Wilson would be in a dilemma, now, Jed knew. If the man asked who took the bullets, he'd be admitting he brought a firearm on the trip. It had happened before, and in every case the guest never said a word afterward.

"You don't have to leave," Jed said. "It's cold out there."

But she'd committed herself and although there was a hint of doubt on her face, he knew she'd go.

"Come back in if you get cold," he said.

She grunted the curse at him again as she backed out through the door trailing her sleeping bag and pad. Before disappearing into the night, though, she paused and looked in.

"I nearly forgot," she said. "He also has a satellite phone."

Jed's eyes widened. "He does?"

Her mouth curled into a sneer. "And he's got a file folder filled with aerial photos," she said, "just like those ones you tried to hide from me when I came in."

And she was gone.

Oh shit, Jed thought. *This I didn't expect.*

Gracie didn't know what time it was during the night when she snapped awake at the sound of blows or thumping footfalls outside the tent, or heard what she thought must be the grunting of a bear. Or a man or woman being wordlessly beaten.

Part Three
Back of Beyond

23

Gracie was late to breakfast. She'd barely slept until the last few hours as the tent walls fused with morning sun, and when she finally awoke she was sweating in her sleeping bag and Danielle was already gone.

She stood and stretched and yawned. Her face felt dirty and her hair was matted to the side and took furious brushing to set right. Danielle's sleeping bag was crumpled and puffy on the pad. She vaguely remembered her sister cursing and grunting as she pulled her clothes on earlier.

Outside the tent, it was cold, still, clear, and breathtakingly beautiful. Bright white sun danced on the ripples of Yellowstone Lake and electrified the dew in the grass. A bald eagle cruised along the surface of the water, talons dropped, fishing. Far across the water was the smudge of an island in the lake. Boils of steam rose from vents and dissipated in the clear morning air. She smelled woodsmoke from the fire and heard subdued voices from the kitchen camp.

Her father stood on the path between her and the morning fire, hands in the pockets of his jacket, head down, feet set on opposite sides of the path as if blocking it.

She thought, *Ambush.*

As she walked out into the wet grass to go around him, he said, "Gracie, please. We have to talk."

"Nothing to talk about."

"I didn't like how things developed last night," he said. "I don't like to see you go to bed angry with me."

She snorted and rolled her eyes and passed him. He fell in behind her, speaking low so he wouldn't draw the attention of the group already eating breakfast.

"I wanted you and Danielle to get to know her, get to like her," he said. "I wanted you two to get comfortable with the idea of us together. I wanted you to *want* us to be together, for me to be happy and for us to be happy. I guess what I'm saying, Gracie, is I want your blessing."

She stopped and turned around. He was right behind her. She said, "You use words girls use when they talk to each other. If I want to talk to girls I'll talk to girls, not my dad. If you want to be with Rachel then tell me and be with her. I'm fourteen years old. I don't give blessings. You're the dad, be the dad," she said. "And man up. That's all I ask."

She left him there with his mouth open but no sound coming out.

She expected chiding for being late but no one said a thing and she realized the moment she stepped into the campfire ring that something was seriously wrong. All she received were brief and furtive glances. She felt as though she'd just blundered into the middle of an argument and stopped it cold.

Danielle sat with Justin on the same log they'd occupied the night before. Walt sat near them, as did Rachel Mina, who eyed her coolly. The Wall Streeters stood and held their plates aloft, as if they had an appointment to keep. The menu was scrambled eggs, bacon, hash browns, toast, and coffee. Although the food looked and smelled good, no one appeared to be really eating it. Donna Glode sat alone. She looked pale and sick. Strands of her hair fell into her face and the food on her plate was untouched. She stared at the fire although the flames were hard to see in the morning light.

Who was missing?

Jed, who was behind the kitchen station, said, "Hey, girl, come over here and get some breakfast. Get your dad to come eat, too."

She looked around for Dakota but couldn't locate her.

Dumbly, Gracie started to go get her dad but he'd joined her. He looked under his brow at her, as if trying to transmit a message.

They got tin plates and eating utensils. She glanced over her shoulder at the others.

She said, "Where is Mr. Glode and that guy Wilson? Where's Dakota?"

Her dad said, "I think that's what everyone was discussing when you walked up."

Jed gave her a scoop of eggs and three strips of bacon. He said, "I sent Dakota back on the trail to find a couple of strays."

Gracie waited for a further explanation, but Jed ignored her. He was studying the others around the campfire with an almost scary intensity, she thought.

Gracie sat by Danielle and her sister reached over and patted her on the shoulder, as if touching base. It was an unusual and warm gesture, Gracie thought.

She listened in. Tristan Glode and K. W. Wilson hadn't come to breakfast because they were gone. Their things had been cleared out of their tents and both of their horses were missing.

"No," Jed said to answer a question from James Knox, "I can't say it's ever happened before. I've had the few rare unhappy customers, but I've never had any who up and went home. Especially on my horses."

"I don't see them sneaking away together," Walt said, to snickers from Knox and Drey Russell.

Jed said, "I wish they would have talked to me about it. Being on your own in Yellowstone is dangerous."

Gracie found herself watching Donna Glode, seeing what kind of impact the speculation was having on her. After all, her husband had left her. But she didn't look distraught, Gracie thought. She looked *guilty*.

This was confirmed when Danielle leaned over and whispered in her ear, *"She didn't spend the night in her tent with him."*

Gracie nodded slightly to indicate she'd heard but didn't give her sister away by looking at her or responding. Gracie noted how Donna glanced repeatedly at D'Amato, hoping, no doubt, he'd share a wink back. As far as she could tell, D'Amato pointedly didn't turn his head toward Donna. And he seemed much more inhibited than he'd been so far. In fact, he looked ashamed, like a little boy. His two friends shot glances at him while they ate, as if seeing him in a new light.

Walt said, "Do you think Dakota will find them and talk them into coming back?"

Jed said he hoped so. He looked stricken as well, Gracie thought. Maybe a little unsure of himself, for the first time. Like he had too much swirling around in his head. "I wish we knew when they left," Jed said.

That's when Gracie said, "I heard something last night. Am I the only one who did?"

She was. With Rachel observing her very carefully, her dad asked what she'd heard.

"It's hard to describe," she said. "I heard some feet thumping around outside and a kind of grunt, like someone got the wind knocked out of them. I didn't recognize anyone or hear any voices, just the thumping and the grunt. I thought it might have been an animal in the camp."

Her dad said, "Why didn't you wake me up and tell me?"

Gracie looked over, her eyes dead. "I wasn't sure whose tent you were in."

"Meow," Danielle whispered.

Her dad turned red and looked quickly away. Gracie felt both good and ashamed at the same time. She expected a glare from Rachel, but the woman eyed her stoically. As if assessing her for later.

"What time did you hear it?" Jed asked, ignoring the others.

Gracie shrugged, and chewed on a piece of bacon.

"I mean," Jed said, "was it right after you went to bed or was it closer to this morning?"

"A few hours after I went to bed," she said. "After midnight, I'm sure. I didn't look at my watch, but I'd guess two or three in the morning."

Jed nodded to himself, as if fitting this new information into a narrative.

"So they could have five or so hours on us," Knox said. "I don't see the point in going after them, then. By the time we caught up to them they'd be at the parking lot."

"Maybe," Jed said, worried. "But they might not have gotten that far while it was dark."

"I still don't see the two of them together," Walt said. "I'd guess they're traveling separately in the same direction."

Russell said, "Fools. On their own they might get lost."

D'Amato cleared his throat. "I volunteer to go after them. After all, it's my fault . . ." He didn't finish the sentence.

"You're not going anywhere on your own," Knox said flatly.

"They'll be okay," Russell said. "It's their deal, not ours. It was their choice to leave."

Jed nodded and addressed his comments to Donna. "I don't think they'll get lost or anything. Hell, the trail just parallels the shore of the lake nearly all the way back. There are a few side trails, but they'd follow our tracks from yesterday. I'm sure Dakota will find them. That girl can *ride*."

Walt said, "It just doesn't make sense to me. Just because there was a disagreement on which trail to take—it just doesn't make sense."

Gracie's dad agreed. Rachel said nothing.

Donna Glode said to the fire, "You don't understand. Tristan is all about control. And last night he lost it." She looked over at D'Amato. "You're not the reason he left. *I'm* the reason he left."

D'Amato stared at his boots, still pointedly ignoring her. No one followed up with a request to Donna for clarification.

"But why Wilson?" Rachel Mina asked. "Why did he leave? He didn't seem that concerned about the vote or which trail we are going to take."

"Who knows about that guy," Walt said. "He was a hard guy to read."

Knox agreed. "It doesn't break me up too damn much that guy's gone. He seemed kind of strange from the start, I thought."

"Hear, hear," Russell said.

"Tristan is another matter," D'Amato said, as much to himself as anyone. "I think maybe it would be a good effort on my part to go try and get him. I want to do this. I want to make things right."

"Forget it," Donna said, ending the discussion. "He won't listen to you, of all people. And he's never listened to me."

She stood and turned to Jed. "I know exactly what he'll do, so you might as well prepare for it. He'll go straight to the top, to the superintendent of the park, and demand that your license be taken away for deviating from the scheduled trip. And I would be surprised if he didn't get his way. That's the way he is."

It was only for a second, but Gracie thought she saw real fear in Jed's eyes.

"Dakota will find him," Jed said, assuring no one.

Gracie found the whole scene fascinating and a little sickening. There was no filtering of words or emotions for the sake of Danielle, Justin, or her. She felt suddenly older and more mature but she didn't like the feeling.

Jed said to Gracie, "What you probably heard last night was one or both of them clearing out their tents to leave. Maybe one of them tripped on a tent stake or something."

Gracie shook her head. "I don't think it was that."

"Then what was it?" her dad asked, suddenly perturbed. "If you can't say what you heard, maybe you shouldn't say anything at all."

Gracie felt her face flush. She knew his anger had more to do with her snub of him than anything else. She said softly, "It sounded more like a fight."

No one said anything. The silence around the fire became oppressive.

Finally, Jed said, "I don't see much sense in discussing this any further. It's time to eat up, pack up, and mount up. We're burning daylight, folks."

The sound of hoofbeats filled the awkward silence, and everyone turned toward the sound.

Dakota rode up and reined to a stop. She was alone.

"I couldn't catch them," she said.

Gracie looked up to see Jed glaring at Dakota, his hands knotted into fists at his side.

Dakota didn't meet his eyes.

Gracie walked with Danielle back toward the tents. When they were far enough away from the adults, Danielle said, "Fuck this. This trip sucks. Why couldn't we go to Mexico or a beach or something?"

Gracie shrugged.

Danielle said, "Who cares if those two guys are gone or what trail we take? It's just stupid. I'm glad that creep Wilson is gone anyway, so he won't be sneaking around trying to look at me when I go to the so-called toilet. And I want to take a hot shower."

"What do you think about Dad and Rachel?"

"I guess I would have liked to have known about it before we did this," her sister said. "But Dad needs to get a life. This might help. Maybe he won't be so clueless and intense all the time."

"That's all you think about it?"

Danielle shrugged. "She seems kind of cool. I don't have anything against her."

"I don't know her well enough to say," Gracie said.

Danielle said, "What I think is if the rules of this trip are everybody sleeps around with everybody else, then they ought to just say so and I'll stay with Justin. He can rub my back and tell me how beautiful I am and we'll see what develops."

Gracie sighed and unzipped their tent so they could repack their things for the day's ride. As she did she saw Rachel Mina come out of a green and blue tent with her sleeping bag bundled in her arms. Gracie thought she looked angry and puzzled, as if trying to struggle through a difficult problem. Then their eyes locked for a moment and Rachel's face softened and changed. Rachel took a deep breath, blew a strand of hair out of her face as if she'd just made a momentous decision, and let her sleeping bag drop to a pile at her feet.

"Uh-oh," Gracie said.

"What?"

"She's coming over."

"Who?" Danielle asked, then saw Rachel working her way through the other tents toward them. "Oh, her."

Gracie looked around. There was nowhere to run.

"Hello, Danielle," Rachel said. "Hello, Gracie."

"Hi," Danielle said. Gracie stood and nodded.

"We haven't officially met," Rachel said, looking from one sister to the other and extending her hand. "I'm Rachel."

They shook her hand.

Rachel said, "I wanted to take this opportunity, since we're away from everyone, to set the record straight regarding your dad and me."

Gracie braced for it.

"I want you to know something," Rachel said, talking mainly to her. "I don't want to be your stepmother. I don't necessarily want to be your best friend. But I want to get along with you and I hope you'll give it a shot to get along with me. We all know the situation, even though the truth came out much more awkwardly than I wanted it to.

"I'm very, very fond of your father. I know he feels the same about me. We're both lonely, and there's a very good possibility we'll be together in the future. That's where you two come in."

"Hey," Danielle said, "as long as you don't try to run my life, I'm okay with it."

Rachel still spoke primarily to Gracie. "I've been around the block. I don't try to pretend your father is young, single, and carefree. I know he's got a family. And I know he absolutely adores you two girls. This isn't an either/or situation unless we make it such," she said. "Do you understand what I'm saying?"

Gracie said, "I'm not sure I do."

Rachel said, "You two are the most important people in his life. I recognize that fact and I admire it and I'd never try to change it. If we can't accept each other and get along, I'll step aside. I won't force him to make a choice and he doesn't need to. Most men are trying to do the right thing but they don't know how. That I've learned. They don't understand what we want and need and expect. They assume we think love is a zero-sum game—either he goes with you or he goes with me—which it isn't. I know he's attracted to me, and I to him. I could draw a line in the sand. But I won't, because then I'd be with a man I don't respect and you'd have a dad you resented. What I'm saying," she continued, "is we're not rivals. Not either/or. You've already got a mother and from what I understand she's a wonderful woman. I look forward to meeting her as well. I don't plan on disliking her or resenting her."

Gracie said, "You talk to us like we're adults."

Rachel said, "And I plan to continue to do that. I'm too old to start playing games, and this . . ." she waved her hand over her head to indicate the situation they were in that morning, "is an incredible distraction. If we don't talk now and talk bluntly, who knows when we'll get the chance?"

Danielle said, "Hey, I'm here, too," attempting to break up the two-way conversation.

"You are," Rachel said. "And I'm sorry. I just had the impression you weren't the one I'd need to convince."

Danielle started to argue, then rolled her eyes and said, "I'm not, I guess."

Rachel turned back to Gracie. "And what about you?"

Gracie hesitated and felt her sister and Rachel Mina looking at her. She said, "I need to think about it."

"*Gawd,*" Danielle sighed. "Gracie, you are such a little—"

"No," Rachel said, holding up her hand to silence Danielle, which impressed Gracie because it actually *worked,* "that's perfectly fair. I'd probably say the same thing."

And with that, she turned and went back to her tent to pack up.

Gracie and Danielle watched her in silence until she was out of earshot.

Danielle said, "I have to admit, that was pretty cool. I like her, even though I still don't see what she sees in Dad. I mean, I could live with her around, I think."

Gracie nodded, although she wasn't yet ready to agree. She didn't want Danielle to think Rachel had won her over so quickly, even though she nearly conceded to herself she had.

Danielle giggled. "I was kind of hoping she would have said she *did* want to be our best friend, though. That's the way you get stuff, you know? There's nothing better for a girl than to have two sets of parents competing for your affection, and buying you things to make you like them more, you know?"

Gracie looked at her sister with disgust. "What planet are you *from,* anyway?"

"Planet Danielle," her sister said with a lilt. "It's a good and happy place. And it has hot showers and cell phone service."

Jed waited until everyone had dispersed before tracking down Dakota, who was picketing her horse with the others. His voice was tight and low. He said, "Why in the hell didn't you keep going until you found them? Do you know what this might mean?"

She slid the saddle and pad off, leaving a sweaty matted square on her horse's back. "No, what does it mean?"

He reached out and grasped her shoulder, preventing her from turning away from him. "It means he'll go to the Park Service, that's what it means. I could lose my contract, is what it means. Why didn't you track him down? Why did you quit on me before you found him?"

She broke eye contact and let her gaze slip to his hand on her shoulder. She wouldn't speak until he let go, so he did.

Dakota said, "I lost them, Jed. I followed their tracks for two miles and then the tracks just vanished. I can't figure out why they left the trail or where they went. I rode another half mile to see if they got back on the trail, but they didn't. I don't know where they are, but I didn't want to say that in front of our clients."

Jed shook his head. "They just disappeared?"

She nodded defiantly.

Jed felt a weight lift. If Tristan and Wilson had wandered away from the route they might never get back to the trailhead.

"Should we notify Search and Rescue?" Dakota asked.

"No," Jed said. "Not yet. Those two might realize the error of their ways and come back yet."

He ignored the puzzlement in her face.

While they were packing, Gracie asked, "Did you hear anything last night?"

"No. I had a bad dream about something, but I forget now what it was about."

"So maybe you heard what I heard."

"I don't know," Danielle said. "Maybe. But who cares? He's great, isn't he? Justin, I mean."

"You think they're all great at first. This one is, but I'm sure you'll screw it up somehow."

"*Shut up.*"

Gracie cinched her sleeping bag stuff sack and started to carry it and her duffel toward the horses. On the way, she stepped off the path into the moist grass and bent down. The sod was churned up in several places exposing soft black soil. She looked up at her tent, which was twenty yards away. "This is where it happened," she said to Danielle.

"This is where the noises came from. Nobody tripped on a tent stake. It's too far away from the tents."

Danielle stayed on the path. She looked from Gracie back toward the camp. The adults were still milling around.

"So what are you saying?" she asked.

Gracie said, "I'm not sure. But there's something really wrong going on. Something evil. Two grown men supposedly just left us in the middle of the night without a word to anyone. We're supposed to believe that two guys who've known each other for a day get together and make a plan like that? Why didn't anyone hear them or notice they were taking two horses? And did you see the way Jed and Dakota were treating each other? Or how Donna Glode and Tony D'Amato are acting?"

"I didn't notice."

"I know you didn't. And why the big deal about taking another trail?" Gracie said. "We wouldn't know what trail we're on, anyway. Why does that matter?"

24

Cody Hoyt rode a tall gelding paint named Gipper behind Bull Mitchell's black horse through a dark stand of lodgepole pine trees that seemed to have no end, on a trail that was so overgrown it barely existed anymore, and he called to Mitchell, "Are you sure you know where we're going?"

It was mid-morning and up beyond the interlaced canopy of trees the sun was out and the sky was intense blue and cloudless. They'd been riding for four hours straight without a break and Cody felt quarter-sized spots on both inner thighs burn through his jeans into his flesh from leather ridges on the saddle. He knew little about horses except he'd never much liked them and he had the distinct impression Gipper thought the same about him, evidenced by the way the horse would drift off the path toward overhanging branches that, if Cody wasn't alert, would have knocked him backwards out of the saddle to the ground.

It was still moist in the trees from a brief rain shower that came at dawn as they set out, and raindrops clung like tears to the tips of pine needles. Occasionally, there was a break in the canopy and light streamed through like jail bars. But mostly they'd been in the shadows on a trail that barely was and Bull Mitchell hadn't said three words to Cody although the old man mumbled plenty to his horse.

Mitchell trailed a packhorse with full canvas panniers and Cody rode his gelding behind them both.

Cody inventoried their weapons. Both he and Mitchell had rifle scabbards lashed onto their saddles. The scarred and faded wooden butt of a scoped .30-06 stuck out of Mitchell's scabbard and a black polymer adjustable butt stock for a departmental AR-15 poked out of Cody's. Mitchell's rifle looked substantial and serious, Cody thought, while his high-tech semiautomatic rifle resembled a kind of toy. He'd switched out the thirty-round for a ten-round magazine so the rifle would slip into the creaky leather sleeve that simply wasn't designed for it. Cody's .40 Sig Sauer was clipped high on his belt, making the weapon difficult to get at but at least it didn't rub along the saddle. Mitchell had strapped on a long-barreled .44 Magnum single-action Ruger Super Blackhawk revolver. Like his rifle, Mitchell's handgun was rubbed nearly clean of blueing and the wooden handgrip was worn and scratched. He wore the .44 Magnum in a holster that covered most of his thigh. It was a bear weapon.

"I said," Cody repeated, "are you sure you know where we're going?" Mitchell pulled his horse to an abrupt stop, which caused the packhorse to do the same. Gipper used the occasion to stop, dip his head, and eat grass.

"I heard you the first time," Mitchell growled. His voice was so deep it seemed to vibrate through the ground. He sounded annoyed.

"Well?"

"What do you think?" Mitchell said.

"I think we've been riding in these trees for a long time and even I can see we're the first people to use this trail in years," Cody said. "So it's a little hard for me to believe we're going to catch them on it."

Mitchell shook his head as he looked away, as if deeply disappointed.

"What?" Cody asked.

"I got a question for you," Mitchell said, turning his horse around so he could glare at Cody and leaning forward in his saddle with both of his huge hands on the horn. Cody had learned from his Montana outfitter uncles that true horsemen—unlike himself—would rather turn their mounts around than turn their heads. "Why the hell did you hire me if you're going to question every damn thing I do?"

Cody shifted his weight, trying to find a position in the saddle that eased the burns. "It's just this trail we're on. It's obvious it hasn't been used in years and there are places I can't even tell it's there. So naturally I—"

"Naturally you start yapping at me," Mitchell said basso profundo, "when you should be keeping quiet."

"I want to know what's going on. You can't expect me to just sit here for hours wondering where we're going."

Mitchell reached up and tilted his cowboy hat back and rubbed his forehead. "I thought you wanted to catch them," he said.

"I do."

"Then the only way we're going to do it in a timely fashion is to ride cross-country and cut all the corners. We should intercept the main trail by early this afternoon. They'll still have about half a day on us but with all those rookie riders and trail horses, we'll make up plenty of time."

Cody nodded. "Thank you for that. All you needed to tell me was you knew where you were going and you had a plan."

Mitchell shook his head again.

Cody said, "All you had to tell me was you were familiar with this sort-of trail we're on and that it will eventually run into the main trail where Jed is."

Mitchell said, "I ain't never been on this trail in my life."

With that, he grinned crookedly and turned his horse back around and clicked his tongue to get him moving again.

Cody moaned and patted his shirt for his cigarettes.

Cody and Bull Mitchell had approached Yellowstone Park from the northwest in the dark pulling a beat-up horse trailer. They'd hidden Cody's

Ford in an empty outbuilding at Jed McCarthy's compound and transferred his gear to Bull Mitchell's rig. Mitchell drove a dented F-250 pickup and sipped from a plastic go cup of coffee, and Cody tried to get some sleep since he hadn't gotten any the night before. Every time he closed his eyes his mind swirled with Technicolor visions of cabins burning down, hotels burning up, conspiracy, and betrayal.

He'd finally dozed for a few minutes when he was jolted awake by a violent pitching of the truck. When he opened his eyes and reached out for the dashboard to find out what had happened, he saw they'd turned off the highway onto an ancient two-track that skirted a dark river and vanished ahead in a bank of dark timber.

"What's this?" he'd asked, groggy.

"Old Indian trick," Mitchell said.

"What the hell does that mean?"

"Means we sure as hell can't drive through the gate at the park and explain to the ranger who you are and why we're bringing horses in without taillights, so we're sneaking in through a back door."

Mitchell gestured vaguely ahead in the dark. "This is an old fire and service road nobody's supposed to know about. It's from the old days when the Park Service actually provided service and put out fires, so we're talking a really long time ago. We can get pretty deep into the park without anyone knowing we're here."

Then Mitchell added, "I hope. They might have blocked it off."

Cody asked, "How long has it been since you were on it?"

Mitchell shrugged and sipped at his coffee. "Seven, eight years," he said. "Maybe more."

"Jesus," Cody said. "What if it's blocked?"

"We'll figure something out," Mitchell said, and shrugged. "Always do. I got a chain saw in the back in case we need to cut trees and a winch on the front in case we get stuck. Of course, I haven't tested either one out in a few years, so let's just hope they work if we need 'em. I got shovels and a handsaw if they don't. At least I think I do."

When Cody just stared, Mitchell said, "Keep in mind this is Yellowstone. Anything can happen here and plans always go wrong. It's just the nature of the place."

The road was passable, although Cody and Mitchell twice had to get out of the truck and cut a path through fallen trees.

"This just seems wrong," Cody said, lifting green branches out of the way of the idling F-250.

"It is wrong," Bull Mitchell said, revving the motor on his chain saw to keep it running. He was haloed by oily blue smoke.

"Breaking into a national park seems like breaking into a church," Cody said.

Mitchell snorted and said, "That's a result of too much indoctrination in public school and too many Disney shows. It's great country—you'll see—but it isn't all sweetness and light. Charlie the Lonesome Cougar would happily take a chunk out of Bambi's tender throat. This place will eat you up and spit you out if you're ever off your guard. Especially where we're going."

Dawn rose pink and cold and sudden waves of rain lashed at the trees and drummed on the hood of the truck but went away as suddenly as they'd come.

Cody told Mitchell about the fire in his room at the Gallatin Gateway Inn as Mitchell eyed him warily but didn't utter a word.

Cody let the story trail off without sharing his suspicions about Larry.

"Got a question," Mitchell said, minutes afterward.

"What?"

"Why are your hands shaking like that?"

Cody had held up his right hand. Mitchell was right.

"DTs?" Mitchell said.

"I guess."

"Let's hope you don't have to aim your gun at anything," Mitchell said.

"Mind if I smoke?"

"Damned right I mind."

As they saddled up in a treeless alcove at the end of the service road, Cody admired Mitchell's experience and abilities. Although the old man moved slowly, there wasn't a wasted step or gesture. Mitchell had obviously spent his life around horses and outfitting, and he saddled the horses, filled and balanced the panniers, and tied a series of intricate outfitter knots over the cargo practically in the dark.

When Mitchell pointed toward the paint horse and grunted, Cody asked why he was called Gipper.

"Last good president," Mitchell said, as if the answer had been obvious.

"Don't cross him neither," Mitchell warned. "He ain't as affable as he looks. Just like his namesake, and his owner: *me.*"

After five straight hours of riding Cody noticed a subtle increase in hue within the forest and more bars of sunlight. Soon there were large enough openings in the canopy he could see blue sky and distant strings of high-altitude cirrus clouds and finally the trees fell away and the horses broke through over a ridge and the whole bright green world, it seemed, was laid out in front of them. The day had warmed considerably and the wind was so slight it barely rippled through the grass. The sun was straight over their heads and the air was thin and smelled of pine and sage from the valley below and it smelled so fresh he was afraid it would unclog his lungs and slough off the tar and nicotine and give him a coughing fit.

Bull Mitchell paused his mount. Cody wrestled with Gipper until the gelding finally understood he was to keep walking alongside the packhorse, and Cody pulled his horse to a stop abreast of Mitchell.

When Cody looked out over the vista of green carpeted saddle slopes with tree-choked river valleys, massive red-veined geological upthrusts that bordered the eastern horizon until they gave up and became mountains, and the vast sprawling tableau of Yellowstone Lake miles ahead and below them, he said, "What big country."

Mitchell grunted and reached back into a saddlebag for his binoculars. "Don't fall in love with it," Mitchell said. "It's guaranteed to break your heart."

Cody used the pause to dismount. His legs were stiff and his knees felt as if they'd been tortured on a rack to bend them inward. He hobbled toward the packhorse and began to unbuckle one of the panniers where he'd seen Mitchell pack his duffel bag.

"See anything?" Cody asked Mitchell.

After a long pause, Mitchell said, "I see a herd of elk, a couple of coyotes, and an eagle. And a whole meadow filled with buffalo chips. Must have been a hundred of them critters there not long ago."

"I meant the pack trip," Cody said, irritated.

"Nope."

Cody withdrew his duffel and dropped it on the ground. It hurt to squat. As soon as he opened it his stomach clenched. Manically, he rooted through the clothing and the gear.

"Shit!"

Mitchell didn't look down from his glasses, but asked what the problem was.

"My cigarettes," Cody said. "I bought a carton of them for the trip. I know I bought a carton and I remember packing them."

Mitchell was silent.

Cody stood up and felt a wave of pure panic. Then he kicked the bag. "Shit. They must have been in the duffel bag that burned up. *Shit.*"

Mitchell said, "It's a long way to the nearest convenience store."

Cody stanched an impulse to pull his Sig Sauer out of his holster and shoot the outfitter right there.

Mitchell shrugged. "Now's as good a time as any to quit, I suppose. I did it years ago. Just stopped. No big deal."

Cody rubbed his face. It felt as if there were tendrils of sinew inside his body tightening up, waiting for the familiar shot of nicotine to relax them. The sky began to spin and the earth itself seemed to undulate, like slow waves across a pool. He patted his pockets, hoping he'd find a spare pack. He rooted through his coat and his saddlebag. In the bottom of a saddlebag he located a cellophane pack that contained . . . *two* cigarettes. Cody felt as if he'd won the lottery.

Mitchell said, "Might as well save 'em."

Cody said, "Bullshit," and lit one up. He'd figure out later when he'd have the last one.

As he sucked in the smoke his body relaxed and seemed to moan with delight. The sky stopped spinning and the valley below stilled.

Cody asked, "Does Jed smoke?"

"Not that I remember."

"I bet somebody in that group does," Cody said, swinging himself painfully back into the saddle. The sores on his thighs burned instantly. "Which is another reason to find 'em fast."

Mitchell clucked his tongue and his horse stepped out. He said, "I'm not sure I'm getting paid enough money to come out here into the wilderness with a desperate man withdrawing from alcohol *and* cigarettes."

"Please shut up," Cody said.

Mitchell laughed. "First you chew my ass for not talking, and now it's *shut up*," he said. "Make up your damned mind."

"I know one thing," Cody said twenty minutes later, as they descended toward the valley floor. "If I can't find some cigarettes pretty soon I'm likely to rip the heart out of the guy we're chasing with my bare hands and feed it to him."

Mitchell said, "So who are we chasing, anyway?"

"Hell if I know."

Cody rode in silence, consumed by the maelstrom in his head. He recounted the conversations he'd had with Larry and the information Larry had conveyed. The pieces of the puzzle had been laid out on the table by Larry, along with a few more he'd added himself, so the logical sequence should have been for the two of them to start assembly and come up with a viable theory or conclusion or at least to be able to discard unworkable scenarios. But if Larry had been working against him, could he count on *anything* his ex-partner had said? Were there even other victims at all? Was Larry the puppet master pulling his strings, leading him to where Larry wanted him to go? Or was it simply a matter of Larry getting Cody out of the picture and out of the way? There was no place in the country more isolated than where he was right now, Cody thought. If Larry's plan had been to get him out of the way, he couldn't have succeeded better.

So was there any validity at all to Larry's information? Was it even true that the last Web site Hank Winters had looked at was the one for Jed McCarthy's pack trip? Or was that all part of Larry's misdirection, too?

He weighed the possibility of turning around and going back. That way, he could wring Larry's neck and blow up whatever game Larry was playing.

They were in the middle of Camp One before Cody even realized it. Only when Bull Mitchell stopped his horse and swung down to the ground did Cody notice there were rough squares of flattened grass on the plateau where tents had been and an alcove in the trees with a fire pit.

"Jed's doing a good job," Mitchell said, with a lilt of admiration. "He's running a low-impact outfit. You wouldn't even know they were here last night except if you knew the exact location. No garbage or human sign except where they flattened the grass."

Cody dismounted as well. He thought he knew why real cowboys liked to sit their horses so long: it hurt too much to get off.

He leaned against Gipper while the blood flowed into his legs and the pain receded. He watched Mitchell roam the campsite and thrust his hand into the fire pit. When he came back wiping the ash on his jeans, he said, "Yup, they were here this morning. The rocks are still warm and the ash is moist from when they put the fire out."

"Any idea how long they've been gone?"

Mitchell said, "It's hard to get everybody up, fed, and get an entire camp packed up. My guess is that they were probably on the trail by nine. So four or five hours is all."

Cody swallowed. He tried to imagine his son in the camp just hours before. He hadn't seen him since last Christmas. He wondered how tall he was now, and how long his hair was.

Cody started to ask Mitchell how long it would take for them to catch them when he noticed Mitchell looking down toward the shore of the lake and squinting.

Cody turned, and said, "What are you seeing?"

Mitchell said, "I thought I caught a glimpse of something down by the water. Something moved. You see it?"

Cody couldn't see well enough through the trees so he shifted to his left. Branches were parted enough for him to get an unimpeded view all the way down the slope to the shore of the lake.

"Wolves," Cody said. "At least three of them."

One wolf was jet-black, another was silver, and the third was mottled gray. Cody could see they were feeding at the water's edge.

25

Gracie lagged behind her sister on the trail, putting distance between Strawberry and Danielle's horse. It seemed odd to her there were four fewer riders ahead on the second day.

Despite his friend James Knox's disapproval and Jed's pleading, Tony D'Amato had decided the only way he could live with himself was to track down Tristan Glode and try to persuade him to come back. Drey Russell thought D'Amato was on a fool's mission, but agreed to ride with him. Their plan, they said, was to rejoin the group at Camp Two. Grudgingly, Jed had given the two his maps and told them to look for a marker on which trail to follow when they came back.

Gracie noticed how Dakota watched the exchange in silence, shaking her head.

It had warmed up enough that Gracie had stripped off her hoodie to her T-shirt. Although she could still see Yellowstone Lake to her left, the path had climbed away from it and they'd gained hundreds of feet of elevation. The rhythmic *clop-clop-clop* of the horses soothed her and reminded her she was in a beautiful, wild place on a perfect summer day and that not everything was horrible. That Rachel Mina had smiled at her with a hint of sympathetic understanding while they were saddling up had buoyed her more than she would have thought.

But all of the questions remained unanswered.

"Everything all right up there?" Dakota asked from behind her. "You need to keep up, girl."

Instead of goosing Strawberry into a faster walk, Gracie reined her horse off to the side of the trail so Dakota could catch up. The trail was not so narrow or the trees so close as they climbed that they couldn't ride side by side for a while.

When Dakota caught up Gracie fell in beside her.

"Nice day," Gracie said.

"Yes it is." Dakota looked over with a hint of suspicion.

"You do this a lot, right?" Gracie asked.

"This is my third summer. So yeah, a lot of pack trips. Most of them are quite a bit shorter than this one, though. This is the big one of the year."

"How'd you meet Jed?" Gracie asked. "Are you two a couple?"

Dakota smiled slyly. "Right to the point."

Gracie tried to smile back innocently.

"I met him in Bozeman," she said. "I was in my third year at the university and I was helping pay the bills by barrel-racing and riding horses for rich folks. There are quite a lot of rich people who've moved to Montana and they like the idea of owning horses but hardly any of 'em know a thing about them. But horses need to be ridden, and I put an ad in the *Chronicle*. Pretty soon, I was getting paid for going out to ranchettes and riding their horses for them to keep the animals in shape and to keep them well trained. Getting paid to ride horses is just about the coolest thing in the world, you know."

"That sounds pretty fun," Gracie said.

"So one of the ladies I worked for got divorced and decided to sell out and move back to L.A.," Dakota said. "Jed bought all three of her horses. In fact, Strawberry there was one of them. So I delivered the horses to Jed at his place and we started talking and he offered me a job as wrangler. Seems his last guy wasn't dependable. I started off as his wrangler and, well, you know. We were already spending a couple of months together day and night, so pretty soon we figured we might as well share the same tent, I guess."

"I sort of know what that's like," Gracie said. "I mean, Danielle is my sister."

Dakota laughed. "Yeah, even I can see how pretty she is."

"So do you love him?"

"Jesus, girl," Dakota said, actually blushing.

"It just seems . . ."

"It seems like what?"

"You seem really different from each other."

"You mean because he's older?"

"That," Gracie said, "and he's your boss. But you don't seem to be the kind of person who needs a boss. And he's not like you at all, you know?"

Dakota went silent for a few moments and Gracie feared she'd offended her. "I'm sorry."

"It's okay," Dakota said. "I'm just trying to figure out how to answer.

"I guess," she said, "it's kind of an unusual situation. I never knew my dad except that he worked in the oil fields in Wyoming, and when I grew up the only thing I could do well was hang around horses. I trust horses more than people, even though they can be knuckleheads. At least they're innocent knuckleheads, though. They never do anything because they're mean, only because they're scared or spooked or trying to get away. But they aren't mean, like people are. When I talked to Jed he pretty much said the same thing. Plus, do you know how hard it is for a girl like me to find a partner my age who isn't an idiot? So many of the guys my age are slackers who are just plain scared of girls in general and me in particular. I get tired of waiting for them to grow up, you know? I don't think I can wait forever. I tried to find someone to take me as I am, but pickings are slim, girl."

Gracie nodded. "So what's he like? I mean, when he isn't being the boss?"

"I can't believe you're asking me these questions," she said. "And I especially can't believe I'm answering them."

"He seems mysterious," Gracie prompted.

"Oh, he is that. He's always got something going," she said. "Did you know he was a poet? He's published a couple of books of poetry. Can you believe that?"

"Is it good poetry?"

"I can't tell," she laughed. "It's beyond me. I mean, I get parts of it, but it's really difficult to understand. He's even won a couple of awards for it, I guess. And there have been times when he reads it to me. It sounds beautiful when he reads it out loud because he has so much passion, but it's not like I understand most of it. I pretend I do, but I don't. I think he's kind of frustrated more people don't recognize his genius."

Gracie peered ahead, trying to see Jed McCarthy in a different light.

"Is he nice to you?" she asked Dakota.

"Much of the time," Dakota said.

"But not always."

"No," she said. "He can be the most obtuse son of a bitch I've ever met sometimes. Worse than a mule. And when he gets a new idea in his head, like a new poem or a new way to make more money, he gets pretty full of himself. I think he prefers his own company to anyone else because he's the only one smart enough to stand himself, if you know what I mean. That's when I feel like throwing in the towel and just hitting the road."

"Are you feeling that way now?"

Dakota looked over and gave Gracie a long searching look. "How did you know that?"

"I watched you two earlier."

"Sometimes I just can't figure out what's going on under his hat," she said. "And this is one of those times."

"Why do you think Mr. Glode left?"

Dakota sighed. "Mrs. Glode," she said.

"Simple as that?"

"It's a hell of a lot more complicated," Dakota said. "I think the two of them were hoping they'd find something out here they didn't find. There have been other couples on these trips looking for the same thing. So at least I can sort of understand that."

"What else?" Gracie said.

"Wilson," Dakota said.

"You mean you don't know why he left, too?"

Dakota nodded. "I'm going to tell you something nobody knows," she said. "I didn't stay with Jed last night. We had a fight and I slept outside by the fire. At one point I had to get up to pee and I walked up above the tents into the trees. In the moonlight, I could see somebody lurking around. Kind of moving real slow and deliberate—walking back and forth from the tents to the lake. I sort of snuck down there and I saw it was Wilson. I don't know what the hell he was doing, but he gave me the creeps. He was just out walking around."

"Did you tell Jed?"

"Not yet. His head is too far up his butt to listen to anyone."

"What do you think Wilson was doing?"

She shrugged. "I don't know. But it looked like he was planning something, or waiting for someone. Maybe it was Tristan Glode, but that doesn't make much sense to me."

Gracie thought about that.

"Maybe it was Wilson and Mr. Glode who had a fight?" she said.

"Maybe. But you're the only one who said they heard anything."

"Don't you believe me?"

Dakota said, "Let me put it this way. I believe you think you heard something."

Gracie said, "But why would they leave together after that? And what would they fight about? I mean, if it was Tony and Mr. Glode at least they'd have a reason."

"I know. It beats me."

"I didn't hear an argument," Gracie said.

Dakota shrugged. "I don't know what the hell is going on, but something is. You look ahead of us at all those people on horses in this setting, and you think, what a perfect thing. But what you don't know is what's going on in everyone's head, and what they might be thinking about everyone else.

"That," she said, "is the reason I prefer horses."

Jed had pulled his horse and mules off to the side of the trail to let his clients ride past. When Gracie and Dakota reached him, Jed said, "Dakota, you take lead for a while. I'll tail up."

Gracie saw that Dakota wanted to argue but clamped her mouth closed, pulled her hat tight, and urged her horse and mules on. Jed fell into place where Dakota had been but he didn't stay there long.

He said, "So, you enjoying the trip so far?"

There was something disconcerting in the way he asked, she thought. Like he couldn't wait to get past the formalities. Like he kind of enjoyed playing with her, enjoyed reeling her in with his soft voice.

"I guess."

"What about your sister? She seems like maybe this isn't her dream vacation."

Gracie had to smile at that.

"Thought so," he said.

"I wanted to ask you something," he said. "I saw you talking away with Dakota. What on earth were you girls chatting about for so many miles?"

"Nothing in particular," she lied.

"Really?" A hint of sarcasm.

"Girls do that," she said. "We just talk about nothing for hours. You know, clothes, nails, shoes. Girly things. That's just how we girls are."

He chuckled. "You are a pistol," he said. "Now really, what were you two talking about for so long?"

Gracie squirmed in her saddle. She wondered why it felt like it had gotten warm, like those car seat heaters did in her mother's Volvo. She said, "I asked her how she liked her job. Since I like horses and all."

"Ah," Jed said. "And she told you what?"

"She said it was pretty good most of the time."

"My name come up?"

"Of course," Gracie said. "You're her boss."

Up until that moment, she hadn't noticed the sheath knife on his belt that lay across the top of his thigh. She guessed it had always been there amidst the things he wore, but she'd just not focused on it before.

He said, "Females always talk too much."

She didn't know if he meant her or Dakota. Or both. He had looked away from her but there seemed to be a lot going on in his head.

"Are we going to find those two guys?" she asked.

"Oh," he said, almost vacant, "we'll find 'em."

26

Bull Mitchell roared and fired his .44 Magnum over the backs of the wolves. The concussion in the epic stillness was tremendous and Cody flinched and came back up with his ears ringing. The big slug slapped the surface of the water twenty feet out and all three wolves wheeled toward them on their back haunches.

Cody could look into their black eyes and see their long red teeth and pink-tinged snouts and he instinctively reached for his Sig Sauer. He'd bought bear spray the day before in Bozeman but it had been in the duffel with his carton of cigarettes so therefore he didn't have any. He couldn't get over how doglike they were, yet they weren't dogs. They had the eyes of dogs and the fur of dogs, but they were wild, big, and menacing. The black one had yellow-rimmed eyes that seemed to burn in their sockets.

"Hold on," Mitchell said. "Stand tall and tough. They want to protect their food but we've got to face 'em down and show no fear."

To the wolves, Mitchell barked, "Get the hell into the woods where you belong. Now get . . ."

To emphasize his point, he ratcheted back the hammer on his Ruger and fired again, this time exploding a plume of swamp mud from a depression five feet in front of the wolves.

The black alpha male—Cody guessed he'd weigh 175 pounds—woofed and exhaled and loped away along the shoreline to the south. The silver female followed and Cody caught a glimpse of something long and blue that reminded him of sausage swinging from her jaws as she ran. The mottled wolf, likely also a male, Cody thought, followed her without conviction, as if he'd wanted to fight. He couldn't believe how fast they ran or how powerful they looked, like ghosts with teeth.

"They might not have gone far," Mitchell said, "so keep your eyes open."

"My God," Cody said, and lifted his hand. "Look at this. I was so scared my hand *stopped* shaking."

Mitchell chuckled while he withdrew the empty brass cartridges out of the revolver and replaced them with fresh hollow-point shells.

"I'll keep this out and cover us," Mitchell said, chinning toward the shoreline where the wolves had been. "You might as well keep that little popgun of yours in your holster. It'll just make 'em mad if they decide to come back."

The first thing Cody noticed as they approached the shoreline was the smell. Mingling with the thin warm air and algae-tinged odor from the lake was a primal whiff of musk from the thick hides of the wolves and the dank metallic smell of viscera.

A tangle of partially submerged driftwood stretched from the shore into the lake for twenty feet. A scum of algae sucked in and out of the water-worn branches of the structure as if being inhaled and exhaled by the structure itself. There was a deep shadowed undercut beneath the driftwood.

The body was half in and half out of the water with the head on the beach, face to the side. Its legs were submerged in the water and pointed down toward the undercut at such an angle that the feet could hardly be seen in the murk. The body appeared to have no arms.

Male, thin, pale, middle-aged, the waterlogged skin alabaster white except for the jagged gaping holes between its ribs and between the legs. All the soft internal parts had been torn away and eaten by the wolves. The clothing on the victim—a lightweight long-sleeved shirt, baggy cargo pants, cowboy boots—had been flayed into ribbons by the teeth of the wolves. The dark sand beach was trampled with canine paw prints, some slowly filling with chocolate-milk-colored swirls of water. The deep indentations of their claws looked like small-caliber bullet holes in the sand.

"Oh man," Mitchell said.

It wasn't Justin. As soon as Cody was assured of that, he felt his cop blinders descending like the shield of a motorcycle helmet. The shield would help him disengage from making a personal connection with the dead body and treat it for what it was: meat whose soul and life spark had long since left it. The wolves had certainly understood that.

Cody turned the body over to find that the arms weren't missing after all. The wrists had been bound with wire behind its back.

He bent down and found handholds beneath the arms and tried to pull the body fully out of the water but it wouldn't budge. He frowned.

"Are you going to give me a hand?" Cody asked Mitchell.

"Nope," the outfitter said. "This is your department."

Cody looked up for clarification.

Mitchell chinned toward the dark timber to the south as they both heard the muffled crack of a branch. "We interrupted those wolves," he said. "They like to eat their fill, then drag what's left into the trees and cache it for later. I'm sure they're watching us and they probably think we're stealing it from them. Keep in mind some of these wolves don't have much fear of man anymore, if they ever did. All these wolves have known for the last couple of decades is that every time they encounter any humans, the Park Service rangers rush in and cordon off the area to keep the people away from them. These critters have learned they have nothing to fear since it's obvious they've been put on the top of the food chain. That's fine for the wolf population, but the ramifications aren't so pretty for us two-legged creatures.

"So if they decide to come back, I want to be ready."

Cody said, "Okay."

He tugged again but the body was held tight by something under the water that gave only slightly. Then he saw the cord wrapped around the ankles that vanished into the hole beneath the driftwood structure. He waded to his thighs in the water. It was startlingly cold for midsummer, so cold it stung. He followed the cord down with his fingers until he could get a good grip with both hands, and he grunted and leaned back, putting his back into it. Whatever the cord was attached to gave and Cody grunted again and walked backwards toward the sand until he was on dry land. His effort spun the body around as well as revealed the large round rock intricately tied to the other end of the cord. He kept yanking until both the body and the rock were out of the water.

For the first time he noticed another length of cord around the victim's neck, so deeply imbedded into the flesh he'd missed it earlier. A two-inch length stuck out from a tight knot, with the loose end slightly frayed. Cody recognized it as nylon parachute cord—a staple of hunters, hikers, and trekkers everywhere.

Cody said, "Whoever did this tied rocks to his feet and neck and dropped them under the driftwood, dragging the body beneath the surface. Whoever did it probably thought no one would ever find the body. They didn't count on the wolves fishing him out and biting through one of the cords."

Mitchell grunted. He looked pale and a little gaunt, and he did his best to scour the trees for signs of the wolves and avoid looking at the body.

Cody dropped to his hands and knees and crawled around the body, looking over every inch of it. He guessed the victim was in his late fifties or sixties and had been in pretty good shape. Unfortunately, his eyes, throat, belly, and genitals had been eaten away.

"Ah," Cody said, bending in close to the victim's head and turning it so the grotesque features no longer faced him, "Here we go."

There was a one-and-a-half-inch cut under the man's right ear. It was J shaped, with a jagged entry at its wide end tapering to a narrow slice slightly above the jawbone.

"Knife wound," Cody said. "The puncture looks deep enough the blade likely went all the way into his brain. An instant kill. Since the thick part of the blade points toward the back, I'd guess the killer came at him from behind, probably grabbed the man's hair and pulled back, then shoved the knife in hard. Perfect placement, too. The killer could have stabbed the guy in the back or reached around and slit his throat. But he went for the single-thrust kill."

Mitchell grunted.

Cody recalled Larry's findings: *Gary Shulze... The difference here is it appears there was a deep puncture wound into his brain... caused by a knife blade driven into his skull and withdrawn.*

"Let me get my camera and my file," Cody said. "We'll treat this as a crime scene, as low-tech as it is."

"You're the cop."

"I'm going to get my file of the applications for the pack trip," Cody said.

Mitchell said, "I'll go with you to cover you and I'll bring the horses down here with us. Wolves like to eat horses, too."

While Cody photographed the body, the scene, the rope, the rock, and the wounds with his digital camera using his camera case in the shots for perspective, Mitchell ate lunch. The outfitter sat on a large rock with his back toward the lake and his .30-06 across his lap and gnawed on pieces of jerky and washed them down with water. His eyes swept the timber from side to side.

Cody knew he'd fouled the scene. He'd moved the body and walked and crawled all over the sand next to it.

"If it wasn't for that knife wound," Mitchell said, "I might have thought the poor son of a bitch could have been mauled by wolves and then sunk in the water to hide him away from more mutilation."

Cody nodded. He'd been replaying scenario after scenario in his mind for the past half hour.

"It's happened before," Mitchell said. "In the deep backcountry like this, folks leave a dead body so they and the Park Service can come after it once they get out. Packing a body along just invites bears and mountain lions and such. It's like trolling for predators. It's not a good idea."

Cody didn't respond. He pulled his duffel out of the panniers and withdrew the file folder.

It didn't take long. He said, "My guess is this is Tristan Glode, president and CEO of The Glode Company of St. Louis. He look sixty-one to you?"

Mitchell grimaced when he looked over. "Yup. Could be."

"He fits the physical description here in the applications," Cody said. "There's only two other older men on the pack trip. One is named K. W. Wilson and there isn't much background on him. The other is Walt Franck, His Richness, and I know that son of a bitch and this isn't him. Which is kind of a shame."

"Want some jerky?"

"No," Cody said. "I want a cigarette."

"Sorry."

"I wonder what he did to deserve this," Cody said. "Knifing a sixty-one-year-old man. His wife's on the trip, it looks like. I wonder if she's involved or if we'll find her body up ahead. I can't see her just going along after her husband's been killed. And how many in the group saw it happen? And what kind of hell are they going through now?"

Mitchell shrugged.

"Do you have a GPS?" Cody asked. "Mine got burned up in the fire. I'd like to get the exact coordinates here so we can let the rangers know to come get the body."

Mitchell said, "I know the exact location of Camp One. I'll tell 'em."

"There may be more forensic evidence around here," Cody said, looking up toward where the tents were pitched on the grassy shelf. "A crime-scene crew could find something if they got here before too long. Maybe where the killing took place, or footprints, or pieces of parachute cord. Or blood. It's not unusual to find the blood of the killer at the scene of a knifing. It's amazing how often the assailant cuts himself with his own knife during a struggle. Lots of times they don't even know it until later."

"Yeah," Mitchell said with a slow smile building, "I watch them shows on television. The CSI folks would get here and we'd know the whole story and catch the bad guy in forty-eight minutes flat."

"It doesn't work like that," Cody said.

"And it sure as hell wouldn't work here," Mitchell said. "I promise you that. It'll likely rain this afternoon and wash evidence away, or the wolves will come back and clean things up. Nothing works here like normal, like I told you earlier."

Cody sat down heavily on a rock next to Mitchell.

He said, "I've never been on a crime scene before when it was just me. Usually we've got evidence techs and forensic guys on the way, not to mention all my own equipment. I can't even communicate with anyone except you. I feel so goddamned helpless."

"So maybe we better get on our horses and find the rest of 'em," Mitchell said. "That's the only way we're going to know what's happened here."

"Yeah. So you said earlier we have to leave the body?"

Mitchell nodded. "We ain't takin' it with us, that's for sure."

"Then what do we do with it? Sink it back into the lake? Bury it?"

"Wolves'll come back," Mitchell said, shaking his head. "There won't be nothin' left. There's only one thing we can do."

Cody said, "Hang it up?"

"I know where the food pole is," Mitchell said, struggling to his feet, his back popping. "A hundred yards up the mountain away from the camp. Unless Jed moved it. We can run the body up the pole until the rangers get here."

"Man."

"Unless you've got a better idea."

"I wish I did."

It wasn't easy. Cody got kicked in the face with Glode's boots as the body was pulled up into the air. Mitchell had dallied the rope around his saddle horn and walked his horse toward the north until the body was raised twenty feet into the air. Cody looked up. Glode's arms were splayed straight out to the sides from the rope looped under his arms. His head was cocked to the side and his legs hung straight down. The body turned slowly as they tied the rope off after wrapping it around the sap-heavy trunk of a lodgepole pine.

"Birds'll get at it," Mitchell said, "but there isn't much we can do about that. This is about as dignified as we can get for now."

Mitchell tied the rope off. "Things have changed around here in more ways than one," he said, as much to himself as to Cody. "If anything, they've gotten a hell of a lot wilder and more dangerous than they used to be. The grizzly bear population is *way* up, and there's nothing going to keep it down. And the reintroduction of wolves has changed the whole ecosystem. I've heard old-timers compare this wolf deal to introducing street gangs back into inner cities where the gangs had long since been wiped out. I'm not sure I'd go that far," Mitchell said, "but it sure has changed things. There are a hell of a lot more critters around that can eat us than there used to be."

"Great," Cody said.

As they rode away from Camp One the trail was instantly recognizable. It was churned up by the hooves of multiple horses and mules.

"One thing I'm sure you noticed, being the detective and all," Mitchell said over his shoulder as he rode, "was that rock holding the body underwater."

Puzzled, Cody said, "What about the rock?"

"I guess I mean the knots on it."

"What about the knots?" Cody asked, annoyed.

"You didn't recognize the style of knots used to secure that rock to the line?"

Cody sighed. "I'm getting tired of being strung along here."

"Diamond hitches," Mitchell said. "Damned near perfect ones. Not the easiest thing to tie in the world, but probably the best damned knot in an outfitter's arsenal."

Cody felt his face go slack.

"Think about it," Mitchell said again.

Cody reached back into his saddlebag as he rode and found the satellite phone. After staring at it in his hand for a few minutes, he powered it on.

It took two minutes to boot up, find the satellite, and come back with full reception.

He had five messages. All from Larry.

27

As Gracie and Dakota topped the hill they found the others. Jed had ridden ahead and gathered everyone off to the side of the trail and they
sat their horses and looked back at the stragglers.

Dakota said, "Oops, looks like we let them get too far ahead of us."

"Are you in trouble?"

"Naw, I can handle it."

Gracie saw where Jed had tied a red bandana on a sapling to indicate
to D'Amato and Russell—and possibly Tristan Glode and Wilson—
where to turn off.

Jed said to Dakota, "You need to keep the hell up."

Dakota lied, "Gracie was having a little trouble with Strawberry.
We got it all worked out."

Jed narrowed his eyes and looked from Dakota to Gracie and back.
Gracie could tell he wasn't sure he was buying the explanation.

Her dad rode over to her. "Everything okay, honey?"

"Fine," Gracie said.

He rode close alongside and reached out and touched her cheek.
"I'm sorry about earlier."

"Me too," she said.

She could see the relief in his face. He said, "We still do need to talk."

"I know."

"Danielle, too. We all need to talk. I thought it would be easier on this trip but we're constantly with everyone else."

Gracie nodded, and he touched her again and walked his horse back to his place in line.

She said, "Dad?"

When he turned, his face filled with concern, she said, "Danielle and I talked with her. She seems nice."

He beamed, and said, "She is."

"Okay," Jed barked, gesturing toward a thick copse of trees at the edge of the meadow, "this is where the trail breaks off. And if everyone will keep in line and follow me and not wander too far behind," he glared at Dakota, "we should all be okay."

And with that he turned his horse and gathered his mules and set off across the meadow. To Gracie, it didn't even look like a trail.

Where are we going?

She turned and looked over her shoulder at Dakota. Dakota shrugged and extended her arms palms up in a *who knows?* gesture.

28

Cody wanted to hurt someone, break something, unleash holy hell. He'd chewed up two packages of Stride gum and drained his Nalgene bottle, pretending the warm plastic-tasting water was 100-proof alcohol, but it wasn't. His cravings for nicotine and booze pulled at him from the inside like talons and he thought, *One cold beer, one cigarette, that's all I fucking ask. That, and my son.*

The single cigarette he had remaining was in his breast pocket, but he'd sworn to himself to save it for when everything was over and Justin was safe. As he rode past pine trees he wondered what their bark would taste like if he stripped it, crumbled it into powder, and inhaled. When he rode Gipper over small streams of water he looked down and wished it came from a brewery.

His head swam and he couldn't concentrate, but there was one thing he knew and he finally said it to Bull Mitchell.

"You need to turn around and go home."

Mitchell acted as if he hadn't heard him. He rode ahead, comfortable in his saddle, his shoulders wide as if telling him to shut up and go away.

They were an hour from Camp One, an hour from where they'd found the body. They hadn't talked, but Cody recognized that Mitchell had picked up the pace and made his horse and the packhorse work harder than before.

"I said, you need to turn around now and go home," Cody said again.

Mitchell didn't turn his head. He drawled, "And why is that?"

"Because I promised your daughter I wouldn't put you into a bad situation. But we're in one. We've got a dead body and who knows what we're riding into. The deal was you'd guide me. I figured we'd find them and you could hang back and let me do my job. But we've got a dead man hanging from a tree and this isn't what the deal was."

Mitchell rode along.

Cody said, "This trail we're on is all churned up by Jed's horses. An idiot could follow this, it's like a highway. I don't need you anymore and your daughter does. Your wife does. I'll return the horses when I'm through."

Mitchell chuckled drily, and said, "Will you now?"

"Yes. Go back to the truck and trailer and I'll meet you there when this is through."

Mitchell rode along.

"I'm not kidding. It's not a negotiation. I'll pay you what I promised because you delivered. You got me here and pointed me where I need to go. Like I said, any idiot could follow their trail now that we're on it."

"And you're the idiot?"

Cody said, "Pretty much, goddamn it. I've got it covered. Go back to the truck, relax, and I'll see you tomorrow or whenever."

"You're sure?"

He said it in a way that led Cody to believe he might have been thinking the same thing.

"I'm absolutely sure."

Mitchell conceded, "There is a pretty obvious trail."

"Yes, there is."

"An idiot could follow it."

"Yes."

"If I get back to the truck, you want me to call the Park Service? Tell them about the dead man?"

Cody hesitated a moment, thinking about the ramifications. He knew the Park Service would respond but probably not quickly. The logistics of ordering up rangers or a helicopter would take hours, and maybe more time than that. He should be on Justin by then. He said, "Yes, call 'em."

Mitchell seemed to be thinking about it. He said, "You think I'm too old and feeble to finish this job?"

Cody said, "Jesus, no. But I made a promise to your daughter. I want to keep it."

"Damn her."

"She's just looking out for her dad. I'd like to think Justin would someday do the same for me," he said, wondering if that would ever happen.

Mitchell clicked his tongue and turned his horse around. Cody saw disappointment in his face. As he rode by headed the opposite direction he handed Cody the reins to the packhorse.

"Dally the rope around your saddle horn once and keep it loose," Mitchell said. "That way, if she gets spooked she won't take you with her or take you down. But don't forget she's there."

"Okay," Cody said, taking the rope.

"There's four days' worth of food in the panniers and some oats for the horses tonight. Feed them before you feed yourself and hobble them up. Make sure they get to water and brush 'em good. They haven't been out much."

"All right."

"Take care of yourself," Mitchell said, looking into Cody's eyes. "And take this," he said, pulling his .44 Magnum from his holster and handing it over butt first. "For bears."

"I don't need—"

"The hell you don't," Mitchell said. And rode away.

————

Cody was sad to see him go, and more than a little scared being completely and totally alone. Not that he didn't do his best work by himself, but Bull Mitchell had a sense of confidence and purpose in the wilderness Cody could never match, or try to. It was as if the last of his confidence was riding away. He kept glancing back at the packhorse, willing her to behave. Willing her to pretend he knew what he was doing.

He slid the long barrel of the .44 Magnum beneath his belt on the left side of his body so he could pull it—if necessary—with a sidearm draw. It was heavy and ungainly. But if the wolves came back or a grizzly blocked him on the trail he wouldn't hesitate to fire. Mitchell's observation about the many animals who could eat him had resonated.

29

Jed McCarthy led his clients west through dark and close stands of timber broken up by lush mountain meadows humming with insects. The alternate trail they had taken was faint, no more than an unpopular game trail at times, but he was sure he was on the right one and he didn't dare stop and check his materials because he didn't want anyone behind him to doubt he knew where he was taking them. Leaders, if they were true leaders, led. They didn't dither, they didn't doubt themselves. They led. He'd made that point to Dakota numerous times, back when she chose to listen to him. He didn't know what her deal was now, which was her loss, not his. And he really didn't care.

His stomach growled with tension and his hands were cold. He didn't slow his pace or turn around, but he raised his right hand to his face and used his teeth, one finger at a time, to loosen his leather glove. Then he tucked it between the saddle and his Wranglers. Still looking ahead, he let his bare right hand creep back to the right nylon saddlebag, where his briefcase was. He worked his fingers inside and probed for the handgrip of his weapon, found it, and squeezed. The weight and texture of it reassured him. He was glad it was in easy reach.

They emerged into another grassy meadow and he clucked his

tongue and led the mules off the trail over to the side against the wall of trees to make room for the rest of the riders.

When they were gathered he smiled at them because they looked apprehensive and they didn't know why he'd stopped or what kind of news he might have for them. Dakota squinted at him, trying to guess the reason for the pause, as she rode past the group and over to the side. Everyone dismounted.

"I'm gettin' a little concerned about Tony and Drey," Jed said. "I thought they would have caught back up with us by now. Least I hoped they would."

Knox, their friend, said, "Me, too." He seemed alone and uncomfortable without his buddies to bounce his comments off.

Jed shot a glance over at Donna. She looked back with no reaction at all even though he'd not mentioned her husband.

Jed said, "I'm thinking it's possible they might have ridden past my red bandana back there and not gotten on the right trail. That's the only place I think they could have gotten confused, even though these horses leave sign like we're an army on the march or something."

He let the implications of that settle in, before he said, "So I'm thinkin' I might ride back there and find those guys before they get too far down the wrong trail."

He could tell by the dark looks on three faces in particular—Ted Sullivan, Rachel Mina, and Walt Franck—they didn't like his idea at all. He didn't even look over at Dakota because he could feel her eyes burning twin holes in his neck.

Walt said, "You're gonna *leave* us?"

"Just for an hour or so," Jed said, keeping it light. "I'll ride hard down where we were, find those guys, and ride hard to get back. We should meet back up with you about the time you folks get close to Camp Two."

He nodded toward Dakota and said, "Dakota knows our camps as good as I do or better. You don't need to worry about her guiding you at all."

Dakota's voice was tight. "What about your mules?"

"I'll leave them with you," Jed said, looking over at her and showing his teeth. She glared at him but said nothing back. He knew she'd hold her fire until later, when the clients couldn't hear her. Which is why he'd set up the whole scene to take place in the open.

Ted Sullivan cleared his throat. He said, "I'm not worried about Dakota leading us to the next camp, not at all. But I'm kind of wondering if it's the best idea for you to go back for them and leave the group."

Jed laughed drily. "Hell," he said, "I always leave the group when I need to on any given trip. It ain't unusual. Sometimes I need to go back for something—like a camera—that somebody left in camp, or sometimes I have to ride ahead and check trail conditions. Luckily," he said, again tipping his hat toward Dakota, "we have this fine hand here to take over the outfit when that happens."

Sullivan nodded conspicuously, as if to convince Jed and the others he had no further objection.

But Rachel Mina had fire in her eyes. She said, "We started this trip with fourteen people. Then last night we lost two. Today we lost two more. And now *you're* leaving?"

Jed said, "Think of it as more food at dinnertime for everybody else."

Walt chuckled, but that was it.

"Sorry," Jed said. "I shouldn't joke. But really, wouldn't you rather get two and possibly three of the group back before dinner? That may not happen unless I go after them."

"Still," she said, "what if something happens to you? What if you get injured? This is *your* trip. How are we going to know what to do or where to go? We're in the middle of nowhere and you gave your maps away to Tony and Drey, so we won't even have those to go by."

Walt nodded as she talked.

Donna Glode put her arms up, palms out, as if to quiet the crowd. Everyone turned toward her. She said, "Given what's happened, I would suggest we abort the trip. There's no reason to continue on as far as I'm concerned. I suggest tomorrow we go back to the vehicles and consider this trip the disaster it's turned out to be."

Silence. Gracie looked from face to face to see if anyone agreed.

Jed kicked at the dirt with obvious anger, but said softly, "I've never quit a trip before. But it's up to everyone else. Any takers on Donna's idea?"

No one spoke. Knox finally said, "I'm not in favor of going back until my friends find us or we know what happened to them."

Walt jumped in, "Mrs. Glode, some of us don't have the, uh, emotional investment you have in quitting. We paid good money for this. I'm not in support of going back yet."

No one else spoke until Jed said, "Okay, it's settled. We'll find our strays and revisit this topic if necessary. But please keep in mind if you decide to quit you'll be missing out on some great scenery and experiences. And now that we've agreed, I'm going to go find those missing boys."

"I'm going with you," Knox said. "They're my friends."

"Not a good idea," Jed said flatly. "I'm going to ride all out to go get them. I'm talking balls-to-the-wall, if you ladies will excuse my French. Unless you can guarantee me you can keep up, it's not a good idea."

Knox flushed and said, "You know I can't. This is my second day on a horse."

"Then with all due respect, fall in behind Dakota and I'll deliver your buddies to you.

"See you at Camp Two or before!" he said, climbing up and spurring his mount. He loved the feeling of his horse digging in and taking off, the hundreds of pounds of bunched muscle between his legs. Of being untethered from this slow gaggle of city-bred dudes who looked on at him with dumb eyes and stupid faces.

As he rocketed through the meadow he tipped his hat at each and every client, and most of them grinned back.

He knew he looked pretty damned dashing.

Gracie had to relieve herself but was not interested in locating any far-off portable toilet so she stepped into a thick copse of pine trees to find James Knox there zipping up. He was as startled as she was.

"You don't want to go all the way up the hill either, I take it," he said. "Sorry."

"No, I'm sorry," she said. "I didn't know you were here."

He waved her concern away. He said, "When you were looking at us last night, what were you thinking?"

She was surprised how direct he was. She stammered, "I don't know. I've just never met anyone from New York City before, I guess."

Knox flashed a quick grin. "We probably disappointed you."

"Not really."

He put his hands in his jeans pockets and leaned against the trunk of a tree. He was looking at her but he seemed distracted. "It would probably surprise you to know in real life the three of us are pretty serious people. People think we're just a crew of cutups, but that's just one week a year. We're hard workers and we don't screw around. What happened with Tony and—that woman, Donna—that was unusual. I'm sorry it happened, and I know Tony is busted up about it."

She nodded. He seemed to be talking to himself as much as to her. His skin looked waxy and drawn as if it had been drained of blood. He looked older than she'd thought before.

"We've been good buddies for almost twenty years," he said. "The three of us. We all started together on the Street. We've been in each other's weddings, helped each other out. Tony was supposed to have been in the World Trade Center that morning on 9/11 to meet a client, but he didn't make it because he was hungover from my bachelor party the night before. That just goes to show you how fate works, you know? You're young, but you know about 9/11, right?"

"Yes."

He nodded. "Our wives always say be careful on these trips. They say don't do anything stupid. We tell them we don't. This kind of stuff never happened before. That's not why we go on these adventures, to screw around. Now my friends aren't here and I get this sick feeling," he said as he gestured toward his heart. "I get this sick feeling . . ."

Then it was as if he woke up. He looked at her, shook his head, and flashed his smile again. "Why am I telling you this?"

"I don't know."

"What I'm trying to say, I guess, is friends are important. You've got to stick by them, even when they screw up."

As he left the copse he reached out and patted her on the shoulder.

30

After a half hour of lone riding, Cody pulled up at a clean small stream that crossed the trail and painfully climbed down to let his horses drink. He hated depending on two animals he neither knew nor trusted, but he had no choice and his thought was to treat them well and maybe they'd reciprocate.

As both horses lowered their heads to suck up the cold water, he went a few feet upstream to fill his own bottle. He'd purchased a water filter kit, but it, like his cigarettes, had been in the duffel that burned up. Giardia contamination was the least of his worries. He thought if he got it, it would at least take his mind off no cigarettes or alcohol. To drive the point home, he drained a quarter of the icy unfiltered water and topped his Nalgene bottle and sealed it.

While the horses rested—oh, how he admired their dumb animal ability to grab a nap whenever they could—he sidled up to Gipper and withdrew the satellite phone again.

The first of Larry's messages was blunt:

"*Cody, where the hell are you? You said you'd turn your phone on. Call me back on this number as soon as you get this, partner.*"

"Partner" was said with heavy sarcasm.

Cody said, "You'd like me to do that, wouldn't you, *partner.*"

Then the second message:

"Hey, I don't know what's going on. I tried your cell and they said it wasn't a working number. Which means you turned it off—stupid move—or your phone fucked up. Either way, you need to call me as soon as you can. Things are happening here. I'm on it. I'm starting to connect the dots and it's getting real fucking interesting. Call me."

His voice was urgent and elevated. Cody fought his instincts to return the call. Larry sounded excited. Cody said, "You'd like that, wouldn't you?"

But he retrieved the third message:

"Cody, goddamn you. I know about the fire. I had a hunch and called the Gallatin Gateway when I heard about it and found out you registered there. And I talked to the Bozeman PD and Gallatin County Sheriff's Department and found out you couldn't be located but the fire started in your room. By the way, there's an APB out for you. They want you for questioning and they suspect you of arson.

"What, are you on the bottle again? Are you flushing your life down the toilet and taking me with you? I can't believe I lied. I hope you understand what I'm saying. I lied for you—again. Why am I doing this? What kind of dumb shit am I, anyway? I lie for you and you won't even call me back.

"Then I start thinking: I know you. I know how you think. You're a conspiracy-minded bastard and you probably suspect somebody fingered you. Assuming you didn't set the fire yourself by getting hammered and passing out in bed with a cig hanging out of your mouth, of course. But only you know if that's the case. And if it wasn't, you're wondering who fingered you and sent the arsonist. Right? Am I right, you jerk? Did you think it was me, the guy who is covering for you every step of the way and keeping you in the loop? You son of a bitch, I know how you think. And I'm disappointed in you to the point where I'm done with you. I'm over you. I heard you were never any good to begin with but I didn't listen. You're a half-breed white-trash asshole who doesn't know enough to trust the only friend he's got—"

Cody felt his ears go hot as the message timed out with Larry yelling at him. He staggered back until his shoulder blades thumped a tree trunk. He lowered the phone and thought about it. Usually, when someone attacked him personally—like Jenny—he agreed with them, he deserved it. But this was . . . confounding. Either Larry was the most evil manipulator he'd ever run across—and so many of the scumbags he encountered were able to justify anything they'd done with a straight face—or he'd misread completely what had happened and why.

Larry was good, Cody thought. He'd rattled him. As intended, he thought. Because nobody but another cop would think as many moves ahead.

Cody raised the satellite phone and retrieved message number four.

"Okay, you ingrate. That's the best word I can think of for you. Either that, or you forgot the sat phone and your cell and in that case you're just a fucking idiot, which seems more and more possible. I wouldn't be surprised anymore if we found you in some drunk tank in Livingston or Ennis or maybe back where you belong in Denver. I've pretty much given up on you, I want you to know that.

"But if you ever get this and actually listen to it, I want you to know something. You need to find them—the pack trip your son is on—and call in the location. I've got the Park Service and the Feds alerted. They know what I know, and that this thing is bigger and worse than either of us thought. I've almost got it dialed in. And man, you're not going to believe it. You're in the middle of a shitstorm neither one of us anticipated. It goes back to the dead alcoholics, and I'm honing in on the explanation. But I'm sure as hell not going to leave it on your fucking message mailbox. So call me. I can't say all is forgiven, but you don't know what you're getting into. It's worse than—"

The message time ran out. Cody felt the hairs stand up on the back of his scalp. He took in a long quivering breath and punched the buttons on the phone for the last message. Larry whispered.

"I don't know where you are or even if you're getting this, Cody.

But the shit has hit the fan. They know you're gone and where you are. You're fucked, and so am I. I never thought it would come to this. Call me."

There were no more messages from Larry on his satellite phone.

Cody withdrew the last cigarette from his pack and lit it and inhaled it as if it were angel's breath. Either Larry was the best actor in the world, or his messages were genuine. He leaned slightly toward the latter.

31

It had been thirty minutes since Cody thought he'd heard gunshots. Two of them, two distant heavy *booms,* far up ahead of him. If the wind had not died to a whisper a few minutes before, he thought, he might not have heard them at all.

They'd come just seconds apart. He'd reined in his gelding and cocked his head and listened further but there was silence. And slowly, with the sound of water pouring over smooth river rocks, the breeze picked back up in the treetops and returned with a whispery white noise just loud enough to swallow up any more distant sounds.

Since then, he'd questioned himself as to what he'd actually heard. The forest was full of creatures and sounds. Having grown up around hunting and guiding with his father and uncle in Montana, he'd never put any stock into the old saw, "If a tree falls in the forest and there's no one to hear it . . ." Because in his experience, nature could be raucous, sloppy, and loud. Especially in a place like Yellowstone that teemed with large-bodied ungulates and bizarre natural phenomena. Although gunshots were the most likely, the faraway sounds could have been trees falling, branches snapping, rocks being dislodged, or thunderclaps. He'd heard that big grizzlies searching for grubs to eat were known to knock over big rotten trees and uproot small ones, and moose sometimes scratched themselves so vigorously on trunks and outcroppings that they knocked them over. Plus there was the internal pounding coming from his own body.

He wished his head was clear and his guts and muscles weren't screaming for nicotine to bring them back to level. Blood that seemed thin and panicked and needy coursed through his ears and whumped at his temples, trying to burst out of his veins as if they were a ruptured hydraulic hose. His vision had restricted and he saw black curtains closing and cutting down his peripheral vision. He knew he was capable, right then, of doing just about anything for a cigarette or a shot of bourbon or both. He cursed his dependency and his weakness while at the same time justifying it to himself because of the situation he was in.

At the time that he'd heard the sounds he'd withdrawn the AR-15 from his saddle scabbard and jacked in a .223 cartridge and laid it over his pommel. He kept riding while the churned-up trail of hoofprints turned deliberately off the main trail toward a copse of trees to his right.

That's where he saw the red bandana tied to a branch and wondered why Jed McCarthy had left the trail and where he was taking his clients. And why someone had left a marker.

At times the new trail was so narrow Cody had to brace the rifle butt on his thigh with the muzzle pointed up so it wouldn't get caught in a tree branch or overgrown foliage on the sides of the trail that seemed to reach out to grasp at his arms and knees. Gipper walked deliberately and haltingly as Cody pushed forward, and he had to keep nudging and kicking him to keep moving. He knew sometimes horses could sense danger ahead, but he also knew horses were sometimes simply overly cautious and tentative. He found that his mouth had become dry as his heart raced.

The lodgepole pine trees had closed in around him. They weren't tall but they were dense and so closely packed it would be difficult for a man to walk through them without turning to the side. It had been so long since the trail had been used, long silky remnants of spiders' webs, broken by Jed's party ahead of him, fluttered like ghosts from boughs over his head. It was as if he were riding through a shroud.

He heard a grunt, and he thought: *Bear.*

Gipper heard it, too, and the horse planted his feet and leaned backwards with his heavy haunches. Gipper's ears cocked forward and his nostrils opened and he snorted either a warning or a cry of alarm. Cody brought the rifle up to his shoulder one-handed, aiming it vaguely ahead of him, keeping a hold on the reins with his left hand. The packhorse, oblivious to what was going on, walked into Gipper's hindquarters and jostled Cody's shaky aim.

There was another grunt, this time closer, and a heavy footfall. It was coming toward him, whatever it was.

Cody didn't know whether to dismount or stay in the saddle. He longed for solid footing, but knew he couldn't slip gracefully to the ground and not risk losing control of the horses. If he was on the ground and they decided to panic and run off, he was stuck. The rifle just seemed to be in the way.

There was a flash of color through the thin trunks ahead. Beige and red.

A low moan, *"Naugh."*

"Who's there?" Cody called out. His mouth was so dry his voice cracked. "Who is it? Identify yourself. I'm a cop."

A man on foot lurched into view, startling Gipper further and the gelding crow-hopped, fouling Cody's aim. As he tried to gain his balance in the saddle, he dropped the reins to the ground. The only thing that stopped Gipper from turning completely around was the wall of thin trees on both sides of the trail.

"Easy," Cody said, as much to himself as to Gipper, "Easy . . ."

The man, an African American wearing jeans, a once-beige shirt soaked almost entirely in glossy red blood, and a look of horror and anguish, cried out again and pitched forward onto his knees on the trail.

Clumsily, with both of his horses stutter-stepping, Cody dismounted and managed to gather up Gipper's reins. While he was tying his horse to the trunk of a thick aspen tree, the packhorse jerked back and the lead rope unraveled from Gipper's saddle horn. Cody reached out for it as it pulled away, missed it, and he stood seething and confused for a few seconds, watching the packhorse gallop away back down the trail. He could see chunks of dirt flying from the horse's hooves and the panniers flapping hard, spooking the horse further.

The drumbeat of the hooves and occasional snap of dry twigs faded away. Cody spat out a string of curses and kicked at the ground.

Then he turned toward the injured man.

Never in his career had Cody confronted a dying man. In nearly every case, the victim was already dead—in many cases for days—and Cody could observe with clinical detachment and dark humor. Bodies were no more than heavy wet bags of organs, muscle, tissue, fat, and bone bound together by a taut wrapping of skin. He studied those bags for likely offered evidence of what method was used to douse the flame of a soul inside.

Cody sat on the trail. He'd never cradled a stranger's head in his lap before while the man cried real tears and choked on pints of his own blood when he tried to speak.

"Jesus," Cody said, elevating the man's head by raising his own leg, trying to find a position where the victim wouldn't have to make the gargling sound. "I don't want to hurt you."

The man shook his head quickly but couldn't form words yet. He was still lucid despite appearances. But, Cody knew, he wouldn't be for long. The victim was bleeding out before his eyes and there wasn't a single thing either of them could do about it. Bull Mitchell's field first-aid kit had been in the panniers of the packhorse. But even if the horse hadn't run away, Cody wasn't sure he could have done anything to save this man's life.

He'd known the end of this story as he approached him minutes ago. There was a hole the size of a fist in the man's back, the exit wound. It was inches deep and pulsating. Cody dropped down to the trail and turned the man over. The victim had watched, his eyes clear and sharp. The entry wound was the size of a nickel and it was framed by a hole in the fabric of his shirt. The hole in the cloth, just below the breast pocket on the left side of the victim's chest, was burned black on the edges in an outline that resembled a blooming flower. The reason for the pattern was powder burns—meaning that the shot had been made practically point-blank. The weapon had been of large caliber. Cody saw no other bullet wounds but there didn't have to be any.

Cody said, "I'm not going to lie and tell you you'll be okay."

The man closed and reopened his eyes. Not out of disappointment, but a means of signaling Cody that he understood.

Cody could feel blood from the exit wound soaking into the denim of his trousers. It was warm.

"Can you hear me?" Cody said.

Again, the man blinked.

"Are you with the pack trip led by Jed McCarthy?"

Blink. *Yes.*

"Is there an older boy on the trip? Named Justin? Seventeen, eighteen?"

Yes.

"Is he okay?"

Yes.

"Man, I don't know what to do. There's no way to stop the bleeding."

Yes.

"Did you see who shot you?"

Yes.

"Can you try to talk? Can you please try to tell me what happened and who did it?"

Yes.

The man closed his eyes and swallowed painfully. Cody looked skyward for a fresh thought or a signal that would give him—and the gunshot victim—some kind of hope. Or something he could do to make this poor man more comfortable.

He felt the man die. It wasn't a sound or a movement, but a sudden absence of firmness in his lap. Cody looked down. "Not now," Cody pleaded. "Not before you tell me what happened."

The man's eyes were still open but there was nothing behind them. His mouth was slightly open and red inside, the color of candied cherries. Cody reached up and closed the eyes, pulling the lids and hoping they'd stay that way. They did.

Cody rolled the body off his legs. In death, it seemed twice as heavy as before. He stood unsteadily. His muscles ached from riding and he was covered with a man's sacred lifeblood; his jeans were black and sticky and orange half-moon-shaped pine needles stuck to the denim. He bent over and dug through the victim's clothing and found a wallet and flipped it open. André Alan Russell, resident of Manhattan. Cody remembered the name from the file he took from Jed's office.

As he'd done earlier in the day, he photographed Russell's body and wounds, knowing while he did it that the shooting had happened someplace else and this wasn't the crime scene. He wondered how far Russell had come from where he'd been shot. He dragged Russell's body off the trail. Before tucking it in beneath a massive fallen tree and covering it the best he could with heavy logs and branches, Cody looked skyward for a moment, then looted all of Russell's pockets looking for a package of cigarettes that wasn't there. Cursing, Cody then covered the body. The cover wouldn't prevent predators from finding it—probably nothing would—but he hoped he could return with help to get the body out before it was torn up.

He kept Russell's New York driver's license but cached the wallet and the contents of the man's pockets in the crook of the aspen tree he'd used to keep Gipper around.

Since Mitchell's GPS was gone and he couldn't get a reading of coordinates, Cody found a T-shirt in his saddlebag and ripped it up and tied one strip to the cover where the body was and another on a low overhanging branch at the trail to mark the location. He scribbled in his spiral notebook what he'd found and what he'd done with the body and Russell's possessions.

When he was through he stood and wiped sweat from his face and took off his hat to cool the top of his head. He could see no trace of Russell's body beneath the cover he'd put on it, but he knew it was there. And the image of Russell's last attempt to speak would be with him forever.

Back on Gipper, Cody contemplated turning around to try and retrieve the packhorse, but he feared the animal was still running and was miles away. He couldn't afford to let more time elapse between him and Justin.

He nudged his horse and Gipper reluctantly stepped back on the trail. As he walked his mount, Cody reached behind him into his saddlebag for the satellite phone. He'd thought long and hard about the situation he was in and had decided he couldn't take any more chances on his own.

Because now there were two bodies, and he had no reason to think there wouldn't be more.

He turned on the phone and watched the display screen. It was working, but there was no signal. He looked up; the tree cover was too thick. He'd need to wait until he rode into a clearing where the phone could hook up with a satellite. Clipping the phone to his belt next to the Sig Sauer, he cautiously rode on. He could smell Russell's blood on his clothing and it mixed with the odor of his own fear.

Things were happening ahead of him. He was hours and miles behind the pack trip, but closing in. He couldn't wrap his mind around the motivation for the murders but it was obvious whomever was behind it was entering a new stage. The killings leading up to the pack trip departure had been meticulously planned to resemble accidents or suicides. A good deal of thought had gone into them.

Tristan Glode's body had been well hidden. It was possible, Cody thought, the murder had taken place out of view of the others on the trip and they may not even know it had occurred. But Russell was different. He'd somehow managed to get away and he'd not been pursued, probably because the killer knew his victim would bleed out. But unlike the murders preceding Russell's, there was no indication of careful planning or execution. Russell had not been chased down and disposed of to hide the crime.

Which meant, for one reason or another, that the situation had grown desperate. Desperate men, Cody knew, were capable of anything.

As was he.

A few minutes went by and Cody checked the phone to see if he'd acquired a signal yet so he could call Larry. He looked up ahead of him and saw a pair of splayed boots that belonged to a third victim.

Gipper woofed and started to backtrack furiously.

Filtered sun shimmered on their coats and he could see at least one massive round head and the humps on their backs and the bulge of heavy muscles beneath the fur.

He'd have to fight off a feeding grizzly sow and her two cubs to identify the body.

32

With Gipper in a panic—backtracking blindly, woofing, eyes white and almond-shaped, ears pinned back—Cody jerked on the reins and tried to stay in the saddle. He knew his reaction was as out-of-control as his horse's and he wasn't helping the situation, but he didn't know what to do. The big brown grizzly sow looked up with a mouthful of red meat. The two cubs—one auburn, the other brown like his mother—scrambled back over the body and fell in behind her giant haunches, peering out at him with black eyes.

Cody managed to crank Gipper's head to the side and stop him from scrambling long enough to slide his right boot out of the stirrup and swing down to the ground with his rifle. Gipper pranced as if he was electrically charged and pinned Cody to a tree trunk, crushing the wind out of him, then crow-hopped back toward the trail. Cody slipped off the side of the horse, stunned and gasping for breath, and felt the reins being pulled away through his fingers.

Gipper was gone, crashing through the timber straight away from him, bouncing through the tight grouping of trees, leaving behind showers of broken branches and pine needles. He could hear his horse grunting and feel the hammering of his hooves on the forest floor through the soles of his boots.

Cody swung the muzzle of the AR-15 toward the body and the bears. The cubs had turned their heads away to the right, transfixed by the panicked run of the horse as it crashed through the trees. The sow, though, locked her eyes with Cody and stretched out, guarding the body with her baseball-mitt-sized paws. The long red strip of flesh swung back and forth in her jaws.

"Get away," Cody hollered, fitting the butt plate of his rifle to his shoulder, aiming down the peep sights and fitting the front sight on her arched left eyebrow. *"Get the hell away from there."*

The auburn cub switched his attention to Cody and stood up. He was only three and a half feet tall, a nascent miniature of his mother. His front paws curled down and rested almost comically on his bulging belly. Although he wanted to, he didn't look formidable except for the blood on his snout.

The brown cub mewled and shot out from behind his mother on all fours, scrambling over the body, straight toward Cody.

"Get back, little guy," Cody bellowed, stepping toward the charging cub and stomping his lead foot while fixing his sights on him. *"GET BACK!"*

The cub came within ten feet before stopping abruptly. It was a deliberate false charge, a bluff move apparently hardwired into grizzly bears that often worked, but Cody refused to run and wouldn't fire and reveal himself unless he had to. Because he knew if he harmed the cub the sow would be all over him before the ejected brass hit the ground. The .223 rounds from his rifle might slow her, but they wouldn't likely stop her.

Standoff.

He couldn't run because the grizzlies could chase him down. Even the cubs had flashing claws and teeth.

Gesturing with the rifle, he advanced several steps as aggressively as he could manage. He screamed at them and bellowed for them to leave and ended up coughing raggedly in what ended as a series of rough barks.

The brown cub wheeled and ran back to his mother. As soon as he reached her, the sow snorted and jumped back from the body, then spun and crashed away into the timber, followed inches away by the brown cub. The auburn cub remained standing on his hind legs.

"You better go, too," Cody growled.

The auburn cub seemed to suddenly realize he was alone, and he fell to all fours, yelped, and scampered into the woods.

Cody lowered the rifle, closed his eyes, and let out a long chattering breath. He looked down to see if he'd fouled himself and he was relieved to find out he hadn't. Over the next minute, he felt his heartbeat slow down. He propped the rifle against a tree trunk and rubbed his face with clammy hands, thinking that the sensation of receding adrenaline was not unlike the first stages of a hangover.

He sensed the bears had not gone far. As he approached the body he held the rifle out in front of him and swept the timber on both sides with his eyes. He could still feel his heart beating hard, and the tips of his fingers and toes ached for nicotine to stop the nerve ends from jangling.

He winced. The smell of fresh blood and exposed stomach contents was acrid. Shards of flesh were ripped from clean white bones and the pile reminded him of the aftermath of a Thanksgiving turkey.

Trying not to look at the mutilation directly, he kept his head to the side while he rolled the body over. The underside was not as torn up. In the back pocket of the trousers he found a wallet. Inside was an EasyPayXpress Unlimited MetroCard for the New York subway system, $480 in cash, assorted credit and business cards, family photos of a very large and dark-haired clan, and a New York State driver's license identifying the victim as Anthony Joseph D'Amato.

D'Amato's clothes had largely been torn away and they'd bunched beneath his back. Cody rooted through the shredded clothing and felt something crackle. It was the familiar and fantastically welcome sound of crinkling cellophane, and Cody dropped manically to his knees and ripped at the bundle with both hands.

Within a slit and blood-spattered double Ziploc bag was a crushed, half-empty pack of Marlboro Lights.

"D'Amato," Cody said, "bless you for being a secret smoker."

It was obvious one of the grizzlies had swiped the plastic bag with claws that sliced through the cigarettes to the skin below. Cody rooted through the pack, breathing in the sweet smell of powdered tobacco, and found three intact cigarettes. The longest one had a small smear of red on the side of it.

He looked at it for a second and conceded that yes, he was smoking a dead man's last bloodstained cigarettes.

He lit up and sat back and inhaled, looking around for the bears, half expecting them to come barreling out of the forest like demons to rip his throat out while his defenses were down.

And he wasn't sure it would be the worst way to go because at least it would be epic and quick.

He left the body of D'Amato on the trail until he could figure out what to do with it. He had no rope to hang it, and it would be a matter of time before the bears came back. His camera was gone with Gipper.

Cody bushwhacked through the brush in the general direction his horse had run. As he shouldered through tree trunks and stepped over downed timber while smoking his cigarette, he felt it was getting lighter. He walked toward the light and within ten minutes stepped out of the trees into a small grassy clearing.

The satellite phone had a signal. He punched the number for the cell phone Larry had said to call. Reception was clear and he heard it ring on the other end. Four, five, six rings. No voice mail prompt. Cody let it ring, figuring Larry would eventually hear it and pick up.

While he waited he slowly pivoted in the meadow so he could keep his eyes out in every direction. He held the AR-15 muzzle down in his right hand. The safety was off. There were no signs of bears, or wolves, or his horse, or whomever had killed Tristan Glode, Russell, and

D'Amato. And before them, the string of recovering alcoholics including Hank Winters.

Two minutes later, Cody was surprised when he heard a click through his earpiece. Someone was on the other end.

"Larry?" Cody said.

Breathing.

"Larry, is that you?"

No other background sound. Just rhythmic breathing. Cody checked the display on his phone to make sure he dialed the correct number. He had. A phone rang somewhere in the background. It was a familiar ring.

"Who is this? Can you hear me?"

The breathing quieted and there was silence but the line was still open. Cody recognized the action as when someone places their hand over the microphone to muffle sound.

"Speak to me," Cody said. "Say something. I'm calling on official police business. *This is an emergency.*"

After a beat, the line was disconnected.

Battling doubts and tendrils of cold fear rising up from his lower stomach, he punched in the numbers again. He did it deliberately, making sure he didn't misdial.

The recorded message said the number was no longer available.

Cody lowered his handset and stared into the sky. It hadn't been Larry, he was sure of it. And it hadn't been a stranger answering an unfamiliar phone, like if Larry had inadvertently left the phone unattended on his desk or at a restaurant.

Whomever answered kept quiet until Cody identified himself. Until Cody had spoken, revealing himself. As if he'd been waiting for the call for quite some time.

And the ring in the background—before it was muffled—was as familiar to him as the sound of his alarm clock. He knew it because it was how the obsolete phones rang in the Lewis and Clark County Sheriff's Department headquarters.

Deep in the timber, in the direction of the trail, he heard a branch snap.

Cody kept the satellite phone on and clipped it back on his belt. He squinted toward the wall of trees to the east where the sound had come from.

There was the click of steel on rock, a distinctive sound. Then the snort of a horse.

Gipper?

Wrong direction, Cody said to himself while raising the AR-15. He wished he had his gear because he very much wanted to replace the short magazine in his rifle with a thirty-rounder.

He heard the squeak of leather and another footfall. His mouth went dry.

A horse was coming. Maybe more than one. It was approaching in a deliberate manner that meant someone was in the saddle.

He lowered himself into a shooter's stance and took a deep breath.

33

As Jed approached Camp Two walking his horse behind him the conversations stopped abruptly.

"My horse went lame," he said. "I didn't get very far on him before he pulled up hurt."

"So you didn't find them?" Knox asked, distressed.

"Didn't get that far," Jed said.

"Jesus," Knox cried to the others, "is anything going to go right at some point?"

Jed knew he had to extricate himself and turn their attention to other matters. He thought, *Get out ahead of the situation and take over in the lead again.*

He was heartened that no one actually confronted him as he entered the camp. Although Dakota, Rachel Mina, and the girl Gracie seemed to view him with challenge and fear—fear was okay, challenge wasn't—none of them said a word. Which meant they were ceding control of the situation to him, at least a little. He shot a glance at the dad. Angry fathers could be a force to themselves. He hadn't expected Ted Sullivan to take him on and the man didn't.

Whatever they'd been saying about him was suddenly off-limits now that he'd shown up. It used to bother him a little when he'd overhear his clients criticizing him or the decisions he made, but it didn't anymore as long as it didn't evolve into open revolt, which it never had. Jed understood how groups worked. A bunch of strangers thrown together sought common ground, and that common ground was often the outfitter who'd brought them together. He was the common denominator among clients of different social strata and interests. So in order to converse, they'd have to find something to either celebrate or bitch about, and that usually turned out to be him, one way or another.

Jed said to everyone, "Look, folks, I know you're all worried about what's going on. It's crazy to have lost those people, and I'm damned sorry it happened. I'm also damned sorry I took off after them on a horse with a bad wheel." He gestured toward his bay.

"What I need to ask you folks," he said, "is to remain calm. Please remain calm. I can kind of tell there are all sorts of conspiracy tales flying around and all sorts of speculation. That's natural. But you're here in this fine camp with plenty of food and comfort. There's no reason to be worried about anything."

Knox stepped out from behind the kitchen setup. "Jed, I'm worried as hell about my friends. I wish I would have gone with you to find them."

He said to Knox, "I'm going back after them but I've got to switch horses. I need a better mount."

Suddenly, Rachel Mina asked, "What did you do to them?"

It felt as though a shard of glass had been shoved under his skin.

"Excuse me?" he said, still maintaining his smile.

Her eyes flashed. "I said what did you do to them? Tristan, Wilson, Drey, and Tony? Did you hurt them and leave them back there?"

Jed slowly removed his hat and stared at the inside of it. He ran his fingertips along the leather sweatband inside, as if testing for irregularities. He felt his stomach contract and it hurt a little to breathe.

All eyes were on him.

"Ma'am," he said after a beat, "I don't have any idea at all what you're talking about or what you're asking me."

From across the camp, Ted Sullivan said, "Jeez, Rachel . . ." He was aghast.

"You heard me," she said to Jed. "You're picking us off one by one. I want to know why. I want to know what your game is and what you're after. I mean, look at us. We're no threat to you—"

"Jesus, Rachel," Ted Sullivan said to her. Then to Jed, "Man, I'm really sorry. I don't know what got into her." He strode across the camp with his arms out toward her.

Sullivan said, "Rachel, really, I've never known you to jump to conclusions like this." As he approached her she turned, said, "Ted, stay away. Don't touch me."

Sullivan's two daughters watched the scene open-mouthed. Jed couldn't tell which side they were on.

"This is getting out of hand," Walt Franck said, slapping his thighs from where he sat on a log and using his hands to push himself to a standing position. "This isn't helpful in any way." He gestured toward Jed and said to Rachel, "This man has spent the best part of a day trying to track down a couple of his clients who left voluntarily in the middle of the night.

"If I can fault him for anything, it's for letting Drey and Tony take off on their own this morning to try and make things right. But given the circumstances," Walt nodded toward Donna Glode, who looked back nonplussed, "I would have probably done the same thing. But no one threw them out, or pressured them to leave. To accuse him of . . ." He couldn't say it. He shook his head as if ridding his thoughts of the unpleasant words. "It's just crazy," he said.

"He's right, Rachel," Sullivan told her. "You're not being helpful or positive. Please, let's take a breath and calm down." He grasped her by the arm and tried to spin her away, but she shrugged him off.

"She might be right," Gracie said, looking straight at her dad. Luckily, Ted Sullivan dismissed his daughter with an angry wave. The girl's face turned crimson.

Jed said bluntly to Rachel, "I ain't going to lose my temper here, lady. I know it's a stressful situation. But making accusations with no proof at all isn't helping anything."

He looked around the camp for assurance.

And he got it from everybody, he thought. The only people who wouldn't meet his gaze were Gracie and Rachel Mina. Dakota looked back, but she did so with an upward tilt of her chin and slitted eyes. Like she was making some kind of decision about him.

A beat of silence, then two. Rachel Mina was being led away by Ted Sullivan. Jed watched them go, and noticed that after they'd cleared the camp and were in the trees Sullivan tried to hug her and reason with her, but she pulled away and stomped off alone. After she left, Sullivan stood in the trees with his head down and his shoulders slumped, a sad portrait of a weak but useful man, Jed thought. In a moment, Sullivan turned on his heel and walked the opposite way from where Rachel Mina had gone. Probably to break down and cry, Jed figured.

Jed turned his attention to Dakota. "Please take this bay down to the corral and pick me out the best horse to ride and get it saddled up so I can go after our wayward boys. I've got to gather some more gear because I may be back pretty late. I'm not coming back without those strays."

"Thank you, Jed," Knox said.

Jed nodded, in his best friendly-like reaction.

He walked the bay to Dakota, who still eyed him coolly. She took the reins, as instructed. That's all he needed from her at the moment.

Gracie, Danielle, and Justin walked side by side toward the collection of tents on the grass. Justin and Danielle were holding hands, but Danielle seemed distracted and vacant.

"Those people are just making me crazy," Justin said, "They're turning on each other instead of pulling together. I wish we could all go home now."

He seemed to be waiting for agreement from Danielle, which didn't come.

Danielle said to Gracie, "I can't believe Dad acted like that. He really dissed you, didn't he?"

"Mmmm," Gracie said. "He dissed Rachel, too."

Danielle said, "I thought he might take Rachel's side and yours, too. I mean, he's our *dad*. You don't want your own dad to side with the other guy."

"Mmmm."

"I guess that's one thing," Justin said. "My dad probably would stand with me. He's like that. I guess I never really thought about it before."

"Lucky you," Gracie said.

"You know what?" Danielle said, letting go of Justin's hand and stepping in front of him next to Gracie.

Gracie said, "What?"

"I'm not sure we can trust him."

"Mmmm."

"I don't," Danielle said. "Not anymore."

Dakota led Jed's bay to the temporary electric corral. As she walked the horse the voices from the camp faded behind her. Jed was holding court; explaining to Knox, Walt, and Donna how he was going to go back down the trail and come back with Drey and Tony, at least. Saying he couldn't promise Tristan and frankly didn't care all that much about Wilson although he'd like to get all his horses back. That he'd likely be back deep into the night or early next morning at the latest. Explaining to Knox, once again, that he didn't need his help.

As Dakota turned off the electric fence charger and parted the string, she glanced up the hill toward the camp. Knox, Donna, and Walt were still there. Jed had apparently gone to his tent to retrieve gear or clothing he would need for a longer trip. Rachel and Ted were off quarreling—or avoiding each other—somewhere.

Her eyes swept the trees and the tents. The three teenagers were by themselves, walking away. No one was watching her from the camp.

She picked up her pace and practically dragged the bay along behind her. The horse limped badly but she couldn't care about that now. The grass was teeming with grasshoppers and they shot away like sparks through the air as she crossed the meadow. A plump one landed on her left breast and she brushed it away. There was a thick spruce in the middle of the makeshift corral and she led the horse behind it, so the trunk was between her and the people in the camp.

Before opening Jed's saddle panniers, she looked around again. She was in the clear.

She fumbled with the straps of the dual panniers and loosened the top flap. Stretching on the toes of her boots, she pulled the lip of the bags down and peered inside. Jed's handgun was on top. She thought she got a whiff of gunpowder.

She pushed his rain gear aside and found his briefcase on the bottom of the pannier. Grasping it by the worn handle, she pulled it up and out. Jed's rolled yellow raincoat came out with it and fell to her feet.

Using the back of the bay like the surface of a desk, she placed the briefcase on it and unsnapped the hasps. They sprung up with two solid clicks.

The manila folder she'd glimpsed the night before in their tent was on top of his other materials and she could see the corners of the printouts peeking beyond the stiff file cover.

She took a deep breath and centered the file folder and reached for the smudged tab to open it.

The white flash in front of her eyes was not another grasshopper, but the blade of a knife wielded by someone who pressed into her back, pinning her to the side of the bay. It sliced so deeply through the flesh of her throat she felt the steel scrape on bone.

34

The sounds in the trees became more pronounced; twigs cracking, the click of hooves against rock, the squeak of leather on leather, the nickering of horses. He felt more than saw the presence of heavy-bodied beings approaching en masse. Cody thought, *How many of them are there?*

He glanced down at his rifle. Likely not enough bullets. And if they were armed? He might need to pull his Sig Sauer when the rifle was empty.

Then a deep-throated shout: "Cody?" The voice carried through the trees.

Cody closed his eyes and took a deep breath and stood up. "Bull?"

"Where the hell are you?" Mitchell grumbled.

"Here. Ahead of you, I think. In a clearing."

"Gotcha," Mitchell said, "so don't shoot me. I'm coming toward your voice."

"I won't," Cody said. "Who is with you? How many of you are there?"

"Just one," Mitchell said.

Cody didn't know if that meant just Mitchell or another. Nevertheless, he could feel heavy weights release from the tops of his shoulders. "I've got to say I'm glad you came back."

"It's taking me a while," Mitchell grumbled, "seeing I've been gathering up loose horses for miles."

Cody lowered his rifle and waited. He could hear Mitchell and the horses coming, picking their way through the timber and brush, but he couldn't see them yet.

Finally, a horse head with a white star blaze on its forehead pushed through the brush. Mitchell's horse.

"There you are," Mitchell said, and Cody could see him. He was a big man but he sat the horse as if they were conjoined, and Cody had trouble discerning where the horse stopped and Bull Mitchell began.

"Damn, I'm glad to see you," Cody said. "Why'd you come back?"

"Hell, I don't know," Mitchell said. "As Hank the Cowdog says, there's a thin line between heroism and stupidity."

Cody found himself grinning at the answer. "Then you'll probably want your gun back."

"Yup."

Mitchell was leading Gipper and the packhorse that had run away. Behind them, tied with a series of lead ropes, were four more horses. The first three had empty saddles.

The last one, a gray, had a rider. Cody was surprised and instinctively raised the rifle again. A dark man, hatless, glowered back at him. So there *was* another. The man rode oddly, shifting around subtly as if he were trying to maintain his balance, as if he were simply cargo. That's when Cody noticed the man's hands were cuffed behind him and he'd been lashed by the waist and legs to the saddle with rope he'd last seen looped on Mitchell's saddle.

"Says his name is Wilson," Mitchell said. "I don't care if you shoot him because he's been nothing but trouble. But I was thinking you might want to talk with him, first."

"K. W. Wilson," Cody said, "fifty-eight, Salt Lake City. Or, as I like to call you, Suspect Number One."

Wilson didn't react. Cody noticed the contusion under Wilson's left eye and his bloody and fattened lower lip.

"Doesn't like cheese," Cody said, remembering Wilson's trip registration.

"I had to thump him a couple times," Mitchell said, patting the butt of his rifle. "He didn't want to work with me very much."

Cody thought Wilson didn't give off any indication of fear—or innocence. Like so many criminals he'd encountered in lockup over the years, Wilson's bearing was a dismissive mix of arrogance and regret. Not regret at what he'd been picked up for, but regret he'd been caught.

Cody nodded. He wondered if he was meeting the killer of Hank Winters and the others.

"I found a couple of things on him you might find interesting," Mitchell said, leaning back and digging into his saddlebag. He produced a six-inch Buck knife in a sheath and a stubby handgun. He handed them both butt-first to Cody.

Cody inspected the revolver, a snub-nosed .38 Special. It was a double-action Taurus six-shot revolver made of stainless steel with rubber grips. It had a two-inch barrel. He sniffed the muzzle and cracked open the cylinder.

"Two rounds have been fired recently," Cody said to Mitchell, who nodded.

Cody snapped the cylinder home, spun it, and pointed the gun at Wilson. Wilson didn't flinch. Cody said, "This is an odd choice of weapon to bring up here. It's not big enough for bears and hard to hit anything at a distance because of the short barrel and fixed sights. I used to carry one of these as a backup in an ankle holster in Denver, but I knew this kind of piece is strictly for self-defense and it's only good for close-in work. Meaning," he said to Mitchell without taking his eyes off Wilson, "he was right on top of D'Amato and Russell when he shot them. Probably a couple of feet away, max. They knew him well enough to get close. I doubt it was an ambush. He probably looked right into their eyes before he pulled the trigger."

He slid the gun into his belt and drew the knife out of the sheath. The blade had been wiped clean but there was dark gummy residue where the fixed blade met the brass guard. Cody dug some out with his fingernail and tasted it. "Blood," Cody said, then spat it out. To Wilson, "This is what you used on Tristan Glode, then. More close-in work."

He circled around Wilson and came up from behind him. He could sense the man start to stiffen, possibly anticipating the stab of the knife. Cody reached up and pressed the point of the blade to Wilson's spinal column just to make him jump. But what he was interested in was an intimate view of Wilson's bound hands.

"You've got blood under the fingernails of your right hand," Cody said. "Looks just like the blood on this knife. There's blood spatter on your cuff, too, it looks like."

"Oh," Mitchell said, digging something silver and square out of the front snap pocket of his shirt and flipping it through the air to Cody. "Something else. Check *this* out."

Cody fumbled the catch and reached down in the grass for the object. "I was hoping it was a pack of cigarettes," Cody said.

"Nope," Mitchell said, "Wilson's camera. You might want to take a look at some of the shots in there to see if there's anyone you recognize. While you do that I'm gonna tie these horses up and get Wilson down."

"I'll help you," Cody said, doing the math. He assumed the three riderless horses had belonged to Tristan Glode, D'Amato, and Russell.

Mitchell swung off and put his hand up to Cody. "Stay there, if you don't mind, pard. The only thing you seem to know about horses is how to lose them."

Cody shrugged. "True enough." He pushed buttons and flicked toggles on the digital camera until the display came alive. The first dozen shots were obviously from the departure area. People milled around eyeing horses, their faces mixes of excitement and anticipation as they got ready to get under way. There were vehicles in the background and glimpses of a long horse trailer with JED MCCARTHY's WILDERNESS ADVENTURES painted along the side.

As he advanced through the photos he tried to match up faces with the names and descriptions he'd memorized from the file he'd borrowed.

The cowboy with the mustache was obviously Jed himself, shadowed by a younger woman in a floppy sweat-stained hat. He recalled her name: Dakota Hill.

The older stiff couple were the Glodes. Cody recognized Tristan and winced. He'd been a regal man in bearing with striking silver hair, cool blue eyes, and a prominent chin.

The father and his two teenage daughters were the Sullivans; Ted, Danielle, and Gracie. The youngest girl appeared to be much more animated than the older girl, who looked bored.

A single woman, open face, attractive, looking away from the camera as if she was furious about being photographed by him. Rachel Mina. Her face reminded him of the glare Jenny had once given him when he photographed her as she stepped out of the shower. It was the last time he ever did anything like *that* again. Cody wondered why Suspect Number Two was so angry at Wilson.

Three men posed on their horses like the characters from the movie *Three Amigos*. The shot would have been amusing, Cody thought, if he hadn't seen D'Amato's and Russell's mangled remains a couple of hours before.

And there were Walt and Justin, sitting side by side on horseback. Cody felt his heart race. Justin looked older and more mature than when he'd seen him last. He had a weariness in his eyes and an easy smile as he looked over at Walt in the photo.

Cody whispered, *"Yes."* Until that second, he hadn't been absolutely sure Justin was on the trip.

The last three shots were taken in deep timber. Although not focused well, Cody could see they were of the two Sullivan girls. One was using a camp latrine.

He looked up as Mitchell untied Wilson from the saddle. Wilson stared straight ahead.

Mitchell said, "I found this guy about a mile from where I left you. Apparently, he'd gotten off his horse to pee and the horse ran off. I seem to be surrounded by goddamned amateurs. I heard him yelling obscenities and I sneaked into the trees. I finally found him chasing his horse around a meadow with that pistol in his hand, like the horse was gonna be threatened by him. He's as good a horseman as you."

Cody studied Wilson's face while Mitchell talked. It was inscrutable.

"I watched him for a while. His horse finally stopped trotting at the edge of the meadow and Wilson here walked right up to it from behind. He didn't know that when a horse pins its ears back and positions his butt toward you you need to get ready for a kick," Mitchell said, and chuckled.

Mitchell said, "Laid Wilson out. Caught him right in the chest. I rode out there to see if he was okay and he woke up going for his pop-gun. So I had to thump him a couple times. I took the liberty of borrowing a set of handcuffs from your gear. I hope you have a key somewhere."

"Maybe," Cody said.

Wilson reacted with a jerk of his mouth to the side when he heard that. Mitchell dismounted and tied his horse to the trunk of a tree with a lead rope. Now that he'd climbed down from his mount he looked old and he moved like a stiff old man, Cody thought. Mitchell limped down the line of horses he'd gathered to the gray. When Mitchell got the ropes untied he slid Wilson off by grasping the back of his belt and pulling. Wilson's boots thumped onto solid ground.

Mitchell said, "I'm officially turning him over to you now while I get these critters some grain and water them."

Mitchell put his big hand in the middle of Wilson's back and shoved. Wilson stumbled toward Cody but managed not to trip and fall.

Cody said to him, "Is my son okay? His name is Justin. He's seventeen."

Wilson stared back, noncommittal.

Cody studied Wilson's face for any kind of tell, but the man's eyes were black, still, and unyielding. He took it as an encouraging sign, assuming there would have been at least a flinch or glimmer of reaction if something had happened to Justin.

"So that's the way you want to play it," Cody said. He noted the twin horseshoe impressions on the front of Wilson's shirt where he'd been kicked. As Cody walked up to him he imagined Wilson's chest must be badly bruised. Although the man was two inches taller, Cody was thicker. "I heard the shots and found Russell and D'Amato," Cody said. "We located Tristan Glode's body earlier. You've left a hell of a mess."

Wilson looked back through heavy-lidded eyes.

Cody gestured toward a pedestal-like rock that jutted out of the grass. "Sit."

Wilson didn't move until Cody prodded him with the muzzle of the rifle, then he did so grudgingly. Wilson grunted and settled on the rock and looked at Cody with bored contempt.

Before speaking, Cody made sure Mitchell was out of earshot. He said to Wilson, "Do you know who I am?"

No response.

Cody felt himself smile as his demons took over. He said, "Do you know who I am?"

Wilson didn't even blink.

"Let me tell you who I am, then. I'm Cody, and I'm an alcoholic."

Wilson twitched. At last, a chord was struck.

"Thought so," Cody said, and swung the butt of the rifle into Wilson's face. He could hear the muffled snap as the man's nose broke and feel the cartilage flatten through the stock of the rifle. Wilson cried out and tumbled over backwards off the rock into the grass.

Cody bounded forward and straddled the rock and pressed the muzzle of his AR-15 into the flesh between Wilson's eyes, which had misted from the pain. Blood coursed down the sides of Wilson's face from the twin spouts of his nostrils. Cody growled, "Let me tell you who I am. I'm the scariest fucking cop you'll ever meet. My son is on that trip and you murdered the best man I ever knew. We've been finding the bodies you left behind all fucking morning. I haven't had a drink in days and I smoked my last cigarette two hours ago. All I want is an excuse to kill you five times over and piss on your remains. Do you understand me?"

Wilson's eyes were open wide. He looked bloody and scared.

Cody said, "What, you expected to hear your Miranda rights?"

He moved the muzzle a few inches to the right and fired into the ground so close to Wilson's head it creased his scalp and furrowed through his hair above the temple. The concussion was deafening in the quiet woods, and when Cody's ears stopped ringing all he could hear were Wilson's terrified curses.

"Jesus Christ, you shot me. You son of a bitch. You can't do this to me. *You're a cop.*"

Cody said, "Yada-yada-yada. Tell me something I don't know."

"Cody," Mitchell called from the timber, "everything all right?"

Cody didn't look up. "Everything's fine," he said.

He moved the muzzle back over where it belonged between Wilson's eyes, said, "Now tell me, is my son okay?"

"He was fine when I saw him last," Wilson said. Then: "You busted my nose." He pronounced the last word *node.* "And I can't hear out of my right ear." *Cadt.*

"I'm just getting started," Cody said softly. "Now what I'm going to do is ask you a series of questions. Your job is to answer each and every one of them with absolute truth and clarity. I've interviewed hundreds of dirtbags like you in my life and I know when I hear a lie. If I hear one it's the last thing you're ever going to say. Do you hear *that*?"

Wilson nodded.

"Good. Tell me why you killed Hank Winters."

"I didn't kill him, I swear."

"You're an idiot," Cody said, feeling his face get hot. "We've got bodies all over Yellowstone Park. I've got the gun you used and the knife. Now you're going to tell me you're innocent?"

"I said I didn't kill *Winters*, whoever the hell he is," Wilson hissed. "I've never heard of the guy. It wasn't me who did that. It wasn't me, I swear it."

Cody paused. "Are you going to try and tell me you didn't kill D'Amato, Russell, or Glode, too?"

"No, I ain't going to tell you that."

"But you know who killed Hank Winters?"

Wilson nodded so slightly Cody almost mistook it for a tremble.

"Do you know why?"

Another barely perceptible nod.

"So what in the hell is going on?" Cody said, pressing the muzzle and front sight against Wilson's forehead hard enough to draw blood.

35

"Is he gone?" Danielle asked Gracie.

"I think so."

They were in their tent, waiting for Jed McCarthy to leave camp. Gracie had unzipped the front flap wide enough to see. She could see the aluminum cooking station and James Knox pacing but her field of vision was blocked in back of her. The trail was beyond the camp over a rise. If Jed was indeed gone she hadn't seen him ride away. But the sounds of the adults talking was muted and random, the sounds of nervous small talk. If Jed was still there she would have heard his voice, which seemed to cut through the air like a saw.

The afternoon sun lit the nylon walls and it was hot inside and Gracie could smell the dirt and perspiration on her body and Danielle's. She couldn't remember ever going two days without a shower, much less two days outside being coated by dust, wood smoke, horse, sweat, and a new smell: fear.

"So we're agreed?" Gracie said, sitting back on her sleeping bag. "We'll gather up Dakota and Rachel and get out of here."

"Don't forget Justin," Danielle said.

"He'll want to bring Walt," Gracie said, a hint of a whine in her tone. "Walt will be the good politician and he'll probably tell everyone what we're doing and want them to come, too. Then it'll be all of us and we're back to where we started."

"With this pack of losers," Danielle said. "But as long as we go home, I don't care. And I can't just leave Justin." She'd brought a file along as well as red polish and she was methodically grooming herself finger by finger. "By the way, I saw where Dad hid the keys to the rental car. He put them by the gas cap and closed that little door. So when we get back we can drive right on out of here." Then, "Man, I want to take a shower and clean this trip off of me. Except for Justin."

Gracie put her head in her hands.

"You don't understand love," Danielle said solemnly.

"You've known him for *two days*," Gracie said.

"Like I said. You don't understand love. I hope someday you will," Danielle said, studying her nails. "But you'll need to lose the attitude."

Gracie flopped back on her sleeping bag and kept one hand over her face.

The silence went on for a while, Danielle working on her nails and Gracie sweltering and miserable. Finally, Gracie said, "What about Dad?"

"I thought you said you didn't care about him, the way he treated you."

"I said that," Gracie said, "but I was mad at him. We can't just leave him here."

"Why not?" She sounded half miffed and half bored. Danielle seemed more than amenable to let Gracie make all the profound decisions, and didn't seem to like the idea of her waffling because that required her to once again become involved in the discussion.

Gracie said, "Because he paid for this trip and everything's gone wrong. I feel sorry for him, you know? I'm not sure Rachel even likes him anymore, and that was the whole point. I mean, besides us bonding with him in the wilderness and all of that. He's going with us."

"I like Rachel," Danielle said. "She's cool. She treats us like adults. Like we matter."

"Yeah.

"Unlike Dad, I mean."

"Yeah."

"I think he doesn't know whether we're little girls or young adults, so he goes with what's most comfortable to him—meaning we're his little girls. He can't think of us as real people. That's why he doesn't believe me when I say someone is spying on us or believe you when you say you heard something happen in the dark outside the tents."

Gracie spread her fingers apart on her face so she could look at her sister with wonder. Rarely did Danielle say something that made her think.

"What?" Danielle asked, defensive.

"Nothing."

"Anyway, wouldn't it be weird if Rachel turned out to be our friend even after she dumps Dad?"

"I hadn't thought of that."

Danielle said, "That's the kind of thing I think about all the time. You know how so many of our friends say they wish their parents could get back together? Well, I never think that. I think Mom is better off without him. I think he's kind of embarrassing, to be honest. He'd rather make that idiot Jed like him than show respect for his own daughters."

Gracie sat up and shook her head at her sister. "You're talking about our dad."

Danielle shrugged. "Really, basically, he's just another dude. He's got to show me something to get me to think otherwise, and I haven't seen it."

"Danielle!"

"Hey," she said, sliding her nail file back into its plastic holder like a sword into a sheath, "that's what I feel. So why shouldn't I say it?"

"Maybe you should think rather than just feel," Gracie said. "It's possible, you know."

Danielle shrugged. "Yeah, if you're a pathetic loser, I guess."

Gracie flopped back down on her back. "This is the worst trip I've ever been on."

Danielle said, "Welcome to Hell-o-stone Park, sister. Maybe we'll see some wolves and bears and birdies and other stupid animals on the way out."

Gracie moaned.

Danielle leaned over on her and put her lips to Gracie's ear. "Now let's go find Dakota and Rachel and my boy and Dad and get the friggin' hell out of here."

They avoided the camp and skirted along the edge of the trees toward where the horses were picketed.

"We'll ask Dakota to get our horses ready," Gracie said. "I can help her. Then we'll find Rachel."

Danielle nodded.

Shadows lengthened across the open ground as the sun sank beneath the tops of the trees. The temperature dropped a quick ten degrees in the shade.

"Leaving in the dark might be a problem for us," Gracie said.

"I don't care when we leave as long as we leave," Danielle said.

"There's Rachel," Gracie said, seeing her coming up from where the horses were. Their dad wasn't with her. And something was off about the way she walked; arms crossed around her like she was hugging herself, head down. She appeared deep in thought.

"Rachel," Gracie called.

Rachel's head snapped up. Her face was drawn and white.

"What's wrong?"

Rachel took a deep breath, as if trying to gain control of herself. She said, "Oh, girls, it's horrible. I just found Dakota down there. Somebody slit her throat and killed her. It just happened. Her body . . ."

Gracie gasped and Danielle froze beside her.

"This isn't a joke, is it?" Danielle asked.

Rachel shook her head and gestured behind her. Her eyes were rimmed with red and she looked like she could collapse. "There's so much blood," she said, and opened her arms so they could see it on the front of her shirt. Rachel said, "I turned her over to see if she was still alive, but . . ." She couldn't finish again. She was trembling.

Gracie gasped and covered her mouth.

"Could it possibly have been an accident?" Gracie asked, her voice trembling.

"No."

"Did you see anyone?"

Rachel turned away, deflecting the question.

"Rachel," Gracie said, "who did you see down there?"

"She saw Jed," Danielle said. "Jed did it."

Rachel nodded her head and tears streamed down her cheeks, making them glisten in a shaft of sunlight.

"Oh my God," Gracie said, reaching out for Danielle so her legs wouldn't collapse. "She saw Jed kill Dakota."

Rachel nodded, apparently unable to speak.

"We've got to get out of here," Danielle said. "*Now.*"

Gracie watched as Rachel's horror transformed into anger. She reached out and grasped both sisters and leaned into them.

"Your dad and I were down by the horses. We heard them arguing and we hid. That's when Jed did it. And he just left her there and took his horse. He just left her there in the grass."

Danielle covered her mouth with her hand.

"Your dad asked me to get you out of here. He said he'd stay in the camp with the others and try to keep Jed under control until we're gone. Get your horses," she said. "I'm going to lead us out of here."

Gracie felt a flood of relief. Then: "What about everyone else?"

Rachel's eyes flashed. "I don't care about them and I don't know if we can trust anyone but each other anymore. It's time to take care of ourselves now. The rest can be on their own."

Gracie swallowed. "Even Dad?"

"I know," Rachel said, gripping her arm harder, "but it's what he asked me. He's going to quietly tell the others what we saw and get them to help him jump Jed and tie him up until we can get help. He doesn't want you two in the camp in case things go bad."

"Justin's coming with us," Danielle said, pulling away from Rachel and folding her arms over her breasts. "I won't leave him behind."

Rachel grimaced, but she seemed to realize she'd come up against an immovable object.

"Get him," she said. "We leave in five minutes."

Gracie and Danielle walked up the hill into the camp. They tried to not betray their anxiety or their plan. Gracie noted that Danielle was better at deception than she was, and she could only imagine how she looked so she covered her head with her hood and kept her eyes down. Jed wasn't there, and neither was her dad.

What was going on?

She followed her sister to where Justin was sitting on a rock. Danielle approached him, held out her hand, and Justin took it with a quizzical but amused look on his face. She led him away.

Walt didn't say a word.

As they led Justin back toward the horses, Gracie chanced a look over her shoulder. Donna Glode, Knox, and Walt stared at the fire, absorbed in their own thoughts.

36

From the edge of the clearing where he was resting the horses, Mitchell called, "Hey, Hoyt. When you get a minute you may want to come look what this guy has in his saddlebags."

Cody didn't ease up on the pressure he was applying with the muzzle of the rifle. He said, "In a minute, Bull."

But he noticed something pass across Wilson's bloody face.

"Christ," Wilson said. "You're Cody *Hoyt*?"

"That's right."

"Shit, I should have figured it out. I knew your uncle Jeter. We used to drink together at the Commercial Bar in Townsend."

Cody let up a bit simply because he was trying to process what Wilson said.

"You're a damned Hoyt," the man said. "A damned *Hoyt*." As if it meant something.

"Then who the hell are you?" Cody asked. "I've never heard of anyone named K. W. Wilson."

Wilson clammed up, and Cody stepped back and kicked him hard in the ribs. When the man grunted and curled away, Cody dropped on him with a knee in his back and snatched his wallet out of his jeans pocket.

The Montana auto license was in the front sleeve. "Jim Gannon," Cody said. "Shit, I know that name."

Gannon, like his uncle Jeter, was an outfitter who used to work out of Lincoln. Cody had never met him, but he'd heard stories. Gannon was a hard-drinking, hard-charging fourth-generation Montanan. He had a reputation as a poacher and a wild man, and Cody remembered hearing he'd been brought up on charges and had his outfitting license revoked and his hunting lodge shut down.

Cody said to Mitchell, "Bull, you know who we've got here?"

"Jim Gannon," Mitchell said, ambling over. "That's what I was going to show you. He's got a bunch of personal crap in his saddlebag with his name all over: 'Property of Jim Gannon.' I told you we were dealing with an outfitter. Hell, I thought he looked familiar. I guess I must have seen his picture in the paper once when they brought him up on charges."

Cody swung his rifle back over. "Why'd you register for this trip as someone named Wilson?"

Wilson/Gannon rasped, "Why d'you think?"

Cody said, "So Jed or anyone else in his office wouldn't recognize the name. It would have seemed kind of suspicious for a bent guide like yourself to pay all that money to go on a trip with dudes."

Gannon nodded, still trying to get his breath back from the kick.

"I think you should just shoot him now," Mitchell said, leaning against a tree. "He gives outfitters a bad name. I never knew him because he wasn't in the Montana Outfitters and Guides Association. Hell, he doesn't even know how to handle horses worth a damn."

"So I ask again," Cody said, "what the hell is going on?"

Gannon gathered himself and sat up with a moan. "Every inch of me hurts," he said.

"More is about to," Cody said, and shot him in the knee.

"Jesus!" Mitchell said, jumping back. "Why'd you do that?" The spent casing landed between his boots.

Cody said to Mitchell, "I've seen this particular method of inter-rogation work pretty well before." Thinking about the year before in Denver. It had certainly worked then, to a point.

Gannon howled and grabbed his mangled leg with both hands. Cody hoped he wouldn't pass out from shock before he started talk-ing. Nevertheless, took careful aim at Gannon's other knee.

"Please, no, no . . ." Gannon begged.

"Hoyt, I don't know about this," Mitchell said, shaking his head.

"Tell me why you're on this trip," Cody said to Gannon.

"We're trying to find that plane," Gannon shouted, fighting through the pain. "That goddamned plane that went down."

"What plane?" Cody asked, but as he said it he recalled something Larry had said. Something about a disabled private airplane flying south toward Yellowstone that was spotted by citizens in Bozeman but never reported missing by anyone. The incident had caused the assembling of the interagency Homeland Security search and rescue team and that was when Larry said he met Rick Doerring of the Park Service.

"That goddamned plane that went down last winter," Gannon said through clenched teeth. Black blood seeped through his fingers, which were laced around his shattered kneecap.

"What's in the plane?"

"Jesus. Money. Jesus. Drug money."

"Why go with Jed? Why didn't you just come up here on your own and go get it? Why involve all these people?"

Gannon was starting to shake. His teeth chattered. "It wasn't my fucking idea. Jesus, I'm going to bleed out and die."

"Let's hope," Cody said. "So whose idea was it? You said 'we.' "

"My partner. All my partner's idea. All of it."

Cody took a deep breath, fighting back the urge to shoot again. Mitchell hovered, shaking his head.

Cody said, "So your idea was to what? Come up here with Jed's clients and break off and find this damned plane? Use him so he could lead you here?"

Gannon nodded his head. "Yeah, that. We wanted to come on our own but with the snowpack and the flooding, this was the first time we could get to where we think the plane crashed. When we found out Jed was leading his clients where we wanted to go—and would be the first to get there anyway—we signed on. Believe me, there wasn't supposed to be all this trouble."

Cody gestured with the rifle, urging Gannon to keep talking.

"None of this other stuff—those three stupid guys back there—was supposed to happen. But that idiot Jed decided to take a different trail, and one of 'em—Glode—got mad about it. That and his wife going down with D'Amato. So he said he was going back on his own. We couldn't risk him getting back to the vehicles and telling the Park Service where we were going. What if they sent rangers after us? They might locate the plane before we did."

Cody thought the likelihood of the Park Service sending rangers to tell Jed McCarthy to get back on the established route was crazy and unlikely, but he didn't want Gannon to stop talking, so he urged him on.

"So I went with Glode. I tried to talk him into going back with the others, but he was stubborn and had a bug up his ass and he wouldn't turn around. And you know what happened. I had to stop him."

Cody took a step toward Gannon, still aiming down the sights at his other knee. "Why take out D'Amato and Russell, then?"

Gannon closed his eyes. His chin shook. "They wouldn't have found Glode or me and they might have gone all the way to the parking lot looking for us. There was a good chance they'd call the Park Service and report a couple of missing men. It was a worse situation than what happened with Glode, because at least that guy deserved it."

"So you shot them both point-blank when they found you," Cody said. "And left them to bleed out or wait for animals to find them. Thinking they'd be mauled beyond recognition if their bodies were ever found and maybe not even point to you."

Gannon rocked back on his haunches holding his knee. He said, "This whole damned thing is a clusterfuck. Everything's gone wrong."

Cody said, "So why did Jed take the other trail?"

"I don't know, I don't know . . . it's all his fault this happened."

"He didn't kill three people," Cody said, "or put my son in danger."

Gannon writhed in pain. "Worse," he said. *"Worse."* As if that somehow lessened his own guilt.

"So your partner is still with the others on the pack trip?" Cody said.

Gannon nodded, his eyes closed, his mouth contorted.

"Which one is he? Jed?"

Gannon either couldn't speak or refused to say.

"I said—"

"Damn you!" Gannon bellowed as his eyes shot open. He glared at Cody with unbridled hate. "You're a cop. I know you're playing rough and you'll think of some story to cover you later. I know you won't kill me. But I damned sure know she will."

Cody felt the hairs on his neck stand up. *"What* did you just say?"

37

Jed McCarthy was angry and anxious and almost missed the game trail he was seeking to go up the mountain. That Dakota was miffed at him was one thing. But to blatantly disregard his instruction to bring him another horse, to vanish like that leaving only his saddle on a stump, was another. And why did she take the lame horse with her? Where in the hell did she go when she should have been getting dinner ready for his clients?

So he'd gotten his own damned horse from the herd and put his saddle on it and ridden out of there.

"Women," he said, as if it were a curse word.

He wondered if she'd be there when he got back to camp. He wondered whether—hoped—Tristan Glode, Tony D'Amato, and Drey Russell had returned as well. He didn't care about Wilson, never had.

If they were all back his world would be in order again, even if Dakota had split the blanket for good. He could cope for the rest of the trip without a petulant Dakota dragging him down.

He'd make sure that future didn't have any women like Dakota in it, he thought with a crooked grin.

As he wound his way up the mountain directly west away from the trail he caught a glimpse through the trees of a J-shaped glacier on the side of a mountain face. He recognized it and nodded to himself, then reached back and undid his saddlebag to compare it against the Google map printouts in his file. The file was missing, and he bellowed, "Dakota! *You bitch!*"

He thanked God she hadn't dug deeper and found the satellite phone. He'd never even told her it existed, or that he brought it along on every pack trip just in case he got into some kind of trouble. He was afraid she'd make a casual reference to it and a client would hear her and want to use it. Pretty soon, he'd have clients lined up wanting to call home, check on their kids, call the office, and so on. He was a purist about the wilderness and about the experience he wanted to impart on his trips, and that experience had very much to do with isolation and forcing his guests to not keep in contact with home.

But this was different. This was about *him*. He punched in the number he was told not to call under any circumstances until he was done with the trip and it rang three times before it was picked up.

"What?"

"This is Jed. I've got a problem."

"I know who the hell it is. It's not a good time."

"I said I have a problem. I need your help."

"You've got more problems than you know, Jed. I've been trying to reach you for two fucking days. Don't you ever turn that thing on?"

"No," Jed said. "I told you. I don't even tell anyone I have it. If someone heard me talking on it—"

"I know, I know, you already told me, for Christ's sake. But given the circumstances, I thought you'd at least *check* it."

Jed said, "Someone took the map."

Silence.

"I said—"

"I heard you! How in the hell did that happen? Who took it?"

"Don't worry," Jed said. "I know who it is and I'll deal with her later. She works for me. Correction: *worked* for me. I don't think she's smart enough to figure out what we're even looking for. But right now I'm practically there. I can see the glacier. I need you to send me that map again as an attachment. You can do that, can't you?"

"If she's got the map she might figure it out."

Jed took a deep breath and looked up at the sky. "She won't figure it out. I'll make sure she doesn't. I'll make up a story about something—don't worry about it. Right now, I need another copy of that map. Can you send it or not?"

A long sigh. "I told you it wasn't a good time. I'm on the way somewhere now. I've got to deal with a problem of my own."

"Are you on duty?"

"Yeah. But what I'm doing is off the books."

"Can you send it to me when you get back to your office?"

"Yeah." He was distracted. "Yeah, I can do that."

"How long before I can expect it, then?"

"I don't know. Forty-five minutes at the latest. Providing there's no one around."

Jed nodded. "Okay then. Good. So what's the other problem you referred to?"

"There's a cop after you."

Jed felt his insides contract. "*What?*"

"There's a cop after you. His name is Cody Hoyt, and he's completely fucking nuts. His son is on your trip, I guess. Jed, he somehow thinks there's a connection between some murders and someone on your trip. That's why he's after you."

Jed shook his head. "I don't understand. What murders?"

"The last one happened up here a week ago. He thinks whoever killed this guy—his name was Winters—is on your pack trip. He wants to find him."

"So what are you telling me?"

"To watch out. I lost track of him two nights ago in Bozeman, but he was definitely headed your direction."

"Are you saying he's in the park?"

"I don't know. I'm going to find out. That's where I'm headed right now. I know a guy who probably knows where he is."

"He's in the park?" Jed said again.

"I told you, I don't know."

"And what do you mean he thinks there's a killer on my trip? Who in the hell is that supposed to be?" Thinking: *If anyone, it's Wilson.*

"I don't have a name. I don't even have a description. I'm not sure *he* knows."

"The boy must be Justin because he's the only boy on the trip."

"Okay."

"Why in the hell would a killer book a pack trip? This makes no sense."

"I know, I know. I'm just telling you what I know."

"Look," Jed said, trying to keep his anger at bay, "You told me you'd take care of the back end. You told me all I'd need to worry about was finding that wreckage and you'd handle your end and make sure nobody put things together. You fucking told me you'd use all your . . . influence . . . to make sure I was the only one looking for that plane."

"I know all that. You think I don't?"

"I don't know anything," Jed said, shouting into the mouthpiece, "except you assured me you'd handle your end. What the hell is going on here? Can't you control a single fucking cop?"

A long sigh. "He's gone rogue. Nobody can control this guy. Believe me, I thought I'd put him out of the picture, but somehow he got away."

Jed said, "So what do you want me to do? Do you want me to just turn around and forget everything? Do you want me to quit? Well, I can't do that because I'm here. I see the glacier. This whole trip has fallen apart and I've got clients gone and angry and I'll probably lose my business if any of 'em tells the Park Service."

"Just calm down, Jed. I'll handle my end."

"You've fucked up your end, if you ask me."

"Look, I'm here. I'm ten minutes away from his house. I've got to go inside and get some answers. I'll call you back as soon as I know where Hoyt is. And I'll send you that map and the GPS coordinates the minute I get back to the office. Just don't fucking panic."

Jed said, "You'd better make this right. The rest of my damned life depends on it."

"I will. Don't worry. Now keep your phone on."

38

At the same time, two and a half miles away, Cody and Bull Mitchell hoisted Jim Gannon up over a high branch. They'd decided based on what Gannon had told them they had to move as quickly as they could to overtake the pack trip, and bringing along the wounded Gannon and four extra horses would slow them down. Using tape and bandages from Mitchell's first-aid kit, they'd bound up Gannon's knee the best they could and tied his hands and feet together. Mitchell had fashioned a seat harness out of rope they could use to lift him.

"Give me a couple of minutes," Mitchell said, breathing hard from the labor of pulling on the rope with Cody. "I need to get these spare horses picketed so they'll be okay."

Cody nodded and unhooked the satellite phone and powered it up. He had a good clear signal and no messages. He started to key in the number for Larry's secret cell phone, thought better of it, and called Larry's ex-wife's cell. She was a real estate agent and was never without it day or night.

"Cindy Olson."

"Cindy, this is Cody Hoyt. I'm out of town and I need to reach Larry."

"Oh, it's you. The man who shot our coroner."

It seemed like ages ago, Cody thought. "Yes, well, there's a good story that goes along with that but I'll need to tell you at a better time. Right now, it's urgent I get ahold of Larry."

"Ah," she said, "you probably tried his office and his cell but he didn't pick up."

"Sort of."

"Then you probably didn't hear. I'm surprised you didn't, since you two have such a deep bromance. Larry's been suspended. You can reach him at home, I suspect. Suggest to him that he spend some of his downtime looking for work because he's got a child support payment coming up."

"Why was he suspended?"

"Guess, Cody." And she hung up.

He called Larry's house. He lived outside of Helena near Marysville on U.S. Highway 279.

"Larry," Cody said.

There was a beat. Then, "It's you, you son of a bitch. Where *are* you? Did you get my messages?"

"I got 'em."

"Then why in the hell didn't you call me back?"

Cody said, "I don't have time to explain, but in a nutshell I got paranoid. I didn't want you to know where I was because of that fire in Bozeman."

"What are you saying?" Larry sounded hurt. "You thought I had something to do with that? Is that what you're saying?"

"I don't know what I was thinking," Cody lied. "Blame it on the DTs. I'm fucking miserable, but we got the bad guy. Or at least one of them."

"Who is it? And who the hell is 'we'?"

Cody outlined hiring Mitchell, and the trail of bodies leading them to Gannon. "He's here now," Cody said. "We hung him up in a tree so the bears and wolves won't eat him. The Park Service can cut him down and take him to a clinic. Not that I really care about that, but we'll need his testimony to nail his partner, who is also on the pack trip."

"His partner?" Larry sounded genuinely baffled. That made Cody feel better toward him.

"A woman."

"Ah, Rachel Mina," Larry said. Cody leaned into the phone, shocked Larry knew the name. "Although that's not her married name, which is Rachel Chavez."

"How do you know that?" Cody asked.

"You dumb shit, it was what I was trying to tell you when I called. I didn't know about Gannon, but I did know about Rachel Mina Chavez. It's called police work, and I think I connected all the dots. Of course, that's before they suspended me for withholding what I knew about *you*."

Cody felt his head begin to spin. "Tell me what you know," he said.

Larry sighed. Cody could anticipate from that sound Larry was going to roll it out in the only way he could. He glanced up to see if Mitchell was still taking care of the horses and saw he was. And Jim Gannon swung slowly in a circle over his head, passed out. The late evening sun made a long shadow across the meadow of Gannon's figure, and in silhouette it looked like the outfitter was hanging from the tree by the neck.

"We were looking at the wrong angle with those murders," Larry said. "At least I was. All I could think of was alcoholics. So how do we get a connection between all these alkies in four different parts of the country? The thing I was trying to figure out was if it were possible they were all in the same place at the same time, like we talked about. Like an ex-alcoholic convention or something. And if not that, something to do with their jobs. But their professions didn't lend that any hope. They might all travel from time to time, but not to the same places or for the same reasons. I couldn't figure out how to put them in the same place at the same time, or to have something in common to link them besides drinking. To all be exposed somehow to whatever would later cause them to be murdered."

Cody said, "You've got to get to it, Larry. We need to get going."

"I know, I know. But do you remember when you told me Winters said no matter what, you can find a meeting?"

"Yeah."

"So I got together with the brains at ViCAP and they were able to access his travel records. Winters flew exclusively on Delta out of Helena, so it wasn't difficult. Man, that guy was all over the west but nothing jumped out at us. But one of the FBI boys thought to pull the records from Shulze as well, thinking if we could cross-reference just one flight or destination between them—put the two of them in the same place at the same time—we'd have something to go on."

Cody started to pace back and forth through the grass. Adrenalin rushed through him.

Larry said, "October 27 of last year, both Winters and Shulze were on the same flight bound for L.A. They probably didn't even know the other was on the plane. Shulze was going to some academic conference at UCLA and Winters was connecting through LAX to Sacramento. But here's where it gets interesting: the flight didn't make it to LAX for two days because it got diverted to San Diego."

"Diverted?" Cody asked. "Why?"

"Wild fires," Larry said. "October 27 last year was the worst of the fires out there. They closed LAX for two days because of the smoke, and all the inbound flights were diverted to other airports. Winters and Shulze found themselves in San Diego October 27 and 28 with nothing to do.

"So we kept digging. William Geraghty was diverted to San Diego on a United flight for the same two days, and Karen Anthony was there visiting her sister."

Larry said, "So imagine the situation. Four alkies away from home. Three killing time at the airport hanging out, just waiting for an announcement so they could get back on their schedules, surrounded by airport lounges and bars and high tension all around. Karen Anthony is there with family, but keeps getting those old urges. So in that circumstance, where would they go?"

Cody said, "To an AA meeting."

"Bingo," Larry said. "So I find a detective in San Diego and run this theory by him and he buys it. So he starts doing the research and calls me back within an hour. An hour! And he tells me the specific AA meeting they all went to at a church. He even says he has photos of them going into and coming out of the meeting. He sends them to me and goddamn it if he isn't exactly right. I've got entrance and exit photos of Hank Winters, William Geraghty, Gary Shulze, and Karen Anthony."

"Hold it," Cody said. "Since when do the police run surveillance on who goes to AA?"

"Never," Larry said. "Unless they've got heavy surveillance going on somebody else who happened to go to the meeting. Like Luis Chavez, the now deceased head of the Chavez drug cartel based out of Tijuana. Seems he saw the light like all of these folks and would cross the border once a week to attend the AA meeting."

"Chavez," Cody repeated.

"Rachel Mina's ex-husband."

"I'm getting lost," Cody said, pacing faster.

Larry said, "It's no secret the cartels are at war. We know that. But what this San Diego cop tells me suddenly clears things up. Seems Chavez had a daughter named Gabriella who was a junior at the University of Colorado in Boulder. Gabriella was apparently the apple of his eye. She was from his first marriage, before he married Rachel Mina. The cartel fighting Chavez sent some guys north to kidnap Gabriella from the house Chavez had bought for her, and held her for ransom. They wanted Chavez to give them Tijuana and pay them millions in exchange for her. They knew he'd do anything—*anything*—

to get her back. Apparently there was bad blood between Rachel and this girl, but that didn't matter to Chavez. So Chavez literally cashed out. We're talking *tens of millions* of dollars here, Cody. They agreed on a drop location in our country on neutral ground. The speculation was they took Gabriella to Jackson Hole, but nobody can confirm it. But that's where Chavez's plane was headed when it apparently had engine trouble and never made it. So the bad guys assumed they'd been stiffed. They didn't believe Chavez's claims that the plane went down with their money inside, and it was beside the point because whatever happened they wouldn't get the loot. So those bastards took Gabriella with them to Laredo, Texas."

Cody felt his scalp crawl. He said, "Now I remember what happened to her."

"That's right," Larry said. "They murdered her and beheaded the body. After that, from what my San Diego guy said, it took just days for the bad guys to move in on Chavez's territory and take over. There was a bloodbath involving his holdouts, and Rachel wanted to fight, but Chavez was a broken man and let it all happen. When he started showing up at the meetings in San Diego the cops thought he was planning his comeback or something, but they didn't know at the time he'd lost his will to live or fight. But that's why they were watching the meetings. And shortly after that meeting," Larry said, "Chavez was found with a bullet in his brain down in Mexico."

Cody's head was spinning with all the information when suddenly it clicked. "Chavez told the story in the AA meeting," Cody said. "He told it to Geraghty, Shulze, Anthony, and Hank. He was confessing his sins, preparing to kill himself or be killed. But because everything that's said in those meetings is confidential and a lot of the time it's pure bullshit, nobody told."

Larry said, "But Rachel never knew that, and she wanted her money back and didn't want anyone else getting bright ideas. The San Diego detective said the Chavez cartel owned enough Mexican cops who were privy to what the San Diego cops were doing that they probably had copies of the photos. So Rachel knew who was in the meeting and who she had to shut up. By the way, Rachel was suspected of being involved in her husband's death, but the Mexican police never arrested her before she vanished. Now we know what she's been doing."

"Jesus," Cody said, glancing up at Gannon, slowly turning in the rope harness. "So she traveled across the country to find everyone who'd been at that meeting. She wanted them all out of the picture before she came here. She must have contacted Gannon thinking: he's an outfitter from Montana, he'd know his way around the park, where the plane with the money crashed."

Larry said, "Gannon probably came pretty cheap."

Cody said, "But how could an airplane crash in a national park and nobody know about it?"

"It's simpler than you think," Larry said. "You know about all the reports we get about aircraft taking off and landing on private strips. Those drug guys disable the tracking beacons and they don't exactly file flight plans. The plane might not even have been registered. If it was flying north to south to Jackson instead of the other way, it wouldn't have attracted any undue attention. And the big thing is no one reported it missing. Our task force was assembled because a couple old folks thought they saw a plane that didn't look healthy flying toward Yellowstone. If it crashed somewhere close to where you are there sure as hell wasn't anyone around to see it come down."

Cody nodded. "So the only people who knew what was in the plane or where it likely crashed were Chavez's inside guys. Not even the bad guys knew where the plane was coming from. Rachel got her info from her husband's inner circle, but she had no way of getting here on her own. Except for Jed McCarthy's pack trip."

Bull Mitchell mounted his horse and signaled to Cody. He was ready to go. Cody waved a *just a second* wave.

"This Rachel," Cody said. "She must be a hell of a looker or a hell of a charmer."

"Both," Larry said. "A stone-cold manipulator with an ice cube for a heart."

Cody said, "She managed to get acquainted with all the victims. I wonder if she played her Rachel Chavez card on them? Maybe she called Hank and said, 'You met my husband in San Diego. He thought you were a wonderful man and he wanted me to give something to you for maintaining his confidence.' Knowing Hank and the importance he placed in mentoring and trust, he'd buy it. Especially coming from a woman."

"That's what I figured, too," Larry said. "She used their bond of confidentiality against them. Shulze and Geraghty, for example, never even told their wives who they were meeting. And she cleaned up her tracks by burning down the homes she killed them and took things like AA coins—anything that would prevent us from connecting the dots."

Cody paused. Gannon's shadow now stretched all the way across the meadow into the bank of trees. He said, "You said you called the Feds. So they're on their way?"

"Should be. I haven't talked to them since this morning, when I got suspended. I didn't tell them about you because I didn't know where the hell you were. I kind of thought you might be in a drunk tank in Ennis, so they don't know you're there."

"I'll watch for helicopters," Cody said. "I haven't seen anyone but killers and dead bodies all day."

"I'd be surprised if they show up tonight," Larry said. "I can't see them trying to find you guys or the pack trip in the dark."

"Shit."

"Yeah."

"I'm going to kill her, Larry."

"Don't tell me that."

"She's dead," Cody said. "She just doesn't know it yet. For what she did to Hank and the others, for putting Justin in this situation, she's going to die."

"Ah, man . . ."

He glanced up. "We've got Gannon for testimony. We don't need her to make the case."

"Cuff her," Larry said. "Bring her in. Hell, I want to meet this dame and look into her eyes. I want to see for myself what's there."

Cody walked toward his horse. Mitchell was clearly getting impatient. Cody said, "Larry, one more thing. I called that cell number you gave me earlier today. Somebody picked up but wouldn't say anything. What was that about?"

A long pause. "Shit, Cody, I don't know. When did you call?"

"Around ten."

"That's when I was in Tubman's office getting my skin peeled off for not telling him you'd left Helena."

"Where was the phone?"

"In my briefcase. Next to my desk. Oh shit," Larry said.

"Somebody answered your phone," Cody said. "Somebody listened to me. Somehow they know I'm here."

"I can't imagine who . . ." Larry said. Then: "Hold on a second. Somebody's banging on my door. I'll be right back."

Cody said, "Somebody's been tracking me, Larry. Someone tried to burn me alive on the way here."

He realized Larry had stepped away.

Cody heard the receiver thunk on Larry's kitchen table. He heard a greeting, a shout, and a gunshot. Then someone picked up the phone. Cody heard breathing. Like before.

"Larry?" Cody asked.

The connection ended.

39

Gracie asked Rachel, "How did you and my dad meet?" She couldn't get him, or what Rachel had told them, out of her mind.

They were riding down the trail Jed had taken, following his hoof-prints. Rachel, Gracie, Danielle, and Justin. They'd left the camp under Rachel's direction, and they'd moved quickly and quietly. Rachel made a quick trip to her tent to retrieve a backpack that was now lashed to the skirt of her saddle and hung low like there was something heavy in it.

The last moments of the evening sun reached through the trees and lit the snowcapped peaks of the eastern mountains, fusing them with a good-bye wink of neon orange and pink. Gracie had barely had enough time to retrieve her hoodie before they left and she was glad she had. It seemed cooler than it had the night before and she was grateful for the warmth from Strawberry between her thighs.

"I said—"

"I heard you," Rachel replied. There was a cool businesslike edge to her voice, and Gracie recoiled.

"Probably the wrong time to ask," Gracie said. "I'm sorry."

Rachel rode ahead, her face set into the mask Gracie had seen earlier. Gracie thought, *She's distracted. She's leading three teenagers through the back of beyond and she's unsure she can do it. She's distracted.*

"It seems awful to just leave him like that," Gracie said, as much to herself as to Rachel.

"It's what he wanted. Would you rather go back?" Rachel said with the same edge in her voice as before. "You can go back there if you want to. I told you what happened."

"No," Gracie said softly.

"I just had a human being die in my arms," Rachel said, not looking over her shoulder at Gracie or trying to soften her tone. "And I saw the man who did it."

Gracie felt sick.

"We've got to find help," Rachel said. "We've got to get out of here."

From behind, Justin said, "Excuse me, Miss Mina?"

Rachel jerked around in the saddle and looked past Gracie to Justin. "Yes?"

"I'm wondering why we're on this trail? If we're headed back to the trailhead this is the wrong direction, I'm pretty sure."

"It's the trail we're taking," Rachel said.

"I don't get it," Justin said, undeterred. "Seems like we're going the wrong way."

Gracie looked ahead for the first time at the trail itself. It was unmarked except for a single set of horse tracks. She was confused.

"What's going on?" Danielle asked from behind them.

"Nothing," Rachel said sharply. "Just please keep quiet, all of you."

Danielle rode up beside Gracie and leaned in to her. "I've been thinking," she said.

Gracie refrained from expressing surprise.

"Remember when we got to the airport in Bozeman? Dad wasn't there."

"I remember."

"Where do you suppose he was?"

Gracie shrugged. "I don't know."

"I don't know either. But he's the one who made such a big deal out of this trip. Knowing him, he should have been there three hours early pacing around and getting all worried about us."

Gracie nodded. "That does sound more like him."

"There's been something going on since the beginning," Danielle said. "He's been up to something. And why wasn't he in camp like he was supposed to be?"

"There has to be an explanation," Gracie said, unsure of her own words.

"Tell me when you come up with one," Danielle said, and slipped back into line.

Ten minutes later, Rachel said, "Here he goes," and turned her horse from the trail onto a faint game route that went west into the trees. She looked back to make sure everyone was with her. Gracie refused to meet her eyes and kept her head down. She couldn't stop thinking of what Rachel said she saw, and the fuel Danielle had added to the fire.

"This way," Rachel said, spurring her horse onto the new trail.

"Now I'm sure we're headed the wrong way," Justin said.

Gracie watched Rachel carefully. How her chest swelled with a big intake of breath, how her mouth was set, how her eyes looked like slits because the skin on her face was pulled back tight. She turned her head and glared at Justin and seemed to be holding back her words.

"Stay in line," Rachel said to Justin. "And stop talking. I'm trying to save us all."

"It just doesn't make sense to me," Justin said. "I mean, we want to go back to the vehicles and we're heading up into the trees on the side of a mountain. I just don't get it."

"No," Rachel Mina said, "you don't."

"Danielle?" Justin said.

"Don't ask me," Danielle said.

Gracie wondered exactly who was leading them and who Rachel

had become. She felt sick to her stomach and wished she'd talked to her father and at least said good-bye.

And as she watched Rachel ride ahead, she noticed the bulge on her right calf where the top of her boot was. Something pushed out against the fabric of her jeans. Gracie leaned over to her left to confirm Rachel's left calf didn't look like that. It was as if something was protruding out of Rachel's boot top. Like a stick.

Or, Gracie thought with sudden realization, like the handle of a knife.

"I met your father in Minneapolis," Rachel said to Gracie. The tone of her voice was warm, like it had been until recently. Like she was trying to reestablish their friendship. "I was there on business and I was staying at the Grand Hotel. My laptop was acting up and I was frustrated I couldn't get it to work so I went down to the bar. He was at the hotel meeting a client, he said. I told him about my computer and he offered to take a look at it. I brought it down to the bar and he fiddled with it and had it working again in no time flat. Then we started talking."

Gracie said nothing. She felt uncomfortable thinking of her dad in any situation where she wasn't with them. She knew he was a man, and he likely had wants and needs. But she was sorry she'd asked Rachel the question in the first place, and wasn't sure she wanted to hear the answer. And she didn't want to set her off again.

Rachel said, "I told him I'd lost my husband recently as well as my stepdaughter. He said he was divorced but he had two daughters he was devoted to. That's when I first heard about you and Danielle and how much you meant to him. I was touched."

"That's nice," Gracie mumbled.

"Then he told me about you two and this trip. He was so excited and passionate that I just fell for him. We kept in touch and he suggested I come along so I could meet you two. So he could introduce us. I'd always wanted to see Yellowstone Park and he seemed to have it all organized and planned, so I came along. I had no idea . . ." Her sentence trailed off.

Gracie said, "Rachel, he wasn't in the camp back there. Jed was gone and Dad wasn't there."

Rachel nodded in a sympathetic way. Then: "It must be hard to think of your father as a coward," Rachel said. "I can't even imagine what's going through your head right now, so tell me. Maybe I can help."

Gracie didn't want to answer. Something about the way Rachel was asking, in such an intimate way, put her off. The swing from warm to cold back to warm made Gracie feel unbalanced, as if the ground beneath her feet was buckling. Finally, Gracie said, "I don't know what I think."

"That's understandable," Rachel said. "It's the worst when someone you love does something beyond comprehension. It's as if you never knew that person at all. As if your entire life together was based on a set of false assumptions. When it happens, it's like everything you ever thought or knew turns out to be based on clouds and lies. You start to wonder, am I the fool here? Am I the gullible idiot who let a *man* ruin me because he was weak and tainted? It's just so hard when it happens, and it eats at the very marrow of your soul until you either give in or decide to get out there and make your own way. You need to take back what you deserve, what belongs to you."

Gracie said, "I don't understand what you're saying."

Rachel shot a puzzled look at Gracie over her shoulder, then shook her head and shrugged. Gracie got the impression Rachel had said things she didn't mean to say.

"Never mind me," Rachel said. "Sometimes I just get going. You know how it is."

No, Gracie thought. She looked again at the backpack Rachel had strapped to her saddle. Something heavy in it. And Gracie thought about the fact that she hadn't seen Dakota's body. No one had, except Rachel. Just like she hadn't seen her father. She took it on Rachel's word he was there with her when they saw Jed murder Dakota.

As she rode she found herself looking hard at Rachel in a different light. Justin was wrong. There might be good in everybody, but there could also be evil.

Gracie continued to stare while her stomach knotted. There was a bulge next to Rachel's calf that could be the handle of a long knife. Rachel said Dakota had her throat cut.

Gracie couldn't help herself. She lurched to the left and got sick, emptying her stomach on the grass.

Rachel looked back with suspicion masquerading as concern, and said, "Are you okay, darling? Is this whole thing getting to you, poor girl?"

Dusk gave way to darkness.

40

Jed McCarthy dug his headlamp out of his jacket and strapped it on the crown of his cowboy hat. He wasn't ready to turn it on yet because there was still enough light to see, but that wouldn't last much longer.

Even after years of wilderness pack trips, he was still slightly awed by twilight in the mountains when for a short period of time a natural transition unfolded as the wind stopped and the hidden animals became still and quiet and the nocturnal predators began to stir awake. It was immensely quiet and he could hear each footfall of his horse and his own nervous breathing.

Ahead of him, when the trees parted, he could see the massive J shape of the glacier in the bald side of the mountain. The glacier glowed light blue in the afterlight and it looked clean and pure and it seemed to beckon him.

His horse labored up the trail, climbing with a rocking motion. Jed sat forward in the saddle, urging him on. They continued to rise, switching back on sharp corners, but always going up. The pitch of the mountainside was getting so sharp he could reach out and touch the wall to his right at times. As it got darker he prayed the trail was passable and had not been blocked over the winter by rockslides or deadfall.

Finally, the sky opened up and although it wasn't pitch-dark yet he could see the sudsy wash of stars in the cloudless sky. The full moon was rising and would soon take over the sky and keep the mountain illuminated.

His senses were on full alert. He was looking for anomalies. He noted a smudge of pale color in the shadowed branches of a pine tree and it caught his attention because it was out of place. He rode over and leaned and reached deep into the needles to retrieve it. It had some heft but was pliable and he pulled it out. A perfect little bird's nest. Empty. The materials used to build it seemed unnatural, a blending of paper and fabric. He shook it and noted how spongy it was.

Birds and mice made nests of whatever material was available. It seemed to Jed much too far from anywhere for the birds to use man-made fabric, but there it was. What had they found?

He dropped the nest to the ground and rode on.

He was almost unaware of it at first, the dusting of snow on the ground in his peripheral vision. It was scattered and mixed in with the mat of pine needles.

Then he thought, *Snow?* In July?

He looked up. It wasn't snowing, and it certainly wasn't cold enough. Could it have snowed earlier in the day?

"This makes no sense," he mumbled to himself while he pushed his horse farther, up the trail and finally to the top and he emerged on a long flat bench of rock.

He reined to a stop to take it all in. The glacier loomed above him like a dimly lit billboard. The bench was solid rock but puckered in places where shallow pools of water gathered from recent rains. Straight ahead of him, toward the face of the mountain, full-grown pine trees that had found purchase in cracks of the rock were knocked down. He could see where they'd been snapped off because the jagged trunks stood like a line of fence poles.

Snow was everywhere on the ground but it wasn't cold, and he dismounted. His boots thumped on the solid rock, and he led his horse to the side where the snow was thickest, where it was caught in short grass.

He clicked on his headlamp and squatted down. The headlamp pointed wherever he looked, and he reached out to touch the snow.

Scraps of paper. Thousands of them. None bigger than a square inch. It was the same material that had been used to construct the bird's nest. He grasped the largest scrap he could find and lifted it into the pool of light. A pair of hooded and wise eyes stared back from the scrap. He recognized the eyes, and said, "Ben Franklin."

He stood, still holding the scrap between his thumb and forefinger. With his other hand, he reached up and twisted the lens of his head-lamp to make the beam sharper.

At the far end of the bench, beyond the sheared-off trees, looking like the last glimpse of a whale sounding off the coast, the V-shaped tail of the airplane stuck straight up out of a crevice where it had fallen after crashing the winter before.

41

"What is that out there in that field?" Mitchell grumbled. "An elk? It's almost gettin' too dark to see."

Cody looked up and squinted. Ahead of them, to the left of the trail in a moon-splashed clearing, was a horizontal dark form elevated above the grass. The form had been still as they approached but now it moved a few feet to the right. The figure was hard to make out because it was dark against a green-black wall of pine trees.

"Damn if it isn't another stray horse," Mitchell said. The string was behind him. "But it looks like there's something on it."

Cody held his satellite phone up to his ear and was talking with Edna at dispatch in Helena. He was glad she was on duty and he'd ignored her pleas to tell her where he was and what had happened since she'd seen him last. When she took a breath, he said, "Edna, send a car up to Larry's house in Marysville. I was talking to him ten minutes ago and I got cut off. I think something happened to him."

She repeated, "Something happened to him? What?"

"I don't know. But I've called back four times since and he won't pick up. Edna, send whoever you can as fast as you can and warn them there may be someone else in Larry's house. Tell them to nail the guy and hold him. Go!"

"Cody—"

"*Go!*" Cody barked, and punched off.

Mitchell and Cody rode up to the stray horse. Mitchell said, "Be calm, Hoyt. Don't rush it or charge it or you'll make it panic and run away. Don't bark out *Go!* anymore."

Cody hung slightly back and let Mitchell walk his gelding to the horse.

There *was* something on its back. Cody's first thought was it was a roll of carpet or a set of slim panniers the way it hung over on both sides of the horse. He could see the horse didn't have a halter or bridle.

"Easy now," Mitchell cooed to the horse.

It was a bay and it took a few unsteady steps forward as Mitchell approached. Cody said, "He's lame."

"Yup," Mitchell said, slipping off his mount and walking patiently toward the bay. With a movement as quick as it was gentle, he slipped a rope over the bay's neck to keep it in place. The horse seemed docile but Cody could see white on the edges of its eyes. It wouldn't take much to set it off.

"Oh, no," Mitchell said with what sounded like genuine sadness. "We've got a woman this time."

With that, he turned the bay and walked it a few steps into the moonlight.

Her body was draped over the back of the horse facedown. Long brown hair hung limply, obscuring her face and ears. Her hands had been tied under the belly of the bay to her boots to keep the body secure.

Cody gritted his teeth, and said, "Shit."

"Look at this," Mitchell said, pointing to a thin gash on the bay's haunch that glistened with fresh blood. "They tied the body on and gave the horse a prod to get it running away."

Mitchell looked up. "Do you know who she is?"

"I think so."

"Want to make sure?"

Cody tried to swallow, but couldn't. He nodded.

Mitchell gently grasped her hair with one hand and cupped her chin in the other and lifted her face up into the light.

Cody could see the gaping wound across her throat and he tasted bile in his mouth.

"Her name was Dakota Hill," Cody said, his voice dry. "And we're going to go find who killed her before there's no one left."

They approached the camp cautiously, even though Cody's inclination was to storm it like Vikings. He could see a fire going, but only four people around it. Justin wasn't one of them. Rachel Mina and Jed were gone as well.

There were four adults huddling around the fire. The firelight on their faces made them look gaunt and shell-shocked.

Mitchell had agreed to stay back in the trees to cover him with his hunting rifle as Cody walked his horse up. He kept looking for others in the camp. After all, there were nine tents pitched neatly in a meadow to the north of the camp. No one seemed to be in them.

Cody had his rifle out and across the pommel as he rode up. He was locked and loaded. He'd checked his .40 to make sure there was one in the chamber with a full twelve-rounds in the magazine.

Before they even knew he was there, before anyone looked up to see a strange rider approaching from the dark, Cody could feel a palpable sense of doom from the people sitting around the fire. Like they'd given in, defeated.

He recognized Walt immediately. His Richness sat there with his hands hung between his knees, his head down. The skeletal woman must be Donna Glode. The younger, slim man who looked out of place had to be James Knox. And the nervous man, the one who sat by the others but didn't seem to be with them, must be Ted Sullivan.

Cody said, "Everybody stay where they are, I'm a cop."

Walt said, "Cody? Is that you?"

"Yeah, Walt. Where the hell is my son?"

Walt gathered himself to his feet and swallowed. "He's gone, Cody. I don't know where."

"Jesus," Cody hissed, "what do you mean you don't know?"

Donna Glode looked up from the fire. "Four more horses are missing. We think Justin is with the two Sullivan girls and Rachel Mina. They sneaked out of here without a word to anyone."

Cody turned to Ted Sullivan: "Where are your girls?"

"I don't know," Sullivan said, standing with closed fists, "but I want to find them. I'm coming with you."

Cody snorted. "Can you ride?"

"Not really."

"Cody," Mitchell said as he approached from the shadows, "I hate to break it to you like this, but you can't ride worth a damn either."

Cody said to Mitchell, "You'll stay here with these three?"

Mitchell nodded.

Cody said to Walt, "Do you want to come, too?"

Walt sighed and looked away. "I'll stay," he said softly.

Cody shook his head, disgusted. To Ted Sullivan, Cody said, "Come on, then."

42

Gracie noticed how Rachel Mina's shoulders tensed as she spurred her horse from the trail up into the open. Then Strawberry nickered and a horse up ahead nickered back. Rachel didn't turn around in her saddle but Gracie saw the woman's hand move back and untie the string bow on the top of the pack she'd retrieved from her tent.

Gracie was beside herself. She had nothing but speculation to go on but with every foot they rode higher up the trail she became more convinced that everything they'd believed an hour before back at Camp Two was a fantasy. She hurt deeply and wanted to cry out for her dad and for herself.

But there was little she could do. Rachel rode ahead on the trail and both Danielle and Justin were behind Gracie. The steep wall of the mountain hemmed her in on her right and the ground dropped off to the left. She couldn't turn and run, or even turn to talk to her sister to convey her fears. It was getting dark and cold. She had no weapon.

Rachel's horse stepped up and over a solid lip of granite and Gracie could hear hoofbeats clatter on solid rock. In a moment Strawberry was on top as well. Danielle and Justin were right behind her.

Rachel had reined to a stop next to a riderless horse tied to the trunk of a tree. She turned in her saddle and whispered, "I'm going to protect you. Do you understand?"

Justin said, "Protect us? All I see is Jed's horse."

Rachel ignored him. "Everybody get off. We're going to walk the rest of the way. I need you all to keep completely silent, and I mean that."

Gracie looked to the others. Danielle looked miffed. She hated to be told what to do, especially if it involved silence. Justin was confused, and he scowled at the older woman.

Reading the same reaction Gracie had seen, Rachel reached back into the open pack and came out with a large handgun. She waved it toward them.

"Get off," she said. "Now."

"Where'd you get that?" Justin asked, swinging off his horse. "I thought nobody was supposed to—"

"Justin," Danielle said sharply, cutting him off. She slid off her horse as well.

Gracie felt fear grip her insides and seem to clamp her legs to Strawberry. She wasn't sure she could move.

"You too," Rachel said to her. "*Especially* you."

Gracie found the will somewhere and stiffly climbed down.

"Listen," Rachel said to them, dismounting herself. "I don't want you to be alarmed. I brought this for self-protection and I'm glad I did."

She moved closer to them as she talked so she wouldn't have to raise her voice. Gracie noticed Rachel kept the revolver down by her side, but not exactly pointed away from them. And she also noticed that when Rachel climbed down from her horse her pant leg had ridden up and the knobby end of the knife handle in her boot was now out in the open. Gracie shot a glance at her sister and Justin to see if they'd picked up on the same thing. They hadn't.

"Look," Rachel said, leaning closer. "That's Jed's horse but obviously he isn't here. I don't know where he is but we can't be too cautious. We need to walk along here until we can find him. I hope nothing's happened to him or anyone else is up here. But," she said, gesturing toward the gun, "I want to be ready if there are any surprises."

Justin and Danielle nodded. They probably didn't fully grasp what Rachel was saying, Gracie thought, because Rachel made no sense. But she'd said it urgently and with gravity and it had worked on them.

Gracie said, "This isn't about getting out of here, is it?"

Rachel looked over at her with icy contempt. She said, "We can talk later, Gracie. Right now I need you to stay with me here and keep quiet. Do you understand?"

"She does," Danielle said, and elbowed Gracie in the back.

"Good," Rachel said, giving Gracie another glance for good measure. "Follow me."

Gracie couldn't really feel her legs, although they seemed to move okay. She led Strawberry through the darkness behind Rachel, followed by the others. *Protect them from whom?* she thought.

She scarcely registered the snowlike substance gathered wherever there were tufts of grass.

But when she looked up over Rachel's shoulder she saw a shaft of yellow light flash across the tops of the trees to the right, then to the left. The effect reminded her of Hollywood floodlights coursing through the sky from the ground. Then she heard a muffled thump and clank up ahead.

She was about to speak when Rachel snapped on her headlamp and illuminated the white metal tail of the airplane.

An airplane?

"What the hell is *that*?" Justin said.

"Shhhh," Rachel cautioned him, holding a finger to his lips. Then, whispering, "All of you come up beside me. Bring your horses. Stand by me on both sides."

Gracie hesitated. What were they doing?

"Come on," Rachel said, heat in her voice. She was addressing Gracie directly.

Reluctantly, Gracie walked up and stopped on Rachel's right. Danielle and Justin stood abreast on Rachel's left. All of their horses milled and sighed behind them. The thumping and banging continued from the opening of the crevice, out of view.

Rachel raised her pistol toward the tail of the plane, and called, "Jed, you can come out now."

The sounds stopped.

"Jed," Rachel said, "we're here. We know what you've found. You need to come out now."

Gracie held her breath. The night was still except for the gentle shuffling of the horses behind them, nosing along the rock surface for blades of grass.

Suddenly, Jed McCarthy's hat appeared above the rim of the crevice, followed by his face. Rachel's headlamp light lit his features. His brow was furrowed in confusion and his mouth, as always, was hidden by his heavy mustache. He had a headlamp on as well, and the beam bobbed from Justin across to Gracie. That's what she'd seen, Gracie thought, the beam of Jed's headlamp escaping from within the crevice as he moved around down there.

"You found it," Rachel said, "but it's still my money. Now, Jed, we need to see your hands. Pull your hands out and put them out in front of you on the rock."

Then Gracie realized what Rachel had done. She'd gathered them around her in case Jed came out shooting. Not only would Jed think he was outnumbered, but a bad shot would kill a kid. They were standing, unaware hostages, she thought. And she knew at that moment every suspicion she'd had toward Rachel was true.

Jed said, "Yours?" But he pulled his hands out and put them on the rock. He had nothing in them, but the backs of his knuckles were smudged with dirt or soot.

Rachel said, "Mine. I guess I should be surprised someone else was after it, but I'm not."

Jed raised one of his hands to shadow his eyes from the glare of

Rachel's headlamp. He said, "I see you got Justin and Danielle with you. Gracie, too. What, are they part of your *gang*?" When he said the word he grinned. He shook his head and said, "That goddamned Dakota. She just can't keep her mouth shut, can she?"

Gracie thought there must be something wrong with him. Rachel held a gun on him and he was making jokes? Then she realized Jed assumed Dakota had not only told them about the printouts she'd found, but that he thought she was still alive.

Which meant . . .

"Look," Jed said, chinning behind him toward the hidden fuselage of the plane, "I've been down there and it ain't pretty. The pilot and copilot are long dead. They're suspended from their seatbelts and the scavengers have been working on them for months. Worse," he said, looking directly at either the muzzle of the gun or Rachel's eyes or both, "the birds and mice have shredded whatever money is left. I haven't been able to find a single bill that isn't chewed up. That isn't to say maybe if I keep digging I might find a bundle of cash somewhere the rodents haven't chewed through, but I've been at this twenty minutes and I'm discouraged as hell."

Gracie glanced over at Rachel. Her face was frozen into a porcelain mask of rage. Her lips looked almost blue. Her voice was tight and threatening when she said, *"I don't believe you."*

43

Cody spurred his horse wildly up the mountainside on the well-trod trail in the dark. He felt out of control because he was; he'd lost his balance once and slipped down the side of Gipper and nearly tumbled to the ground under his hooves but managed to pull himself upright. A few minutes after, he'd been swept out of the saddle backwards by riding under a low-hanging branch he couldn't see in the dark. Cody's shoulders and back ached where he'd hit the ground and the branch left a gash across his nose that oozed blood. He felt his ear burning where he'd been injured and realized he'd probably left the scab from it back on the branch. Ted Sullivan had done no better, and he'd fallen straight off the back of his horse and said he was pretty sure his tailbone was broken.

Cody relied on his horse to find the rest of the herd up ahead. That, and there was nowhere to go but up.

It was full dark in the trees now except for the perfectly blue-white orb of the full moon that winked down through openings. Cody was astonished how bright it was in the clearings now that the moon was up, and how the stars lit the ground as well, like an upside-down city illuminating overhead clouds. Without electric lights around for dozens of miles, the forest was capable of lighting itself, he thought. *Who knew?*

He was starting to question himself if they were on the right path when he saw a gold splash of light up ahead on the side of a tree. The top of the J-shaped glacier came into view and Cody heard a sharp voice, then another.

Cody pulled to a stop on Gipper and Sullivan's horse slammed into him and both horses crow-hopped away from each other. He held on to the saddle horn and kept his head down but heard Sullivan fall heavily behind him with a grunt. Gipper calmed down, and he looked back, making sure Sullivan's horse was in its proper place and not crowding him again. "Horses, Jesus," Cody said under his breath. "They're worse than kids."

When he dismounted after clearing his rifle from the sheath, he heard rather than saw the thundering of Sullivan's horse running away back down the mountain. Sullivan lay in a heap, writhing. Cody tied off Gipper to a tree trunk and crab-walked up the last twenty feet of the trail before it leveled. As he neared the top the voices got louder.

Painfully, he straightened his legs and rose up until he could see over the lip of the flat rocky bench. Horses blocked his view, but between their legs he could see four people standing side by side with their backs to him. Beyond them was the tail of an airplane and Jed McCarthy's hands waving around in a beam of light as he talked. He appeared to be mostly underground, with only his head and shoulders visible. The dented white metal of the tail stood out in bizarre juxtaposition to the rock and trees that overwhelmed the area, but Cody instantly could see why it hadn't been spotted from the air.

Justin was there. He recognized him because his son towered over the others. Justin held hands with a girl with long dark hair. He could tell by their rigid grip that the situation they were in was tense. A woman he couldn't yet identify but guessed was Rachel Mina was next to them pointing a handgun toward the aircraft. Next to Mina/Chavez on her right was a slim younger girl shifting her weight nervously from foot to foot.

Cody spun and ducked back down and jogged down the trail to

where Sullivan was. The man had managed to sit up and rest his back against a trunk. His face was contorted with pain.

Cody leaned in to him and whispered, "They're up above. All of them. I'm not sure what's going on yet, but I need you to stay here and not make a sound."

"Are my daughters there?"

"I'm pretty sure. There are two girls, but I can't see their faces. But it looks right. My son's there, too."

"Don't let anyone hurt them."

Cody reached out and squeezed Sullivan's shoulder. He noticed how the man was positioned by, in effect, holding his buttocks in the air by digging in his bootheels and flexing his legs to avoid contact between his tailbone and the ground.

"Must hurt," Cody said.

Sullivan nodded frantically.

"Don't yell," Cody said, and left him there. "Let me do my work here."

Jed tried to stifle the grin that pulled on the sides of his mouth. Rachel Mina didn't respond. In fact, the glint in her eyes and the set of her face said *trouble*.

He ignored the teenagers even though he wasn't sure why they were there. They didn't seem to know what was going on, the way their eyes shot back and forth from Rachel to him as if watching a tennis volley. Still, he felt responsible for them. They were his clients.

"Rachel," Jed said, "there's been a big misunderstanding, obviously. We can work this out. A couple of nights ago Dakota handed me some printouts she said she found in Wilson's tent, but she must have been in the wrong damned tent. She must have been in *your* tent.

"I got curious as hell and wanted to see what he was looking for, so I rode up here tonight. How could I know there was a plane crash, or what was in the plane? Come on."

Gracie thought, *He's lying.*

Dakota had said Jed had some kind of scheme going. This was it.

Jed had fed them a story to convince them all to take an alternate route that would get him closer to the location.

He'd left Camp Two to try and find his missing clients, he'd said. So why was he up here on the side of a mountain, at least a mile off the trail?

She stole a look at Rachel Mina. She didn't buy it, either.

So why did he keep smiling?

Cody's sight lines were blocked by the horses and he couldn't get a bead on Mina. He could clearly see her forearm and hand gripping the pistol, but the heavy front shoulders of a horse blocked the rest of her. Shooting guns out of hands was reserved for old Western movies. He needed a bigger and better target.

Feeling his way, he shinnied along the lip to his right. As he did so he got brief vignettes of Justin, Mina, and the girls through the horses' legs, like viewing a set piece through the blades of a slowly spinning fan. He could see Jed clearly now, lit up in Mina's headlamp. Jed seemed surprisingly relaxed, smiling even. Cody had a thought: were Jed and Mina in it together? Was this a falling out among conspirators?

But when he got a quick glimpse at Rachel Mina's face and posture, he concluded it didn't matter. The woman was cold as ice, and determined.

Jed said, "You need to let me crawl on up out of here, Rachel. I've got one foot on a ledge of the crevice and the other on a piece of metal. Either one might give the way I'm balancing myself. If you want, you can come over here and shine your light down this hole. You'll see what I saw: dead guys, and a whole shitload of shredded cash. Below that, it drops down farther than hell. I couldn't even see the bottom of this crevice, even before it got full dark."

Mina didn't budge. He couldn't tell what she was thinking. He was getting tired of looking straight into the wide O of the muzzle of her revolver.

Finally, he said, "Rachel, there's something you've got to know because this is getting old. When Dakota went to the wrong tent the other night she found that gun. Here, let me show you something. Don't worry, I'm not armed."

He slipped his right hand along the rock and cautiously dropped it down out of view, never taking his eyes off her. Wondering if she'd pull the trigger before he could show her.

Gracie braced for an explosion while Jed took one of his hands out of view. The man, she thought, was incredibly brave or foolish. Or he knew something no one else did.

Then she thought she heard something—a grunt or moan—from back beyond the horses and broken trees where the trail came up to the rock ledge. Had someone followed them?

She looked at Rachel out of the corner of her eye to see if she'd heard it as well. If she had, Gracie concluded, she showed no reaction. Gracie guessed Rachel was so focused on Jed and what he was doing she'd blocked everything else out.

Cody wanted to holler to Ted Sullivan to get the hell back. The man had crawled up the trail and was at the lip, peering across the rock toward the scene. He'd grunted in pain as he hefted himself to see.

Cody tried to get Sullivan's attention by waving at him. But Sullivan couldn't or wouldn't look over.

Instead, Cody turned his attention to the plane. One of the horses had shifted slightly to the left and he could see the side of Mina's face clearly. The background was good; the teenagers were to the sides and wouldn't be hit by an exiting bullet or a possible miss.

Cody lowered himself to the rock and pulled the rifle butt to his shoulder and leaned in to the peep sight. Forty yards. An easy shot if his sight lines were clear.

The side of Rachel Mina's face filled the tiny metal ring hole of the back peep sight. He noted her high cheekbones and attractive profile, her smooth skin, the glint of her eye.

His insides churned. He'd never in his life pointed a gun at a woman, much less shot one in the face. The realization and revulsion came out of nowhere.

Jed brought his hand back up as slowly as he dropped it. His eyebrows were arched in a way that suggested he was about to reveal a magic trick. He could sense Mina's trepidation, he thought, and feel it from the others. Not that he was worried.

He laid his fist out on the rock knuckles down and opened his hand. Six bronze-colored .357 Magnum bullets winked in the light of their headlamps. Jed said, "Dakota took these, also."

Gracie turned for Rachel's reaction, hoping it was over.

Rachel shook her head at Jed. She said, "You must think I'm stupid. You have no idea what I've had to do to get here. You actually thought I'd bring only six bullets?"

Jed's mouth opened and Rachel shot him between the eyes. The bark of the gun was sharp and Gracie saw the big tongue of flame. Jed's head jerked back, his hat flew off, and he dropped out of view.

Despite the ringing in her ears, she could hear Jed's body dropping down the crevice, smashing on the sides of the walls, until it landed with a thump several seconds later.

"Girls! Run!" Ted Sullivan bellowed.

Cody cursed and tried to keep track of the sudden activity through his sights.

Justin and Danielle let go of their horses and bolted for the far wall of trees. Mina spun on her heels with her smoking pistol in firing position. The horses, startled by the gunshot and the yelling, backpedaled away from them, then joined together and ran the opposite way from

Justin and Danielle, crossing Cody's view and blocking everything out for a moment as they passed by. The horses plunged over the lip of rock to Cody's right a few feet away and crashed down through the timber.

And when they were gone Cody saw that Mina had grasped the younger girl around her throat and held her in front of her like a shield. The gun was pressed against the girl's temple.

The girl, Gracie, was terrified. But she was taller than Cody thought, and blocked most of Mina's body. When he peered down his sights he could see Mina's flashing eyes, but barely over the top of Gracie's head. He couldn't take the shot and regretted he hadn't fired moments before.

"It's my dad," Gracie said to Rachel, her voice altered by the pressure across her throat. "Don't hurt him, please."

"That's up to him," Rachel said. Then to her dad, "Ted, turn the fuck around and walk back down that trail or you'll get your girls killed. Is that what you want?"

From the darkness, Gracie heard her dad say with a choke in his voice, "No, Rachel."

Rachel said, "Are you here alone? Is anyone with you?"

Cody thought, *That son of a bitch will say the wrong thing.*

He prayed for Mina to shift her position. To move. Even if she'd turn to the right a little he might be able to see the back of her head and put one there.

Thinking, *If only I'd fired earlier . . .*

Gracie said again, "Don't hurt him, please, Rachel. He does his best."

Rachel snorted bitterly. "And we both know that isn't much, don't we?" Then lowering her voice, she said to Gracie, "I don't want to hurt him. I don't want to ever see his face again, but I don't want to hurt him. And I don't want to hurt you. But I want what's mine, and I want to get out of here with it. My life is in that plane. I'm not leaving without it."

Gracie didn't think it was wise to mention Jed said all the money was shredded.

"Ted," Rachel called out, "you never answered me. Is anyone else with you?"

Suddenly, Gracie realized someone *was*. Because although her dad could never communicate well, he'd never *lied*. He wasn't capable of telling a lie, even now. He was probably beside himself, she thought, trying to figure out what he could say. And the fact that he'd said nothing meant yes, someone else was out there.

"Ted?"

Gracie glanced down. Rachel stood with her legs braced behind her. She could see the top of the knife handle poking out of Rachel's right boot.

The pressure of the muzzle eased slightly on her temple as Rachel yelled for Ted to answer her. Gracie took that moment to slump back and let her legs buckle, as if she'd suddenly passed out from the tension. She felt herself slide down Rachel's body. Rachel braced herself and reset her grip on Gracie's neck, but in the moment she did so Gracie felt the muzzle of the gun lift up and away.

She touched the handle of the knife with her fingertips then closed her hand around it and drew it out fast. Before Rachel realized what was happening, Gracie jerked the knife out and away from her, then back as hard as she could in a chopping motion, plunging it nearly to the hilt in Rachel's right thigh.

The whimper that came from Rachel was wholly unexpected and a sound Gracie would never be able to forget. But the pressure on her neck eased and she was able to pull herself away and tumble to the rock.

Cody shot Rachel Mina in the heart twice with a furious double-tap. The woman was likely dead before she hit the ground.

———

Gracie saw the cloud of bright red mist balloon from the back of Rachel's jacket, and felt the heavy gun drop on her leg. She heard the dull crack of Rachel's head as it slammed down against the rock as she fell.

Cody was up and scrambling. He approached Mina's body with his sights set on her head, hoping he wouldn't need to pull the trigger again. He was struck by how small she looked now, like a broken doll. Rivulets of blood streamed from her body and filled cracks in the rock like a spring flash flood hitting the plains.

Gracie was sitting up covering her mouth with her hands.

He said, "You all right?"

She nodded.

"Damn, that was brave what you did," he said. "Gutsy as hell, Grace."

"It's Gracie."

"Gutsy as hell, Gracie."

She nodded and he liked that she knew she'd been tough.

Gracie nodded toward Mina's body. "She's just so . . . *dead.*"

"That's how it goes," he said. Then to the others, "You can all come out now." He almost said, *Even you, Ted, you stupid moronic son of a bitch who just about got your daughter killed.* But he didn't.

Cody looked up to see two figures coming out of the woods. One of them had a flashlight.

"Justin?"

"It's me."

His son shined his flashlight beam up so his face was illuminated. Although the shadows should have looked monsterlike, Cody saw a huge smile and an expression he could only think of as awed.

And for the first time in at least ten years, Justin walked straight up to him and threw his arms around him. Justin said, "My God, Dad. I just knew you'd come. As soon as things went bad, I knew you'd be here."

Cody said, "You *did*?"

"I had faith in you," Justin said.

Stunned, Cody said, "Hell, I didn't."

"I did," Justin said, squeezing harder. "I can't believe you. I just can't frigging believe you."

Cody grunted but hugged him back for a moment.

Gracie ran to her dad, Danielle behind her. He was crying with joy, tears on his face. She helped him walk up over the lip of rock, and wrapped her arms around his waist.

"Careful," he said, sobbing, "I think I broke my tailbone."

"Jeez, Dad," Danielle said, and Gracie could almost feel her sister rolling her eyes in the dark.

Cody said to Justin, "Can you build a fire?"

Justin stepped away. His face was still lit with wonder, and he shook his head as if trying to wrap his mind around what had just happened. Cody felt the same way as his adrenaline crash started to take hold. He noticed his hands were trembling.

"Yeah, I can make a fire. We've had a lot of practice the last couple of days."

Cody nodded. "Then please gather some wood. Maybe you can get your girlfriend to help you."

"Her name's Danielle," Justin said. "I don't know if she's my girlfriend."

"Can she help gather wood?"

"I guess."

"Good enough," Cody said. "I'm going to make a couple of calls and get us out of here."

An hour later, Cody peered down the crevice. The beam of his Maglite wouldn't reach the bottom where Jed's body had ended up. He could

BACK OF BEYOND   359

see bits of clothing and blood on the walls where Jed's body had pin-
balled his way down.

From what he could discern, Jed had been telling the truth. The
fuselage of the airplane had been ripped open by the trees and peeled
back like the lid of a soup can. One wing had come off and likely
fallen to the bottom and the other was mangled and parallel to the
crack in the opening.

Two partially clothed skeletons hung from the cockpit by seat re-
straints. Inside the plane, Cody could see mounds of shredded money
as well as a few skittering field mice. It was possible, he thought, there
could be some intact bundles of cash buried deep or even down on the
floor of the crevice. That would be for the investigators to determine.

He heard a bass thumping in the night sky and turned around. Justin and Danielle had built a massive bonfire that crackled and lit up
the rock walls and the trees and threw off so much light the stars had
retreated into urban mode. Ted Sullivan lay across two downed logs,
suspending his injured tailbone.

Cody said, "Helicopters coming."

In the distance he could see approaching lights in the sky. Two sets
of them. He hoped the pilot of one of them would see the fire from
Camp Two and swoop down for the others, as he'd instructed the dispatcher.

He hadn't noticed Gracie approach him until he looked down. She
was a slip of a girl.

"I want to thank you," she said.

He nodded.

"Justin's really proud."

"That means a lot. Your dad should be proud of *you.*"

"Yeah." She shrugged.

"Don't be too hard on him," Cody said. "He came up here even
though he couldn't ride. He obviously cares about you and your sister."

Gracie nodded, looking over at her father on the downed trees. "He does, in his way," she said. "I feel bad that Danielle and I thought he'd run. Rachel pretty much convinced us. You see, he told us why he showed up late at the airport to get us. It turns out he was late because he was booking a weekend at a spa for us in Billings when we were done with this trip. He'd arrived the day before to meet Rachel and he wanted us to feel all girly again when we went back home. And the reason he wasn't in the camp was because he was feeling sick and resting in his tent. He had no idea Rachel told us that story."

Cody had nothing to say.

"Rachel had me completely fooled," Gracie said.

"She fooled a lot of people."

"Even though she's dead and I wanted her to be, I feel kind of bad. Jed, too."

Cody squeezed her on the shoulder. "You should feel that way," he said. "It's the difference between you and them."

She nodded, not sure.

"I hope you don't mind if I smoke," he said, digging the last of D'Amato's cigarettes out of his breast pocket.

She looked up, said, "Justin said you'd quit."

"Nope," he said, lighting and inhaling as deeply as he could without falling back into the crevice.

Epilogue

MONTANA

Three days later, Cody Hoyt slumped in the uncomfortable chair across from Sheriff Tub Tubman's desk, but Tubman wasn't there yet. Undersheriff Cliff Bodean perched as he usually did on the corner of Tubman's desk, looking down at him. Cody had brought a small briefcase with him filled with statements and his files and another object and had placed it near his feet.

"He said be here at eleven to discuss my situation," Cody said. "So I'm here."

"I don't know where he is," Bodean said, shooting a cuff to look at his watch. He gestured toward the credenza in back of the sheriff's chair. "His hat is here."

"Goddamn it," Cody said, standing with difficulty and walking around the desk to turn the hat crown-down, "the man doesn't *listen*."

Cody sat back down in the chair and moaned. It seemed like every inch of his body still hurt. The gash on his face across his nose was stitched closed and there was a fresh bandage on his ear. His body was a mass of bruises. His knees still hurt from riding the horses.

"Frankly," Bodean said, "I'm surprised he's taking you back."

Cody snorted in response.

"The coroner is likely to use it as a campaign issue against him,"

Bodean said, shaking his head. "You're coming out pretty damned good on this. I don't know how you do it. Larry used to joke about you having illicit photos of him. Is that the case?"

Cody looked up and grimaced. "I'll never tell."

Bodean looked at his watch again. Then: "I hear there have never been as many Feds in Yellowstone for an investigation before. They're practically tripping over each other. They've got FBI, DEA, Park Service, Homeland Security, not to mention detectives from Minnesota, Utah, California, Wyoming, and our state guys. You must have given a lot of statements."

Cody grunted.

Bodean said, "I read your initial one. I noticed you didn't say anything about being suspended while you were there."

"It wasn't relevant."

Bodean raised his eyebrows. "Oh really?"

Cody said, "I could have told them, I guess. But then I'd have to tell them the reason I was there was because I was freelancing on a murder investigation prohibited by my superiors. How do you think that would play in the press?"

Bodean didn't respond.

Cody said, "I've got requests from *USA Today, The New York Times, The Wall Street Journal,* AP, and five cable news shows. I haven't called any of them back. Would you like me to amend my statement before I call them so they know why I was in the park on my own?"

"You can be such an asshole," Bodean said.

Cody shrugged.

"Following up on your statement," Bodean said, "are the other survivors back home?"

"Far as I know. Bull Mitchell is back with his daughter and his wife in Bozeman. I guess he's quite the local celebrity. I owe him a lot of money but he's graciously set up a long-term payment plan. Knox is doing a lot of interviews for the New York press. I've seen a couple of them. As you can imagine, it's quite a story there. Donna Glode isn't talking. Walt went home with his tail between his legs."

"What about the Sullivan family?"

Cody nodded. "They're okay. My son Justin is constantly texting the older daughter. They're scheming something but I don't know what. I plan to keep in touch with the younger one, Gracie. She's a smart little lady." When he said her name he smiled. He couldn't help it.

Cody said, "They found Gannon where we hung him up. He's singing like a bird, from what I understand. Telling the Feds everything he knows. Pieces are falling into place."

"Speaking of," Bodean said, "I understand he's accusing you of torturing him. Of shooting him in the ear and the knee to get him to talk."

Cody shook his head. "That guy. I shot in self-defense. You can check it out with Bull Mitchell. He'll corroborate my story."

Bodean smiled bitterly. "I don't know how you keep getting away with it."

"I chalk it up to clean living," Cody said. "Mind if I smoke?"

Bodean looked at the ceiling tile and took a deep breath.

Cody withdrew a packet of cigarettes from his jacket and tapped one out and lit it. He tossed the spent match on the little placard on Tubman's desk that said NO SMOKING.

Bodean said, "So you say the Feds are putting it all together, connecting the dots. I assume you mean they're getting evidence linking up Mina, Gannon, Jed, and maybe an outside accomplice working with Mina."

Cody studied Bodean's face, letting him go on, but saying nothing.

"That Rachel Mina or Chavez, or whatever," Bodean whistled, "she must have been something. I read all of Larry's files, the stuff he got from the San Diego PD and DEA. He traced her all over the country, to every one of those murders. She operated completely under the radar. I saw photos of her. She was a looker, but not a knockout. She must have been something," he repeated. "A stone-cold killer who looks like the cute girl next door."

"She knew she had to get to Yellowstone," Cody said. "When she met that poor schmuck Ted Sullivan she planted the seed. Of course, he accommodated her. She knew a single woman on a trip like that would draw suspicion, so Ted was her cover."

Bodean nodded. "So as far as you're concerned, she was working with Wilson—I mean Gannon—and no one else?"

He seemed to be prying, Cody thought. He refused to play.

"When's the funeral?" Cody asked.

"Larry?"

"Who the hell else?"

"Tomorrow. I'm surprised you didn't get the e-mail. Wear your Class A's." That was department-speak for dress blues.

"I didn't get the e-mail because I was giving statement after statement in the park," Cody said, annoyed, "and I was still officially suspended, remember? I didn't have fucking *access* to my e-mails."

"Oh, yeah."

Cody felt like standing up and decking him, but he fought back his rage.

"As soon as we've buried Larry," Bodean said, "we're ramping up our effort on going after his killer. Everything gets shoved aside. Finding the bastard who did it is Job One."

"It's about time," Cody said, gripping the arm of the chair so hard he was surprised he didn't leave dents in the wood.

"Jesus," Bodean said, looking at his watch again. "Where the hell is the sheriff?"

Cody shrugged. Then he changed the subject. "Larry always used to lay things out for me in the most methodical way. It used to drive me crazy, but he wouldn't let me rush him. He told me things his way, which was deliberate as all hell and very linear. I used to beg him to get to the bottom line but he'd never get there until he was good and ready after he had the storyline laid out."

Bodean looked puzzled. "So?"

"So pretend I'm Larry," Cody said, "and listen. You might want to sit down until the sheriff gets here. This won't be as good as if Larry were telling it, but I'll do my best."

Bodean started to object, but bit his lip. His eyes showed concern. But he moved around the desk and sat in Tubman's chair and leaned forward holding his hands together, fingers loosely laced.

"The assumption here with the Feds," Cody said, "is it's all connected, as you said. Mina, Gannon, Jed, maybe even Dakota Hill. And given that assumption, there's the assumption Mina's net spread farther out, that she had an accomplice on the outside. Whoever it was tried to burn me alive at Gallatin Gateway and was more successful with Larry. And that suspect is still out there."

Bodean broke in: "I'm confident the Feds will find him with all the cooperation they've got. They can do a nationwide investigation. We're limited to the county—"

"I know all that, Bodean," Cody said impatiently. "Now please shut up and listen. We're doing this Larry's way."

Bodean took a deep breath and held it, then leaned forward. "Go ahead," he said.

"Okay. Things started to go bad for me in Townsend when I left here. I got pulled over by the local cop and spent the night there, putting me a day behind I'll never get back. Who knows how many lives might have been saved if I'd been able to get into Yellowstone and break up the pack trip before they left? I will always be haunted by that.

"It seemed odd to be picked up like I was," he said. "I thought at the time the local cop might have received a tip of some kind, likely anonymous, to watch for my car. That's when I first got the inkling maybe Larry was playing a double game with me. That for some reason—maybe for my own damned good—Larry wanted to slow me down. Save me from doing something stupid."

Bodean nodded for him to continue.

"After that fire in my room in the hotel, I was even more sure it was

Larry. It could have been the perfect death. Whoever did it knew me pretty well. Out of control, suspended, drunk alcoholic, disabled smoke alarm, smoking in bed. It would have been a slam-dunk accidental death. But for some reason I saw the fire and got out in time. No one saw who did it, and I never really thought it was Larry but maybe someone he sent."

Cody noted the small beads of perspiration forming on Bodean's upper lip. It wasn't warm in the office.

"I realized in Bozeman someone was tracking my cell, so I smashed it. Of course, not just anybody can get the phone company to track a cell phone. Only law enforcement can do that, so again, it pointed to Larry—the only guy who knew where the hell I was or why I was going. I've since confirmed that the phone company had a request to track my cell phone and the request came from this office."

Bodean's voice cracked when he said, "That son of a bitch."

Cody raised his eyebrows this time. "Yeah, that Larry," he said with sarcasm. Then: "Later, in the park, I turned on my phone. There were five messages from Larry on it. I listened to them. They're still on the phone, by the way. I could tell from what he was saying and his tone he was working on something big, that he'd found something huge. Now, if his intent was to steer me away from the pack trip, why would he keep investigating? Unless, of course, he was trying to completely mislead me. But that didn't jibe with his tone. He was excited, and angry with me. He wanted to help me. Larry was my partner. I believed him.

"So I called back," Cody said. "Someone picked up his cell phone from the briefcase sitting next to his desk. Larry said it wasn't him because he was getting reamed out by the sheriff at the time right here in this chair. But you know what? He didn't mention anyone else being in the room. And knowing Larry, he wouldn't have left a detail like that out, because Larry didn't leave out details.

"So someone heard my voice and knew I was alive and probably in the park. Any idea who that might have been?"

Bodean's gaze was hard and steady. "It could have been anyone who picked up that phone. You're on thin ice, Hoyt."

Cody conceded that. "But it wasn't just anyone, I don't think, because what would just anyone have learned from my call? Only that I was calling Larry. Nothing else. Supposedly at that time no one knew about my trip south, or the fire."

"I'm confused," Bodean said.

"Sure you are," Cody said. "So whoever picked up Larry's phone knew that I was trying to reach him. And they knew if I was trying to reach him Larry would tell me what he'd discovered. That he'd spoken to the San Diego PD and so on. If someone was involved in the whole mess in Yellowstone, that wouldn't be a good thing.

"I'm guessing Sheriff Tubman didn't decide to suspend Larry on his own. I'm guessing maybe his undersheriff convinced him Larry was going rogue and withholding information about me, as well as what he was learning in his unauthorized investigation. It went right by me when Larry told me you became unhinged when you found out our investigation was pointing toward Yellowstone Park and Jed McCarthy's outfit."

Cody noticed Bodean's hands were now two fists on the desk.

"When I gave my statement to the Park Service, I met Larry's buddy Rick Doerring. Rick confirmed that Jed McCarthy had been around doing some kind of concession business when the interagency team assembled in Mammoth about that report of the disabled plane. Rick said the rumor mill was really cranking along, as usual. Then I remembered something Larry said to me in passing, and I'd almost completely forgotten about it."

"What?" Bodean said.

"The sheriff sent *two* members of the department down to Yellowstone. Larry and you."

Bodean swallowed hard but said nothing.

Cody said, "That's where you met Jed McCarthy for the first time and learned about his pack trips. I'm sure Jed told you all about them because he was a yapper. I'm sure he told you all about his big Back of Beyond itinerary, since that was his pride and joy, not to mention his cash cow.

"But that isn't the only task force Undersheriff Cliff Bodean belongs to, is it?" Cody asked. "You're also our official liaison to the DEA. So later, after you got back from the park and everyone forgot about the airplane since no one reported it missing, you heard the rumors and read the reports about the Chavez cartel and the kidnapping. You put the dates of the kidnapping and the plane disappearance together and found they were days apart. There was a rumor the exchange was to have taken place in Jackson Hole, but it never did. So you got out a map and drew a line between Bozeman, where the plane was last seen, and Jackson, where the plane was supposed to land. I did it myself last night. That line goes straight through the Thorofare country of Yellowstone. Practically on top of Jed's route."

Bodean tried to laugh it off, but it sounded like he was barking, Cody thought.

"So you contacted Jed," he said. "I guess you probably met with him a few times and laid it all out. You shared your information and made him maps. You agreed to cover his back on the law enforcement side—make sure nobody decided to suddenly look for that plane—if he'd actually retrieve the cash."

"This is insane," Bodean said.

"No, sorry, it isn't."

Bodean said, "You're trying to connect me with Rachel Mina. I never knew Hank Winters from Adam. I swear."

Cody said, "I believe you. Nice try. But this is where everyone investigating this has it wrong. The thing is, there is no connection between you and Mina and Gannon, is there? The key to this mystery is that it *wasn't* connected. It was two completely independent schemes both working to find that plane, but unaware of the other. There was

Mina and Gannon on one team, and you and Jed on the other. Two schemes, one trip, one destination. I don't think even Jed and Mina figured that out until the very end."

Bodean wiped the sweat from his lip. His face was drained of color. He said, "You've got nothing."

"I didn't until this morning," Cody said. He leaned forward in his chair. "Until the FAA investigators pulled Jed's body out of that hole. He had a satellite phone, too, Bodean. He'd made one call on it and it was to your private cell number."

"It must be a mistake," Bodean said.

"And something else," Cody said, reaching for the briefcase he'd brought. "I had Edna look over the logs the night Larry was killed. You know those GPS units we all have under our cars? Well, I disabled mine, but you never did. It shows your midnight trip to Bozeman to try and burn me up. And Edna found you took a trip up to Marysville twenty minutes *before* I called her to send a car. Either you're real fucking prescient, or you killed Larry."

Bodean said softly, "Do you realize what you're saying?"

"Yup," Cody said. "I'm saying up in Deer Lodge those convicts are gonna *looove* you. A former undersheriff? Man, you'll have plenty of dates, I'd guess. And if you think the prison guards are going to protect a cop killer, well think again."

Cody opened his briefcase and took out the bird's nest he'd found near the crevice and spun it across the desk so it landed between Bodean's fists.

"Look," Cody said, "it's made of money. A nest made of money. You thought you'd have one of your own and now you do. Pretty cool, if you think about it."

Then he reached into his pocket and plucked out the microphone. Said, "Heard enough? If you guys don't come in here in the next five seconds I'm going to rip his throat out for killing my best friend."

Cody stood aside as the FBI agents rushed in the room, followed by a hang-dog Sheriff Tubman.

As they stood Bodean face-first against the wall and cuffed him, and before they could read him his rights, Cody said, "I wanted to shoot you in the head, myself. But the sheriff said no, that would hurt his reelection campaign, so he made me go through all this."

One of the FBI agents gave Cody a withering glance. As did Tubman.

"I'd start with his knees," Cody said. "That makes 'em talk, believe me."

He turned to Tubman. "Look at it this way, sheriff. You've eliminated a rival."

Cody trudged across the lawn toward Jenny's van. Justin sat in the back, no doubt texting Danielle Sullivan. Justin looked up and nodded.

"Tell her to say hello to Gracie for me," Cody said.

He swung in beside Jenny and gave her a quick kiss. She didn't seem affected by the sudden breaking of her engagement to Walt. "I hope you've picked a smoking restaurant," he said.

"I was thinking Chubby's in Clancy," she said, pulling away from the curb. "The sign out front says 'Greatest Food You'll Ever Eat.'"

"Sounds promising," Cody said.

"Cody," she said, "it has a lounge. I know you'll probably want to toast Larry's memory . . ."

"I know," he said. "But I can't do that kind of thing anymore. I made a promise to Larry."

Acknowledgments

The author would like to sincerely thank the many friends, relatives, and colleagues who assisted in the research, reading, editing, and publication of this novel, starting with Investigator Cory Olson of the Lewis and Clark Sheriff's Department in Helena, Montana, and including Investigator Larry Platts, Sheriff Leo Dutton, my friend Pam Gosink, and forensics guru D. P. Lyle, MD.

Thanks always to my first readers: Becky Box Rcif, Molly Box, and Laurie Box.

Thanks also to John R. Erickson for the use of the lines from *The Original Adventures of Hank the Cowdog*, Puffin Books, 1983.

It's an absolute honor and privilege to work with the excellent and enthusiastic team at St. Martins Minotaur, including Sally Richardson, Andy Martin, Matthew Shear, Matthew Baldacci, Hector DeJean, and the absolutely peerless Jennifer Enderlin.

For Ann Rittenberg: You. Are. The. Greatest.

C.J.BOX

THE JOE PICKETT SERIES

|1

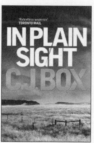
|2

|3

|4

|5

|6

|7

|8

|9

|10

ORDINARY MAN
EXTRAORDINARY
HERO

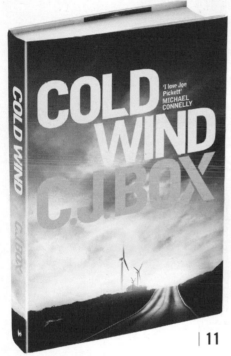

| 11

JOE PICKETT, Wyoming game warden, has taken on eco-terrorists, rogue federal land managers, animal mutilators, corrupt bureaucrats, crazed hitmen, homicidal animal rights advocates – all in the pursuit of justice.

Through it all, he has remained true to himself and his family.

COLLECT THEM ALL...

 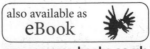

R 6-16 ✓